EAT

(ΣΔT Book One: Sigma)

Jesse Brown

First published in 2023
Edited by Nick Hodgson
Cover design and layout by Jessica Brown for Func.ton Design
www.authorjessebrown.co.uk

ISBN 978-1-7384290-0-4

For Jean and Luke

Acknowledgements

First, I'd like to thank you for purchasing this copy of EAT. That you saw the cover and thought, "heck yeah let's give this a try" means the world to me.

This book existing amongst all the other books out there may not seem like a remarkable achievement. However, I think any endeavour of this size deserves acknowledgment, because it's bloody hard work, and it doesn't happen in a vacuum.

With that in mind I would like to thank my editor, Nick Hodgson, who took on this project with great care, patience and skill. Thank you to Sam, who has read this about as many times as I have, and given valuable feedback such as, "I had to put down what I was eating" and, "God, I hate this character". I'd also like to thank Paul for providing feedback for me while he was supposed to be writing campaigns for our Force and Destiny tabletop RPG group. Thank you to George, who not only provided valuable feedback but also had to listen to me talking about this non-stop for many, many months. A huge thank you to everyone who had read this prior to print, including my poor relatives and colleagues, who had to read the early drafts.

Finally, thank you to my late grandmother, who said this book was good, and that's really all the approval I need.

Prologue

We're the rabbits now.

Blind, bleeding, suffering...mad. We finally became the victims of our own folly. We tried to play God, but therein lies the problem.

There isn't one.

-

Daisy skidded around the corner, sucking breath into burning lungs, feet pelting hard against the wet pavement. Sirens wailed behind her—so close that she could see the fluorescent red and blue lights ricocheting off the puddles and surrounding buildings. Rain dripped from the lip of her hood into her eyes. She blinked it away, clutched the metal briefcase tighter to her chest and hopped a fence, darting down a narrow side street.

No time for mistakes. Caught now, she'd be tried as a terrorist, a traitor, a war criminal. They'd get her for something, that was certain. Worse, the whole thing would be covered up, and all this would have been for nothing. The evil would continue unseen, unchecked. *Just get to the van*, she told herself. People needed—no, not just needed—they *deserved* to know the truth.

Lucas had been caught already. Too bad. He knew what he was getting into when he demanded to be on the mission. Seemed funny to call it that, in hindsight. Oh well. Get the samples and get to the van. That was all they had to do. *Just get to the van.* The rest would be taken care of.

1

Bloody Introductions

This isn't Casey's.

The light burned from somewhere above, stark and imposing, searing the back of Caede's eyeballs. She groaned, screwing her face up in torment as she tried to squirm away from the glare, twisting her body over until she could no longer see it. Her forehead rested on something sharp and gritty. It hurt. Everything hurt. The ground beneath her lurched, rising and falling, so cold she could barely breathe, as if she had been caught by a tide and swept out to sea. A pounding began somewhere deep inside the back of her head. Nausea followed. She lay still, eyes clamped shut, muttering curses at no one in particular.

Shadows danced in and out of her periphery, teasing glimpses of the night before. She didn't recall having anything to drink. But there it was, the-day-after agony, and there she was, freezing her arse off somewhere unfamiliar with a head full of storms, and a mouth full of bile. Finally, she opened her eyes and the grey stone slabs beneath her shifted into focus. She was outside, lying on a cold, hard pavement.

This isn't Casey's.

The thought carried more urgency this time. She must have left the pub at the end of her shift without issue–no having to frog-march out any rowdy locals or deflect Danny's advances. So why was she outside, asleep on the pavement? How long had she been here? And where was *here*, anyway? She tried to stand and failed. Numb and leaden in the bitter autumn air, her legs wobbled and collapsed, sending her sliding back to the ground. Panic rose from her guts and burned the back of her throat. She gulped it down, telling herself that it was just the cold.

She flexed her frozen fingers, coaxing the warmth back into them, one by one. Pins and needles followed, shooting up her arms, tingling her skin as the blood began to flow. She did the same with her toes, then her feet, then her legs. Soon, she had warmed enough to sit up and rest on her knees.

The pavement sharpened and blurred with every blink as she sat waiting for her head to stop throbbing and for the nausea to pass. A frigid breeze snaked around her, and she shivered, clutching her cardigan tightly against her skin–as if the flimsy thing could provide any warmth. She couldn't tell if it was just condensation lining the thin wool fabric, or if it had been raining. Typical if it had. It was always bloody raining. And the air sat heavily around her as if more would soon be on its way.

It had been dark when she left the pub. Hadn't it? Where was her coat? No answers came. She put her hands to her head, finding a band of some sort clamped over it, and she pulled it down. It was a set of novelty pink bunny ears, forced on to her by Danny under the guise of uniformity, despite the fact that she despised fancy dress, even on Halloween. Casey's wasn't even supposed to be open. The quarantine was still in place, which included the closure of all pubs and restaurants. But it was for a private party, Danny had said, and the money was too good to turn down. She threw the ears aside in disgust.

Her foot nudged something soft and wet, and the smell of rust hit her nostrils. Rust and something else. Something metallic, unsettling and malevolent, hanging thick in the air like a fog. It smelled of rust and…rot. The throbbing in Caede's head returned and peaked, exploding into searing pain. Bile bubbled in her throat once more and she fell forward, retching and heaving at the pavement. She reached for her face and found it wet. Lowering her hand, she stared at the red liquid coating her fingers. The scent of metal struck again. She looked up.

All around her were dead bodies.

They were strewn everywhere, sprawled across the pavement, contorted and lifeless as abandoned marionettes, their strings severed and left to decay in the wind.

A ringing noise filled Caede's ears. The scenery blurred. She sat there, breath caught in her throat and eyes burning, unable to believe what was in front of her. So many people dead, and she was sitting right in the middle of them. Was it a bomb? Another terror attack? This was the outskirts. The suburbs. There was nothing important here. But it had to be a bomb. There was no other way to explain it.

Closest to her lay a man, his eyes staring vacantly up at the sky, nose bloody, lips dry and peeled back into an empty wail. Caede tumbled backwards, gasping, and landed on something cold and rigid. She turned to see her hand resting on the greying torso of a woman lying face down on the ground, brown leaves and dirt entangled in her hair. Almost on top of her was a man in a jogging suit, headphones dangling from his bluing, bloated neck. Both lay still, oblivious to their surroundings.

Caede yelped and tried to scramble away. But another body–a man in a suit this time–blocked her path. He looked fresher than the others; his skin was still warm and deep brown, and not yet swollen. At first glance, he could have been asleep, but his eyes were wide open, and great purple welts and crimson gashes marred his face. His smart suit was dashed and torn, the soft grey fabric splattered with brown and red stains. Black hair that had once been gelled and waved now lay matted against his head, encrusted with blood. One of his eyes had no colour in its iris. It was as if he had been attacked by a wild animal. But what kind of animal could have done that?

Outstretched in front of him were the remains of his arm, broken and twisted, bent at sharp angles like the wing of a bird, shards of fractured bone protruding through purple skin. His hand was shrivelled and curled into a blackened fist, leathery and gnarled like an old glove. The nails on this hand were long and thick, almost like the talons on a parrot, or an eagle, or any bird-like creature.

Caede gagged and tore her head away. Where the hell were the emergency services? Who would you even call for something like this? Ambulance? The police? She glanced around for her bag, spotting it on the pavement a few feet away, just past the glassy-eyed man in the suit. She grimaced and crawled towards it, hands and legs shaking as she reached over him. Eyes closed, she snatched up the bag, clutching it to her chest as she rifled around inside for her phone.

Her fingers met the familiar leather case. With a click, it opened, and she stared at the phone screen. The date showed November 2nd, 2030. There had to be something wrong with it. The thing was rubbish anyway. Cheap crap, probably damaged after being left in the cold overnight. That seemed like a reasonable explanation.

She unlocked it and checked the screen once more. Only three percent battery left. It was fully charged when she left for work. How could it be so low now? Using the GPS to get home would be out of the question. She shouldn't have needed it anyway, but with her head fuzzy as it was, navigating her arse from her elbow would have been impossible, let alone getting back to her house. It had to be a concussion. No other way to explain it. She rifled through the bag once more for her smartwatch. Danny preferred the staff didn't wear them while on shift. They looked clunky, he'd said, and mentioned something about being on social media while working, despite it not actually having social media capabilities. And where was Danny now? The light on the screen flickered for a moment before dying completely. *Shit.* No matter. The pub was only a few minutes' walk from her house, and there was no reason for her to be anywhere else in the city. No, she wouldn't need the GPS.

She returned the watch to her wrist to recharge, waiting a few seconds for it to absorb the tiny electrical current produced by her skin before it started back up. The time and date flickered briefly before disappearing back into the black square screen. 16:36, Saturday, November 2nd, 2030. *What?* The phone wasn't broken, after all. And that meant Kai had been left alone for two nights in a row. Two nights, all alone. She checked the phone again, flicking her thumb across the screen as she checked her recent calls list. There were over a dozen missed calls from him. *Shit.* What if it had been a terror attack? He could be injured, trapped in the rubble of their house, buried alive in the debris. Or worse. She checked the screen again. The calls had all been made on the night of her shift. Her face felt hot. Tears spilled down her cheeks and chin. Anything could have happened to him, and she would have had no idea.

Hands shaking, she held up the phone and said, "call Kai."

The dial tone sounded, and the phone rang.

"Hello?" Kai answered.

Caede stifled a relieved sob and pressed the phone to her ear. "Kai! It's me, are you okay? Are you safe?"

His reply came in a flurry of panicked squeaks. "Oh my God, Caedey! Where have you been? Have you seen what's outside? You need to get home now! I didn't know what to do. I haven't tidied up, by the way."

"Kai, Kai! Calm down," she replied.

She lowered the phone and let out a long breath. Kai was alive. Alive and safe.

"I don't think I'm that far away, okay?" she said. "I'll be home soon and—"

The phone cut off; the battery giving up. Caede swore and thrust it back inside the bag. As she looked up, she spotted the street sign for St. Mary's Road. The same St. Mary's Road that joined the street to her own house. She'd been lying on that pavement, not two minutes from home, for God knows how long. Had she been there for two whole nights? A sharp, stabbing sensation took root just behind her right eye.

Shakily, she stood and began making her way over the bodies. First, the suited man, then a woman who lay face down with lank, brown hair, clumped and stained with patches of red. Caede swallowed the knot in her throat and looked away. Better to pretend they weren't there for now.

She had taken only a few steps when a faint moan rose from somewhere beyond the pile. Caede whipped her head around to find the source, and a flicker of movement caught the corner of her eye. From a junction where St. Mary's Road merged with the high street, next to some parked cars, a man moved. He was completely naked, and covered in what looked to be burns, his flesh taut and raw, and paper thin, veins visible and pulsing under the epidermis. One of his arms was clamped to his side, as if it had melted and become stuck there. With the other, he dragged himself painfully along the ground.

"Hello?" Caede called, heading towards him. "Are you okay? Oh my God, I thought I was the only one alive, I..." she trailed off.

Something wasn't right. The man stopped moving and turned towards her, twisting slowly on the spot, shoulders leading, his head lagging behind as if his attention were elsewhere. When he finally faced her, he opened his mouth to speak. No sound came out. Instead, he fell forward, coughing, gagging, lurching violently. Out of his mouth fell a ribbon of reddened spit, then fleshy lumps of brown that collected on the ground at his feet.

The man needed help. But with no phone battery, and the nearest hospital half an hour away, Caede faltered. What could she do without a first aid kit? *Get home, use Kai's phone to call an ambulance, and let the professionals deal with him.*

"Don't worry!" she called. "I'm going to get you some help, okay? Everything's going to be fine."

The man opened his mouth to speak again, but this time, a hissing escaped his lips. It was a cold, ghostly rasping that caught Caede's foot mid-step and danced shivers across the surface of her skin. The man was on the verge of death; she was sure of it. Urgency tugged at her, and she started towards him once more. Suddenly, the man began twitching and convulsing, as if in the throes of a seizure, his eyes rolling wildly in their sockets as he shook on the spot. More red, then thick white mucus bubbled from his open mouth. The sound turned Caede's blood to ice, and she found herself anchored to the ground, fighting the urge to scream. Then the man fell heavily onto the pavement and lay still. She stared, hands clamped over her mouth, too afraid to move or speak. A few seconds passed.

Do something, she thought. *Don't just stand there. He's going to die if you don't-*

Suddenly, the man rose. He didn't push himself up with his arms. He just *rose.* The veil of pain was seemingly lifted from him too, as if he'd simply forgotten the damage to his body. Not a minute ago, he was barely standing. Now he turned his head this way and that, first up at the sky, then to the buildings, his eyes swivelling around, investigating the scenery before finally settling on Caede. The breath in her throat snagged as his gaze met hers. Instinct screamed at her to get away, to run, but her legs refused to move. The man tilted his head, regarding her like an animal inspecting its prey. Then he lunged.

Caede screamed. She must have screamed, though it felt as if no sound was coming out. And the scream seemed to shock the man, because he froze mid-step. Confusion filled his face, then upset, then pain. He raised his good arm to his head, eyes closed and face contorted, a cry escaping from his open mouth. Caede stepped back. Her shoe caught something and slipped underneath her. The world spun upwards as the back of her head met the ground, and suddenly everything was black.

2

Rust and Rot

Terry Howard, entry 07.01.2030

Thus far, we have successfully replicated the desired effects in our 'smaller' test subjects, which is promising. Not promising enough, according to Raj. The people upstairs want human trials to begin. I have tried to explain to them that Rome wasn't built in a day, but they don't want to hear it.

We are pushing the boundaries of life and death here. I suppose it's what we've always done, isn't it; delay the inevitable embrace of the void? And there are still those who delight in drawing it closer to whomever they deem deserving. It's not a stretch to guess which direction we have taken here. And they don't seem to care how we do it, as long as it's done. It's fitting, I suppose. We were made in God's image, were we not? And just look at what he has created. I'm keen for this project to reach completion, but to say I have reservations about its use is an understatement.

This all makes me think of the rabbits; eyes swollen shut, forced to suffer the agony of Myxomatosis at our hands, all because we wanted to control the population. What did they ever do to deserve such cruelty? What does anyone do, I suppose. And this project? It's no better; nothing but eugenics under the guise of cure.

I am tired of this. The people upstairs want their results. If we don't make some progress soon, my career is over. Perhaps that's for the best.

-

Two nights had passed since Caedey left for that 'emergency' shift. She was only supposed to be a few hours. She wasn't even supposed to be there. Kai checked his phone again. The last message from his sister read, "Don't call. Stay inside, lock doors. Will be home ASAP xxx."

In the time since, he had eaten his way through the snacks and instant noodle pots in the cupboards. Now he was standing at the fridge, face bathed in its white glow as he reluctantly eyed the contents. He'd already missed breakfast by sleeping in. His stomach knew it, gurgling and groaning with every step, sounding the call for more food, more fullness. A single apple sat sadly at the bottom of the vegetable drawer. There were eggs on the door shelf. Was the situation desperate enough for proper cooking? For fruit? There was half a loaf of bread in the cupboard. Eggs and bread? That could work.

As the eggs bubbled in the pan, Kai picked off the mould spots on the bread crusts and stared absentmindedly out of the kitchen window at the dingy back garden, with its moss-covered cement paving and rust-speckled iron furniture. Some potted plants leaned against the surrounding walls; a Japanese maple tree with no leaves, some twigs in a faded metal planter with 'herbs' written on it, and a dying lavender bush. On the table sat a used jam jar filled with cigarette butts and rainwater.

It was quiet out there today. Same as yesterday. The night his sister left had been filled with screams and sirens wailing, the crunch of glass, metal squealing as it collided with brick... Terrified, Kai had called Caede every minute, receiving no answer. Until she'd sent the text message. Some men had knocked on the door the next day, claiming to be from the army or the police. He couldn't remember which, but he hadn't let them in. Instead, he'd hidden in his bed, curled up in a ball, staying as quiet as possible until they went away and left him alone. He thought they were taking people out of the city because of the riots, but he didn't want to go anywhere. Not without Caede.

Worse, the internet was down, so he couldn't even talk to his friends. At first, the whole thing was exciting. Funny, even. They'd joked about leaving their houses to bag themselves some new trainers, just like with the riots of the year before. Then, when the excitement wore off and things started to feel more real, they'd messaged each other frantically, checking in via their group chat, comparing news stories and giving regular updates on each of their situations. But the replies, at first a cascade, quickly slowed to a trickle, before drying up altogether. Then Kai was alone.

Kai wasn't sure which was more frightening: the unsettling silence, or the entropic screams that sporadically shattered it. Both seemed to seep into the walls of the building, the air, even his skin. It made his hair stand on end and the inside of his mouth dry.

The cat hadn't returned either. It was normal for her to stay out, but Kai wished he had thought to keep her indoors. She might have been hurt in all the chaos. *She'll be fine*, he told himself. What would Caede say? She knows where home is. Besides, outside were the *things*.

Kai finished his egg sandwich and topped up the cat's food bowl, just in case. He dumped his plate in the sink before remembering the rules and put it in the dishwasher. The sudden vibration of his mobile phone against the kitchen counter cut through the quiet. He leapt for it, yanking it from its charge cable, and pressed it to his ear.

"Hello?"

"Kai! It's me," came the voice. "Are you okay? Are you safe?"

He slumped in relief against the cupboard door. Caede was alive! He took a few breaths and put the phone back to his ear.

"Oh my God, Caedey! You told me to call if there was an emergency! Where have you been? Have you seen what's outside? You need to get home now! I didn't know what to do. I haven't tidied up, by the way."

"Kai, Kai, calm down." There was a pause on the other end of the line, as Kai could hear his sister sighing.

"I don't think I'm that far away," she said, "I should be home soon and–" The phone cut off.

"Hello? Caedey? Caede? Hello?"

Kai dropped the phone and ran to the front door.

On the porch, he froze. *The things.* They were everywhere. Just lying there on the pavement below, their eyes open and empty. The smell of metal hit the back of his nose. Just like in the hospital. The memory played unbidden, as if on a reel. Try as he might, he couldn't stop it. The bright white lights of the hallway. The whooshing and beeping of machines somewhere in a nearby room. Someone coughing. The smell of metal and chemicals in the air. Caede staring into her hands. His grandfather in the other room, convulsing over a hospital bed while his grandmother stood, arms around him. Doctors and nurses waited around the bed, their faces apologetic and sagging behind surgical masks. His mother's hollow face, eyes open and empty. The last time Kai ever saw her.

He slumped back and leaned against the front door, chest tight and heart pounding. The air seemed to thicken around him and he swayed, clutching the door handle with his eyes clamped shut and his mouth full of chalk. His coat suddenly felt heavy, claustrophobic and sweat-drenched. He kept it on. After a few seconds, the spinning stopped, and the hammering in his chest calmed. He pushed himself away from the door and continued on.

At the base of the steps was their tiny front garden, paved and barren, short of a hedge lining the black iron fence that met the pavement. Beyond that was the road. And the *things*. Hands on the rail, he steeled himself and slowly followed the steps down. One of the things stared up at him through the bars of the garden gate as he descended. It was Mrs Webber, their neighbour, and her little dog,

Rocky. Kai had walked Rocky for her a few times. He liked Rocky, with his fluffy coat and bold attitude. Now the tiny body of the Pomeranian lay rigid next to his owner, dried blood lining his gums. Eyes open and empty. Kai swallowed down the chalky taste and moved away from the pair, choosing to hop over the fence further along the garden.

The streets surrounding Kai's home were formed of terraced houses, with space on the road for parking and little else, typical of a South London suburb. The road running parallel was wider and had a bus lane for commuters heading into the city centre. Small shops lined the pavement; a local newsagent, some charity shops, and a popular fried chicken place. Casey's pub was a short walk from home, fifteen minutes at a relaxed pace. Sometimes, when Caede worked day shifts, Kai would take the bus after school to meet her there, and they'd walk home together. The underground was also an option, but Kai didn't like it. Too loud, too dark, too smelly, and in the time it took to get to the platform and wait for the train, he could have walked to the pub and home again. Now, the road was empty and silent, with abandoned cars spread across its surface, their doors left flung open.

Kai scanned the pavements as he walked, checking bodies with a glance before moving on. He reached the end of St Mary's Road and stopped. They were everywhere. Bodies littered the street, splayed every which way between the cars, some lining the pavement, others piled up against the buildings. Kai gagged as the metallic air pressed down on him, creeping into his nose and mouth.

Before moving to London, his parents had kept chickens. One night, a fox got into the coop. Maybe it had dug under the fence; maybe they'd failed to secure the door properly. Either way, it had slaughtered all the hens. The fox had taken what it could carry and left the tattered remains of the rest for the family to find the next morning. He remembered the smell then, of metal and rot, and the static in the air above the birds, like the smoke that hovered briefly over a snuffed-out candle.

Kai tore his eyes away from the nightmare just in time to spot some movement further along the road. Was someone running? He ducked down behind a car and closed his eyes, hoping he hadn't been noticed. A sudden scream tore through the silence, sending the hair at the back of his neck on end. *Caedey?* Without a second thought, he jumped up and sprinted towards the sound. Rounding the corner, he skidded to a halt and ducked back, chest heaving as he hugged the garden wall of a terraced house. Something was standing a few metres away on the other side. Leaning against the brick, breath held, Kai slowly peered around and snuck a glimpse.

The thing was crouched, stooped over, as if searching for something. It was the same height as a grown man, but it looked all wrong, all bent and angular, as if a human had been stuffed into a plastic bag and was struggling to get out. Taut melted skin stretched across the thing's back like an ill-fitting leather coat. One of its arms was pinned to its side, all shrivelled and fingerless, as if it had been melted there. The other, deathly thin and withered as a husk, was outstretched and reaching for something. As the thing moved, it twitched and retched, juddering with every step as if in agony. Just looking at it turned Kai's guts to ice.

Without warning, it stopped and fell to the pavement, shaking and twisting. A weird choking noise left its mouth and the skin on its back split, exposing the raw, pink flesh underneath. It fell still for a moment, then heaved itself back up. Something about it had changed. Head tilted to the sky, it seemed to sniff the air like an animal. Then it dropped again, retching and twitching once more, its spine flexing and eyes rolling as it flailed around. With a sickening crack, its back arched and lengthened. The pinned arm fell free and dangled limp at its side.

Kai wanted to run, return home and hide under his duvet, but his feet remained cemented to the pavement. Instead, he stood, staring open-mouthed at the creature as it continued, falling, rising again, changing more and more with each collapse.

Finally, it stood and stayed upright. It raised its face to the sky, and a wail erupted from its mouth, filling the air, crashing against the sides of the buildings and bouncing back in distorted echoes, causing Kai to press his hands to his ears and grind his teeth together. The skin on its back loosened. With a shiver, it shrugged off the old pelt, and it landed in a heap on the pavement. The creature stopped howling, freed now, and it stretched itself out like a cat, but slicker, narrower, with a thick tail and short, thin legs. Its flesh was now white and shimmering like a fish.

By its bony feet lay a small cluster of bodies. As Kai studied them, he could make out the black uniform and the mess of ash-blonde hair of his sister. Kai darted forward and leapt under a parked car, shimmying himself forward to get a better look. From this new angle, he could see the woman's face. *Definitely Caede.* She didn't look like the other corpses, either. They were all grey and swollen, and he could make out the red flush of her cheeks in the cold air. She must be alive. Somehow, he had to get to her.

The creature opened its mouth once more. With a scream, it unhinged its jaws, splitting the skin along the sides of its lips. It thrashed its head from side to side, spraying the pavement with blood. A cloud of black liquid erupted from inside its gaping mouth and dissipated into the air with a hiss. The liquid fell, hitting a nearby body. Bubbles formed on the flesh of the corpse as the liquid ate through it, exposing the white bone underneath. An acrid smell hit Kai's nose, and he gagged, banging his head on the underside of the car. Pain shot through his body, and he yelped before he could stop himself. Too late, he clamped his hands over his mouth. The creature whipped its head around and their eyes locked.

Where a human face should have been was a white expanse, with pale, blank eyes, flattened nostrils and a wide, frog-like mouth lining a set of elongated jaws. It stared at him, head tilted as if in curiosity. Then, it lowered itself, shifting its weight onto its belly, and moved, gliding in a zigzag over the corpses with unnatural grace, slithering towards him. Its lips peeled back, and out of its mouth flickered a long, black tongue.

Hands and feet scraping the asphalt, Kai wriggled backwards, whimpering in terror. The creature, more a monster now, slid closer, its glassy eyes alert and full of interest. Kai shimmied from underneath the car and rolled onto the pavement. Acid burning in his throat and chest pounding, he crawled alongside the parked cars towards Caede's body. As he reached the next car along, a hiss caught his ears. Kai turned in time to see the monster flicking its black tongue at him, its eyes narrowed into menacing slits. No point in hiding anymore. Kai leapt up and hurtled towards his sister. He jumped over the bodies, seized Caede's arm and shook. Nothing. He gritted his teeth and shook again.

"Caedey, come on, wake up!"

Before he could do anything else, the monster struck. The blow came from behind with the force of a hammer. He hit the pavement hard, ears ringing and white spots filling his vision. He caught a movement to his left and threw himself sideways just in time to avoid the second strike. The monster flew past him, slamming into a parked car with a heavy crunch. Legs wobbling and head spinning, Kai scrambled onto his feet. Too slow, he tried to run. The monster's tail whipped around, hitting him in the gut; with a gasp, he returned to the ground. The taste of metal filled his mouth, and the scenery blurred. Seizing its chance, the beast recoiled and sprang forward, its mouth stretched open like a bear trap. Adrenaline kicked in, and Kai rolled out of its path once more.

Furious now, the monster threw open its mouth, emitting an ear-splitting screech. Kai clamped his hands over his ears and screamed in terror. A sudden silence forced his eyes back open. He looked up to see the monster throwing its head around, spraying the black liquid into the air once more. Too late, Kai jumped back. A glob of the hot tar hit his arm, bubbling away the fabric of the coat. Then it met flesh, and Kai screamed. The monster hissed and arched, ready to aim again.

Kai leaped behind a car, barely escaping the spray that followed. Lungs straining and heart pounding, he leaned against the car door. His arm felt heavier somehow, like a dead weight hanging uselessly against his side. His skin burned under the black acid and made his eyes water. He needed to get out of there. *Not without Caedey.* As if by fate, he heard a low moan. The blood pulsed in his ears. Was it Caede? He scanned the pavement, desperate to find something to defend himself with. The car. Maybe it would have something. He tried the door, but it was locked. He stifled a frustrated sob, eyes darting around for anything he could use. He saw a discarded pile of scaffolding pipes poking up over the wall of a front garden. Too far away to reach, but if he was quick, he could run, hop the garden wall and grab one. He poked his head around the car to glimpse the monster. Its attention was drawn towards Caede as she stirred. He took his chance and sprinted to the wall. A solid-looking section of pipe sat separated from the pile. He grabbed it and ran back, holding the pipe high in the air.

"Hey!"

The monster stopped and turned its ghostly face to meet his. Legs wobbling, he took a breath and banged the pipe against the pavement, sending a confrontational clash ringing out into the street. The monster answered it with a furious hiss and began gliding towards him. Kai choked down a shiver and held the pipe close, ready to swing.

23

3

Dinner For One

Justine Pearson, entry 04.03.2030

Yes! Bloody finally. It works. Thirteen works. I'm treating myself to the good stuff tonight.

It's far more sophisticated than strains eleven or twelve ever were. Better than we could ever dream! The next few months are going to be very interesting. I can't wait. We'll have to keep an extra close eye on the subjects, but so far, so good. If the modified strains continue to behave accordingly, we should see dramatic cell reproduction in all subjects within the next seventy-two hours.

Terry is still griping about the funding, and I swear the other day he was comparing us all to rabbits. For Christ's sake, Terry. Of course the military's paying for this. No other bugger wanted to, that's for sure. Bloody hypocrite. He's still here, isn't he? Still turns up for work every morning.

People are suffering. We need to do what we can to help, even if, yes, it means shaking hands with the devil.

This new strain, though. My God, it's grand.

-

Jonathan tipped his head back and chugged the last few drops of liquid, savouring the warm haze that followed. It was the last of the booze in the flat; a moderately priced Japanese whiskey gifted to him by a friend some years ago. Under any other circumstance, he would have preferred to save this bottle, keep it sealed for a special occasion, but the beer was all gone, and soon he'd be dead. It would be a shame to go without at least having a sip. He'd eaten the last of the food too, all but the stale remains of some pizza. And since Tara had left, he didn't feel like going out to get more.

So, he sat there, on the sofa, in the same T-shirt and jogging bottoms he'd worn for the last week, gazing at the tower of empty takeaway boxes on the floor. Even in a quarantine, you could rely on takeaway. He'd piled the boxes up high enough to use them as a makeshift side table, and now he couldn't be bothered to throw them away. Tara never would have let things come to this, but Tara wasn't here anymore now, was she? Two weeks and not even a sodding text. She'd left half of her shit in the flat too, as if she wanted to leave him hanging while she had her fun with Mike. Taken the cat, though, hadn't she? *His* cat. He'd loved that cat.

A few days had passed since the event. *Event* was the best way to think of it. He didn't want to call it anything else. Plague sounded too grim, despite the drama outside. Nights of sirens and riots, police knocking on every door urging people to leave, now, evacuate for your own safety—every damn door in the block except his. Not that it mattered if they had.

Jon let the bottle slip from his hand. He watched as it landed on the rug with a hollow thump and rolled away. In a few hours, its effect would wear off, and he would be lucid and alone all over again. He could just stay put, lie down on the sofa, starve to death and leave it at that. *Not quick enough.* If he didn't do it now, the hunger might eventually become too much and his innate instinct to survive would take over. Room spinning, he stood and wobbled to the front door.

As he opened it, a wave of putrescent musk flooded in from the hallway, knocking him backwards with a startled gasp. He folded in on himself, choking and heaving at the floor, hands gripping his knees. The cause of the smell was lying in front of him in the hallway. One of them he recognised as his neighbour, Mrs Brown. The old woman had lived across from him with her husband until he'd passed away. Since then, they'd formed a sort of friendship, quick chats in the hallway and the like, often when he was in a hurry to be somewhere. Jon swore at himself. How long had she been there? In the panic, the sirens, Tara leaving, he had forgotten to check up on her. He hadn't even heard her fall. Now she lay face down, half inside the open doorway of her apartment. A thick, fur-lined hood hid her body from view, but judging by the smell, she'd been there a while. Unquestionably dead. Guilt burned the back of his neck and face.

The body of a younger woman in a leopard-print dress and fluffy coat lay further down the hallway, a high-heeled shoe in one hand, legs blocking the entrance to the lift. The doors closed, hit the girl, re-opened with a ding, then closed again. She could have been one of the students who lived in the building, but he couldn't tell. Jon wondered if she and Mrs Brown had died at the same time. Regardless, neither were getting back up anytime soon.

He considered heading into Mrs Brown's apartment to see if she had any food worth taking, but quickly abandoned the idea. It would only delay things. And he would have to step over her to gain access to the property. He shuddered as horror-movie scenarios played out in his mind, of Mrs Brown reaching up to seize his ankles as he stepped over her. For a while, he just stood there in the hallway. Was it worth taking the lift? Or would the stairs be better? The girl blocking the lift doors answered with silence.

Jon scolded himself for being afraid of some bodies. He was a grown man, for Christ's sake. Opting for the stairs, he turned away from the dead women and sprinted down the hallway.

Every step up to the roof was an effort. It was as if his feet had worked out what he was planning before the rest of his body and were trying to drag him back to the apartment. He bounced drunkenly from wall to rail, swaying as he made his way up. By the time he reached the top floor, he was drenched in sweat, cursing under his breath about not keeping fit. He wondered what his obituary would read, if there were one. *Jonathan Taylor: graphic designer, alcoholic. Died trying to get up a flight of stairs.*

Warm light filtered into the stairwell as he pushed open the door, and an icy wind whipped his face, bringing with it the cold nausea of sobriety. Dusk stretched across the horizon to welcome him, wrapped in velvet hues of mauve and pink. The clouds had cleared, and the sun beckoned from beyond the skyline as it descended, impatient as him to put an end to the day. When he was a student, Jon would have welcomed the sight of a clear evening sky. It brought back memories of trips to the beach in summer; sitting on the sand wrapped in a blanket, eating fish and chips and watching the stars come out. The weather would be nice now, wouldn't it? Rained all year round, except for today. *Fantastic.*

Fighting the rising nausea, Jon lurched towards the edge of the roof and stepped up onto the parapet, glancing down at the corpse-covered pavements below. Soon he would be joining them. His face felt wet. He rubbed the tears away roughly with his sleeve and shifted closer to the edge. Eyes closed, he lifted his foot. *Let's go, lad.*

A high-pitched scream tore through the air from somewhere below. Jon yelped, losing his balance, and he tumbled backwards, landing on the gravel rooftop with a crunch. Chest heaving, he turned painfully onto his back and swore out loud, first at the sky, then at himself.

"Fuck! Fuck, fuck, fuck!"

He stayed there on the gravel, letting the stones pinch the back of his neck and hands, listening to the blood pump in his ears.

"Flippin' 'eck," he said to no one in particular. "What the fuck am I doing?"

Silence answered.

He forced himself to stand up and looked over the edge for the source of the scream. At first, he saw nothing but a cluster of askew cars, abandoned in the road, and the bodies. Then some movement in his periphery nudged his head. Down by the corner of the road, someone was running–a young boy, being chased by a large, white figure. Some kind of creature–a dog, maybe? The kid swung at it with a metal bat, or pipe. That didn't deter the creature; it leapt forward, and a red mist filled the air. Another scream rang out through the street.

Jon was already on his way, leaping down the stairwell one flight at a time. He burst out of the main entrance of the tower block and stopped dead. The scene looked like an apocalyptic nightmare, piles of corpses lining the roads as if they'd been mown down by rapid gunfire. He checked the ground for shell casings and found none. It was unbelievable. He'd never seen–or smelled–anything like it. It was one thing to see them from the window from three storeys up. He could distance himself, pretend they weren't there. Here, there was no escaping it. For a moment, he couldn't feel his feet, and the alcohol still sitting in his belly threatened to return to his mouth.

But they evacuated everyone, he thought. *How could so many...*

Jon ran to the other side of the building and along the street where he'd seen the boy, stopping just short of the sign for St. Mary's Road to hug the corner of a house and peek around. He scanned the scene until he saw the creature. It stood as tall and wide as a grown man, but was long and slick, like an eel, pale and translucent, its skin a texture that reminded Jon of an undercooked egg. The vision turned his stomach, and he whipped his head back around the corner, acid clawing the back of his throat.

He poked his head around again. The boy was on the pavement, crawling away from the creature, trailed by a long streak of red. He didn't have much fight left in him. The creature stood over the boy, mouth open wide, blood dripping from its chin. Wishing he hadn't finished off the whiskey, Jon hopped from one foot to the other to shake off the fear, psyching himself up. *Just get to the kid.* He took a deep breath, hurled himself around the corner and sprinted full pelt towards the creature.

Jon had once enjoyed rugby as a hobby. Something to do at the weekend, and a good excuse to go to the pub afterwards for a quick pint with the lads, before returning home to the missus. It was something to do while Tara was at her yoga lessons with Mike. Kept him fit for a time until, like everything else, it became an effort.

The creature turned too late to avoid the impact. With a heavy grunt, Jon tackled it to the ground. Its head met the pavement with a crack and it stayed there, unmoving. Jon hopped up and ran over to the boy.

"Come on, lad, time to go," he said, pulling the kid up.

Thick, dark blood poured from the boy's side onto the pavement. Jon grimaced and heaved him onto his shoulders. "Hold on, alright?"

"My sister…" the boy croaked, pointing a shaking hand towards a small cluster of bodies in the middle of the road.

Jon followed the boy's hand until his gaze rested on the figure of a girl lying on the ground next to the pile.

"She's alive?"

The boy nodded weakly; hand still outstretched. "Please…"

"Alright then," Jon replied, "let's go."

At first glance, the girl appeared fresh out of her teens, and as if she'd seen better days. Blood and vomit plastered her pale face and purple bags hung from her closed eyes. Jon sat the boy down next to him and reached out to the girl, nudging her gently.

"Ey up. Come on, love," he said. "Wake up. We've got to go."

No response. He shook harder.

"Come on, we need to go!"

Her eyelids fluttered, and she stirred, groaning and coughing. Jon dragged her up and reached for the boy's arm, only to find a space where it should be. He heard movement behind him. Grabbing the boy's other arm, Jon heaved him back onto his shoulders.

"Alright you two," he said, "time to go."

The creature was already stirring as the three shuffled past. Jon swore under his breath and quickened his pace. Soon enough, from behind him came a hiss. He gritted his teeth and sped up again, ignoring the sweat dripping into his eyes, yanking at the girl's arm. The girl groaned, tripping and stumbling, and the boy lay like a heavy stone on his back, but he didn't dare stop.

"Come on, you can do it," he huffed, urging the girl on. "Keep going. Not far now."

He didn't dare to look back, either. Once it had regained its composure, that thing wouldn't be far behind, and he wasn't leaving the two youths outside with it. The main door to the block approached. With his elbow, he heaved it open and shoved the girl inside. He dropped the boy off his shoulder and slammed the door closed, the deadbolt clicking reassuringly. Jon lifted his head to see the blank, white face of the creature staring at him through the door's window. He cried out and tumbled backwards, expecting it to smash through the glass and make its attack. Instead, it just stood there, studying him, as if he were an animal at a zoo and the thing had never seen one of him before. For an age, he held eye contact with it, too afraid to look away. Just as his eyeballs began to burn, the creature turned and left.

Jon remained sitting on the floor, staring at nothing, while his heart hammered against his ribcage. Remembering the others, he turned around. The girl was staring at him, wide-eyed, both fearful and furious, as she gripped the boy.

Jon put his hands up. "I'm not gonna hurt you," he said gently.

"Don't just stand there," she replied. "Fucking help me!"

Jon looked down to see the girl was clinging to the boy's arm. The boy's face was white as a sheet, grey almost, and thick blood poured from the space where his elbow and forearm should be. Beads of sweat were scattered along his forehead.

"Do you have a belt?" she said. "Something to stop the bleeding? Anything?"

Jon yanked off his T-shirt and handed it to the girl. She tied it around the boy's arm in a knot, taking one end.

"Here," she ordered, gesturing to the other side. "Pull!"

Jon obeyed, pulling the T-shirt tight as he could. The boy winced in pain and tears streamed down his face, but he didn't squirm. *He's in shock,* Jon thought. The girl swore to herself as she gripped the shirt. Jon gritted his teeth and waited. Finally, the blood slowed. Jon lifted the boy and, turning to the girl, said, "You take his legs. Third floor."

She sprang into action, and together, they began carrying the boy up the stairs towards the flat. With every step, the boy groaned in pain, and slick blood dripped from the T-shirt onto the stairs, causing the girl to slip and knock her shins against the metal stair guards. Grimacing, she kept going. They carried the boy inside and laid him on the kitchen floor.

"Do you know first aid?" said the girl.

"Uh…"

"Do you have a first aid kit? Any bandages?"

Besides witnessing a guy lose a finger in a printing press a few years ago, Jon had never dealt with anything first aid related. And even then, he wasn't first aid trained. He had a kit somewhere— didn't he? Had Tara taken it with her? How old was it? *Think.* Was it in the bathroom? *Come on, think!* Jon got up and skidded into the bedroom. The first aid kit was sitting on a shelf above the bed, partially hidden by a thick layer of dust.

He ran back to the kitchen.

"What about this?" he said.

She took it and tore it open. "It'll do. If we can stop the bleeding, he'll be fine."

"What do you need me to do?"

"I need hot water and rubber gloves."

"I'll put the kettle on."

The girl growled in frustration. "These bandages are tiny! Do you have any towels?"

Jon pulled open some cupboards and drawers. His guts churned and his face itched. The boy's lips were turning blue. He found the tea towels and hurled them at the girl. Sweat poured from the boy's forehead as the girl worked. The adrenaline was wearing off. Soon the boy would be lucid and in agony. Jon swore silently to himself.

The kettle clicked. "Water's boiled," said Jon. "What now?"

"I need it in a bowl. Do you have salt?"

"What?"

"Salt! To disinfect the wound."

Jon tipped half a carton of salt into a dish and filled it with the hot water.

Blood dripped in thick globs over the girl's shaking hands, causing them to slip clumsily around as she tried to clean the wound, and as the hot water met the boy's skin, he winced and cried out.

"Hold him still," she ordered.

Jon obeyed, wrapping his arms around the boy. Tears streaked down the boy's face, but he kept still. Finally, the girl finished cleaning and wrapped the boy's stump in gauze and bandages. They replaced the T-shirt with a tightly wrapped tea towel, and, satisfied that the bleeding had stopped, Jon and the girl carried the boy into the living room and laid him on the sofa to rest. The girl sat herself on the floor beside it, watching the boy intently.

"It's not ideal," she said. "But he'll live."

"Are you sure?" said Jon.

The girl shot him a look, and immediately he regretted opening his mouth.

"Yes," she said. "But he needs to get to a hospital."

"There's one about a half-hour walk from here."

"I know," she replied. "We live round the corner. We should go now, we–"

Jon put his hand up. "Not yet."

"Why?" she protested, suddenly angry. She stood quickly. "You can't keep us here!"

"No, no," said Jon, waving his hands. "He needs a hospital but think about it. That thing's still outside waiting for us. We don't know what the hospitals are like right now, and I don't think phoning for an ambulance is gonna work."

Eyes glassy, the girl lowered her face. She stared at her brother, then her legs buckled, the last ounce of her strength fleeing, and she slumped to the floor. Tears spilled out over her eyes and down her face.

"This is all my fault," she whispered.

Jon stood on the spot, unsure of what to say. The universe had gone to shit. There was nothing he could do for her; nothing to make it better.

And look at you. Can't even kill yourself right. Useless.

Somehow, the thought had taken Tara's condescending fucking tone. His own voice cut through.

Shut up.

You're just standing there like an idiot! Why don't you do something?

Shut up.

Why are you just standing there? Why can't you just do something for once?

Shut up!

What are you so afraid of?

The question sat heavily over him. His face felt wet, and his head thumped. Before he knew what he was doing, he was on the floor, wrapping his arms around the girl.

"It's going to be okay," he said. "I promise."

The girl clamped her arms around his waist and sobbed.

4

First Aid Training

A few minutes had passed since the pair of strangers had arrived at the flat. The boy lay on the sofa, breathing deep and steady as he slept. By some miracle, the bleeding had stopped, and he'd even kept down some water and painkillers. As if they'd make a difference. The kid's arm had been torn off at the elbow joint. *Almost like a shark attack*, Jon thought, but it didn't look too bad, all things considered. Besides the exposed bone, the tear seemed pretty clean. If they could get the boy to the hospital, he would likely survive. And if they couldn't....

Jon wondered if the local pharmacy stocked surgical kits and bone saws. Antibiotics wouldn't be an issue, at least. Tara had piles of meds, enough to supply a Camden nightclub for a month. Bandages…those were another story. Gauze, too. All Jon had now was an extremely old pack of plasters in the bathroom cabinet. He made a mental shopping list as he watched the boy's chest slowly rise and fall.

The girl sat on the floor next to the sofa, one hand resting beside the boy's head, the other holding Jon's mobile phone to her ear. Every so often she'd glance up to check on the boy, place her hand on his forehead and stroke his hair.

Things had been awkward since the hug. It felt like the right thing to do at the time, but in hindsight, Jon was a complete stranger–a potential predator, even. Worse, he hadn't showered in about a week. Worse still, his shirt had been wrapped around the boy's arm, so he'd been nude from the waist up when he'd hugged her. He dug his fingers into his temples and rubbed vigorously.

To distract himself from the embarrassment, he headed to the kitchen to clean up the blood. It was everywhere, saturating the laminate floor, the skirting boards, even the cupboards. It seemed like too much blood for an adult to lose, let alone a child, and the kid was skinny too, frail as a newborn lamb. He shouldn't have survived that attack, but there he was, sleeping it off as though he'd grazed his knee.

The damp cloth in his hand knocked something small and metal. Jon glanced down. On the floor was a gold engagement ring with tiny white diamonds encircling a deep blue sapphire. It was the ring he had bought for Tara a few weeks prior. He was planning to propose, but hadn't been able to find the right moment. Probably for the best. But how did it get here? Had Tara seen it? Had she tried to take it with her and lost it? He supposed it didn't matter if she had. He slipped it into his pocket, finished cleaning the kitchen floor, and headed for the bathroom to shower.

Clean, and fully dressed now, he returned to the living room and took a spot on the floor next to an old leather armchair by the balcony window. Given to him by his father when he'd left Yorkshire, the chair was his favourite piece of furniture, and the subject of many arguments with Tara. She hated it, calling it old and ugly, said that it didn't fit in with the modern aesthetic of the apartment. She couldn't understand why he wanted to keep it. Jon rested his head against the well-worn leather and pressed the tips of his fingers together as he tried to think of a way to break the ice. Another hand-me-down habit from his father, exercised during times of unease as a way of expressing anxiety without relinquishing his outward stoicism.

The girl huffed and put the phone down. "No answer," she said. "I've tried everyone."

"Aye. I thought that might be the case," Jon replied. "It's alright. I'll help you get him to the hospital."

"You don't have to do that."

"I don't mind. My calendar's empty."

The girl nodded and said nothing.

Jon gestured at the girl's apron. "You work at Casey's?"

As if she'd forgotten she was wearing it, the girl glanced down at herself. "Oh. Yeah. Part time."

Jon shifted his weight, his hand finding its way to the back of his neck.

"Nice place," he said. "Been there a few times with the lads from my rugby club. I'm sure I've seen you there before, actually, now that I think about it."

The girl pulled a face. "Oh…" she said, pausing. "Hang on. I remember you lot. You were the idiots who broke the pool table."

"Uh, yeah. Sorry about that."

Jon fidgeted again. Why was his mouth dry?

She thinks you're a serial killer.

Shut up.

"So, uh," he continued, "what's your name?"

"Caede," she replied. "This is my brother, Kai."

"Nice name. Celtic?"

"My mum was Welsh. You?"

"Jonathan, but just call me Jon. It's easier."

"Okay," the girl, now Caede, said. "So, what do you do, then?"

"Graphic designer," he replied. "Mostly freelance now. You said you work part time–you a student?"

"Yeah. Master's degree."

Caede turned briefly to her brother, her fingertips brushing gently against the boy's pallid forehead as she checked his temperature. A soft expression settled on her face and she appeared tender–motherly, even.

"Thanks for saving us," she said without looking up. "I thought I'd hallucinated that thing."

Jon nodded at his hands, fingertips pressed together again as he thought about the creature and its blank, nightmarish face.

"*Thing* seems about right," he said. "Don't think I've ever seen anything like it. Well, 'cept maybe in a horror movie."

"Same. I don't even know what to think of it," Caede replied. "It was a person, then it… changed into something else."

Jon raised his head. "It looked like a giant snake to me, or a fish. Are you telling me that thing was a person?"

"Yeah, a man. He was all burned, like he'd just escaped from a fire. I thought he was dying. I must have passed out 'cause I can't remember much after that, not until getting here."

Jon leaned back against the side of the armchair. "Is that the first one of them things you've seen?"

Caede opened her mouth as if to answer, then paused. "There were some weird-looking bodies out on the road," she said finally. "Like they'd been, I don't know, mutilated or something. One of them looked like…" She stopped and shook her head. "Sorry, this will sound stupid. They looked like a bird. Their arm was all, you know, bent at odd angles. Like a wing. I don't know how else to describe it."

Jon sighed, tucking his hands behind his head. "You're right, that sounds mad. If I hadn't seen that other one, I would have thought you'd had too much to drink…. Ah, shit."

Caede glanced up. "What is it?"

"I was gonna offer you a cup of tea, but I've got nowt here."

"It's okay, I'm not thirsty."

"Are you hungry?"

"No. I feel a bit sick, actually."

"When was the last time you ate anything?"

"I can't remember."

Jon stood. "Alright. You need to eat something or you're gonna keel over. I'll check next door and see if there's anything in there. You wait here."

Caede looked up. "It's fine. I'll help," she said, standing, her hands settling on her hips in a matter-of-fact manner.

"No, no," Jon replied. "I don't want you going. It could be dangerous."

"More dangerous than being in an unfamiliar flat with a man I don't know, with a child I need to protect, who could be used as leverage in return for my compliance?"

Jon's hand returned to the back of his neck. *Touché.*

"Woah, woah," he said, laughing nervously. "Listen, love, the only thing I'm a danger to is myself–consider yourself lucky, anyway. You could still be outside with a real monster if I hadn't..."

He paused. Caede raised an eyebrow.

"Ah...look, I'm sorry," he said. "I didn't mean it like that."

"It's fine," she said with a wave. Checking on her brother one last time, she headed to the front door. "Come on then."

Jon couldn't bring himself to look at Mrs Brown as he stepped over her. Caede winced at the sight of the body, stepping over with one hand clamped over her face.

Mrs Brown's flat was almost a cliché of an old person's home. No doilies to speak of, but the living room was cluttered with china figurines, crocheted blankets, and pot-pourri bowls. Commemorative plates lined the shelves of a heavy oak display cabinet. The walls were mint green and adorned with photo frames; images of smiling people, loved ones and relatives, most likely. But as far as he knew, Mrs Brown had lived alone since the death of her husband, and rarely had guests.

Mrs Brown had once told Jon, during one of their chance meetings in the hallway, that going up and down the stairs every day was the secret to her good health, and that if she were to move to a bungalow or, God forbid, an old age home, she'd be dead within a month. A pang of sadness crept over him at the thought of her spending the winter of her years alone, in a flat in South London instead of a picturesque countryside cottage, only to meet such a sorry fate.

In the kitchen cupboards, he and Caede found canned food, tea bags, milk, a loaf of bread within its use-by date, and some packs of biscuits. Inside the fridge, they found a few pre-prepped meals sealed in plastic containers. A quick sniff confirmed they hadn't gone off, so they set aside the tubs on the kitchen counter next to the cans and some carrier bags they'd found under the sink. As they packed up the food, Jon found his eyes flickering upwards, glimpsing Caede. Despite her frail stature, she seemed ragged and aged, as if she'd spent her life beaten and weathered by turbulent storms, and her body had kept a score of every blow. It was as if she wore a mask of malaise and exhaustion that couldn't be scrubbed off with the layers of blood and dirt.

"Your brother seems to be doing alright," he said. "We can eat and head straight to the hospital if you want."

Caede paused and gazed at the kitchen side, turning a can of baked beans over in her hands. "He needs a doctor, but I don't know if he can make the walk in his current state."

"Alright, well, let's eat and see. If he's too weak after we've had some food, he can always rest here and we'll go pick up some supplies."

"What if that thing comes back while we're out?"

Jon thought about it. The creature knew what building they were in, but would it be able to find his flat? Could it smell them? For all he knew, the thing could have bloody X-ray vision.

"No idea," he muttered. "I don't know what it's capable of. If he stays in the flat and keeps quiet, it might not find him, but he'll be a sitting duck if it does. If we try to take him with us, there's the risk that we might be putting him in more danger if it's still outside."

Caede nodded in consideration. "Okay."

"I could head to the hospital, get an ambulance or someone who can help?"

"And leave us alone here? How do I know you won't just lock us in and come back with a bunch of your mates?"

"Alright, I could stay here, and you go get someone."

"And leave my little brother in the care of a stranger?"

"What's your plan, then?"

Caede kept her gaze on the tin and said nothing.

"Tell you what," said Jon. "I could carry him. He's pretty light. I reckon I could get him there. Then he doesn't have to walk, and you don't need to worry."

She put the tin down and placed her hands flat against the counter's surface. "Why are you doing this?"

"Eh?" Jon's face warmed.

"Why are you doing all this?"

Caede looked up, her eyes burning an accusation into the cupboard in front of her. "You obviously don't need anyone to help you. And, like you said, if it wasn't for you, we'd still be out there with that thing. You don't even know us."

"I said I didn't mean it like that-"

"I know," she replied, putting a hand up. "But you're right. You saved my brother, and you've taken us into your home, and now you're offering to help us get to the hospital, and..." she trailed off and sighed, turning her face to meet his. "Why?"

Jon met her stare, and a lump rose in his throat. With a grimace, he gulped it back down and wrenched his face back towards the counter. Cheeks burning, he took one of the tins in his hands and turned it over. Maybe if he stared at the label hard enough, she'd stop looking at him with those eyes. Those grey eyes. Eyes that looked like they could have been blue once, or maybe hazel. He couldn't tell. It was as if her soul had been burned, and all that remained in its place were ashes and mistrust.

"Uh..."

He faltered and glanced at her. An unfamiliar ache formed in his chest. Why was he helping? Wouldn't anyone? They needed help. He'd helped. Simple. He'd done enough now, though, surely. The pair were alive, safe–safer than they would be outside, anyway–so why not just let them go, be on their way? He could finish his dinner for one on the roof and that would be that. And yet... His vision blurred as the despair resurfaced. Jon rubbed it away with his sleeve and sniffed.

"Just seems like the right thing to do, I guess."

He didn't look up. It wouldn't help to see her reaction and, if he was being honest, he didn't want a stranger to see him in such a state. This was the first human contact he'd had in days. The last thing he wanted was to be bawling like a little kid in front of them.

"Well, thank you," said Caede. "I don't know how I can ever repay you, but thanks all the same."

"Yeah, well," Jon said, straightening himself. "Seems the world's gone to shit. Makes sense for people to be helping each other."

Now that the risk of crying had passed, he looked up, shrugged and tried a smile. It felt awkward and lopsided. Caede met his eye, then dropped her gaze back towards the counter. He thought he saw the faintest of smiles forming. The unfamiliar ache returned, and with it, a voice telling him to stop being an idiot.

They bagged up as much food as they could carry and headed back to Jon's flat. Inside, they found Kai awake and shivering on the sofa.

"Hey," Kai croaked. "Where'd you go?"

"To find food," said Caede. "How are you feeling?"

Kai groaned, shifting his weight as he tried to sit up. "My arm hurts."

"It will be okay," replied Caede, her voice soft. "We're going to get you to a hospital, but you need to eat something, okay? You've lost a lot of blood."

"I'm cold."

"I'll get a blanket," said Jon.

Kai kept his face down and stared vacantly at the floor, perhaps trying not to cry. Caede was kneeling next to the boy, her voice gentle and soothing.

"Don't worry about it, okay? Are you hungry?"

"I feel sick," he sniffed.

"Try to eat something. I'll make a cup of tea. We found some biscuits next door. How's that sound?"

"Okay."

Caede headed towards the kitchen, but Jon cut her off, striding in front of her. "I've got it, don't worry," he said, hopping to the sink to wash his hands. "Not to be rude, but you look like you could do with some warmer clothes."

Caede looked down, examining herself. It was clear from her attire that she hadn't planned on being outside for any length of time. She wore only a skirt, vest top, and a flimsy-looking cardigan. The small apron he'd noticed earlier lined her waist, with 'Casey's' embroidered on the pocket, was drenched in red. Her shoes looked like those flimsy plimsolls a lot of girls would wear in summer, and her tights were laddered to the point of no return. If the three of them were going to be heading to the hospital, she'd need something far warmer.

"Ah. Yeah, I guess," she replied, voice quiet. "I need to wash as well. Do you have anything I can borrow?"

"Actually, I do," said Jon. He dried his hands and gestured towards the far end of the living room. "Through that hallway, door's on the left. My ex left a bunch of her shit 'ere and hasn't bothered picking it up, so help yourself."

Caede snorted. "Okay."

"There's an ensuite in there as well, so you can have a wash. Clean towels are on the shelf by the shower; you can't miss 'em."

Caede hesitated, her eyes flickering to her brother.

"He'll be fine," said Jon gently. "I promise."

She turned slowly and headed towards the bedroom. Jon stepped into the kitchen and busied himself by drying up some mugs. Kai lay quietly on the sofa. *Too weak to do much else,* Jon imagined. Caede must have been unsure about leaving her brother alone with him. *Could you blame her?*

He hoped she wouldn't judge him too harshly as he thought about the state of the bedroom. Dust coated the shelves, and empty beer cans littered the bedside tables. The bed hadn't been slept in for days. Clothing and belongings had been piled on top of it in anticipation of Tara returning to collect them, so he'd been sleeping on the sofa instead–not that he could have slept in that bed anymore. If Caede hadn't thought he was a creep before, she certainly would now. Jon heard the shower turn on and the water spraying as it hit the floor tiles. Then he heard a scream.

The mug fell from Jon's hands, bounced off the kitchen counter, and shattered on the floor. He swore and ran into the living room.

"Caede?"

The boy hadn't moved from his spot on the sofa and for a second Jon wondered if he'd imagined the scream.

"Caede?" he called. "You alright?"

No response. *Shit.* What if she'd passed out? Slipped and whacked her head? He moved to the bedroom and tapped on the ensuite door.

"Caede?" Jon repeated. Maybe he hadn't said it loudly enough. Tara's voice filled his head again. *She could be drowning in her own vomit right now, and you're just standing there. She could be dead. A dead girl in your bathroom and her injured child brother in your care.*

Shit, shit, shit.

He closed his eyes and opened the door.

"Caede? You alright?"

A small voice came from inside the shower cubicle. "Help me…"

Jon blinked, looked down at the pile of clothing on the floor, then at Caede. She stared at him through the glass shower door, wide-eyed, curled up under the water in the corner of the cubicle, back pressed against the tiles of the far wall and hugging her knees.

"Don't look!"

"I won't," said Jon, putting his hands up.

Caede twitched her head frantically at something above her, on the other side. It was a large spider, suspended on a thread between her and the shower door, unmoving. *One of those false widows*, he thought.

"It's a spider."

"Don't you think I know that? Can you just get it, please?"

"Are you sure?"

"Yes! Get it out!"

"Okay…"

Jon stepped further into the ensuite and stopped at the shower door.

"Alright," he said. "I'm gonna open the door, okay?"

"Just hurry up!"

He slid open the shower door and scooped up the spider. Stepping out from the ensuite, he caught a glimpse of her still crouching under the water.

"Can you close the door, please?" she said.

"Uh, yeah," he said. "Sorry."

He left the bedroom, face hot and nausea rising in his throat.

Jonathan Taylor, voyeur and pervert.

Taking a breath, he returned to the living room, dropping the spider out of a window to continue its life of ambushing people in bathrooms elsewhere. Kai shuffled up from the sofa.

"What happened?"

"Spider," Jon replied. "False widow."

"Oh. She hates those." Kai sighed and sank back into the cushions. "My arm hurts."

"It will do," Jon replied. "Just try to take it easy, alright?"

"Okay."

Jon headed for the kitchen to heat some food and pour a cup of tea for everyone. As the water bubbled inside the kettle, he contemplated. The hot water or heating may not have been working in the flat, but the electricity seemed to be fine. How long would it last? Was there a backup generator for the flats? Would he know how to work it? The kettle clicked, and as the steam snaked along the cupboard doors towards the window, Jon gave thought to the possibility of asking Caede and her brother if they wanted to stay with him. It was a nice change from being alone and, let's face it, better than standing on the roof. The alternative was getting the pair to the hospital, saying goodbye, and heading back home to finish what he started. Only that didn't feel so appealing now.

5

Home Invasion

Jon and Kai quietly picked at the food as they waited for Caede. She emerged a few minutes later, sheepishly stepping into the hall. Now it was free of the dirt and blood, he could see her face clearly. The cold water from the shower had brought a flush of colour to her cheeks. Her hair, ash blonde, was clean now, and combed into a loose ponytail. Her face still wore its mask of trauma, and her stony eyes carried dark bags underneath them, held there by some inner exhaustion that couldn't be cured by a decent night's sleep. Jon wondered how many days she'd spent hunched over a computer screen after nights of working at the pub.

She wore a blue knitted jumper, the one he'd bought for Tara as a Christmas present the year before, and a pair of old jeans, ones with rips in the knees. They looked too big for her, and the jumper hung loosely from one of her shoulders. She stood awkwardly in the doorway, shifting her weight and wringing her hands. Jon hopped from the sofa, offering her the space.

"Here," he said. "Food's ready."

Caede sat down. "Thanks. I picked these up from a pile on the bed. Is that alright?"

"Uh, yeah, that's fine," Jon replied. "Funny story. I got that jumper for my ex last Christmas. She's never worn it."

"That doesn't sound funny."

"Yeah. I don't know why I said that."

"I can take something else if you want?"

"Nah, it's yours now. She's probably not coming back for it."

"Oh, sorry. She's probably…"

"Dead?" said Jon. "Who knows?"

Caede and Kai glanced at each other.

"It's alright," said Jon. "I've made my peace with it. We weren't married. I wasn't making an effort, and she'd started seeing her personal trainer five times a week. Should have seen it coming, really."

"Oh well," replied Caede. "Her loss, right? What's he got that you haven't?"

"A magic dick and a six-pack, I imagine."

Jon handed a plate of food to Caede and sat on the floor next to the sofa.

"So, scared of spiders, eh?" he said.

"Not all of them," she replied flatly, without looking up. "Just the ones like that. I was bitten by one when I was little and had an allergic reaction. I had to be rushed to hospital."

"Ah, sorry. I didn't mean anything by it."

"It's fine."

He looked down and noticed her feet were bare. "You're gonna need some shoes if we're heading out."

"Oh, yeah," she replied, glancing at them, as if to confirm the fact. "Don't suppose your ex left any trainers or anything?"

"I'll have a look," Jon replied. He disappeared into the bedroom and after a minute, returned with a clean pair of socks and some well-worn running shoes. "I hope these are okay. They're a bit used."

The trainers had seen better days, but they had to be miles better than the tiny pumps she'd been wearing. At least now she would be able to run properly if the creature was still out there.

After eating, Caede inspected Kai's arm, her face neutral as she looked at the wound. Jon leaned forward, glancing at Kai's face. It was clear the boy was Caede's brother, with his straw-blond mess of hair and steely eyes. And, like his sister, he wore trauma on his face like an iron mask. Something about him was off, though. Maybe it was the blood loss, or the light in the flat, but the kid looked a funny colour. Kind of grey. And there was a fine coating of what looked like lanugo on his cheeks and neck. It didn't make sense. And the creature that attacked him…would a bite be contagious? Was it like a zombie movie, one bite, and that was it? Would the kid turn into a creature too?

The fresh clothing hung loosely off Kai's slim frame–Jon's smallest available, an old T-shirt and hoodie he hadn't worn in about a decade–but was far better than the blood-soaked shirt he had on. Warmer too. Caede helped the boy change while Jon waited in the kitchen, elbows resting on the counter. She appeared under the archway that separated the two rooms, holding her plate and Kai's old, bloody T-shirt.

"Is there anywhere I can put this for now?"

Jon rested his back against the counter and nodded to the sink. "Pop it in there; I'll sort it out when we get back."

Jon met her eye. She wore a strange expression, one he couldn't quite place.

"Ignore me," he said quickly. "Leave it in the sink. I'll get it washed for you."

"Thanks."

"Let's hope there's someone still alive at the hospital, eh?"

Caede settled herself against the archway, cast her eyes down and said nothing. Jon shifted his weight. His hands found the pockets of his trousers and planted themselves firmly inside.

"Sorry," said Jon. "That came out wrong. There'll be someone there, right? Worst-case scenario, we'll find another hospital. We've stopped the bleeding, so we've got time. We can figure something out. It'll be fine, I promise."

Caede's head tilted up, and she shot Jon a look. "Who are you to promise that?"

Jon rubbed his face with his hands. She was right. He turned to the drawers under the kitchen countertop and rifled through one, pulling out a packet of cigarettes and a lighter.

"Want one?" he said, waving the box like a white flag.

Caede's stance softened, and she let out a sigh. "Yeah," she said, leaving the plate and shirt in the sink.

"Sorry," she said. "I'm just really scared, and I don't know what to do. He's my little brother. I'm supposed to protect him."

Jon handed her a cigarette. She pressed it to her lips and sparked the lighter, letting the tiny flame flicker over the end of it. Jon lit his own, and they stood next to each other, leaning against the kitchen counter in silence.

"They're a bit stale, sorry," said Jon.

"It's fine."

She drew in a breath and closed her eyes as if to savour the rush of the nicotine, before letting the smoke pour slowly from her open mouth.

"I'm surprised you smoke," said Jon.

"Why?" said Caede.

"Most people vape nowadays."

"I read somewhere that vaping is worse for you."

"Probably. I'm not one to talk… Listen. You asked before why I was helping you," said Jon. "Truth is, I had a bit of a near-death experience today. Changed a few things, you know?"

He chuckled sadly and looked down at the cigarette. "You two really messed up my evening."

"I guess that makes us even for the pool table," she said quietly, taking another drag.

He caught her eye, and she regarded him for an uncomfortable amount of time, as if assessing him. He held her gaze, unsure if he should look away or not. The whiskey threatened to make its return.

"You alright?" he said with a gulp.

"I dunno," she said, casting her eyes to the window. "I'm waiting for the moment I wake up and all this was some weird, fucked up dream. I feel like I'm in shock."

"Seems about average for me," said Jon, half laughing again. He stuffed his hands back into his pockets, leaving the cigarette to balance on his bottom lip. "I'm half drunk, I've had an argument with a member of the opposite sex, and I'm smoking, even though I said I'd quit…. The boy's new."

Caede sniggered and took another drag.

"I am grateful, honestly," she said. "I've always thought people were kind of selfish. Our mum died when I was a teenager. Cancer. When my dad found out it was terminal, he filed for divorce. Turns out he'd been having an affair with one of his colleagues. When my grandparents took custody, he didn't even fight for us. I haven't spoken to him in years. I don't even know if he's alive."

"Shit," said Jon. "I'm sorry."

"It is what it is."

"My ma went the same way," said Jon.

"I'm sorry," said Caede. "I don't know why I brought it up."

"Look," said Jon. "I know you don't know me, and you got no reason to trust me. But I'm a man of my word. I'll get you to the hospital. And, you've probably got somewhere already, but you're welcome to stay here till all this blows over. Safety in numbers n' all that… Only if you want to, mind."

"Thanks. I'll think about it."

They packed a rucksack with some basics. Not knowing how long they'd be at the hospital, Jon decided some food and a change of clothes would probably be enough. He paused. Would that thing still be out there? Would they need weapons? Even if he had any in the apartment, he wouldn't know how to use them. He hadn't fired a gun in years, and that was only at a clay pigeon ground for a stag weekend. In the end, he settled for his Swiss Army knife. A present from an uncle well over a decade ago, and he'd never used it for anything before, but he supposed that it might come in handy.

Caede had borrowed a ropy-looking denim jacket from the pile of clothing in the bedroom. "I couldn't find any winter coats," she said. "I guess I can always find something warmer in one of the shops—if the looters haven't taken them all. Do you think it'll count as shoplifting if I just took a coat from somewhere?"

"I won't tell if you don't," said Jon.

Kai sat upright on the sofa, quiet and patiently waiting. His eyes were red and puffy.

"You alright, bud?" asked Jon.

"I feel dizzy," said Kai, looking down at his arm.

Jon put his hand on the boy's forehead and whipped it away again. Heat radiated off it like a furnace. He couldn't understand it. Not that he knew many kids, or much about fevers, but he knew skin shouldn't be that hot.

"It'll be okay," said Jon unconvincingly. "Let me get you a jacket, hang on."

Jon headed to the bedroom and grabbed a coat from the wardrobe. He was about to leave when he remembered the ring. It would only get lost if it stayed in his pocket. Better to put it back in its box for now. He reached for the bedside table and opened the drawer, finding the small velvet ring box at the back, stuffed behind a mountain of socks.

That's odd.

The ring was already in its box. He looked at the one in his hand, then the one in the box. At a glance, they were almost identical. On closer inspection, he realised the gems were different colours. And the ring he'd bought for Tara was slightly larger, the sapphire lighter, the diamonds an alternating mix of white and yellow. He frowned. The ring in his hand must have belonged to Caede. Maybe it slipped off while they were seeing to Kai? Regardless, it looked expensive, and she'd want it back.

He returned the box to its drawer and headed back to the living room, the ring in his hand.

"Hey, Caede," he said. "I think this is..."

Before Jon could finish his sentence, a tremor swept across the apartment. The building shook as if a train had hit it, filling the air with the sound of glass and metal crushing and grinding against each other.

"What the fuck was that?" Caede gasped.

"I don't know," said Jon. "Can't be good, whatever it is."

"It's the monster," said Kai, his voice shrill and trembling. Any colour the poor boy might have had left in his face drained from him.

Jon threw on a coat, handing Caede the rucksack. "Time we headed out, don't you think? Yeah?"

Caede and Kai nodded in response.

"Come on then," said Jon. "Electric's still working; we can take the lift down."

"Could we hide?" said Caede. "It doesn't know exactly where we are, does it?"

"No!" Kai whispered, looking up at his sister with eyes full of fear. "It can smell. It'll find us."

"That and the blood trail we left up the stairs," Jon added. "I don't know about you, but I don't want to find out if it's smart enough to follow it."

Jon lifted Kai onto his back and headed for the front door. He gazed out of the peephole before opening it enough to allow a sliver of light to spill across the floor and dissipate into the empty corridor. There was nothing but silence on the other side. If the creature was inside the building, he couldn't hear it. He closed his eyes and listened more intently. Somewhere below, glass and rubble crunched underneath something–not like something was stepping on it. Like a heavy form was dragging it along the ground. Jon tried to remember what the creature looked like. It didn't have arms or legs, or it didn't seem to when he'd tackled it. Could it even get up the stairs?

He couldn't tell how far away it was–as if that mattered. If they didn't move now, they might lose their chance. Together, they sprinted for the lift and jumped inside, just in time to see the creature appear at the stairwell door.

Jon hammered the ground floor button. "Come on, come on, hurry the fuck up!"

An explosion of glass and metal reverberated through the corridor. The lift mechanism whirred into life, and with a lurch the doors began to slide together. Just as they were about to close, they jolted open again. The dead girl's leg was still blocking the entrance.

"Shit!"

Jon kicked the corpse away, and the doors began to close again. Suddenly, the creature's face burst through the gap. Jon yelped and tumbled backwards. Caede leapt forward with the rucksack, swinging it hard. It collided with the creature, knocking it violently back into the hallway. The doors closed, and the lift began to move. The screech of twisting metal followed.

"It's coming after us!" Caede yelled.

"It'll get stuck in the lift shaft," said Jon. "Soon as the doors open, run for it, alright?"

There was a heavy jolt, and the lift lurched, bowling the three over. Caede and Kai screamed. Jon clung to the handrail, fighting the urge to throw up as the lift shuddered and squealed under the weight of the creature. He wondered if the cables would last much longer. *Only one floor to go.* Not far to fall if it came to it. The lift slowed to a halt, reaching its final destination. Caede readied herself to run. Jon lifted Kai once again onto his back, wrenched open the outer doors, and they piled out of the lift, hurtling towards the street outside.

62

6

Arachnophobia

The lobby door was hanging on one hinge and glass shards covered the floor. Caede sprinted ahead to clear a path for Jon and Kai, and the three of them spilled into the street. The shrieks and wails of the creature pursued them as it thrashed inside the lift shaft. They ran until the building disappeared from view and the air fell quiet once more.

Lungs heaving for breath, they continued on, turning into the council estate. It was a rabbit warren of tight, winding alleyways and hovels of grey cement blocks and black roof tiles, half of them falling apart thanks to government cutbacks.

They finally stopped running and settled to rest in an alley. Caede slumped against a wall, sucking air into her burning chest. Jon set Kai down on the pavement and rested his hands on his knees, eyes closed, and sweat dripping from his brow as he panted.

"I think we can walk now," he said finally. "Super smell or not, I don't think snake man's getting out of that lift shaft anytime soon."

Caede snorted. "Snake man? Is that what you're calling it?"

"What? Makes sense, don't it? What would you call it?"

Caede shrugged in response.

"Alright," said Jon. "Snake man it is."

Caede shook her head and stood. "Let's keep going."

"Alright–gimme a sec."

The three continued towards the hospital. Between checking the direction and the street signs, Caede found herself glancing at her new travelling companion, half suspicious that she had fallen into some kind of trap, half worried she'd offended him by coming across as ungrateful. But the man had no reason to help them, and nobody just helped. He'd already done enough by taking them in. If his story about his near-death experience was true, maybe this was just catharsis, some new lease on life, or 'come-to-Jesus' moment. Maybe he believed he owed them some sort of life debt. *Oh God,* she thought. *What if he's some kind of religious nut?*

The strain of carrying Kai's weight was showing now. Sweat dripped from the man's hair–a mop of chestnut brown that had gone far too long without a trim–and his jaw sat tight against the rest of his face. Still, he soldiered on. The man had belonged to the local rugby club, she remembered, and she could believe it, even if it looked like he'd let himself go a bit. Broad enough in the shoulder to hold his own in a scrum, certainly. Strong enough to overpower her if he wanted to. Not that it would be a challenge in her current state. Throw a poor diet and years of excessive cardio into the mix, and a strong enough breeze could take her out. There wasn't much choice in the matter. Kai was too weak to make it to the hospital without being carried. All Caede could do was trust this stranger and hope that his intentions were honest. He'd gotten rid of the spider, though, hadn't he? *Not before having a look,* she thought.

The man turned back and caught her looking. She shot her head towards the floor and hoped he hadn't noticed her scrutiny.

"You alright?" he asked.

Caede raised her head and saw that he'd stopped and was looking at her with concern.

"It's nothing," she said. "I'm fine. Do you want to swap out?"

"Nah, s'alright. Can do this all day, me."

"Only if you're sure."

He grinned, or at least tried to, and turned back.

The last embers of daylight had faded, fully surrendering to the fluorescent glow of the streetlamps as night set in. Shadows crept like ghosts over the nearby cars and buildings, and Caede jumped at every shape that met her periphery. The breeze didn't help. It swept through the trees and bushes, puppeteering them, turning them into whispering, dancing monsters that waved to her as she passed by.

From the ground, the bodies watched silently with frost-tinged hair and eyelashes, following Caede's every step. She swallowed a shiver and turned her gaze up towards the streetlights. How much longer would they last before the grid finally stopped working? Was all of London affected, or just the south? What about the rest of the country? Was it like this everywhere?

Puffs of steam billowed from her mouth and dissipated into the cold air as they reached the train station and marketplace. Less of an actual market space as one would expect it to be, it was a long, narrow street that ran below the overground station, filled with stalls and food trucks. A week ago, this street had been bustling with life, music, movement, each stall decorated in vibrant colours, heaving with local produce, handmade goods, second-hand goods, and items you didn't ask too many questions about, like car parts and computer components. Suddenly it was all gone, and only the metal skeletons of the stalls remained. One had been knocked over and lay on its side, contents trampled into the pavement.

An oppressive silence hung over them as they tip-toed through, sending spectres crawling into Caede's imagination, taunting her as she trod over the debris. She considered the possibility of more creatures existing, all of them similar to the snake-thing that had attacked them.

That thing hadn't caught up to them. Hopefully it was still trapped in that lift shaft, but she couldn't shake the feeling that, at any moment, she would hear its ghostly hiss right behind her. Bile burned the back of her throat at the thought. But if more of them did exist, where were they?

After a while, they reached the car park and main entrance of St. Luke's Hospital. The building stood on the corner of two adjoining major roads that led into the city centre, its imposing silhouette visible even in the darkness. A wall of trees and shrubs protected its grounds and the lower windows of the building–no doubt planted to reduce noise pollution and dirt from the nearby road. The plants contrasted with the stark, modern architecture of the area, offering a snippet of the natural world to the city dwellers who lived around it. Their shadows twisted across the grounds as if they were reaching out for the building, trying to claw their way inside.

As the three approached the entrance, Caede looked up at the black, empty windows and her heart sank. Either the building was abandoned or locked down. Jon lowered Kai off his shoulders and tried the main entrance doors, but they held fast. Caede peered into the lobby on the other side of the glass.

"That's weird," she said. "It looks so quiet. Part of me thought the hospital would be heaving right now."

"Looks like it's been closed for days," Jon replied.

"That makes no sense," said Caede. "Why would you close a hospital while all this was going on?"

"No idea." Jon rested his hands on his hips and sucked his teeth in frustration. "It's gonna be a right pain in the arse to get inside now."

"Could we smash the glass?" Caede asked. "Break a window?"

Jon shook his head in response. "Too risky. Could set off an alarm, and we don't know how many of those things are out here. But look, it's locked for a reason, right? I bet someone's in there."

Caede looked around, eyeing the scenery with suspicion. "Let's just hurry, whatever we do. I don't like being out here."

Something was shuffling around in the bushes nearby. A small animal, maybe; a fox? She turned her head towards the sound, following it with her ears as it moved.

Voice low, she leaned into Jon's ear. "Did you hear that?"

Jon paused and then looked up, squinting into the dark. "No, what is it?"

"Something moving. Over there."

Jon frowned. "I can't hear anything," he said. "You got super hearing or summat?"

"Shhh."

Caede closed her eyes, trying to focus on the sound. Whatever it was, it had moved on. "I think it's gone now."

"Might be a fox," Jon said. "They're normally out by this time."

"Yeah, maybe," Caede replied, unconvinced, as she stared into the nearby shrubs. She checked her watch. *November 2nd, 18:15.* Were foxes out this early?

"Well, whatever it was, let's get inside," said Jon. "The sooner we're indoors, the better."

He picked up Kai, and they headed to the side of the building and into the multi-storey car park, following the luminescent marked path towards the entrance doors inside. The light of the streetlamps filtered in from outside, illuminating the silhouettes of the cars resting peacefully in their spaces, as if the carnage outside had never existed. A puddle reflected it back at Caede. Water dripped steadily from one of the ceiling beams. Jon and Caede weaved between the cars, keeping low and quiet, listening out for any signs of life.

"We should be able to get into one of these doors," he said. "They're electronic. Power looks like it's out, so it'll only be spring bolted right now. Credit card will see to that."

"How on earth do you know that?" said Caede.

"My brother's a locksmith."

"Really?"

"Nah. Just watch a lot of YouTube."

"Very funny."

Jon wiggled the card into the gap where the deadbolt met the door. It hit metal and nothing happened. Jon pushed the card in further. It bent and slipped, falling through the gap to the other side of the door.

"Bugger," said Jon, deflated. "Okay. Let's try the next level. There might be an older door upstairs. You know what this means, though?"

"What's that?"

"Someone's locked this from the inside."

Using Jon's phone as a torch, Caede led the way towards the car park staircase. Even though it was open to the elements, the stench of piss rose from the cement steps and hung in the air like a miasma. It was hard to tell which was worse, the smell of the bodies or this. She held her breath as they ascended to the next level.

Stepping onto the next floor, Caede looked around to see a path running between the columns of parking spaces to a door on the other side marked FIRE EXIT. She aimed the torch beam over it and noticed the rubber seal didn't line up with the frame.

"I think the door's open, it-"

She stopped. A loud tapping echoed from the level below.

"Can you hear that?" she asked.

Jon stopped. "Yeah," he replied. "Could be water dripping?"

"It doesn't sound like water."

The pair stood still and listened. There was a faint shuffling and a clicking that sounded like heeled shoes on a hard floor, or the ticking of a clock, only it was out of sync, uneven.

"Could be another survivor?" said Caede.

"Maybe."

The sound entered the stairwell. Jon gently nudged Kai.

"Hey, bud, can you stand for a minute?"

"I think so," said Kai.

"It's alright," said Caede, "I'll hold him."

Jon lowered and let Kai slide off. Caede took him and looped his remaining arm over her shoulder.

"Wait here. I'll check it out," Jon whispered.

Caede handed him the phone, and he aimed it at the doorway. The beam cut into the darkness and disappeared down the stairs. From inside came a low moan, soft and juvenile, like a child's. Caede tightened her grip around Kai's waist, taking a step backwards. A tiny figure appeared in the doorway, a young girl, no older than Kai. She stood on bare, blackened feet, her shoulders hunched, wearing a hospital gown and flimsy-looking pyjama bottoms. Long, matted hair hung over her face. In the torchlight, her exposed limbs appeared thin and pale as bones. Jon held his hand up to Caede and Kai, signalling for them to stay behind him as he stepped slowly towards her.

"Hey," he said. "Are you okay? Do you need some help?"

The girl looked up. "Help?"

"Yeah," he repeated. "Do you need some help?"

The girl stared up at him with wide, vacant eyes as she repeated Jon's words back. "Do you…need some…help?" *Tck.*

"No, poppet, I'm fine," said Jon. "I'm asking if you need help. Are you alright?"

"Jon?" said Caede, taking a step towards him.

"It's okay," he replied, waving her off. "I got it."

Tck. Tck.

Unease knotted around Caede's stomach. As the girl spoke, Caede couldn't see her mouth, or anything else underneath the matted strands of hair, except for a pair of glittering black eyes staring at Jon. Her head twitched and shuddered as she spoke, but the rest of her body remained still as a shop mannequin, her arms hanging limp at her side. And there was that clicking sound. Where was it coming from? Caede had an urge to run.

"Jon," she said. "Something's not right."

Without looking back, he nodded. "Alright. Just head to the door."

The girl looked at Jon, head tilted. *Tck.* "Do…you…need…some…help?"

The three took a step back. Caede held Kai close and whispered in his ear. "Get ready to run, okay?"

Kai nodded.

Tilting her head further, the girl stared, unblinking, at Jon.

"Help?" she repeated. *Tck.*

As if awakening from a deep sleep, the girl lifted her arms and stretched them outwards in an arc. She did the same with her legs, lifting each one and twirling her extremities as if she were warming them up from a long sleep. Then she rose. She just *rose.* Caede stared, frozen, as she watched the girl's feet leave the floor. Four long, grey limbs unfurled from the girl's back, filling the doorway as they lifted her into the open space of the car park floor. Suddenly the girl was above them, hovering in the air like a nightmarish marionette, her black eyes glittering as she gazed at the three. Like a *spider.* A scream rose in Caede's throat and stayed there, snagged behind gritted teeth. She felt Kai tighten his grip on her shoulder.

"Jon," she said. Her voice sounded hoarse and distant. "Get away from it…"

The clicking sound filled the surrounding air, in time with the girl's limbs lifting and falling, each following the other in uniform succession as if she were testing them out.

"Help," said the girl. She smiled. Lines formed across her pale face, first faint, then deeper as the skin creased and split. With a crack, the girl's jaw swung open and fell. Two large, black fangs curled out from the void within.

Jon said something. She couldn't hear him. Her feet were already moving. Without looking back, she dashed towards the door. Jon shouted something. Kai stumbled and cried out. Caede gripped her brother tighter and dragged him along. *Just get to the door.* Jon shouted again. Her hand met the metal handle and she tore the door open, heaving Kai over the threshold before leaping in herself. She turned back, hand outstretched to grab Jon, to pull him to safety, to get him away from that *thing.*

"Jon!"

Clouds of steam poured from his mouth as he hurtled towards the door. The monstrous girl was close behind him, her bony arms outstretched. He reached the door. Their fingertips touched. Suddenly he was no longer moving, but staring blank faced, his eyes wide. Caede glanced down to see thin, white threads wrapped around his chest. Too late, she jumped forward to grab him. He was already out of reach, flying backwards through the air. With a sickening thud, he hit the ground and lay still. Black eyes staring hungrily, the girl floated above Jon's body, twirling the threads between her fingers as she pulled him towards her. A groan escaped his lungs. Opening his eyes, he turned to meet Caede's.

"Go!" he gasped.

7

Accident & Emergency

"We've got it!"

"Okay, [CENSORED], head back."

"We're on our way now. Can't believe we did it!"

"Just get out before you get caught. I've sent the van round. Get it all on camera and get back here in one piece."

-

As of posting this entry, I can confirm that our special investigations team have completed a raid on a hidden facility, right here in London, and found proof that the military, our government, are creating illegal biological weapons. I have included the footage and screenshots via the video link below.

Our team has secured samples of what an anonymous source informs us is called "Sigma Delta Tau." It's a military funded gene-editing technology. You know what this means, people. It's going to be just like the pigs all over again.

The warmongers of this country have been allowed to continue, unchecked and unpunished, for too long. We need to hold them accountable. It's bad enough our rights are stripped away, year after year—microchip ID just to vote. Spied on every hour of every day. And now, you and I, the taxpayers of this nation, are being forced to bankroll government-sanctioned mass murder.

How many of our loved ones have been used as throwaway bodies for the war machine? How many of us have gone hungry, gone cold, because of this pointless effort?

-

Saturday, second of November. Twenty-one days until I'm married. Ravi lay on the floor of his office, staring vacantly up at the off-white ceiling panels. It wasn't really his office. He'd commandeered the room in the absence of its previous resident; some upper-managerial type who didn't bother themselves with patients or paperwork. They were in no position to argue about it, what with them being dead and all. Ravi could have claimed the entire building, and no one would argue with it. Well, no one but Efia and Holly. They might have something to say. But right now, they weren't there; they were out foraging. He would have joined them, but at the time he couldn't face going outside again. Not out *there* again. Efia, Holly, and him. All that was left of the St. Luke's Hospital staff.

Ravi followed the patterns on the ceiling panels, hoping if he studied them hard enough, it would push the thought of it all back to the inner sanctum of his subconscious. In its place came the faces of his family. His exuberant sisters, his ferocious mother, his father sat in a beanbag chair, restringing a guitar. Farha, asking him what he thought about this colour satin for the chairs at the wedding breakfast. He wondered why they called it a breakfast when it was served in the evening.

They'd planned to attend a local wedding fair that day, but he'd been stuck in A&E. He closed his eyes and watched Farha's face light up at the mention of free cake samples and brochure collecting. They'd already made all the arrangements, but there was going to be an antique car she'd wanted to see at the event; she could arrive at the temple in style. The weather had been perfect for it; clear skies, no rain. Sunshine all day.

It had rained since, though–rained all day and night, in fact. And instead of eating cake samples, he was on a hospital floor with only the dead for company. In his mind, he and Farha were at the fair, laughing, bickering over the cake flavours. Planning their new lives together. Two kids? No. Three. His sisters could teach them guitar and bask in their cool aunt status. His dad would cook far too much food and go overboard with the snacks. His mother would have delighted in telling them all kinds of tall tales. Everything had been falling into place. Promising career, loving family, dream wedding. It had taken only a week for it all to crumble to dust. The smiling faces of his sisters, his parents, Farha, all blurred and faded as the tears poured.

When he heard the shouting, he'd considered going to investigate. It was the right thing to do, but he had taken all he could, and these new cries were only distracting him from his melancholy, from his memories. Instead of leaving the office, he curled into a ball, held his hands over his ears, and wept.

The shouting died down, and Ravi sat up. He knew he should have investigated. It could have been Efi or Holly... What if it was his family coming to find him? No, they'd been evacuated with everyone else—he hoped. Guilt urged him up off the floor and dragged him into the hallway towards the source of the sound.

Treading tentatively through the dark corridors, he passed the main reception and paused, peeking through the glass doors to see if anyone was hanging around outside. The reception was smart-tech-powered, and couldn't be shut down without some electrical know-how, so the three remaining survivors settled for locking just the inner doors. Made of smart glass, the outer doors absorbed radiance much like a solar panel and powered the reception area, making it self-sustaining. Part of a 'Go-green' government initiative. All the newer hospitals—and those with successful grant applications—had them installed. Solar panels on the roof, smart-glass front doors. Saved the National Health Service millions every year, apparently, but didn't seem to slow the tide of cutbacks and corruption scandals.

Ravi, Holly and Efia had done their best to close off as much of the ground floor as possible, including the A&E department. It was full of bodies, and they didn't want to be anywhere near them. If any survivors came looking for help, they could treat them somewhere else, in one of the cleaner wards upstairs. Fortunately, the windows on the ground floor were all barred, and the doors were locked save for a fire exit leading to the car park, which he and Efi agreed to use as their way in and out of the building.

From his vantage point, he could see into the reception, but beyond that, only darkness, and the pale slivers of light that slid across the glass of the outer door. Ravi shivered and retreated back into the hallway.

He wondered if this was the best course of action. Should he have brought something? A knife, perhaps? There would be no point. He was in no position to defend himself either way, or anyone else, for that matter. He was a sensible, middle-class British man who drank tea, read books, avoided tabloid newspapers, and always remembered to phone his mother. Civilised. Still, bringing something, anything, might have been prudent.

He continued on, heading towards the access door. When he reached the stairwell, his ears picked up the sound of two people, strangers, arguing. They must have found the door, but how had they gotten in? Efi would have closed it as she always did. Perhaps it was Efi who let them in. They could be survivors needing help.... Or they could be something else. Palms sweating, Ravi stood at the base of the stairs, agonising over whether to find out who the trespassers might be, or sneak back to his office and pretend they weren't there. He straightened himself, adjusted his jacket, and stepped into the hallway.

A boy sat slumped against the wall next to the door, deathly pale. One of his arms was far shorter than the other and wrapped in towels. A young woman was looking out of the doorway, calling for someone. She closed the door and shook her head.

"He's gone."

The boy squirmed, trying to get up. "We can't just leave him!"

"We don't have a choice, Kai," said the woman. "That thing got him."

"You don't know that!"

"I literally just saw it," she said, kneeling down to reach for him. "Now come on, we need to go."

"Hello?" said Ravi.

The woman jumped and spun on her feet to face him. In the low light she appeared frail and dishevelled, eyes raw and swollen, but blazing with fury. Her fists were curled into tight balls, ready to fight, like a cornered cat protecting its kitten. She stepped in front of the boy and glared at Ravi, lips peeled back to reveal her teeth.

"Who are you?" she demanded.

"I'm sorry?" said Ravi.

"I said, who are you? Do you work here?"

"Yes, I work here. Did Efia send you?"

"Who?"

Ravi pushed up his glasses and pinched the bridge of his nose. He walked over to the door, checked the lock, then peered out into the car park. Only darkness. Where the hell were they?

"Are you a doctor?" said the woman. "We need help."

She gestured to the boy on the floor. He sat up and turned to show Ravi the crudely wrapped remains of what should have been an arm.

"He's lost a lot of blood," she said, her voice softer this time.

Ravi kneeled down to look at the boy. Finding Efi and Holly would have to wait for now.

"You came to the right place," said Ravi. "Let's get him upstairs so I can have a proper look at him."

The woman took the boy's good arm and looped it over her shoulder, lifting him up. "Thank you."

"Who were you calling just then?" Ravi asked.

"Another survivor. We met him earlier," said the woman, her voice quiet. "He helped us get here. Then this *thing* attacked us. We ran, but… he didn't make it."

The woman looked down and shook her head.

"I'm sorry," said Ravi.

She sniffed. "It is what it is."

8

The Doctor

The ceiling panels faded in and out of focus. Kai sat in a wheelchair by the door of the ward, drifting as he watched Caede and the doctor scrub up. Nausea washed over him in waves, and he gripped the handle of the seat with his good arm, trying to focus on not throwing up. For a moment, he wondered why they were in a hospital. Then he remembered they needed help. Why did they need help again?

Caede's voice echoed in the distance as she replied to the doctor. "Just tell me what to do."

"Okay," said the doctor. "Arms out, put these on. Oh, here, take these. And this hair cap."

Kai wondered if this was what dying felt like. If it was, it seemed okay. The pain in his arm had faded, and in its place was a floating sensation, as if he were lying in a deep pool of warm water. Caede and the doctor lifted him out of the wheelchair, and he drifted over to the operating table, floating, watching the ceiling panels dance around him. The doctor said something, but Kai couldn't hear him. Caede replied, her voice foreign and intelligible.

Kai looked up at her. "I wanna finish this level first…"

"Shh," she whispered. "It's okay. Just relax, alright? Everything's going to be okay."

She was stroking his hair. Their mother used to do that. Her eyes were watering. *Why is she always so sad?* Kai returned his gaze to the ceiling. The room appeared dark except for a light above him. Its brightness stung his eyes. He grimaced and closed them.

Caede's voice cut through the haze. "What do you mean, you've never done this before?"

"I said," replied the doctor, "I haven't operated on an arm before. Plenty of people lose fingers and toes, but few people come in missing an arm. Would you prefer to do it and I watch?"

"Alright, calm down. I was only asking. What do you need me to do?"

"Hold his arm here…. No, here. Good, good."

Kai looked down at his remaining arm. It seemed a million miles away. Caede swayed as she hooked something up to it.

"We need to work quickly," the doctor assured. "He's in Haemorrhagic shock. You're sure about his blood type?"

"I'm sure. You know what you're doing, right?"

"No, I'm just pretending to be a doctor. I'm actually going to harvest his kidneys for the black market. Bloody hell!"

"Fine, I get it! What else do you need me to…"

The world faded away as Kai drifted into unconsciousness.

***

"Take this please," said Ravi, handing Caede a bloodied scalpel. "Okay."

She kept her eyes away from it as she dropped it into a metal tray, alongside a variety of other instruments, settling them on Ravi as he worked. Beads of sweat formed on his forehead and his eyes narrowed, focused on the task in front of him. Glare from the overhead lights cast deep shadows over his face and etched fine lines into his forehead. The lights had lasted far longer than expected, considering that they were running from the solar batteries alone. According to Ravi, they were powering the rest of the equipment too, and at less capacity.

"Dab, please," said Ravi.

Caede obliged and dabbed his face with a pad before discarding it into the tray. Her eyes returned to Kai, who lay in a deep sleep, peaceful and unmoving under the effects of the anaesthetic. Had they administered enough? Too much? Without a proper surgeon or anaesthetist, it was hard to say. Ravi had assured her that, despite having never performed this exact procedure before, he had some surgical training, and felt confident he could close up the arm with few complications. It was better than nothing, and better than trying to work with Kai awake.

Caede looked over at the heart monitor, the drip, and the tubes protruding from Kai's body. He looked so small. Not since the funeral had he seemed so small. She checked his face, relieved to see some of the warmth returning to it little by little. He still looked grey, not just pale. It was concerning. Ravi had informed her that Kai would need to stay at the hospital for at least a week to recover, time she could use to piece together the missing memories between her last shift and waking up on the pavement. In the present, when she tried to recall the days leading up to that night, a headache was all that came.

"Pass me that dressing, please?" said Ravi.

Caede passed it, glimpsing what remained of Kai's arm. The first aid she and Jon administered had saved Kai's life, but it paled compared to the handiwork of a professional. In the few hours they had been inside the operating theatre, Ravi had smoothed the bone, removed the damaged skin and stitched it all up neatly. He stood up straight and stretched, yawning.

"It's done," he said. "He just needs to rest, and hopefully within a few hours he'll be awake again, provided I haven't administered too much anaesthetic."

Exhaustion and relief enveloped Caede, and she leaned heavily against the table. It had been a long day, and the adrenaline that had been holding her up was now gone.

"Will he be okay?" she asked.

"He should be fine," Ravi replied. "Though he might be nauseated for a few days. We'll have to keep the wound and the dressings clean. I assume you'll be staying here with him while he recovers?"

"Where else is there to go?" said Caede sadly.

After wheeling Kai's bed to a private patient suite, the pair took it in turns to use the bathroom and fetch food. Caede found a group of untouched vending machines in one of the hallways and helped herself to some chocolate and crisps from one, and two cups of coffee from the other. Hardly nutritious, but it was better than going hungry. She sat cross-legged in an armchair beside Kai's bed. Ravi sat on a sofa nearby, coffee in hand.

"So," she said. "What exactly happened here?"

Ravi stretched out his legs and closed his eyes. He took his glasses in his hand and turned them over, as if in contemplation, gathering his thoughts before giving his answer, perhaps even reliving the events and trying not to break down. It was a hard question, but it needed to be asked, and she needed to know. She'd been unconscious for God knows how long, with no memory of the nights before, or even the week before, for that matter.

"Unfortunately, I don't have the full picture," he replied. "We had a few people come into A&E with vomiting, diarrhoea, the sort of symptoms you would expect from a viral infection. We get a few in at this time of year. It's flu season. Suddenly, we were swamped. We didn't have enough beds to hold them all. We followed quarantine procedure, notified authorities, and sent off samples for analysis, believing it to be another Ebola outbreak like the one in 2027. But the tests came back negative. It spread quickly. There was nothing we could do. Then the military came in, took most of the bodies, tested us, and left us here when we came back clean, told us to stay and report any more cases that came in. Everyone else was evacuated. They said they were taking the surviving patients to facilities outside of the city. I don't know where."

"So, not everyone is dead, then."

"Lord, no. I also don't know why they just left us here. They just said to carry on doing what we're doing, that things will eventually return to normal. Whatever that means."

Ravi rubbed his temples. Dark circles hung under his eyelids and his face sagged. He shook his head and pushed his glasses back up his nose.

"What about you?" he asked. "How did you and your brother get here?"

"I can't remember much. I woke up outside, around the corner from my house. I thought maybe I'd been spiked or something, but then I saw all the bodies. I must have passed out right after. When I woke up again, this guy, Jon, was standing over me."

Caede cast her eyes down to explore the inside of the cup. "He saved us from that... *thing*."

"And you feel okay, yes?"

"I've probably got a concussion, but I'm fine."

"I can take a look at you, if you want?"

Caede shrugged. "Honestly, it's fine."

Ravi nodded. "Okay. If you start to feel nauseated or dizzy, let me know. Tell me more about the thing. Did it look human?"

"Yeah," she replied, glancing up. "I can't really describe it. It was a man. Then it changed."

She paused, her eyes moving to the operating table. "Kai must have come out to find me, because he was there when I woke up. Then we came here to get help.... You've seen them then, those things?"

Ravi stared at the floor, voice low as he spoke.

"I've been calling them chimaera," he said. "Some of the patients, they started *changing*. Similar to the man you spoke about. They began suffering with the same symptoms as everyone else; high fevers, vomiting, bleeding. Then, parts of them started falling off, or growing. One person grew a tail…. Disturbing stuff, truly. Stuff of nightmares. If someone had told me this, I wouldn't have believed them. I would have said it's impossible.

"We thought it was another stage of this mystery illness, but it was only affecting some people, not all. Almost everyone else who contracted the illness died of organ failure and fluid loss, but these people…. The army took them. Some went of their own accord; others got a bit aggressive and had to be sedated…"

Ravi paused. "You said this other survivor rescued you. Did he kill the chimaera?"

"No, it got trapped in a lift shaft," said Caede. She shivered and stared down at her hands. "I should have gone after him," she said. "I should have helped him. He helped us and I left him out there."

"You had to help your brother. You did the right thing."

"Is Kai going to become one of those things?" she asked.

"It's hard to tell," replied Ravi. "His temperature was very high, but I can't see any other symptoms."

Caede nodded and said nothing.

"What about the rest of your family?" Ravi asked. "Had any luck contacting them?"

"No," she replied. "My nan and grandad aren't answering their phones. Neither's my aunty. You?"

"Nothing, I'm afraid. Nothing in days."

"Sorry, this might sound rude, but when this was all happening, why didn't you just leave and join them?"

"It was fear at first. If this was an infection, I couldn't risk spreading it to my parents. After things quietened down a bit and our tests came back clear, I went home to check on them, to make sure they were okay. But they weren't there. I tried calling their phones, but there was no answer."

"I'm sorry."

"It's okay, I don't think they..." Ravi trailed off. "I assume anyone evacuated would have to follow a quarantine procedure before they're allowed to travel anywhere. My aunt and uncle have a house in Kent. If my parents and sisters were allowed, they would probably head there."

"Why not go, then? You clearly don't have whatever this is. You could be with them right now."

"By the time I realised I wasn't going to change or die, people were already rioting, and the military had closed off the bus routes and the underground. It looked like all of London had been put into quarantine. And, we were explicitly told to stay here and report any new cases. I also don't want to risk the possibility that I might be immune, or asymptomatic. If it's on my clothes, on my hands, anywhere on my person, someone I love could contract it."

Ravi trailed off and fell silent, no longer able to face talking about it. The pair sat quietly after that, waiting for sleep to take them.

9

Wicked Webs

Justine Pearson, entry 06.05.2030

There was a break-in at the lab over the weekend. Christ, this is the last thing we need. Gabriel said the CCTV picked up a group of people raiding Lab B. I told Raj we should have employed another guard, but no, apparently we're on a limited budget. As if the military is short on money! It's ridiculous. They couldn't get a couple of extra soldiers to man the gate?

Luckily they only took older samples, strain 9 I think — completely dead, that one. Couldn't even get Sigma to properly infuse with the viral bodies, so at least it won't kill anybody. Still, I dread to think. We can't have untested product out in circulation, that would be disastrous. Could you imagine the scandal?

Lab B is in a right state now, of course. The idiots smashed a bunch of the samples so it has to be completely sterilised. That's literally weeks of work down the drain. What bothers me is that they knew where the lab was, and they were specifically after the Sigma samples. They knew where to look.

Call me paranoid, but I don't think they could have done all this on their own. And I think I know who helped them.

Caede had shouted something at him inside the car park, but he couldn't hear her. He hit the ground hard and rolled over, feeling a crunch from somewhere deep within his ribcage. Then he saw the monstrous girl, grey and bug-like, with her cold eyes staring into his as she loomed over him. Only darkness after that.

"Eurgh…"

The chill from the floor bit into his bones and burned his already bruised ribs, and his head pounded, brains thoroughly scrambled from the fall. Had he fallen? Or was it that the alcohol had finally worn off, and he'd passed out? Not important. He was still alive, though. That was something. It was something, wasn't it? The relief was unexpected, almost alien. His eyes creaked open, finding only dark shapes and shadows. Wherever he was, it was unfamiliar. And fucking freezing.

Oh, said Tara's voice. *This is definitely better than the roof. Great way to go. Now you can really savour it.*

Shut up.

A shuffling noise caught his ear, coming from somewhere nearby, but his eyes hadn't adapted to the darkness yet. He tried moving his arm, but it wouldn't respond. Same with his legs. They were stuck fast against some unfamiliar obstacle, held together as if he'd been tied up. He tried to sit up and failed, then tried turning his head only to find it also stuck. His eyes darted around, trying to find a source of light or familiarity, as memories of the attack flooded back into his mind.

He remembered Caede shouting, hand reaching from inside the doorway as the girl dragged him down the stairs. That must have been how he'd fallen unconscious. He gagged, his breath caught in his windpipe, stifled by vomit. He choked it back down, gasping. Was he sick? Concussed? Had the girl bitten him? Was she venomous? All those legs and teeth reminded him of a spider. If she was anything like the snake man, who knew what she was capable of? But he could still breathe. If she wanted him dead, he would be. Straining his eyes, he glimpsed down at himself, cursing when he saw the thread. Thick and white, it covered his body completely, sealing him in like a cocoon. A haze filled his head, and the sound of his own racing pulse filled his ears. He gasped for air and wriggled in desperation to free himself from it.

After a minute of unsuccessful flailing, Jon stopped and reminded himself not to waste his energy. He calmed his breathing and began rocking himself back and forth until he could build enough momentum to roll onto his side. The view was better at this angle; a few feet away, he could see a sliver of dim light peeking under what could have been a wide door. It must have been a storage room or garage. Eyes now adjusted, he glanced around and spotted a few tattered boxes stacked against the opposite wall, all covered in the same ropey threads that were wrapped around him. The shuffling noise returned, behind him this time.

Jon rolled over and came face to face with a woman. Blue eyes stared at him, wide and vacant, the sockets sunken in around them. Grey lips hung open with teeth visible, forming a silent "O". Curly red hair lay matted against her face. Loose white thread hung off her mummified body. Jon yelped and wriggled backwards, reeling at the sight. His leg caught the corpse, knocking it back, and it rolled away, dust crumbling off its surface and dissipating into the air.

The shuffling continued, louder now, and faster. Jon froze. In the room's corner, he could see another cocoon, squirming and writhing against a wall. It reminded him of a body bag...or an egg sac. Dread rose from his stomach, bubbling up into his throat and stinging the back of his mouth. Afraid to move, he stared, watching in horror as it thrashed. Suddenly, a small ripping sound came from the bag, and something began to squirm out of it. He squinted into the darkness and realised that it was a finger, then a hand, as the person inside began tearing their way out.

Jon wheezed in relief.

"Psst! Hey," he whispered.

The hand stopped moving, as if startled, then started up again, the movement more desperate, encouraged by the sound of his voice.

Jon gritted his teeth. "Shhh!"

If the monstrous spider girl was nearby, he didn't want to risk summoning her.

"I'll help you," he said. "Just, uh, give me a second."

He wriggled towards the cocoon, untangling his arms and legs bit by bit as he squirmed, freeing himself enough to stand and kick off the last of the threads. Stretching out his aching limbs, he walked over to the bag and tore it open. A woman burst out, coughing and gasping.

"Ah, God!" she said between gulps of air. Arms flailing, she ripped away the rest of the cocoon. "I thought I was going to die in there!"

He gestured, raising a finger to his mouth.

"Shh! I don't want to alert that spider-girl thing!"

The woman shrank into herself at the mention of the creature.

"Did you see it?" she said.

"No," replied Jon, "but I can't imagine she'd stray far from her–
"

"Holly?" said the woman, looking around. "Holly?"

"What?"

"My girlfriend. We went out for supplies and that thing got us."

"What's she look like?"

"Short, white girl. Red hair. I was sure she was in here with me."

Immediately, Jon thought of the corpse. Could that have been the woman's girlfriend? What colour was her hair, again? He realised he'd been silent for too long.

"Uh, no, just a dusty old corpse, sorry. Is there any way out of here?"

"No idea," said the woman. "She must be with Ravi then…. Give me a second. I can see bugger all in here."

"Probably for the best," said Jon.

As if she hadn't heard him, the woman turned around, stretching out her arms until they brushed the surface of a wall.

"Feels like concrete," she said. "We've got to be in a garage or something. If it is, that light down there must be the door."

Together, the two traced the wall, their fingers finding corrugated metal at the end.

"It's a garage," she confirmed, "and I bet it's not locked."

The woman kneeled down and began pushing against the bottom of the door.

"It's too stiff. Give me a hand, would you?"

"Wait!" said Jon. "What if the spider's outside? We don't have anything to defend ourselves with."

"Speak for yourself. I've got a machete."

"Where did you get a machete from?"

"You're not from around here, are you? It doesn't matter where I got it. It's useful."

"And how useful was it when you got caught?"

"Shut up and help me open this!"

Jon obliged and leaned down to help. His ribs ached, the pain in one sharper and brighter than the others. It jabbed at him as he lowered himself to the base of the door. *Definitely broken*, he thought. No matter, he could deal with it once he was back at the hospital. Hopefully, by then, the boy's arm would have been seen by someone. He suddenly remembered the ring in his pocket and pressed against it with his free hand, feeling its outline against the fabric. Another reason to get back to the hospital. Caede would be missing it. And if he was being honest, it would be nice to see them both again.

If they're not dead.

Shut up.

He moved himself into a more comfortable position to push against the door. As he turned to press his shoulder against the metal, he caught a movement in the corner of his periphery, somewhere behind him. Above him. Slowly, he reached out and tapped the woman's arm and gestured, pressing his finger to his mouth. The woman looked up. Jon watched as her eyes widened in horror and he turned, following their gaze. At the far end of the garage, curled up in a corner of the ceiling, dangled the spider, her black eyes open and glittering with malice.

"Shit!"

The spider unfurled herself and descended, arms outstretched, ready to seize the pair. Jon yelped and threw himself to the side, landing hard. He blinked away the stars in time to see the woman pull a machete out from her belt. She swung it, catching the spider's arm, slicing a deep gouge into its white flesh. The spider hissed in fury and recoiled before lunging again, jaws gaping open, black fangs ready to strike. Jon wriggled backwards and collided with something–a pile of cardboard boxes. He tore one open and began rummaging through it.

A scream filled the air, and he glanced up just in time to see the spider looming over him, her porcelain face cracked open wide as if to swallow him up in one piece. Without thinking, he launched the box at her. A shoe flew out of it and struck her in the eye, and she reeled backwards, hissing and limbs flailing. A leg caught Jon in the gut, knocking the wind out of him. Pain surged through him and he keeled over, clutching his waist. The other survivor wasn't doing too well, either. She was on the floor, hands wrapped around one of her legs. He glimpsed a movement to his left. The spider was on the wall, clawed feet clamped to the concrete as she circled, eyes on him.

His hand found another box, and he tore it open. Inside was a large hammer. He seized it, held it up in front of him, waving it at the spider as if it were a sword. A groan came from his right and the spider snapped her pale face in its direction to the woman. Tempted by the weaker prey, she moved, propelling herself along the wall. Jon threw himself forward, striking one of the spider's legs with the claw end of the hammer. He gripped the limb and hacked away at the grey flesh, releasing a thick spray of black blood into the room. The spider screamed and wrenched herself around to face him.

"Get up!" Jon bellowed at the woman.

The spider clawed at him with her fingers and bucked like a wild horse, but he held on, striking again and again with the hammer. Black blood soaked his face and hands and he slipped, landing in a pile of the white, sticky threads. He struggled and tugged against them, but he was stuck fast.

At the other end of the garage, the woman was back on her feet. She screamed and leapt at the spider, machete in her hands. With a crunch, it collided with the spider's face and sank deep into her skull. The spider shrieked in agony and clawed at the machete with her bony arms. Her legs shrivelled up against her body and she shrank back into the dark in a heap. Jon wrenched himself free and ran to the woman.

"Come on!"

Together they heaved open the door. White streetlight flooded into the garage and the pair bolted, sprinting across the road, too terrified to look back or slow down. A ransacked grocery store came into view, its front window smashed and scattered across the pavement. They ran towards it and hopped over the window frame. Glass crunched underfoot as the pair stumbled over debris and a toppled shelf before they reached the counter. Behind that stood a door marked 'staff only'. Jon tried the handle, and it clicked open. They leapt inside, slamming it closed behind them. Jon leaned against the door, breath locked in his throat, ears straining for any sound, any hint that the spider had followed them. Finally, he broke the silence.

"I don't think she's coming."

"Yeah," said the woman. "It would be a bit difficult to follow us with a machete in her face."

"Thank Christ."

The woman tutted and wiped her brow with her jacket sleeve. In the light, Jon could see the woman more clearly. She was tall, with dark skin, wide brown eyes, and short, tightly curled hair, wearing a brown leather jacket, black jeans and chunky boots that reminded him of the punk scene in Camden.

"Christ?" she said. "You think Jesus got anything to do with that thing? No. That's some horror-movie shit right there."

Jon snorted at that, then yawned. The adrenaline had left, and in its place came exhaustion, sweeping through him, making his head heavy and his knees sink. His ribs burned and stabbed at his lungs with every breath. The sooner they got back to the hospital, the better, but it would have to wait for now. He investigated the contents of the shelves, rifling through a few boxes before pulling a pack of cereal bars out of one.

The woman was on the floor, leaning against one of the shelves, inspecting her leg. She groaned.

"I need to stop this bleeding," she said. "Do me a favour, would you?"

"Sure," said Jon. "What do you need?"

"A first aid kit, ideally. If you can't find that…towels, tampons, sanitary pads, duct tape. Whatever you can find that could wrap up a wound. I'm sure you can find something here."

"To be fair, this room looks pretty much untouched," said Jon. "Don't know why. There's been riots for days."

"Pretty certain the rioters were stealing laptops and high-end televisions," the woman replied. "I don't think snacks and tampons were high on the shopping list."

Jon continued searching the shelves. "So, uh, what's your name, anyway?"

"Efia," said the woman. "But call me Efi. I prefer it."

After his search, Jon chewed on a cereal bar while Efi dressed the wound on her calf. Pressing the unrolled tampon against her leg, she winced and grit her teeth.

"These will soak up the blood," she said, explaining her actions with the well-practised tone of someone used to giving others instruction. "The bandages and tape will hold it together until I can get back to the hospital. I'll need stitches by the looks of it."

Jon stopped chewing and looked up, his interest piqued. "Which hospital?"

"St. Luke's," she replied, continuing to bandage the leg.

"I'm headed that way myself."

"Yeah?" said Efi. "Well then, looks like we can be travel buddies."

"You got some relatives there?"

"I work there. I'm a paediatric nurse. You?"

"The kid I was travelling with lost his arm. One of them things tore it off at the elbow."

He needed to come up with a better name than *things* for the creatures, but *monster* seemed too cartoonish. He would think of something later.

"We were heading to St. Luke's. I reckoned there might be someone who could help, but it was all locked up. Then I got snatched by spider girl."

He pressed his hand on his side to dull the ache in his ribs.

"The kid needs help, or he's not gonna make it," said Jon. "I told his sister he'd be fine, but…"

He trailed off. How long had he been in that garage? The streetlights were still on outside, so not too long, he figured. He checked his phone. *Sunday, 5am.* A weight settled in his stomach. He turned away from Efi and rubbed at his face.

"A torn-off arm? Jesus Christ," she said. "Poor boy. I assume you stopped the bleeding?"

"Yeah, but…I don't know. He lost a lot of blood. He's only a little lad."

"If you stopped the bleeding, he should be okay," said Efi. "You'd be surprised how many people lose a limb. It happens all the time. Ravi's at the hospital. He'll help him."

"Ravi?"

"He's a doctor. A good one. They will be just fine."

Jon leaned against a shelf, eyes closed, and let the relief wash over him. Maybe Efi didn't mean it and was just comforting him, but he was relieved all the same. He'd only known the pair a couple of hours, if that, but he found himself fond of them, as if he'd always known them. Caede especially. She seemed to harbour a deep loneliness, and he could relate to that. He knew a thing or two about loneliness. That, and drowning his problems in alcohol. Their company, despite the situation, had felt as though he'd been thrown a life jacket. A second chance, maybe. Maybe they'd just made him feel needed at a crucial moment.

Tara had never needed him, and more often than not, she was away for work. And since he worked from home, he rarely ventured outside for much beyond food shopping or his occasional rugby match. He had become something of a recluse. Old friends from Yorkshire sometimes travelled down to visit, but otherwise they were busy with life, doing grown-up things like getting married, having kids, and staying together for them. He wasn't sure when the depression–and the booze–had taken over. Maybe it was when he and Tara had stopped having sex. Maybe it had always been there, lurking in the shadows, biding its time. He wasn't sure, but he'd spent the last few years in a haze, just existing, taking one day at a time with little purpose beyond rare moments of elation with his friends and the rugby club–until he'd quit, of course. How long had it been since he had shared a genuine moment with anyone?

A tapping noise threw him off his thoughts. It was coming from the other side of the door, from somewhere inside the shop. He opened his eyes and stood up.

"Did you hear that?"

Efi was looking up, eyes on the door. "Yeah," she said, voice low. "Where's it coming from?"

Jon headed for the door and pressed his ear against it, listening to the sound. He could hear movement from the other side. Something crunched underfoot, a jar or bottle perhaps. He lowered himself to Efi, and whispered, "I think we've been followed."

Efi's eyes widened. "You don't think it's her, do you?"

"Maybe. Let's just stay quiet and see. It might not find us."

Jon pushed himself back up. As his hand left the floor, he wobbled, caught Efi's torn trouser leg, and tripped. Efi let out a pained yelp as he landed heavily next to her. The sound rang out like a siren throughout the storeroom, bouncing off the stacked cans and boxes of crisps. Efi clasped her hands over her mouth, but it was too late. The movement and the tapping that accompanied it stopped. Jon stood up and waited. He glanced at Efi, who stared at the door, her eyes wide and her jaw set. Jon followed her gaze to see the handle of the door turning.

Jon watched the door handle tilt down, his breath and heartbeat paused, waiting for the moment it opened. Efi shifted herself backwards, away from the door, and Jon stepped in front of her.

"It's close quarters," he said. "We'll be okay if we're quick. I'll hit it, then we run."

He reached for the nearest shelf and took a large tin, ready to hurl it at whatever was on the other side.

"Speak for yourself," said Efi, as she painfully pushed herself up to standing.

The door handle stopped turning, and a small voice on the other side spoke.

"Hello?"

Jon froze.

"Hello?" the voice repeated.

Jon took the handle of the door in his free hand and held it shut.

"What are you?" he said.

"What?" replied the voice.

"Are you human?" said Jon.

"Um, yeah? I'm not one of the monsters, if that's what you mean."

A sigh escaped him, and he buckled, slumping under the weight of relief. Efi groaned in a mutual expression, leaning her head back against the shelf. Breath returned, Jon pulled himself back up and slowly opened the door. On the other side stood a teenage girl in a hoodie and baggy jeans that were ripped at the knees. Clutched to her chest was a baseball bat. Her hair sat against her shoulders, and must have been dyed blue at some point, but now it was greasy, with yellow bleached strands poking through the faded blue. She stared up at him, bug-eyed and round-faced, expression covered by a surgical mask.

"Um, who are you?" she said, rubbing her eyes with her free hand. "What are you doing in my dad's shop?"

"Sorry," said Jon. He pointed to Efi's leg. "We, uh, needed supplies. We didn't break the window. It was already like that."

"I know," said the girl. "Looters did it. Is she okay?" The girl pointed at Efi.

"I'm fine," said Efi. "I just need a minute."

"Do you want to come upstairs?" asked the girl. "It's safer there."

"You sure?" said Jon. "I mean–we're not, but we could be anyone."

The girl shrugged. "So could I."

Jon helped up Efi and together they followed the girl outside, rounding the corner of the shop to a set of crumbling metal stairs leading up to a side door. The girl fumbled with the rusty lock of the front door and it creaked open. She gestured inside with a shrug.

"You can stay here for a bit. There's food, and the water's still running."

Jon stepped over the threshold, looking around. The place was dark and damp. It looked as if it hadn't been cleaned in a while–if at all. Mould and smears of what Jon hoped was mould lined the ageing wallpaper of the hallway. A thick, unidentifiable smell hung heavily in the air, stale and metallic as the corridor and the piss-soaked lifts in his own apartment block. A small table stood in the hallway, the build-it-yourself kind, covered in a thick layer of dust, and unopened mail. Several pairs of tatty-looking shoes were piled underneath it. Under those was the carpet, deep burgundy and flecked with burn marks and debris. Out of the corner of his eye, he caught Efi pulling a face.

"So, uh, live here with your parents, do you?" he asked.

If there had been anything off about his tone, the girl didn't seem to notice.

"I did, yeah," the girl answered, leading Jon and Efi into an equally dingy kitchen.

She gestured at a dirty, plate-laden kitchen table with a couple of chairs, inviting them to sit. "They're not here anymore."

"What?"

Jon helped Efi into the nearest chair. Her jaw set in a grimace as she rested her weight on the seat; he suspected it had more to do with the filth on the chair than the pain in her leg.

"They fucked off when the riots started," said the girl. "Decided it was their chance to get away, I guess. I was in bed. They didn't even bother trying to wake me up. So, I've been here by myself."

"Christ," said Jon.

"Who just abandons their child?" said Efi, horrified.

"It's okay," shrugged the girl. "They were arseholes. I'm glad they're gone."

The three of them sat in silence while the girl poured water into some limescale-marked glasses. She pulled up a chair and sat down next to Efi.

"My name's Luna, by the way. It used to be something else, but I changed it."

"Well, it's nice to meet you, Luna," Jon replied, shifting on the spot.

His hand met the back of his neck and stayed there. "So, uh, where are we anyway? I don't recognise the road...."

"How far are we from the hospital?" asked Efi.

"This is Belmore Street," Luna replied.

"Strange," said Efi. "I've lived around here for years; never been down this way before."

"Me neither," Jon said, "but I've not been living in London for that long, to be honest."

"The hospital's like a twenty-minute walk from here? It's not far. I can give you directions if you want," said Luna.

"Thank you," replied Efi. "Normally I'd use my phone, but I must have lost it in the attack."

"Mine's got no signal," said Luna. "And the wi-Fi stopped too. I guess it makes sense; there's probably no one around to look after it all."

"Electric's still working, though. Why wouldn't there be phone signal?" Efi glanced over at Jon. "Any idea?"

"Don't look at me," said Jon, holding his hands up. "I'm a graphic designer. I've no clue how this stuff works." He paused and nodded towards the kitchen sink. "Is your hot water working?"

"No, that stopped yesterday."

After resting in the kitchen long enough to catch their breath, the three prepared for the walk back. Efi had suggested packing up whatever food they could carry, since they didn't know how long they would be with no supplies. They sat in the hallway, sorting through tins and boxes, making small talk as they gathered their selection into a backpack. Luna's parents had at least been sensible enough to take most of the food in the shop upstairs for storage early on, so there was plenty to choose from, and most of it non-perishable. Alcohol, too.

"Luna," said Jon. "Your dad got any whiskey?"

"Yeah, why?"

"Mind if I nick some?"

Luna's father had kept a stock of various liquors in the kitchen cupboards, never bothering to hide them from his daughter. She'd had no interest in drinking it herself, seeing it pointless, so she said Jon could have it. He found a bottle of whiskey, necked it, and let the familiar haze wash over him.

From out of nowhere, the image of Caede's slight, almost secret, smile entered his mind. His face warmed. Would she be happy to see him? Ridiculous. They'd only just met. She probably didn't even care about the ring; she'd be too busy worrying about her brother. The back of his neck itched.

Anxious that Efi and Luna had suddenly developed mind-reading powers, he returned to the hallway, his burning face pointed at the floor. Despite the carpets rich, dark colour, Jon could still see various stains on its surface. Crumbs and specks of dirt marred the fibres. There were some dark brown spots he couldn't identify.

"Heads up," said Efi.

A stray tin of baked beans rolled past Jon's hand.

"I've got it," he said.

He leaned over to reach it and missed. The rogue tin carried on past him, stopping at the base of a closed door. He shuffled over to grab it and his eye caught something. Small reddish-brown splatters littered the doorframe, like the specks on the carpet. *Odd*, he thought. Tiny, russet spots were dotted over the aged, chipped paint of the door frame as well, and on the door's handle. On the weathered brass was a distinctive, dark red smear, surrounded by the faint outlines of fingerprints. A faint smell tickled the back of his nose, rising over the musk and the mould; something he couldn't quite place.

"Say, uh, what's in this room, Luna?" he asked, reaching for the handle.

"Don't go in there!"

In a flash, Luna was up off the floor and standing above him, her eyes burning as they stared into his.

"That's my parents' bedroom. No one's allowed in there."

Was that fear in her voice, or rage?

"Oh, sorry."

Jon lowered his hand slowly to the floor and picked up the tin, passing it to her. She glared back at him as she took it.

"Guess your dad really was an arsehole, huh?" he said, laughing nervously. His hand found its way to its safe space on the back of his neck. "He doesn't know how to varnish properly for a start. Look at it. It's everywhere."

Fantastic bluff there, lad. You should be a fucking magician.

He shot a pleading look at Efi, who raised a confused eyebrow in response.

Great lot of help you are.

Luna kept her eyes on him as she walked over to the bag.

"Yeah," she replied, dropping in the tin. "He was."

The three finished packing the food in silence before heading outside. Jon helped Efi limp over the threshold onto the metal railing, supporting her weight with his shoulder and scanning the street below for any movement while he waited for Luna to lock up.

"You coming, Luna?"

"Yeah," she replied from inside the flat. "I just need to get something."

Jon and Efi continued slowly down the rusted stairs. The streets were silent and empty, save for the bodies scattered around. If the spider had survived their earlier fight, it hadn't made much effort to follow them. The thing had a machete jammed into its face, after all. How inclined would it be to chase them? The pair stopped at the bottom of the stairs and waited for Luna.

"What was that look for earlier?" whispered Efi.

Jon glanced up the stairway. Keeping his voice low, he leaned in close to Efi's ear and whispered, "that door handle had blood on it."

Efi's expression remained passive, but her eyes widened just enough for Jon to notice that she was shocked. She opened her mouth to reply, but the clang of boots on metal from above stopped her.

"I'm ready," announced Luna.

Efi's eyes met Jon's for a fraction of a second before turning to Luna. "You okay?"

"Yeah. Let's go."

Luna led the way, walking slightly ahead of Jon and Efi, checking around corners and signalling to them when it was safe to proceed. The heavy silence and the emptiness of the streets sent shivers dancing up and down Jon's spine, making him feel queasy. The cold air of nightfall had kept the bodies chilled and the rot at bay, but the warmth of daybreak was coming, and soon they would begin to smell.

Jon turned his face away from the corpses and focused his attention on his companions. Efi had kept quiet about the door so far, and for that, he was grateful. He tried not to dwell on the blood too much. Thinking about it would only lead to questions, and questions usually led to unwelcome answers. A murder-suicide, perhaps? If so, why spare the girl? Jon decided to wipe the thought of it from his mind, at least for now. *Poor kid*, he thought.

As the three reached the main road, Jon glimpsed a street sign a few feet away. He looked at it, confused, trying to recall where he had seen the sign before, and why. A house party, perhaps? He couldn't think of why he would have been on this street otherwise, and he wondered who he knew that would live nearby. There were no pubs around, and it wasn't a route he had any reason to take. He racked his brains as they passed a row of shops, glimpsing a gym next to a supermarket. Suddenly, he knew where he was. Mike lived on the street next to this one. Mike, the personal trainer with visible abs, who ate nothing but kale and ran for fun. A few times he'd dropped Tara off at that gym, because it had better equipment than the one nearer the apartment, apparently. At the time, he hadn't thought to question her definition of the word 'equipment'. She had even mentioned how lucky Mike was to live so close to his work. Jon wondered why he'd never put the two together before, and his face warmed again. He let out a sigh. No point being angry about it now. She was probably dead.

10

Wolf Pack

The three continued on under the streetlamps with dawn in slow pursuit. The ache in Jon's back, and the stiffness of his joints were enough to tell him he'd been in that damn garage all night. He wondered if Caede and Kai had found the doctor, if they had been able to save Kai's arm, and if they'd managed to get a decent night's sleep. Any other scenario wasn't worth thinking about.

Luna trotted ahead, inspecting a body here and there. Jon and Efi limped behind, slowed down by Efi's leg. The attack from the spider had left a deep gash in her calf. While she had bandaged it enough to stop the bleeding, the surrounding area had become swollen, and, he imagined, quite sore. Efi hadn't complained, but she gritted her teeth with every step.

"You alright?" he asked.

"I'll be okay," she replied, and carried on.

Luna turned a corner just ahead of them, disappearing from sight. She reappeared immediately, frantically gesturing at Jon and Efi to stop. She pointed to a nearby parked car and ducked down beside it. The pair followed, kneeling down next to her.

"There're some men over there," she said, voice low. "They were turning over bodies and looking at them."

Jon stood, peeking over the car before answering. "Okay. You wait here. I'll have a look."

Keeping low, he crept to the corner and glanced round to see a group of five men on the other side of the road, prodding a corpse with what looked like a hiking stick. The road was wide, a major route into the city centre, with several bus stops and a long row of shops lining the pavements. Abandoned vehicles, buses included, sat scattered across it.

One man, taller and broader than the others, rubbed his chin in contemplation, then shook his head. He was an odd colour for a human, almost grey, and there was something weird about his face, too. The man's jaws were elongated, his face more predatory and wolfish than human. The others were no different, each of them almost human in appearance. *Almost.* They had to be like the snake man and the spider girl. If that was the case, it would be better if he weren't spotted.

Another muttered something as they moved on to the next body. They kept whispering to each other, darting their heads around every so often, as if to make sure they were alone.

What were they doing?

Jon stuck his head out a little further and squinted, trying to get a clear view of the group. A smaller man, skinnier than the others, walked among the bodies on all fours. He wasn't just thin either. He was emaciated, and hunched over, almost childlike compared to the rest of the pack. Jon watched, curious, as the man knelt down closer to the ground and sniffed the bodies in front of him.

Another smaller one paced back and forth in agitation, his mouth hanging open, as if panting. He was darker than any person Jon had ever seen before, covered in what looked like thick, black hair. It was as if the man was wearing a novelty gorilla suit. Another one, stockier and rounder in the gut, glanced around, his head darting about in quick, jarring movements that put Jon on edge. That one was brown and peppered with black and grey patches, like a dog. That was it. They all looked like dogs.

The small one suddenly stopped and tilted his head up. He sniffed the air and beckoned the tall one, muttering something in his ear. The leader turned, lifting his head, and sniffed too. Visibly agitated, he said something back to the smaller one, and the group dynamic changed. As if an electrical current had run through them, they became animated, excited, and they all turned their heads around as if in search of something. While the others ran around, the smaller man kept still, holding his face in the air. Then, to Jon's horror, he pointed his head towards him and made eye contact.

Shit.

Jon scrambled backwards and dashed to the parked car.

"We need to go. Now," he said, hooking Efi's arm over his shoulder.

Before anyone could reply, a long howl rang out through the street.

"What did you do?" Efi hissed.

"Nothing!" said Jon. "They...it's like they knew I was there."

He helped Efi up and nodded to Luna.

"Which way?"

Luna glanced around, then pointed towards a side street.

"Go," said Jon. "We'll keep up."

The howls rang out again, this time closer. Luna sprinted down the street, darting to the left. Jon followed, holding onto Efi's waist, the pair barely able to keep up. The men pursued, crowing and hollering wildly. Blood pounding in his ears, Jon grit his teeth and picked up the pace. Nimble as a rabbit, Luna ran, zigzagging between bodies and cars. She could have easily left Jon and Efi behind if she wanted, but she stayed close, looking back every few seconds before continuing on. She led them to an open road and darted across it, heading towards a London Underground station that sat on the corner between conjoining roads. Jon realised they had circled around using the side streets, just a little further down than before.

It was a smart move, but the men hadn't been put off. They were closer now, their voices echoing off the buildings as they howled and yelled, giddy in their sport, like a pack of hounds chasing down a fox. Ignoring the agony in his lungs and legs, Jon ploughed forward, keen to keep up with Luna, who was now at the station entrance. She turned briefly and gestured to him before disappearing inside.

"Oi!"

Jon jumped at the sound of the call and stopped dead, whipping his head around to see the group of men standing behind them some thirty feet away, all grinning as if the chase had been little more than a fun game. Each of them regarded Jon with burning eyes, as if to size him up. The stocky one's gaze flickered briefly towards Efi, and he smiled.

The tall one stepped forward, mouth tilted up in a cocky, shit-eating grin.

"You alright, mate?" he said, nodding at Jon.

Jon shared a glance with Efi. She kept her face forward, giving only the slightest nod of acknowledgement. Slowly, they turned to face the group.

"Hey," said the tall man. The word spat out like a bark, sharp and unsettling.

"Hey," Jon replied, hoping to sound braver than he felt.

The man took another step towards the pair. "What are you running for, mate?"

Jon's lungs were heaving for air, and his legs felt like lead. But if he ran now, and really ran, he could get to the underground station before they could catch him. He could change course, lead the men away from Luna, but then Efi would be a sitting duck. There were enough of the men that they could send half after him and the other half would be free to do as they pleased–whatever that might be. He took a step backwards, keeping his arm wrapped around Efi's waist. She gripped his shoulder in return.

"You don't need to run, mate," said the tall man. "We just wanna talk to you. Not many other survivors out here, you get me?"

His tone made Jon uneasy. It was mocking, reeking of malice, and raised the hairs on the back of his neck. His guts tightened, and a voice in his head screamed at him to run.

"Aye," Jon replied. "I get you."

One man, pale and lanky, had separated from the pack, and was slinking along the abandoned cars, keeping low. Like the others, he appeared to be covered in fine hair, with sharpened facial features and an elongated jaw. A bead of sweat ran down Jon's back. The tall man chuckled. *Bugger.*

"We just wanna talk to you," he repeated.

"So you keep saying," said Jon.

His eyes flickered to the left. Another man, the small one, was flanking on the other side.

"It's about your woman."

"My what?"

Had he heard that right? He turned his face to meet Efi's. Her eyes bulged in terror and her jaw was locked in a grimace. Her fingernails dug into his shoulder. She glanced back at him pleadingly.

"We've got a proposition for you," the man continued.

"Did they see Luna?" Efi whispered.

"I don't think so."

"I don't like this."

"Neither do I. Just hold on to me, alright?"

A shout cut through the air.

"Hey! I'm talking to you!"

The tall man was no longer grinning.

"Yeah?" said Jon, returning fire. "What about her?"

The man seemed to calm, his smirk returning.

"Relax, mate, it's not like that," he replied. "We need her. Like I said, we've got a proposition for you. Our employer requires females to join his…establishment. You get me?"

"I don't think I do, no."

"He'll ask if you want to join his crew. You say yes, you're in. You say no, and, well..."

The stocky one next to him grinned and licked his lips.

The tall man stepped forward again. "Look, mate, I haven't got all day. It's yes or no, innit."

"I'm not your mate!" Jon yelled back at him, taking another step back.

"Listen," said the man. "It's nothing personal. I don't wanna go back to my boss without her. Just give her to us and we'll leave you alone."

"She is not for giving!" Efi bellowed, glaring at the man, her face contorted in fury and terror.

The stocky one laughed. "She's fiery!"

"Get ready to run," said Jon, his voice low. "I won't let them hurt you."

The men were all laughing now. "Come on, mate. Don't be selfish!"

"You heard her," Jon answered. "She said no!"

The tall man's smirk faded. "Your loss, then."

He nudged his head towards the others, and they took off.

"Fuck this!" screamed Efi.

Slamming her foot to the floor, she seized Jon's hand and together they hurtled across the road, the men close behind, yelling and howling as they gave chase. One of them caught up and leapt for Efi. She screamed and punched upward, her fist colliding with the man's jaw. He yelped and staggered, dropping behind. Another arrived in his place. Jon slammed into him with his shoulder, sending him toppling to the floor in a heap. The man stayed down, and they kept running.

They reached the station entrance, threw themselves over the ticket barriers, and skidded down the hallway towards the lifts. Luna stood by the doors, waiting anxiously as she held them open.

"Get in!" she urged, jumping inside.

Efi leapt into the lift. Luna slammed her hand on the door close button. Just before he followed, Jon turned to see the pack stopping at the barriers. The tall one stood amongst them, staring at Jon.

"You don't wanna go down there, mate," he smirked.

"Jon, get in here!"

Efi shot out an arm and dragged him into the lift. He stuck his middle finger up at the men defiantly, the doors closing behind him.

11

The congregation

Terry Howard, entry 07.05.2030

Justine was just in my office, giving me the Spanish Inquisition treatment over the break-in at the weekend. I'm not saying a damn word. She's just annoyed that it was Lab B they raided, and now she has to work in Lab C with Levushka. Serves her right, if you ask me. Sigma could save so many lives, cure so much misery, and we're just using it to make super soldiers. I would laugh if it wasn't so terrifying. People deserve access to this technology. People deserve to know the truth.

-

"It's good news," said Ravi, smiling triumphantly. He stood by the hospital bed, inspecting the drip attached to Kai's arm, making pleased little hums as he checked everything. Caede sat perched on the edge of the bed, cosying herself with a cup of vending machine coffee. Kai was now in one of the private patient suites. Far nicer than the shared rooms, this had a window, television, side table, and a plush leather chair for visitors.

"You're doing very well, Kai," Ravi continued. "The antibiotics seem to be doing their job, and your arm is healing nicely. It's going to be sore for a few days, and you will experience some swelling, but we have painkillers if you need them."

Ravi had expressed surprise at Kai's recovery speed. He'd been unconscious far longer than Ravi predicted; the result of mistakenly administering too much anaesthetic. Ravi had accounted for Kai's age and approximate weight, but not his arm or the blood loss. But after the transfusion and some nausea, the boy was doing well.

"I found a prosthesis that might fit you," said Ravi. "Well enough, anyway. Just don't ask where I got it from and know that I cleaned it thoroughly. We won't find out if it fits until you've recovered. But that won't take long, usually a few weeks, and then some physical therapy."

"Okay," said Kai.

"Here," said Caede, handing him a small beaker. "Have some water. Are you hungry?"

Kai took a sip of the water but shook his head at the suggestion of food. "Do I have to stay in bed for two weeks?"

"Strictly, no," Ravi said. "But it is important you get as much rest as possible. Once you're recovered from the effects of the anaesthetic, you'll be able to go to the bathroom on your own and walk around for a bit, but don't expect to be outside running marathons just yet. How does it feel?"

"I'm not sure," said Kai. "I can't really feel anything. I keep going to move my hand and there's nothing there."

Ravi nodded. "That's normal. It will get easier."

Kai gazed down at what remained of his arm, his eyes glassy. "It's going to be okay, right?"

"Of course," replied Caede. "It's going to be fine. Once your arm's better, we can go home."

Kai looked down at the stump. "It's not though, is it?"

"What?"

"My arm," said Kai, voice cracking. "It's not going to get better. It's gone."

"It could have been a lot worse, Kai," said Caede. "That monster could have killed you."

"I was only out there trying to find you!"

"I told you I was on my way home. You should have stayed indoors."

"If I'd stayed indoors, you'd be dead. The monster would have got you."

"You don't know that, Kai!"

"Yes, I do. And if you just stayed at home when I said, instead of going to work, I wouldn't have needed to go outside to find you!"

"I had to! How do you think we get food on the table? It just appears there like magic? We needed the money, Kai."

Kai huffed and fell silent.

"Just rest, okay?" said Caede. "We'll be home soon enough."

"What's the point? There's nothing to go back to."

Kai slumped against the wall of pillows and closed his eyes.

Caede stood up. "Kai, come on. You won't feel like that when this is all over."

"You should have left me with Nan and Grandad."

"Kai, we've been through this a thousand times. They can't take care of you anymore."

"I wish Mum was here," Kai replied.

"Well, she's not here, is she? Guess you're stuck with me!"

Kai said nothing, but turned his face away and buried it in a pillow to scream. Caede sat down on the edge of the bed, head resting in her hands.

Finally, she sighed, breaking the silence. "Kai. Look. I'm sorry. This is really shit, I know. I don't know what to do and loads of people are dead, and there's literally fucking monsters walking around like it's a horror movie. I don't know what to do, but I'm here. You're here. We're both alive."

"I don't care!" Kai snapped from behind the pillow. "What's the point?"

Caede wrung her hands in frustration. "Stop being such a child!"

She felt a hand rest on her shoulder and turned to see Ravi looking down at her. "Maybe it's best to give him some space," he whispered. "It's been a long few days and we're all tired."

Caede shrugged him off and stormed out of the room. Kai turned away from Ravi, pulling the bed sheet over his head.

"Ravi," he said from under the linen. "What are we going to do?"

"I don't know," Ravi replied. "But your sister is right. We're alive, and that is a blessing."

He sat down in the chair by the bed and removed his glasses, twirling them in his hand as he turned his face to the ceiling. He closed his eyes and contemplated. In times of difficulty, or at any opportunity for that matter, his mother would hug him tightly, calling him her "big squeezy Rav-berry." Something he found extremely uncool, especially after he'd lost all the weight. Oh, to have a hug from his mother now. Tears ran down his cheeks and he wiped them away with a sleeve.

"It's going to be okay, Kai," he said. "You'll see."

Caede thundered down the hallway, huffing angrily with every step. Reaching the stairwell, she stopped and plucked a small pack of cigarettes and a lighter from her pocket. A habit she had tried, and failed, to keep a secret from Kai, hoping he wouldn't take it up. And perhaps Ravi would disapprove as well, what with him being a doctor and all. *Oh well.* She kicked open the stair door and stomped across the roof over to the low parapet. She slumped down against the edge and lit up a cigarette, closing her eyes as she inhaled, letting the calming wave of nicotine flow through her as she absorbed the silence.

Through the glow of dawn, Caede gazed at the now empty office buildings, housing estates and, further in the distance, the distinctive architecture that formed the iconic London skyline. It looked like the type of photographic print one would expect to see decorating the wall in some dentist's office; pleasant enough to look at, but nothing more than a distraction from the root canal waiting in the next room.

Not even a month ago, she'd had few plans other than graduating and breathing new life into her online dating profile. Times were hard on that front; harder still when you had a kid to look after. Lovers were a rare luxury, something to indulge in once work was finished, dissertations handed in. And by the time that had all happened, all she wanted to do was sleep.

Kai was twelve and more than capable of looking after himself. He was laid back for the most part; easy to deal with. But Caede wasn't his mother, and despite her best efforts, she often found herself exhausted and frustrated from the effort of trying to be. Over time, the relationship between them had become strained and distant, with both of them maintaining an ongoing stalemate for the sake of peace and normality. Kai spent most of his time in his room, Caede spent all of hers working, studying or sleeping. She had got herself to a point where her master's was almost finished. Completing the course would have freed up a lot of time, allowing her to explore the world of the living instead of just existing on the outskirts. *And now all this.*

Her thoughts drifted to the night a bunch of idiots had come in and broken the pub's pool table. She hadn't told the men at the time, but the leg on the thing was already wobbly, and idiot number one who'd landed on it–the very same idiot who saved her brother's life not twenty-four hours ago–hadn't realised. If her useless boss, Danny, had fixed the leg when she told him about it, the guy wouldn't have fallen, wouldn't have been offering profuse apologies to her, wouldn't have known she worked there. She hadn't said at the time that she thought he was cute, because at the time, she was the only member of staff working that shift and was too tired and annoyed to ask for his number. And now the guy was dead. *Typical.*

Raising her hand to take another drag of the cigarette, she noticed the barren space on her middle finger where her ring should be.

"Shit!"

How long had it been missing? Where had she left it? Was it in the operating theatre? By Kai's bed? Had someone pried it from her body while she was unconscious on the pavement? Too many questions flew around her, barraging her. The only thing she had left of her mother's, and she couldn't even keep that safe. Kai was right. This was all her fault. Deep down, she knew it was long gone. Probably lining some thief's pocket. Someone with no idea what it meant to her. She clamped her eyes shut and took another drag of the cigarette.

Images of her family crept into her mind, bringing with them waves of grief and nostalgia. She blinked, desperate to escape the oncoming tears. Opening those doors again would only bring unnecessary misery. She had grieved already, enough for a lifetime, even for that poor Jon, who had helped them. *What a way to say thanks.* She stubbed the cigarette out against the wall, suddenly nauseated.

Everyone she'd ever known or cared about was long gone. All except for Kai. She would have to go back down the stairs and make peace with him. She lingered, taking in the scene for just a little longer, then stashed the cigarettes and lighter into her jacket pocket.

As she began making her way to the stairwell, a movement in the distance below caught her eye. She turned towards it and froze.

Down on the road, in a small grassy area of one of the housing estates, stood a small group of people in a circle. Ducking down, she crept to the edge of the roof and peered over to watch the strange congregation. There were ten of them standing in formation, still and silent as statues, their faces hanging solemnly towards the ground. They all seemed to be different sizes, some small and childlike, others standing over six feet in height. One of them was as round as they were tall, and another was hunched over, a large hump sticking out of their back. There was something uncannily human about them, but the more she gazed at the group, the more monstrous their forms became.

One of them tilted their head up, and Caede dropped down, heart pounding. After a few seconds, she peered back over the edge. They were all facing the same direction, away from her, looking at something just out of view. One of them spoke, but the words were swept up by the breeze, and all Caede could hear were vague sounds.

Suddenly they became animated, bristling and bobbing like excited children. A loud clang shattered the quiet, and the group hissed and whooped. They were beside themselves, jumping up and down in a maddened frenzy. The clang was drowned out by an ear-splitting wail. A huge man, larger than any person Caede had ever seen before, stepped into view, dragging something behind him. He had to be one of the creatures, she thought, just like the snake and the spider girl in the car park. He was too tall and broad to be a normal human, easily towering over the rest of the circle.

As the man lifted his arm, Caede gasped and clamped her hands over her mouth. A woman, naked and crying, was hanging by her wrists in his hand. Compared to him, she was tiny and frail, flailing uselessly against his grip like a fish on a hook. The group calmed and fell silent. The man lifted the woman, holding her in front of him, and spoke, his voice rising and falling over the wind. Caede strained to hear the words but couldn't. Whatever he had said to her, it wasn't good. In response, she screamed and kicked her legs against his chest. The man laughed and replied. He raised the woman over his head, taking one of her legs in his other hand, and gripped it as he stepped towards the circle. The others hopped and shrieked with feverous glee and he stood, taking it in, clearly enjoying the reverence, and the woman cried and begged. Lifting her above his head, he roared. Caede shook as she watched in horror.

The woman's screams grew louder, transforming into maddened wails. Caede begged herself, pleaded to herself to move, to do something, anything, but she remained there, hands over her mouth, doing all she could to stop herself from screaming.

With another deafening roar, the man twisted his hands against the woman's limbs and pulled. Blood sprayed high into the air before raining down onto the group, and the woman's torso landed in a heap at the man's feet. The congregation cheered, hissing and howling in glee, arms raised up to the sky as they danced under it. The poor woman lay wailing and writhing on the floor, blood pooling around her. The man held up the torn-off limbs, a leg in one hand, an arm in another, and then threw them to the group. Like starving dogs, they descended, snarling and hissing as they tore flesh from bone, swallowing it in huge chunks. The tall one stood and watched in silence.

Caede had seen enough. Shaking, she crawled away from the edge of the roof, back to the door and, quietly as possible, closed it behind her. She retreated into the stairwell and stumbled down the stairs, sobbing and gasping, the screams of the dying woman echoing behind her.

12

Going Underground

Justine Pearson, entry 07.05.2030

I went into Terry's office and asked him outright if he helped those hippies, and he denied it. Of course he would, but he's a terrible liar. I know he helped them and he can't keep quiet forever. I'm going to express my concerns to Raj and see what he thinks about all of this. The police can take it from there. Apparently, they already have a suspect in custody.

If Terry's behind this, I'll be furious. That idiot probably doesn't even realise what he's done. If those morons had gotten hold of live samples.... Well, luckily we don't have to think about that.

-

"What did he mean by that?" asked Efi. She sat on the floor of the elevator as it descended towards the station platform, tentatively inspecting her leg. The sprint had drained the colour from her face, and she kept her foot raised as she rested her weight, as if to ease the pain.

"By what?" Jon replied.

"When he said we didn't want to go down here?"

"Oh…no idea."

Jon kept his face pointed at the floor as he caught his breath. His ribs sent waves of pain coursing through his chest with every inhale, and now that the adrenaline had run out, he could no longer ignore it. The sooner they got to the hospital, the better. "I think he was trying to scare us."

Efi stopped moving her leg and stared at the floor. "I'm just glad we got away," she muttered.

The elevator slowed to a stop, and the doors slid open. Stark white light filled the lift, revealing the empty corridor that led down to the station platforms. Jon peered out and looked around. On the wall opposite was an informational sign featuring a map of the railway lines and platform guide. The smell of rust and decay filled Jon's nostrils. He pointed his face towards it. Further along, on the corridor leading to the platform, he could see the olive green and cream tiled walls, smeared and splattered with old, dried blood.

"Stay here for a sec," he said. "I'm just gonna check it out."

Efi and Luna said nothing, so he stepped into the corridor and headed over to the map. Giving the image a once over, he confirmed which line would be best to follow, then headed to the hallway on his left.

The stairs were dark and uninviting, and he hesitated before descending. Smaller than many of the central stations, the platform was little more than a ceramic panelled tube. It was empty. The only sign anyone had ever been there were smears of congealed blood on the walls and floor.

An abandoned train sat on the rails, its doors open and the lights on. Jon hopped inside the nearest carriage. It was the same as the platform. No bodies, just more blood and the smell of death lingering in the air. He stepped back out and headed to the front, finding the driver's cabin also abandoned. Satisfied that it wouldn't be moving soon, he left and walked to the back of the train, where the carriages met the mouth of the tunnel and disappeared into darkness. He peered in and shuddered. Weren't there supposed to be lights?

Jon left the platform and headed back towards the lift. Efi and Luna were in the corridor, waiting for him.

"What's it like down there?" asked Efi.

"It's quiet," Jon replied. "No one down there–not from what I could see, anyway. We're only two stops from where we need to be. We could walk through the tunnel to the next station and carry on from there. Those blokes don't know which way we're heading, so I'm pretty sure we can lose them."

He trailed off, frowning.

"What is it?" said Efi.

"Ah, I don't know," he said. "I can't put my finger on it. What the guy said about coming down here?"

"It's the blood," said Luna.

Jon and Efi turned to see her standing over a congealed puddle of blood, inspecting it with the air of a seasoned forensic investigator.

"Look," she said, pointing to various smears along the wall and floor, following them with her finger down the corridor. "There's blood here, but no bodies. They've been moved."

Luna turned her gaze towards the stairs leading to the platform. "I don't think we should use the tunnel."

"We could wait for them to leave," said Jon. "Sneak out and find a way around them."

"I'd rather just take the tunnel," said Efi. "I don't know if you've noticed, but my leg's fucked. We could use the shortcut."

"Really?" said Luna, gesturing at the blood smears.

Efi opened her mouth to answer, but before she could speak, the lift behind them pinged and whirred as it began ascending towards the surface.

"You think that's automatic?" said Jon.

"No," said Efi, voice heavy with dread. "Someone must have pressed the call button."

"Looks like we don't have a choice," said Jon. "Right then. Tunnel, it is."

Efi wrapped her arm around his shoulder and they headed towards the stairs. Jon looked back to see Luna standing by the hall, hesitant.

"I don't like the situation either," he said, holding his hand out to her. "But we need to go."

Ignoring his hand, Luna walked past the pair and headed down the stairs. Jon and Efi shared a glance and followed.

Jon lowered himself from the platform edge down onto the rails and shimmied past the train carriage into the tunnel. Underfoot he could feel a faint vibration – the low hum of the still live line in the centre of the tracks. The tunnel itself was more claustrophobic than he'd imagined. Maybe they could hide just inside the entrance and wait for the men to leave? He stepped back out and helped Efi down from the platform. Luna hopped down behind them.

"The line's live," Jon warned, "so be careful."

The three headed into the lip of the tunnel, pressing themselves against the wall, their breath shallow as they listened out for the men. Soon enough, they approached, snarling and bickering at each other as they descended the stairs. To Jon's comfort, they seemed fearful, voicing their hesitancy to venture onto the platform.

Maybe they'd just leave.

"I don't see why we have to go down there," said one, groaning.

"Just shut up and move, man," said the other, snapping at the first. "You wanna tell Lee we lost her?"

Efi gripped Jon's shoulder, and he began shuffling further into the tunnel.

"Luna," he whispered. "Come on."

Luna didn't move. "I can't."

"Luna, please. We don't have time!"

The footsteps of the men echoed across the empty platform as they drew closer. Finally, Luna took his hand and they descended into the darkness.

Jon squinted, making out the tiny red and green cable lights that hung overhead. The hum from the live line, the crunch of stones under his feet, and his laboured breathing all seemed louder in the oppressive silence. The thick, inky blackness of the tunnel walls seemed to close in on him, and he wanted to run back, try fighting off the men, but he kept moving forward.

"If we keep following this, we'll be at the next platform in no time," he whispered, partly to reassure Luna and partly to reassure himself. "We'll head back to the surface and go straight to St. Luke's from there. Twenty minutes, tops."

Efi and Luna said nothing. He pressed on, taking their silence as acceptance.

"Not like them newer tunnels, is it?" said Jon. "The new ones have got lights in them for a start. Tidier cables, too. I did a project for London Underground a while back, just some ad designs. Lad doing the photos showed me a pic of the new lines, and it's way nicer than this one. South London for you."

"I thought they all had lights," said Efi. "For engineers, you know?"

About five minutes in, Jon started hearing noises. Small clicking sounds, and tapping, coming from somewhere under his feet. Could it be rats? The sound left a sickly ache in his gut and seemed to grow louder the more he focused on it. He kept his eyes ahead, following the cable lights as a guide, and tried not to think about it.

After another minute, the group discovered a hole. Jon was looking ahead, trying to see further into the tunnel, when his foot met air and he yelped, catching himself on some cable supports just in time to stop himself from falling in. Luna tumbled into him and screamed. From somewhere behind him, he could hear Efi swear as she bumped into Luna. He gritted his teeth and held onto the supports for dear life, silently thankful that Luna wasn't heavier.

"Jon, what the hell?" said Efi.

"There's a bloody hole here!"

Across the entire width of the tunnel, the floor had caved in, leaving only the rails and supports in place, exposed like bones sticking out of a carcass. Jon regained his composure and fished his phone from his pocket, turning on the torch. The beam met the darkness and disappeared as the hole curved to the left.

"It's like a whole other tunnel."

"What?" said Efi.

He moved the beam upwards, and it caught something. Jon looked up. The tunnel did have lights, just like the newer ones, but someone, or something, had torn them from their casings. Luna leaned forwards to get a better look at the hole.

"That's massive," she said.

"Yeah," said Jon. "Now get back. I don't want you falling in."

Luna stepped back, moving out of the way for Efi to have a look. She hobbled up to the hole and peered over the edge.

"I can see fuck all down there," she said. "We could climb over it. The tracks are still there."

"Yeah, maybe," said Jon, rubbing his face in contemplation. "If we avoid the live line, we should be alright."

"I think we should go back," said Luna.

Efi snorted. "Absolutely not. Look. There might be a way around it. How do engineers get around down here?"

"No idea," said Jon. "Could there be a service door somewhere? I've seen none, but I'll be honest, I wasn't looking for them."

Jon looked back at the tracks. He was pretty confident that they could make it across, but with Efi's leg, it would be difficult. "Alright," he said. "I'll climb over first, see how far it is to the next station. It shouldn't be far. You two wait here. I'll try to find something to cover the live line while I'm at it."

Luna jumped up. "How do we know you won't just leave us here?"

"Eh? Luna, I'm not gonna leave you. My honour as a Yorkshireman."

"If he did, I'd hunt him down," said Efi.

"Efi, I'm sure there's not a man or woman alive who would see that as a bad thing, but I'll come back. I promise."

Efi chuckled at that. "Flattery won't save you. Now go. Good luck."

Jon nodded and carefully stepped on to the tracks. The live rail hummed like a nest of angry hornets beneath him, waiting for him to make a wrong move. He did not know if stepping on it would be enough to be electrocuted, and he didn't want to find out. Lowering to all fours, and using the track to support him, he crawled slowly over the concrete slats. The hole loomed underneath, drawing him in, and he lurched sideways, head swimming. He imagined noises were coming from it, the same clicking and ticks he'd heard earlier.

"You okay?" called Efi, her voice cutting through the dizziness.

Jon immediately sobered and righted himself. "I'm fine," he replied. "Can you hear that?"

"Hear what?"

"I don't know. Sounds like movement."

Efi craned her head closer to the hole, trying to listen. "Movement?"

"Can't we just go back?" said Luna. "I really don't like this."

"Luna, we're not going back," said Efi. "Those men-"

"I don't care! I can hide, you-"

"Shh!" Jon interrupted. "Listen!"

The clicking noises were growing louder and clearer, as if whatever was making them was moving–and heading in their direction. They were all out of sequence too, more organic in nature than mechanical, almost conversational, echoing across the walls of the tunnel, grating against Jon's nerves. A sickening feeling gnawed up from his guts. Instinct nipped at his heels, urging him to hurry up and get across the gap as quickly as possible. Somewhere far behind him, a howl rang out through the tunnel. He jumped and lost his grip on the rail, almost slipping and falling into the hole.

"Shit!" said Efi.

Jon whipped his head back towards Efi and Luna. "Think you can get across?"

"Just keep going," said Efi, "we'll catch up."

"I can't," said Luna, her voice small and childish. "I don't want to."

"We don't have a choice," replied Efi, nudging her towards the tracks.

Jon turned himself around and reached towards her. "It's okay, just go on all fours like me. I'll help you."

Luna hesitated.

Another howl rang out. At the sound, the clicking in the hole below intensified, agitated and frantic, as if an army of furious insects were squirming around under its black surface.

"Oi!" came a voice.

Efi swore and seized Luna's arm, shoving her onto the tracks towards Jon.

"You do not want them catching you, child," she hissed. "Now go!"

They crawled along the bare bones of the track towards Jon. Further behind, the men were bickering with each other, their whispers carrying, bouncing off the walls of the tunnel. Jon, Efi and Luna all froze, afraid to make a sound.

"Where the fuck did they go?" one of them whined.

"Do I look like I know?" said the other. "I can't see shit down here!"

"Come on. Let's just go."

"You heard Lee. If we don't get her, we'll be offered to Kalinov instead."

"Mate, I'd rather take my chances with the dragon than the freaks down here!"

"Dragon?" whispered Jon. "What's he mean, dragon?"

"I don't know, and I don't want to find out," replied Efi. "Just keep going."

Jon scurried across the gap, then turned and reached for Luna, helping her up. As he motioned to do the same for Efi, the clicking noises reached a peak. For an agonising moment, the three were surrounded by a cacophony of clicks and scraping. Jon ducked, hands clamped over his ears and teeth gritted. As quickly as it came, the sounds quietened, as if whatever was making it was moving swiftly away.

Jon helped Efi up and whispered, "did you hear that?"

"Yeah," she said. "What on earth was it?"

"No idea. I wanna know what the dragon is."

"I don't."

An eerie silence had settled over the tunnel, and Jon wondered if the men had bottled it and left. Maybe the clicking was loud enough to scare them away. If that hadn't put them off, maybe the hole would. Either way, it was quiet now. All the more reason to get out of there as soon as possible.

A short, strangled scream cut through the silence.

"What the fuck was that?" said Efi.

"I don't know," Jon muttered.

He could hear Luna's laboured breathing beside him, sucking in air with small, panicked breaths.

"You alright?" he said.

"Can we just go, please?" she said between gasps.

A second scream erupted from deep within the darkness, shaking the surrounding air.

"Yup," said Jon. "Let's go."

They ran. The screams from the men followed, chasing, clawing at them like wild animals as they fled. The path curved to the left and tilted downwards. It seemed endless, with no sign of the next station, and Jon wondered if he'd chosen the correct route.

The screams faded into silence, and, stamina waning, the three slowed, settling for a pace barely faster than shuffling, but refusing to stop outright. With no breath to spare for conversation, they limped on in silence, dragged by their fear-fuelled feet, the crunch of the gravel and their laboured breathing the only sounds.

13

The Platform

Ambling along for what seemed like bloody ages, they rounded a corner and the tunnel opened out, revealing the remains of the next station platform. Jon stopped. Even with the limited light of his phone torch, he could see the pile of rubble where the platform should have been. The beam met a sign for the exit. Jon lowered the torch and found the archway underneath hidden behind a wall of broken brick and debris.

"What the hell?" he said.

"What do we do now?" said Luna, staring up at the wreckage.

"Keep going," Efi shrugged. "We already know where this tunnel goes. The next station is closer to the hospital, anyway."

"And it's not like we can go back," Jon muttered, turning towards the tunnel entrance. "Whatever attacked our friend back there could still be about. Might even be on its way to us."

With that, Luna sank to the floor and raised her hands to her face. Efi shot Jon a look that he didn't quite understand and limped over to Luna, settling herself painfully down next to the girl.

Luna's voice came between frustrated growls and gasps, her fists clenched and her body shaking. "I can't do this," she said. "I need to get out of here..."

Efi stretched out her leg, grimacing, and put an arm around Luna. "Listen, babe," she said softly. "It's gonna be okay. If we keep moving and stay quiet, we'll be fine. We don't know what happened to those men. And if there is something back there, we'll just feed Jon to it."

"Hey!" said Jon.

Luna sniffed and nodded, smiling faintly at the joke.

"But before we carry on," Efi continued, "I need to take the tape off my leg. It's too tight."

"Fine," said Jon, "but if whatever got those lads comes after us, I'm kicking you in the shin and running."

Efi sniggered and began unwrapping the bandages around her leg until she reached the soaked tampon. Clenching her jaw, she peeled it away, revealing the torn flesh of her leg underneath.

"Oh dear. That's not pretty."

Her calf appeared dark and bruised, the wound angry and swollen. Black lines snaked under the skin, wrapping around her leg like the vines of a poisonous plant. The gash itself wasn't as deep as it looked before, and was no longer bleeding, but Jon could see it was infected, and would need stitches at the very least.

"How is it?" he asked, kneeling next to her.

Efi let out a sigh. Beads of sweat rested on her forehead.

"I'm okay," she replied, before pointing to her leg. "But see that, there? That is blood poisoning."

"Damn," said Jon. "Does it happen that fast?"

Efi kept her eyes down. "Not usually. The sooner we get to the hospital, the better."

While Efi redressed the wound with supplies from the rucksack, Jon kept one ear facing the tunnel, listening for any signs that they'd been followed. Ever present, within the blackness, were the clicking sounds, muffled, quiet, and not all worked up as they were before, but definitely still there. It was all around him, as if he were standing in the centre of a giant hive. The sound seemed to come from within the walls, the ceiling, underneath his feet, everywhere. Even over Luna's sobs of frustration, he could hear it. The more he listened, the more deafening it became, and the more his guts twisted in dread.

"Luna!"

Efi's voice cut through the hum and Jon whipped his head around to see Luna running towards the pile of rubble.

"Luna!" he shouted.

"I don't care!" she replied, pulling herself up onto the platform. "I need to get out of here now!"

She began scrambling up the pile of debris towards the exit archway. The scrape of brick against brick echoed through the chamber as she climbed, grating at Jon's ears and nerves. In response, the clicking grew louder and faster, as if the tunnel itself were alive and bristling with anger.

Jon took off towards the pile. He climbed after her, seizing her arm. "Luna, no!"

"I need to get out of here!"

"Luna, come on. You're gonna get hurt!"

"No! I shouldn't have gone with you! We're going to die down here!"

A stirring from within the rubble caught his ears. The pair froze and fell silent.

"Luna," he said quietly, "come on. We need to go."

She nodded and turned, reaching for his hand, but as she stepped forward, her foot slipped. Jon caught her, but a brick wobbled and fell, smashing against the pile as it tumbled to the ground, landing in pieces on the tracks below. A small cloud of dust followed, dissipating into the air. Jon and Luna stood deathly still, eyes fixed on the rubble as they waited for it to clear. Without warning, another came loose and plummeted down, each knock a hammer strike, filling the air with a fine mist, crashing against the rest of the brick before landing next to its predecessor at Efi's feet. As if a large rock had been thrown into a calm pool, a ripple spread across the pile, bricks all around them shuddering as they began to loosen and tumble down.

Efi was already up, boots back on and waving up at the pair. "Let's go!" she called.

"Luna," said Jon, "we're going now. Efi! You okay to walk?"

"Yeah, I'll be fine. Let's get out of here," Efi replied, testing her weight on her newly bandaged leg.

Jon took the rucksack, slinging it around his shoulders, and the three took off into the next tunnel. As he stepped under its shadow, he turned briefly back towards the platform. Out of the corner of his eye, he spotted something moving in the rubble. Something like a leg, but longer. Thinner.

"Go. Go!" he whispered, and together they took off for the next station, the sound of bricks falling right behind them. Jon stayed behind Luna and Efi, ushering them on, nervously glancing back every few seconds as they stumbled onwards. The clicking hounded them, as constant and oppressive as the tunnel walls, and maddening. *Either attack us or fuck off*, Jon thought.

They continued on, groping the walls for guidance, stumbling and panting with exhaustion, but too afraid to slow down. Finally, Jon caught a glimpse of light ahead.

"The station!" said Efi between gasps.

"Keep going," Jon replied. Soon, fresh air, daylight. The hospital. Seeing Caede and Kai again. *Just get outside.*

Light from the platform washed over them, burning their eyes. Jon stopped, blinking, and looked around. The sign for the exit was right above them, illuminated, encased in stark white light. Underneath stood the archway and corridor to the escalators, the platform, and freedom beyond. The clicking noises had quietened too, as if calmer, content that the intruders would soon be leaving.

Luna climbed up to the platform and ran towards it, disappearing under the archway for a moment. "It's clear," she said, poking her head back through.

"Thank the lord," replied Efi.

Jon helped her onto the platform, then heaved himself up. Together, they headed to the escalators.

"Typical," said Efi as they approached. "The lights work, but these are dead."

"Be thankful it's not rush hour," Jon replied with a grin.

"Jon, I swear to God, I will hit you."

They ran up the escalator steps, Jon striding ahead two at a time, eager to feel the fresh air against his skin. He reached the top and stopped dead, breath caught in the back of his mouth. At the top of the escalator, something appeared in front of him.

It was a small humanoid, hunched over and crouching low to the ground on all fours, its head twitching and clicking jarringly. Bulbous, bloodshot eyes stared vacantly at him. Its face was swollen and balloon-like, with long, silver marks where the skin had stretched and torn. Its mouth hung open, revealing two long, bony mandibles. Muddy rags hung from the wretched thing's emaciated body, its limbs sharp and protruding like the knotted branches of a tree. At the end of its hands were black, brittle-looking fingers, lost to frostbite, infection, or something else.

Just like the spider and the snake man before her, this one must have been human at some point. They had both been horrific, but in Jon's mind they at least seemed lucid, deliberate in their actions, and coherent. The spider even looked human–to an extent. And she could talk. Whatever this was, it was too far gone to resemble a person now, as if its transformation had been too gruelling to survive with any trace of humanity intact. Something was growing out of it, too. A long, white stem, with soft branches sprouting from its centre. The creature seemed confused or in pain. It turned around in circles, clicking and twitching, as if trying to tug itself back from an unknown assailant. Jon gaped at the sight of it, frozen in place as disgust and fear fought in the pit of his stomach.

Two more appeared out of the darkness. One was dragging a body by the arm. Upon seeing the first, the pair clicked furiously at it. The one with the body dropped it and lunged as if to attack the first. It stopped short of making contact and retreated quickly.

The first clicked back, retreating a little, then moving forward, its front limbs reaching out as if trying to touch the other two. They clicked and wheezed angrily in response, and darted back, afraid. Suddenly, the source of the sound in the tunnels became clear. The blood without the bodies became clear. Luna had been right. Worse, that arsehole on the surface had tried to warn them.

A scream rose up from behind him as Efi and Luna reached the top of the escalators. The creatures stopped and snapped their heads around, their bulbous faces locked on the woman and child. Adrenaline coursed through Jon's body, carrying with it a single message to every nerve, sinew, and tendon in his being: run. The world around him jarred to a halt. Almost in slow motion, he wrenched his body around, his eyes meeting Efi's. Her face was contorted in horror and confusion. She moved her lips as if she were shouting something, but he couldn't hear her. Luna stood frozen and wide-eyed, one foot still in the air. The world sped back up.

"Run!"

They pummelled down the stairs, sprinting across the platform. Without looking back, they threw themselves into the tunnel.

14

Patient Discharge

Justine Pearson, entry 08.05.2030

Well, this is just fucking typical. Yesterday I went to Raj's office to tell him I thought Terry might be responsible for the break-in and that he's up to something. Raj basically told me that there's no way Terry helped the activists get access to the lab, and then implied that I'm crazy. So I guess I'm going to have to find proof myself. Fine. As soon as Terry leaves his office, I'm going to go in there and I'm going to find out exactly what he's been planning.

-

Caede burst through the ward doors, an empty rucksack in her hand with the tags still attached as if it had been nicked from one of the hospital shops.

"We need to go."

Ravi and Kai raised their heads in bewilderment.

"What?" said Ravi.

Caede replied. "I said we need to go."

Ravi rose from the armchair slowly. Kai wriggled in the bed as if to follow, but Ravi waved a hand and the boy stopped. "Caede, calm down. What are you talking about?"

Caede stopped and stared at the pair, exasperated. "Didn't you hear the screaming? We're not safe here. We need to go!"

She started gathering up bits and pieces from around the room, stuffing them into the bag as she muttered to herself.

"They were…"

"They were what?" said Ravi.

"They… They…"

Ravi walked over and took Caede gently by the shoulders, turning her to face him. "What's going on? Who is 'they?'"

Caede brushed him off with a wave and kneeled down, scooping vending machine snacks and drink cans into the bag, her face aimed at the floor as she spoke. "The *things.*"

Ravi glanced over at Kai before ducking down next to her. The boy was just watching, no signs of panic on his face, just bewilderment at his sister's behaviour.

"The creatures?" he whispered.

Without looking up, she answered, voice low. "There's a group of them. One of them had another survivor, a woman. They…"

"They what?" asked Ravi.

The answer left her lips as barely a whisper. "They…they were eating her."

Ravi let himself settle on the floor next to her, mind reeling as he absorbed the information. "Eating her?" he mouthed silently.

Caede nodded.

He rubbed his hand over his face and chin, and, after a moment, he looked at her. "Did they see you?" he asked.

"No," she replied. "I don't think so. They were too distracted. There was one.… Oh God, Ravi, he, it, I don't know what to call it. He was like a giant. I've never seen anyone so tall before. It literally pulled her apart. They're hunting down survivors, and they're not far from here. We're not safe if we stay here."

"Very well," said Ravi. "We're going to need supplies then. Kai still needs antibiotics, and he is far from well enough to be walking around right now."

Caede stopped and looked at Kai.

Kai cocked his head in confusion. "What's going on?"

"Nothing, Kai, everything's fine," said Caede. She turned back to Ravi. "Can we use a wheelchair?"

"I suppose so," Ravi replied. "That would limit our travel options, but it could work until we can find a car."

"We just need to get far enough away that those monsters won't find us."

Ravi shifted uncomfortably. "What makes you think they will? Unless we attract their attention, I doubt they will be looking here. We could turn off the lights, stay quiet?"

"No. Think about it. I don't know if they can smell us, or hear us or what, but they are looking for survivors. This is a hospital. Anyone still alive will probably be heading here. If those things have any reason to head this way, or if they can sniff us out, we won't be able to hide for long. We need to leave while they're still eating. If they look for us, they're going to find us. If we don't run while we can, while they're distracted..."

"I understand," Ravi replied. "I can't stop you and your brother from leaving, but Efia and Holly aren't back yet. I can't just abandon them."

"Look," said Caede. "I don't want to be mean, but they've been gone all night. Don't you think if they were coming back, they would be here by now?"

Ravi's face dropped. He gazed at the floor, took off his glasses, and rubbed his face with the back of his hand. Caede waited for his response.

"You're right," he said, sad and quiet. "They didn't have any reason to stay here."

He shook himself as if to shed the malaise and rose. "Alright," he said. "But where?"

"I don't know. Somewhere safer than here."

"We could go to my aunt and uncle's house. It's a bit of a journey, but it's a big place and it's out of the way–there's only farmland surrounding it."

"Would they let us stay?"

"Given the circumstances, I'm sure it will be fine."

"What are you both talking about?" Kai demanded.

Caede looked at Ravi and he nodded. She stood and walked over to the bed.

"So..." she started.

"I heard you," said Kai. "There's more monsters, aren't there?"

Caede nodded. "They're not far away. We need to leave the hospital."

Kai leaned back into the pillows and said nothing. His face was passive on the surface, but his eyes trembled.

"We should leave tonight," said Ravi. "If those things are hunting during the day, they must be sleeping at night just like us."

Caede frowned. "We don't know that for sure, and I don't want to be stuck here if they get hungry later and come back."

"Very well," replied Ravi, "but I need to leave a note for Efi and Holly. We had an agreement to do so if any of us left with no intention to return."

"And what if those things can read?"

"I'll put the note somewhere they won't think to look."

"Can't you just text her? Or phone? Do you have her number?"

"If Efi is hiding somewhere, I don't want to give away her location. I'm not even sure the phone networks are working now."

"I called Kai earlier..." Caede started but stopped. She didn't know why she was arguing. He'd already agreed to leave, and what was the harm in leaving a note?

"I'll leave them a map too," said Ravi. "If they want to catch up to us, they can."

Within a few minutes, the three had packed and were leaving the hospital, each of them armed with a surgical mask, gloves and safety goggles–Ravi's idea. He left the note for Efi with a map book and instructions inside one of the drawers in his office. If Efi and Holly returned, they would know to check there. The house, he had said, was about an hour's drive from London, and ten if they walked. With the wheelchair and rest stops, it could be more like fifteen.

Kai sat in a wheelchair they had borrowed from the accident and emergency department, holding a rucksack filled with medical supplies and wrapped in a blanket that made him look like a swaddled infant. Caede kneeled in front of the chair and softly stroked his head.

"Are you warm enough?"

He nodded weakly in response. She couldn't tell if he was annoyed with her for making them leave the safety of the hospital, or because he was still in pain, but she didn't question it. The warmth had returned to his skin at least. His cheeks were flushed with pink, the grey seemingly faded.

Caede carried the food in her bag, and acted as a scout, darting ahead to inspect corridors and clear the walkway of any obstacles until they reached the car park. There, she paused, watching for any sign of movement. Across the way was the path they had taken to reach the door, where their kind saviour had met his fate. Sunlight poured through the pillars, bringing with it warmth and the soft blue of the late morning sky. Seconds passed, and nothing moved. She waved to Ravi, who wheeled Kai over, and together they left the hospital grounds.

They had discussed taking a car and driving out of the city, but the roads were blocked by abandoned vehicles and scores of bodies, some of them piled into grotesque pyramids. Caede wondered if that had been the work of the military or some kind of government-mandated clean-up squad, either still in process or abandoned mid-task. The air around them reeked of death. It made her want to heave.

Nothing in the streets moved, but she was uneasy, unable to shake the vision of the woman, her bloody body lying on the ground, limbs devoured by monsters as she wailed. The outside was so quiet now. Tiny seeds of doubt began to grow and bloom in her mind. Was she wrong to make them leave the hospital? Was the encounter just her fevered imagination running amok? *No*, she told herself. It had to be real.

Hand jittering, she instinctively pulled out the box of cigarettes, pressing one to her lips as she fumbled around her pocket for the lighter. As the flame danced, she reached for the cigarette and glimpsed some red on the pavement. Dried blood. It could have been Jon's blood. Caede frowned. Kai was right. If she had stayed at home in the first place, Kai would still have his arm, and the man who saved them would probably still be alive, surviving just fine without them. A throbbing started up behind her right eye.

Ravi approached with Kai. "Are you okay, Caede?"

"I'll be fine. It's just a lot to take in."

Ravi gave a sympathetic nod. Caede returned the unlit cigarette to the box.

"Let's go," she said.

15

Man in the Tunnel

Terry Howard, entry 14.05.2030

I have moved off the work entry log to this personal recorder. It's safer, and I can store the files on my home computer instead of the work ones. Justine is becoming more suspicious, but I don't think she will find anything linking me to the break-in. I would find this all amusing, but I'm too stressed. I just want to quit, hand in my resignation, but I can't leave my research to those fiends. All the while I'm still here, I can at least oversee what happens.

There's worse news too. The samples secured by Lauren's team are all dead. They can't prove anything with those, despite posting statements all over their social media pages. No one except the extreme conspiracy enthusiasts will be interested in dead samples and grand accusations. We can't afford to stage another break-in either. It looks as though I will have to smuggle something out for them.

-

Jon panted as he stumbled along, lungs and legs straining from the effort. Efi and Luna followed close behind him, their ragged breaths drowned out by the furious clicking and scuffling of the monstrosities in pursuit. The tunnel walls seemed to narrow and close around him, but then curved, and he spotted a dim, yellow light and an indent in the wall. It was a service door. Jon leapt towards it and tugged at the handle. To his relief, it opened, and he waved the others inside before throwing himself in. He slammed the door shut and gripped the handle while Efi and Luna scrambled for something to block it. They found a section of metal track leaning against the stone wall and together dragged it over, wedging it under.

Tapping followed. The handle twitched under Jon's grip, then stopped. Eventually, the noise died down, and the room fell silent. Jon closed his eyes and slumped down against the door. Sweat dripped from his hair and down his face, and his heart threw itself around the inside of his ribs. His legs and chest burned. Efi fared no better, sliding down next to him as she gulped in deep breaths of air, exhaustion and agony written all over her face. Luna leaned forwards, hands on knees, and heaved. A few minutes passed this way, each survivor solely focused on coaxing the oxygen back into their lungs. As for how long they had been running, exactly, Jon couldn't guess, but the next station couldn't be far, not now. They could hide in this room for a bit, catch their breath, then carry on once the threat had passed. Blinking the white spots from his vision, he jerked his head up and looked around the room.

It was a large storage and maintenance room, from what he could tell, full of metal shelving carrying cleaning supplies, rolls of cable, tools, and a few spray paint cans. The centre of the room was empty and dark for the most part, with a solitary, dim bulb dangling bare from the middle of the grey cement ceiling.

After a while, Efi spoke. "We could have taken them."

Jon snorted. "Are you daft?"

"We could have taken them."

Jon chuckled between breaths. "What was stopping you, then?"

"You were in the way."

Luna stood up and looked around. "It smells like piss in here," she said, wrinkling her nose in disgust.

Efi nudged Jon with her shoulder. "That'll be Jon after he saw those monsters."

He nudged her back with a grimace.

Luna stared at the pair in disbelief. "Why are you making jokes?"

"Because," said Efi, "if I don't, I might cry, and no one wants to see that."

With that, the jovial atmosphere dissipated, leaving the three of them to sit in silence on the floor.

"Can I have some water?" asked Luna.

Jon shrugged off the rucksack and slid a bottle of water to her. She took a long swig, gulping down the liquid until the bottle was almost empty.

"Woah, woah," said Jon. "Don't go crazy. We don't have much of that."

Luna stopped and shot a look at Jon. "If it wasn't for my dad's shop, you wouldn't have any."

"So, we'd be in the same situation we're in now," Efi shot back. "Girl, share the water. We'll find more when we get out of here."

Luna shrugged and threw the bottle at Jon before walking to the other side of the room and slumping down against the wall. It bounced in his hands, almost falling. He looked at Efi as he handed her the bottle. She shrugged in response, as if to say "teenagers," then took a few sips before handing it back. He tipped up the bottle and downed the rest of the water gratefully.

"We've got one more bottle," he said.

Efi nodded.

"I'm tired," said Luna.

"Have a snooze if you want," said Jon. "I'm knackered myself."

"We can rest for a bit," said Efi. "We'll head off once things are quiet out there."

"I need to pee," said Luna.

"Didn't you go before we left yours?" Efi replied.

"I didn't need to then."

"You should have gone, anyway!"

Luna sighed, wrapped her hands around her knees, and rested her head on top of them. Jon felt Efi's weight settle against him. He lifted his arm and wrapped it around her shoulder. Neither of them had slept since the spider attack, and he was pretty sure being unconscious didn't count as rest. He fought the exhaustion for a little longer, then gave in, letting his eyes close and his thoughts drift lazily towards sleep. Memories coasted towards his parents, then to Tara, to his friends, then finally to Caede and her brother. Those two, with their grey eyes, and Caede's faint smile. *Stoic, that one,* he thought. *Hope they're alright.*

Before he realised, he had drifted off.

A loud knock against the door startled him.

"Huh?"

The door banged again, twice. Someone was waiting on the other side, and not very patiently. He grumbled to himself, still half asleep. It wasn't even morning yet.

"Tara, get the door will you, babe?"

"Who's Tara?" asked Efi.

"What?"

Jon sat upright, dazed and bleary-eyed, body cold and aching. It took a moment to realise that he wasn't at home. He was in a dimly lit storeroom, sitting on cold cement, underground, with two people he had only just met.

"Shhh!"

It was Luna, wide awake and pressed against the far wall, hugging the rucksack. She pointed at the door behind them. Confused, Jon turned around and looked up. The door banged again, catapulting Jon and Efi from the floor. They each seized the door handle and gripped it tightly.

"Have we got any weapons?" said Efi.

Jon glanced around. "What about those spray cans? We could blind them, at least?"

"It will have to do."

A muffled, deep voice rose from the other side of the door. "Yo! Anyone alive in there?"

The three froze, glancing nervously at each other.

"Should we let them in?" asked Efi.

"No, don't!" replied Luna.

Cautiously, Jon approached the door. "You armed?"

He hoped he'd hidden the fear in his voice enough to sound at least a little intimidating.

"Course I'm armed," growled the voice in response. "Have you seen outside?"

"You human?" Jon asked.

The voice hesitated. "Uh, yeah, I think so.... Listen, are you gonna let me in or not?"

Jon turned to Efi and Luna. "What do you think?" he mouthed.

Efi nodded, quickly padding over to the shelves, grabbing some spray cans. She handed one to Luna, and they held them, facing the door.

"Alright," he said, "I'm opening the door now. Don't try anything funny."

He let go of the handle, and the door swung heavily open. Jon found himself staring throat level at a man. He considered simply closing the door again, but before he could, the man ducked under the threshold, breathing a sigh of relief as he entered the room.

"Close it back up if you want, mate," said the man, wiping his brow with his arm.

Jon closed the door. The man padded lazily to the other side of the room, away from Luna and Efi. They followed him with the cans, their fingers locked on the spray nozzles. As far as Jon was concerned, they were right to be suspicious. There was something off about the man, and it wasn't just his height. He was a foot taller than Jon–muscular, too, from what he could see in the dim light. Dense, thick muscles, the kind you would expect to see only on prized bodybuilders and genetically engineered pigs.

Jon glanced down at his somewhat softer, rounder belly and shifted uncomfortably, tucking his hands into his jeans pockets. He suddenly regretted letting the man inside, then wondered if he'd even had a choice in the matter.

"So, uh, what's your name, pal?" he asked.

"Does it matter?" the man replied with a grunt.

Jon crossed his arms. It was a 'fuck you' gesture, reserved for meetings with ego-inflated blowhards and arguments with Tara. Efi stood, her brow lowered in equal annoyance.

"If you won't tell us your name," she said, "at least tell us how you got here."

"I was chased down here," said the man.

He shrugged off a heavy-looking rucksack and kneeled down to inspect the contents.

"My name's Samson," he said as he unclipped a sleeping bag from underneath the pack. "Samson, Thomas, Okoye."

He unravelled the bag and sat down, continuing to rummage through the rucksack, pulling out a bottle of water and some tins of tuna.

Efi shot Jon a look and raised her eyebrows. The man seemed unfazed by them. Either he didn't care if he lived or died, or he knew neither Jon, Efi or Luna posed any threat to him. Jon suspected the latter was true.

"How close to the nearest station?" Jon asked.

Samson twisted open one of the tins. "If you go out that door," he continued, "and turn right, less than a minute."

"Great, thanks," said Jon. "We'll leave you to it, then."

"Woah, woah," said Samson. "Where're you going, fam?"

"What?"

"You don't wanna go out there yet. Them things hunt at night."

"What things?" asked Efi.

"Wait," said Jon. "It's night?"

"Yeah," said Samson. "It's like ten already. And the things; they're called chimaera."

"The what?"

"Chimaera. You know, like in the Greek myths. That lion, bird, goat thing. Like a mix, you get me?"

Samson tipped the contents of the tin into his mouth, chugging it down without chewing, like a seagull.

Jon grimaced at the sight and turned to Efi. "Like the spider girl."

"Oh," said Samson. "You've seen her, huh? I think I saw her yesterday. There's some real weird ones out there."

"There's weird ones in here, too," said Jon.

Samson nodded. "The bugs, right? They go outside when it's dark. Take the bodies down here to eat, or something, I don't wanna think about what. There's the dog pack, too. They're like werewolves, but no full moon between them, you get me?" With that Samson laughed, deep and booming.

"They must be the same men who chased us down here," said Efi. She shivered. "They said they wanted women."

"I bet they did," said Samson. "They ain't right."

Efi tutted in response. "What do you know about them?"

"I won't scare you with the details," the big man replied. "Just don't let them catch you when you leave here."

16

Hide and Seek

Justine Pearson, entry 15.05.2030

Terry's done a good job of covering his tracks, that's for sure. I don't think Raj is covering for him, but who knows. I don't think I can trust anyone right now. These people are my colleagues, friends, even! I thought I knew them.

-

Caede shivered. The city centre was grey and silent, the buildings merging with the sky in equal bleakness. She wondered when it was going to rain again. Abandoned cars littered the roads, some of them even merged, left there in mid-collision. Any hopes they might have had of driving out had been dashed for now, so the three continued on foot with Caede scouting ahead, clearing the path of any debris for Ravi as he wheeled Kai in the chair. They had taken some waterproof coats from a local shop, just in case it started raining again. It felt wrong, but considering the circumstances, a couple of coats weren't going to be missed by anyone.

Caede had fashioned a sort of spear out of a broken broom handle, less as a weapon but more to help clear the path and push the odd corpse out of the way. The body pyramids were here too, some over ten feet high. In other areas, the bodies were scattered across the roads and pavements, left to rot where they lay. For those, she plotted routes around, moving the odd one wherever she could. Luckily for the three, the side streets were relatively clear.

Steam built up on the inside of her mask, fogging her goggles. She wondered why she'd agreed to wear the sodding thing. She'd been lying there amongst the bodies for two nights. If she was going to catch anything, she'd have it by now. Her face itched, and her mind kept drifting back to the screams of the dying woman. Her wails resonated against the silence outside, reverberating in circles around her head, until Caede was no longer sure if she was imagining it, or if somewhere nearby, another victim had been claimed.

The three continued at a steady pace for a little over three hours before hunger and exhaustion threatened to overwhelm them. Spotting an abandoned café across the road, next to an alleyway and a laundrette, Caede signalled to Ravi to follow and headed towards it.

The remains of the front window lay scattered across the pavement in tiny, glittering cubes. A faded red and yellow sign decorated the front of the building, designed in the style of an old 1950s diner–a place where you would expect to eat comically large hotdogs and drink tall, frothy milkshakes. She couldn't remember the last time she'd had a milkshake.

The front door hung haphazardly off its hinges, as if it had been torn away from the frame. Caede stepped over the front window ledge, avoiding the doorway, and looked around.

The inside of the café matched the outside theme, with blue-and-white-striped leather benches and chrome-edged diner tables, aged and stained from years of coffee abuse from clientele. Caede inspected one of the menus. No hotdogs, but you could order an all-day fried breakfast, and it came with a free mug of tea. Your typical workman's café. The kitchen was further in, situated behind the service counter, separated by a wide, swinging door with a small porthole window. She cautiously approached it and peeked through. Chrome countertops and emptiness met her on the other side.

The sound of her own blood pumping filled her ears as she slowly pushed the door open, just wide enough to fit her head through. There was nothing but some rotting vegetables on the counter. Leaving the kitchen, she turned back to the café floor. A sudden movement caught her eye. In a corridor ahead of her, opposite the kitchen door, was a storeroom and the customer toilets, the door to the latter creaking to a close. Caede felt the moisture leave her mouth. Her chest tightened and the air around her thickened. The door was old, too heavy and solid to be affected by a gust of wind, and it was too far away from the kitchen door for her to have brushed past it. The sound of her heart pounding returned, and she gripped the broom handle a little tighter. Unblinking, she stared at the door, and began slowly stepping backwards.

Her eyes flickered towards the front window to see Ravi and Kai approaching, waving at her. Ravi opened his mouth to speak, but she shook her head, raising a hand to silence him before returning her gaze to the toilet door. She glared at it, breath held, silently demanding that it close and stay closed. Finally, it stopped moving. The handle of the door was old brass, the catch wedged inside the mechanism, so it didn't click closed. It just stopped. If she wanted it fully closed, she'd have to do that herself. And she wasn't going to do that. The door remained still. Finally, she let herself settle. She exhaled and took a step back. Her foot met something brittle, a plate or bottle, and a loud crunch echoed through the café as it shattered.

The toilet door exploded open. With a shriek, a mass of thick black fur and teeth leapt out, charging at Caede, eyes wide and white as a rabid dog's. She screamed, not realising that she had already raised the broken broom handle up in front of her. The creature stopped moving. It stared at her, almost in surprise. She stared back at it. At him. It wasn't a creature—not like the others she had seen before, anyway. It was more like a person, his face still human, but longer, more canine-like. His eyes were no longer wild and white, they were brown and pleading, and he looked small, young. As young as Kai. He began to cough and gurgle. His eyes watered. Thick red blood frothed from inside his mouth and spilled over his lips. He tried to say something, but nothing came out. He looked down, curling his hands around the broom handle embedded in his chest, then looked back up at Caede.

"Oh, God..." Caede whispered. "I'm sorry... I'm so sorry..."

The boy's lips moved. More blood poured from them. Panicking, Caede yanked the broom handle out and grabbed him, trying to hold him up. The boy moaned quietly and shook in her arms.

"It's okay," she said. "It's going to be okay. We have a doctor, he'll help you…"

Dark blood splattered across the floor, pouring in a solid red line, soaking her clothes. The boy dropped heavily to his knees, then sank to the floor, and lay still.

"Caede!" Ravi shouted, hurdling over the windowpane, tearing through the café. "Caede, are you okay?"

"Get help…" she replied, her voice quiet and distant.

Ravi looked at the floor. "Oh my God! Caede, get away from it!"

"He needs help..."

Ravi grabbed her arm, pulling her away from the boy. "Don't get its blood on you! Come on, we need to go!"

Caede stumbled outside, where Kai was sitting, squirming, paler than ever and shaken.

"Are you okay?" he gasped.

"I'm fine," she replied unconvincingly.

"We need to hurry," said Ravi. "There's probably more of them."

Caede glanced around, spotting a small shop with its window still intact. She pointed towards it, and they hurriedly wheeled Kai over, yanking open the front door and ducking inside. Ravi wheeled

Kai further in behind some shelves and took up a space next to Caede by the window. The pair gazed in horror as two large male humanoids appeared, running into the café. After a few seconds, a howl filled the air. It was more like a wail, haunting and full of misery. A weight sank into Caede's stomach and settled there.

"It must have been a trap," Ravi whispered.

Could it have been? Were they just waiting there for survivors to wander inside? Or was it that their kid just needed to go to the bathroom and had been startled by her? And she'd killed him. Easily, in fact, without a second thought. Her vision blurred.

The men left the café. One was thick and stocky in appearance, the other smaller and slim, and darting about in circles on all fours, sniffing the air with an elongated, dog-like face.

"What are they doing?" asked Ravi.

Another man stepped out from a nearby building. Unlike his companions, this one stood fully upright. He was tall, broad, more human in appearance, sleeve tattoos still visible under a layer of thick grey hair, and he barked an order at them, pointing at the café. The slim one approached, hunched over, holding himself low as if in reverence of the larger man, replying to him, but Caede couldn't make out the words. The tall one entered the café and emerged after a few seconds, his face twisted in fury.

"They were human before, weren't they?" Caede whispered.

"Yes."

"I killed him."

"It would have killed you."

They sat in silence, watching from the window as they waited for the creatures to leave. Eventually they did just that, the tall one leading the others away, disappearing from sight.

"When this was all happening," said Ravi, voice low, "and people began changing, the transformations were incredibly fast. Too fast for some. A lot of them lost their minds. They forgot who they were. I don't think they're human anymore."

Ravi kept his eyes fixed on the street outside as he spoke, his face calm and melancholic. "For some reason, males seemed to be more affected. They transformed faster, days faster than women. Many became violent and unstable. There was nothing we could do but let them go until the army arrived. I think it's to do with the testosterone levels in the body."

"So it might not just be males, then?"

"Anyone with high levels of testosterone… but that's just my theory."

A sniffle came from behind them. Caede turned to see Kai, his eyes wide and pleading. "That's going to happen to me, isn't it?" he said.

"No," said Caede. "You're fine, see? Ravi gave you a blood transfusion. You're fine."

She looked at Ravi. "Right? He's fine, right?"

Ravi nodded.

"I'm going to turn into one of those things," Kai repeated.

"Kai," said Caede. "Listen to me. You're not going to turn into…"

"But look at me!"

A howl rang across the street.

"Not good," whispered Ravi. "We need to go."

Caede took the handles of the wheelchair and pushed Kai through the shop floor. "There's got to be a back door," she said. "We can sneak out there."

"Let's hope they can't smell us," Ravi replied.

17

Rush hour

Terry Howard, entry 27.05.2030

I have spoken to Lauren again, and we're going to attempt to get a few live samples.

Justine and I have begun human trials in the meantime. I wonder how many of our 'volunteers' know what they have signed up for. They are here under the pretence of an experimental cancer treatment. Deplorable. I have tried putting it off for as long as possible. However, the higher-ups are keen to get a move on after that announcement from Russia.

-

Samson rifled through the bag once more, pulling out some packets of crisps and taking a final swig of his water bottle before returning it. He threw the crisp packets over to the others. Jon took a bag and nodded in thanks.

"I don't want to think about that," replied Jon. "I'm just glad they hadn't seen Luna."

"I can take care of myself," said Luna defiantly.

"Oh yeah?" said Efi. Her eyes stayed on the floor of the room, haunted and glittering. "Think of the worst thing that could happen to a woman. That's what they would have done to us. It's what they always do to us. We're nothing but toys to them."

Luna didn't respond.

"See," said Samson. "This is how you have to think. Get complacent, you'll end up dead–or wishing you was. Especially with those pricks. They were probably scum before, but now no one's out to stop them. No police. No prison time. They've gone feral. A good-looking woman like you? Probably thought they'd won the lottery."

Efi snorted in response, disgusted. Jon caught a glimpse of Luna rolling her eyes. She was probably too young to even know what Efi and Samson were talking about. Jon's thoughts turned to Caede. How far were those men from the hospital? How safe would she be there? Would they threaten the boy to get to her? It's what men like that did, wasn't it? He shivered.

Looking back at Samson, Jon felt a pang of envy. The guy could easily take care of himself. He could do a better job at protecting Efi and Luna from those men. The man's jawline alone would put off any potential attacker. What did the guy do for a living, fight bears? When did the apocalypse leave only tall, good-looking men, and then him, as survivors?

"So, when can we leave?" Jon asked, trying to hide his irritation.

"You can leave whenever you want, mate," Samson replied nonchalantly. "But I'd recommend waiting till morning."

"Those wolf guys must be long gone by now," said Jon.

"It's not them I'm worried about."

"The bugs then?"

"Nah. Something worse."

Samson shifted uncomfortably. There was a slight change in his composure, as if the easy-going surfer-dude mask had momentarily slipped. Jon narrowed his eyes. He hadn't been able to see the man quite clearly enough to make him out properly. Yes, he was abnormally tall, but then some men are. Jon couldn't hold that against him. There was something else, though, something about his appearance, his body, something Jon couldn't quite place. Was it his build? Plenty of tall guys also worked out. He could have been a professional athlete, perhaps.

"What are you worried about?" asked Luna.

Samson let out a chuckle. "Same thing as you, baby girl. Same thing as you."

"So, Samson," said Jon. "When I asked if you were human, you hesitated. Why is that?"

Samson chuckled again. "It's complicated."

"What do you mean, 'it's complicated'?"

"You're one of them, aren't you?"

"No, mate. I'm nothing like them."

"What the fuck are you, then?" snapped Jon. "And I'm not your mate!"

"Trust," Samson replied. "I'm nothing like those pricks outside."

"Every one of those things we've encountered has tried to kill us, and you're asking me to trust you? We've only just met you!"

"I haven't attacked you, have I? Look, I've been like this for days now and I feel normal! I'm fine."

Jon hadn't realised, but both he and Samson were on their feet, facing each other, the air around them thick and heavy. Jon ran his hands through his hair and exhaled away the tension.

"Alright. I believe you. So, what now?"

"Now?" said Samson. "I plan to get a good night's sleep. I recommend you do the same."

"You don't look like the other creatures," said Luna, eyeing him curiously.

"I'm the same bloke I always was," he replied. "I haven't changed much, 'cept I used to be a skinny shit, and a foot shorter. Whatever this thing is, it's affecting everyone differently."

"I think it's a virus," said Efi from her spot against the wall.

Jon spun around to face her. "What?"

Luna sat up straight, her face aimed at Efi's.

"I think it's a virus," Efi repeated.

"What kind of virus turns someone into a giant spider?" said Jon.

Luna pointed at Efi's leg, shifting herself away. "How contagious is it?"

Efi massaged her leg, unsure of her own words. "I don't think…"

"How contagious is it, Efi?" Jon repeated.

Efi stared vacantly at her leg, as if she were trying to figure out the answer herself. "I don't know."

"Hang on," said Jon. "Last week the news said this was another Ebola outbreak. Is that what they were referring to?"

Efi nodded gravely. "Yes. But there's only ever been one outbreak in this country and that was in 2027, and it only affected six people."

"I remember," said Jon. "It was all over the news. Got all the xenophobes knickers in a right bunch."

Efi kept her face aimed at her leg. "One of the doctors I was working with had a patient come in two weeks ago. Vomiting, diarrhoea, fever, delirium. Bleeding from multiple orifices. That's why they thought it was Ebola at first. The patient had just come back from Liberia–visiting family, then fallen ill shortly after returning. We called the relevant bodies, set up a quarantine, ordered new PPE. We sent off samples. The tests came back negative."

Efi paused and shook her head.

"We looked at other things. The flu, SARS, Covid-19. We even looked at advanced AIDS cases. This was something else. So, the hospital tried getting in touch with someone, a specialist. They seemed pretty excited at first, but then they stopped answering our calls. All the while, people were still turning up at the hospital. It's flu season as well. You try telling people to stay at home. It won't happen."

Efi looked up at the ceiling with glassy eyes and sighed.

"Then people started dying. They just…dissolved in front of our eyes. Multiple organ failure and dehydration. There was nothing we could do about it. We didn't know who was next to get it. We had all the protective gear on, but that didn't seem to make much difference. Age didn't seem to matter either. The elderly, adults, children, tiny babies…"

Efi sniffed, the tears now pouring freely as she clutched her leg. The rest of the group sat in silence.

"It happened so fast," she continued. "So fast. We didn't know what to do. And then, some of them seemed to get better, only to start changing."

"Into the creatures," said Jon.

Efi nodded. "Then the army came, took a bunch of the bodies and patients and left us where we were. Didn't tell us a fucking thing but to stay put. In the end, it was just me, Holly, and Ravi left. We locked down the hospital and hid. I tried going home, hoping to find my mum, but no one was there."

"I don't know how contagious it is," she whispered. "I don't know how it spreads…. I don't know if I have it."

Guilt tugged at Jon's insides. He sat down next to Efi and put his arm around her. She took his hand and squeezed it, but kept her face pointed down.

"You could end up like me," said Samson. "You never know."

He sat down beside Efi and nudged her gently with his shoulder. "Pretty nice, eh?"

Efi sniffed and chuckled softly, rubbing her face with the back of her hand.

"You alright?" Jon asked.

"Yeah," she replied. "I'll be fine. Just give me a minute."

"Okay," said Jon. "I think Samson's right. We could do with some more sleep before we head off, anyway."

"Stay in here tonight," yawned Samson, waving his hand as he returned to his sleeping bag. "In the morning, I'll take you topside."

He lay down, facing away from the group as if to grant them some privacy and declare the conversation adjourned.

Efi and Luna succumbed to the call of sleep even faster than before. Again, Jon resisted, watching the stranger in the sleeping bag, until eventually his eyes were too heavy to stay open.

He stirred, his back in agony and his right arm numb under the weight of Efi leaning against it. Gently shifting his shoulder, he nudged her. She didn't respond. He nudged again, harder. A moan escaped her lips, feeble and quiet.

"Efi?"

Luna was awake now. She stretched out her limbs and looked over at Jon. "Is she okay?"

"I don't know."

"Is she going to turn into one of the things?"

Jon lowered Efi to the floor and checked her pulse. He opened her mouth and held his hand there, relieved to feel her breath passing in and out. Beads of sweat glistened on her forehead. He pressed his hand against her face and neck and promptly whipped it away.

"She's burning up," said Jon. "Gotta be a fever."

He rubbed his eyes and temples. "Shit."

The sleeping bag shifted, revealing a half-asleep Samson.

"Whassgoinon?"

"There's something wrong with Efi," said Luna. "She's going to turn."

"She's just got a fever," said Jon. "We need to get her out of here."

Samson threw aside the sleeping bag and padded over. Placing his hand on her forehead, then her cheek, he murmured to himself, eyebrows low.

"Shit," he said. "She's on fire. Right, uh, give me a sec to grab my gear and we'll go."

"We should leave her here," said Luna. "She's going to turn into one of the monsters!"

"I'm not leaving her," said Jon. He looked at Samson. "What about the things in the tunnel? You think we'll be alright?"

"Don't worry about them," said Samson. "It'll be fine. Exit's not far."

Jon kneeled down next to Efi. How was he going to carry her out? She wasn't heavy-set, but she was an adult–not small and light like Kai. And she was tall, too, the same height as him. How on earth could he get her all the way to the hospital?

A rucksack landed next to him. "You carry this," said Samson, nodding at Efi. "I'll take her."

"The fuck you will," said Jon. "How do I know you're not gonna do a runner with her?"

"Mate," Samson replied. "I told you. I'm not like the others."

"Fine. Try anything, mind, and you'll have me to deal with."

"Yeah, yeah."

Samson lifted Efi into a fireman's hold and took a position by the door, waiting as Jon and Luna gathered the bags. Pressing his ear against the cold metal, Jon listened. Silence answered.

"I think they're gone," he said, voice low.

The others nodded, and he heaved open the door. The tunnel met him, black and empty as it had been when they first entered the underground. He held the door open, allowing Samson, then Luna, to pass before stepping over the threshold.

They'd barely made it a few feet before Jon could hear the clicking, quiet and distant, but present, and growing.

"Hear that?" he whispered.

Samson and Luna paused.

"Yeah. Better speed up," said Samson, quickening his pace.

The clicking grew louder. Suddenly it was everywhere, enveloping the group in a squirming, screaming cacophony. Jon ushered Luna onwards, and she sped up, scrambling behind Samson. Light cut through the darkness, opening up the tunnel, and the three broke into a sprint.

A sharp pain hit the back of Jon's leg and he tripped, landing face first on the gravel with a grunt. He turned to see one of the monsters gripping his leg in its mandibles. Another appeared next to it, its bulbous face and bloodshot eyes fixed on him. It seized his other foot, and the pair began to tug.

Jon screamed. "Fuck! Get it off me!"

He kicked wildly and clawed at the ground with his hands, but the creatures continued, pulling him backwards.

Luna fumbled with her rucksack, pulling out one of the spray cans from the storeroom and threw it towards Jon. He seized it, aimed and pressed the nozzle. A cloud of luminous yellow erupted into the face of one of the creatures. It screamed and let go, disappearing back into the dark. The other held on. Jon kicked at it with his free leg, catching it in the eye. It fell back, clicking furiously, taking his trainer with it.

Samson grabbed Jon and pulled him up. "You alright?"

Jon nodded. "I'm fine. Go, go!"

They took off towards the light. The creatures chased, angrily clicking and screeching close behind. Jon could almost feel them right behind him, all around him, so close that if he dared slow for a second, they'd seize him again and drag him back into the darkness. The light beckoned, cheering them on as they dashed towards it.

"Just up there on the right!" yelled Samson.

Even with the weight of Efi's body draped over his shoulder, the man leapt effortlessly onto the station platform, turning to pull Luna up with one fluid motion. Jon dragged himself onto the ledge and they ran for the exit. A horde of the creatures followed, all clambering over each other as they poured out of the tunnel entrance.

Samson led the way, sprinting towards the escalators. "They won't follow us outside!" he shouted.

Legs burning, lungs heaving, they sped up the steps, through the hallway, vaulted over the ticket barriers, and without looking back, leapt through the station towards the exit.

18

Run rabbit, run

Justine Pearson 03.06.2030

Terry's gone out for lunch, and he's left his laptop in his office. I want to check it but the door's locked. I feel like I'm losing my mind. What if I'm wrong? What if Terry's completely innocent? What if the lab break-in was just some hippies trying to free a handful of rabbits?

I don't actually believe that, but still, I can't help but have doubts. I may not like the man, but he's a dedicated scientist. He was my mentor, for Christ's sake. And Sigma was his creation. Why would he allow it to be stolen?

And if I didn't have enough to worry about, the suits upstairs are all in a flap over that announcement from Russia. It's like the Cold War all over again, except now we're waving whole men at each other instead of just our dicks.

-

One foot in front of the other. Breathing steady, pace even, arms in. Caede silently repeated the instruction, wheezing in sharp, shallow gasps as she limped along. Blood dripped from the wound, sending sharp pains shooting through her waist, soaking her jogging bottoms. Would it leave a trail? Not that it mattered. All she had to do was get to the tube station, anyway. *A test of endurance.* The words of an old lecturer during her university days.

"For humans, the hunt is not a sprint, but a marathon," he had said, his old voice lofty and patrician, as if he only taught as a way to practise his elocution. He pointed to the white, pulled down screen at the front of the lecture hall. A screen that was probably about as old as the lecturer, she had thought at the time. All the other lecture halls had big television screens in them, like educational cinemas. She supposed it was because nobody wanted to study social anthropology except those seeking a career in teaching it. A cave painting appeared, displaying the crude lines that formed the human shapes, their stick arms raised, holding what looked to be spears, surrounding a larger, round shape on legs that resembled a large prey animal. One of the guys made a comment about it being someone's mum, and a snigger rippled through the hall.

The professor continued on, ignoring the joke. "It is a test of endurance, of which humans are exceptionally skilled. In terms of success rate, no other predator comes close. Other predators rely on speed, poison, or raw power, which has served them well in their respective fields. But we are not like other predators. We do not have claws for slashing, nor long canines for tearing flesh. We're not very fast, and our bodies aren't that strong–not compared to our chimpanzee and gorilla cousins, anyway. All in all, we're quite flimsy. So, how did we make it to the top of the food chain?

"The answer lies in our endurance. Of course, we have our wonderful brains, designed to find patterns, to out-think our opponents–very important for communication and teamwork, absolutely necessary when you're tracking a herd of woolly mammoths. But we Sapiens also have endurance, and this is a significant contributor to our high success rate as hunters. We don't need to be fast; we don't need to be strong. We don't even need to be all that smart. We simply keep tracking our prey until it collapses from exhaustion. And that's just it. Why outpace something you can outlast?"

Caede kept going, one foot in front of the other. *Just get to the station.* It had been over an hour. If they had any sense, Kai and Ravi would be long gone by now. If she kept walking, she might be able to catch up to them. *Liar,* said the other her, from somewhere just beyond her periphery, its whisper barely audible despite the silence.

"Be quiet," she croaked in response.

The plan had been straightforward enough. Ravi would wheel Kai into the launderette next door, hide, and Caede would act as decoy, steering the pack away. She would take the men far enough away that she could lose them, then circle back around. She would meet Ravi and Kai at the tube station further down the road, and they would continue together from there.

That had been the plan.

But as soon as she'd opened the door, something clicked, then wailed, as the ring of the alarm hammered in her ears.

She leapt outside, yelling, "Quick!"

She hadn't expected the pack to flank. But there was the tall one, lips peeled, curled around shining white teeth in a wide grin. From somewhere behind her, among the crash of falling shelves and the screams of torn cardboard boxes, snarls and yells rose up as the others approached. They were chasing them out, like ferrets winding through a warren. And the big one was ready with his net, waiting for her. Without thinking, she leapt forward and barrelled into the man, knocking him against the wall of the alleyway. He seized her arm and she lunged forward, biting down on the soft flesh of his wrist. He yelped and let go.

"Run!" she shrieked.

Ravi bolted out of the shop in the opposite direction, hands gripping Kai's wheelchair, and the pair disappeared inside a building further along. Caede leapt past the man and took off. The man swore and tried to grab her. His hand caught the coat, yanking it off as she squirmed away.

"Get the girl!"

Another voice said, "what about the others?"

"Fuck the others! We just need her!"

Caede ran. She tore herself away from the alley into the high street. The howls of the men followed, sounding the hunt. It would be a test of endurance, to not only lead them away from Kai, but get them away and get back without them catching up. If they were smart, they'd see through it, but their excitement must have overridden their rationale, because they were whooping and yelling in glee as if it was a game. Maybe they didn't need to take it seriously. *Don't underestimate me*, she thought.

After what she guessed to be a couple of miles, she paused, panting, as she rested her hands on her knees. She'd been running at an even pace for about fifteen minutes. When she had been training seriously, she could have covered a couple of miles in less and it wouldn't have fazed her, but that was before the smoking and the late nights. She could hear the men in the distance, howls rising up over the buildings, riding the breeze, drawing closer with every second.

She glanced around, taking in the street. Cars littered the road, abandoned, doors still open. On the pavement, a crow picked at the remains of a body. The first bird she'd seen in days. Startled, it let out a loud, mocking caw, and took flight. As she watched it leave, the window display of a large department store caught her eye.

The lights were still on inside and the front doors were open, the glass smashed and spread across the pavement. If she could lose the men in there and slip away, she could head back to Kai and Ravi, save herself some time. A worry rose up from her gut. It might not be empty. What if there were others in there, waiting for someone like her to stumble into their hideout? Could she use it to her advantage? Would the things fight each other? What if they were just other survivors, like her? What then? The howls grew louder. The men sounded impatient now, excited, relishing in the pursuit. *Animals*, she thought.

Sweat dripped from her forehead, stinging her eyes, and she wiped it away with the sleeve of her denim jacket. She looked down at the damp patch. What was it Kai had said about the snake? Her eyes returned to the department store, and an idea took hold. With a deep inhale, she sprinted for the main doors.

Glass crunched underfoot as she stepped over the threshold. She looked around, studying the layout for just a moment before running to the back of the store. Behind the main tills stood the door for the stockroom. She ran inside and tore off the jacket, hastily rubbing it over her face. Throwing it into a group of clothing rails, she turned and ran back onto the shop floor. Heading for the escalators in the centre, she yanked off the blue jumper and hurled it into the display stands. Next went the T-shirt and jeans, which she abandoned on the escalators. The socks, she balled up and threw behind a till on the first floor. Same for each of the trainers; tossed in opposite directions as she made her way up to the second floor.

From outside, a carnal howl echoed through the street and drifted inside. Caede froze. A chill settled at the base of her spine. *No time to spare now*. A snarl followed, then a yell and a yelp. They were arguing, snapping at each other. *Good*. She darted across the floor towards the sign reading "women's wear". Removing her bra, she threw it to the side, then did the same with her underwear.

Naked and shivering, she ran to the underwear section, seizing fresh garments and yanking them on. Socks and new trainers followed. The sound of glass crushed underfoot startled her, and she froze. The men were inside now. Hands shaking, she fumbled with the laces of the trainers, tying them roughly into knots. Quieter than before, she headed to the sportswear section. Taking a pair of sweatpants from a rail, she hopped as she tried to pull them on, cursing herself for putting the trainers on first. Suddenly, she tripped. Her leg flailed, kicking out. The clang of a metal rail toppling over rang out through the store, clashing from wall to wall. Caede sat, eyes wide at the rail, the blood hammering in her ears. Below, the men fell silent.

A chuckle, cold and triumphant, rose to meet her.

"We know you're here, love!"

Terror snaked through her veins. Scrambling up, she yanked on the sweatpants and took off to the far end of the room, ducking underneath the clothing on the wall rails.

"Where the fuck is she?" one of them barked.

"She can't be far," a deeper voice replied. The tall one? She wasn't sure. "Spread out."

"Her smell's all over the place," a third voice whined, higher in pitch than the others. "This might take a while, boss man."

The deeper voice chuckled again in response, his laughter all gravel and crushed glass digging under her skin. "No worries, mate," he replied calmly. "She can't hide forever."

The words danced around her, delighting in her fear. Instinct begged her to bolt, run for it, but she stayed still, her eyes following the wall until they met the sign for the fire exit. *Calm down. Just breathe.* She could make a run for it while they were on the lower floor. The men were wasting time, sniffing around in the direction of her abandoned clothing, snarling at each other as they tore through the rails and shelves on the floor below.

Just as she prepared herself to move, one of them appeared at the top of the escalator. A small man, skinny and childish compared to the rest of them, stepped onto the floor and sniffed at the air. Something had caught his attention. Caede watched as he turned on the spot a few times before darting off to the lingerie section.

The rest of the men followed shortly after and spread out. Only the large one stood by the escalator, unmoving, his eyes scanning the shop floor.

"Hello, what's this?" said a high-pitched voice, all singsong and cockney.

Caede curled herself into a ball, hands over her mouth.

It was the skinny one, returning to the group with a skip in his step, and her underwear held aloft in his hand.

"Here lads, check this out!" he called to the others. "I've got her drawers!"

The first of the men to approach him was short and stocky, with soft facial features and a round paunch that made him look pregnant. He snatched the underwear from the skinny one and held the fabric to his face, taking a long, deep breath. Bile rose in Caede's throat.

"Yes, mate!" yelled Skinny, running in a circle. "She's taken her clothes off!"

"Clever girl," replied the tall one. "Speed things up, boys."

Breath held, Caede uncurled herself and, body pressed against the wall, she began shuffling towards the fire escape sign. All around her, she could hear the men, tearing through rails and knocking over stands as she moved. Jaw clenched and eyes flickering briefly back towards them every few seconds, she finally reached for the door and pushed it open. A stark metal stairwell met her with a sign pointing in the direction of the exit. She slipped through the gap and began her descent.

Whether it was by a gust of wind or by design, the door suddenly slammed shut.

"Oi!" came a shout from the shop floor.

Caede leapt down the stairs, feet pummelling the metal flooring. The fire door exploded open, and the men piled into the stairwell, howling in sadistic glee. Throat burning, heart in mouth, she jumped the flight of stairs. The impact jarred her shins, but there was no time to recover. Bolting towards the next floor, she wrenched open the door and flew through the shop. Homeware and interiors. *Shit.* She'd gone too far down. She sprinted for the escalators and froze. The tall one stood at the top, staring down at her, his expression triumphant.

"Got you," he mouthed.

Caede screamed and fled. The sign for the kitchenware section of the shop floor met her as she ran, and headed in, frantically searching for something to use as a weapon. The knives were useless, all secured firmly to a wall fixture with metal locks. Yanking at them did nothing; they were stuck fast. Whoops and hollers rang through the air as the men burst on to the shop floor and spread out. She could hear them in all directions. Soon they'd close in. How many were there? Four? Five? *Fuck.*

Caede glanced around and spotted a display of glass bottles and festive hampers. Seizing one of the bottles, she smashed it against the table. The bottle shattered into pieces. Growling in frustration, she grabbed another one. A sudden movement came from the right. She turned just in time to see Skinny approaching. The launched bottle hit him squarely in the leg, bowling him over, and he landed face first on the floor with a heavy crunch. She turned to run, colliding with the stocky one. He seized her with long, hairy arms, gripping her in a suffocating bear hug. She screamed and kicked viciously, her foot hitting him hard on his shins. Stocky yelped and let go, but now Skinny had regained his composure and approached, his face bloody and furious. Snatching another bottle, she swung wildly at the men. Skinny dodged and leapt forward, swiping at her with clawed hands. Her arm shot out and the bottle hit, striking him on the nose. The glass smashed, spraying into his face, and he fell back, swearing.

Then, from behind, something struck her. The back of her head exploded in bright, sharp pain. Before she knew it, she was falling, landing, the wind knocked out of her as she hit the floor. Caede groaned, head spinning. Shards of glass bit into her torso and face. Curling up, she turned over, and there was Stocky. He dropped, landing heavily on top of her, pinning her down. The last of the air left her lungs with a gasp. Stocky seized her wrists and leaned close to her face, grinning wide.

Wild with rage, Caede kicked, writhed, bucked as hard as she could, screamed and spat. But it was no use: she was stuck.

"I love the feisty ones, man," Stocky laughed, gripping her wrists tighter. Pain shot through her arms. He pressed his face into her neck and sniffed.

"Ah, I fucking love this smell." He looked over at Skinny. "Sid, you alright, mate?"

"Bitch broke my fucking nose!" said Sid, sat on the floor nursing his bloodied face.

"Stop being a pussy," said Stocky. "Just get a towel or something."

Tears burned Caede's eyes and her vision blurred. Stocky's laugh pierced her ears.

"Get off me!" she screamed.

The tall one appeared from behind the knife fixture.

"Hold her still," he said calmly.

"I'm trying," laughed Stocky. "This one's feral!"

He looked down at her, his eyes glittering malevolently. "Stop moving so much," he mocked. "You're making me hard!"

"Fuck you!" Caede spat, glaring up at him.

The tall man stepped over, nonchalant and smiling. He kneeled down, lowering his wolfish face to hers.

"Calm down, love," he cooed, voice dripping with malice. "Breathe, alright? We just want to talk to you."

19

Alternative medicine

Justine Pearson, entry 08.07.2030

It's been over a month and nothing's happened. I asked Raj again and he said the investigation is ongoing, and that I need to stop asking about it. Apparently, it has been suggested that there was no foul play from our end, but we will know as soon as they do. Bollocks.

-

Jon vaulted over the ticket barrier and threw himself at the wide-open station entrance, Samson and Luna close behind, with a legion of the creatures nipping at their heels like feral dogs. The group tore out into the open night air, not stopping until the station and the creatures were long out of view.

Jon sat down on the pavement and inspected his foot. "I can't keep this up. I need some shoes."

Samson shrugged Efi back up his shoulder and nodded, gesturing to the path on their left with his chin. "The high street's on the way."

"I know," said Jon, turning to reply to Samson. He had meant to thank him for his help. The guy irritated the shit out of him, but here he was, helping them out of a dire situation for no apparent reason beyond being a fellow survivor. Could he even be counted as a survivor? Jon opened his mouth to speak again and stopped. He hadn't seen it in the tunnel, but now in the streetlight the man not only stood tall and muscular as an Olympic athlete, but he was covered from head to toe in a golden sheen. Of hair? No. *Fur.* It was fur. Combined with the man's statuesque form, smooth facial features, and thick mane twisted into long copper braids, he looked like something out of a Greek odyssey. Something out of a fantasy novel. The man looked fucking majestic. He looked…just like a lion. Jon felt the bitter tang of acid rising in his throat. He spat it away before eyeing Samson again. What kind of virus did *that*?

Samson caught Jon's stare and looked down at himself. "Oh, yeah…that. Weird, innit?"

Jon could only manage a nod. Samson turned and strode ahead. Luna trotted behind him, struggling to keep up. She stared at Samson and glanced back at Jon to mouth something at him. He didn't have the heart to tell her he couldn't lip read.

Samson glanced behind him and grunted. "Don't know what you were expecting."

"Uh," said Jon. "I'll be honest, this wasn't it."

Samson shrugged. "Don't know what to tell you, man."

"I don't get it," said Jon. "Everyone else like you was hostile. Those blokes who chased us. And that spider thing that attacked me and Efi—and she talked! Those blokes could talk too."

"There's others as well," said Luna.

"It's like night of the living furries out here," said Jon. "And so far, they've all been arseholes."

Luna sniggered.

"Maybe they were just arseholes," said Samson. "You get me? Maybe they were pricks before they changed, and this just made them more like it."

"Works for me," said Jon.

"Listen yeah," said Samson. "You don't have to trust me. But trust that your mate is in trouble, and she's fine as fuck. So, I'm gonna help."

"I won't argue with that," said Jon.

The hospital loomed into view and soon they were in the car pack, standing at the same side entrance where Jon had last seen Caede and Kai. They were on the other side of that door, and hopefully they'd be happy to see him. The thought made him almost giddy. He threw open the door and stepped inside the lightless stairwell. Samson and Luna followed.

In the path of Jon's phone torch, drops of dried blood lined the floor by the doorway, leading up to a path of rust-coloured drips on the stairs. Jon thought of Kai, and his guts churned.

Samson looked around. "Right," he said. "Let's do this. Where's the wall map?" He lowered Efi off his shoulder and held her cradled in his arms. She groaned in response. Jon walked over and pressed the back of his hand gently against her forehead. It was still hot, but not as bad as it was, as if the storm of fever must have been passing. Or maybe it came in waves, and this just was a moment of calm. He didn't know.

"Efi," he said. "Efi, you need to wake up."

She groaned again, eyelids fluttering.

"Efi," he urged. "We can help, but we don't know how. You need to tell us what to do."

"Mm-hmm…" she mumbled. "Leg hurts…"

"Efi," Jon repeated, louder and sterner this time. "You need to tell us how to fix it."

She grimaced, but responded, and began whispering fractured instructions, straining for breath with each word.

"Clean room… Clean wound… Antibacterial... clean dressing… Intravenous antibiotics… Vancomycin."

"What did she say?" asked Luna.

"Vanco something," replied Jon.

"I know what it is," replied Samson. "It's an antibiotic."

"Right… Wait, how do you know that?" asked Jon.

"Was on it not that long ago. I was scratched by a cat; got infected."

"Ah, right. Okay. Let's find a room and get to work."

The three headed upstairs for the wards, using the wall-mounted maps to navigate. Jon trotted ahead, opening doors to scope out rooms, mostly to find one suitable for Efi, but also hoping to see Caede and Kai on the other side. The blood trail had ended at the stairs, leaving no further clues as to their whereabouts. Few of the rooms were in any state to enter, let alone treat anyone. Some even housed ripe-looking corpses, their rancid odour sending Jon reeling and moving swiftly on to the next.

Finally, Jon found a room clean enough. It looked as if it had been recently used, with fresh white linens lining the mattress of the bed, and thick but dented pillows sitting upright at the head. A worn lounge chair sat next to it. On the floor by its feet stood an almost empty coffee cup. Jon shrugged off the rucksack, letting it fall to the floor, and headed to the cup to inspect its contents. The smell of stale vending machine cappuccino hit his nostrils.

He glanced around the room and suddenly it was full of clues – snack wrappers, bandages, another cup on a side table. A celebrity gossip magazine laying open on the floor by the window.

"They were here," he said.

He headed back to the door and yanked it open, running into the hallway.

"Kai? Caede?" he called, heading further down the hall.

Samson and Luna looked at each other.

"Do me a favour," said Samson, jerking his head to the door. "Go shut him up before the whole city hears him?"

Luna nodded and trotted after Jon.

Samson lay Efi on the bed, then checked her forehead and pulse. "Don't worry, girl. I got you."

He shot a furtive glance at the door and picked up his rucksack, reaching inside to pull out a sealed plastic sleeve. He tore open the seal and removed the syringe inside.

"You're gonna turn," he whispered. "I can't do much about that. But I got a better option for you."

Efi groaned, stirring a little as Samson jabbed the syringe into the crook of her elbow and emptied its contents, but didn't wake up. He removed the syringe, returning it to the sleeve, and threw it into the nearby waste bin just as Luna opened the door. A forlorn-looking Jon followed, muttering under his breath.

"So," said Luna. "What do we do now?"

"I'm gonna need water, lots of it, and paracetamol."

"What about the antibiotics?"

"Probably find 'em in a locked cabinet somewhere," said Samson.

Before long, Efi was awake and sitting up, drinking water and taking painkillers. She wasted no time administering instructions to Jon and the others with the air of a drill sergeant. Fever tamed, and after a couple of attempts and some colourful language, Jon was able to attach a drip to her arm and get the antibiotics started. Finding the drugs had been tricky. Much of the hospital had been emptied, the supplies looted or simply exhausted. Jon had managed to break open some locked cupboards and taken the contents back to the room. Clean dressings for the wound were applied. Would it need stitches?

Maybe the antibiotics and the dressings would be enough. Efi would know.

She sat upright in the bed, nursing a cup of tea. Samson and Luna were sitting on the floor by the table, dozing quietly. Jon was curled up in the chair next to the bed, eyes closed.

"Any sign of Ravi and Holly?" she said.

Jon stirred from the armchair and stretched his arms. "Nope," he replied. "Nothing."

"That's weird," said Efi. "I was sure they'd be here."

"Someone's been here," said Jon. "The coffee in that cup's still fairly fresh."

"What about your friends? Didn't they need help?"

"Yeah," Jon replied, "they did."

"Maybe they left to get supplies," said Samson. He laid his cards flat on the table and headed over to the bed.

"I don't think so," replied Efi. "Ravi's not the going out type. He's a bit helpless, you know? Doesn't understand hardship. I'm not sure he'd last long out there."

"Ah, posh boy," said Samson.

"Yes, but his heart's in the right place. And he's a good doctor. He wouldn't abandon a patient if they came to him for help."

"And," said Jon, "the kid I was travelling with, Kai, his arm was torn off. There's no way he could get anywhere by himself."

"Okay," said Samson. "So, they can't be far then. I guess there's no rush to go anywhere."

"So, you're staying with us, then?" said Jon.

"If that's alright with you."

"Couldn't hurt."

"At least we're not in that bloody tunnel anymore," said Efi. "Jon, pull the blanket off, would you? I need to see the wound."

Jon obliged, carefully lifting the blankets, then the bandages around the leg. Efi sat forward, inspecting it. Her eyebrows shot up. "That can't be right. This was infected yesterday. Have you started the antibiotics yet?"

"Yeah," replied Jon, "they're in your drip."

"I didn't expect them to work this quickly."

Jon checked the drip before returning to Efi's leg. "Maybe it just wasn't as bad as we thought," he shrugged.

"Maybe," she replied. There was a whisper of doubt in her voice, but she waved it away. "As long as it's healing I can't complain. It's still going to need stitches, though."

20

Little Red

Terry Howard, entry 10.07.2030

Justine won't let up, but I cannot leave yet. There is still too much to do. I need to make sure Sigma-13 is ready.

I wanted to include her in this, but I do not think she would understand. I want everyone to benefit from this. Not just the wealthy, not just the warmongers and the politicians. Every day people are suffering, and we could put an end to it all, if only we weren't so selfish.

-

The tall man spoke again, his face so close Caede could feel the heat of his breath on her skin.

"We just want to talk to you," he said. "We've got an offer for you."

"Hurry up, Lee, I'm dying here!" Stocky moaned.

Chunks of glass bit into her flesh as he shifted and bore more of his weight onto her. The displays, the shelves, and the white lights hanging from the ceiling above began to blur and fall away. The room shifted and spun. Tears burned Caede's eyes. From all around came a high-pitched ringing, a shrill hum electrifying the air. She could hear it, but the men didn't seem to notice. They continued bickering with each other, their voices distant and muffled.

Don't zone out now, whispered a small voice.

Caede blinked. Her own self knelt in front of her. *It's just a hallucination.* A trauma-induced vision dredged up from the depths of her fear-addled mind. Darkness spread through the room, leaving only the other her and the floor around her visible. The men's voices had faded now. The other Caede, the shadow, the spectre, sat in front of her, childishly hugging its knees.

Well, it demanded, *how are we getting out of this?*

Caede closed her eyes, blinking hard, and banished it to the back of her mind.

"Shut up, Mike, you sick fuck!" barked the larger man, Lee. Stocky Mike grunted in response, and the pair continued to argue. Caede felt the grip on her wrists loosen.

Looks like we might have a shot.

"Listen, you fat shit," Lee growled, "we're only alive because I made a deal with those lizard freaks. Do you want to be eaten?"

"Aw, come on, Lee, we got time," Mike whined. "I just want a bit of fun with her."

"Tell that to the dragon."

"What's he gonna do, come find us? We could be out of London tonight. Everyone else has gone up North. We could join them!"

"Like this, yeah? You really want your mum to see you looking like a chunky werewolf?"

"I don't think she'd care!"

"Listen. Either Kal's gonna be eating something today or fucking something today. Your option's hunting or bending over."

"We're already doing both. Yes sir, no sir, lick your arse sir! I'm just saying we were doing fine without the prick."

Hey, look there. What's that? Caede blinked. The rucksack, less than an arm's reach away, laying open. A Swiss Army knife was on the floor next to it.

Lee turned his attention back to Caede. "Ignore him, love," he said. "He just hasn't had any for a while. Look at him though, you get me? Would you fuck that?"

With that, he laughed, voice rising through the room.

Mike chuckled. "Shut up, Lee."

"Just hold her still for me, alright?"

Lee shrugged a rucksack off his shoulders and pulled out a metal tin, opening it to reveal a small plastic bag of pills.

"Is that the new stuff?" asked Mike. He was leaning more towards Lee, nosing the pills, his hands barely holding her anymore.

"Yeah," said Lee. "don't worry darlin', you won't remember anything after you've had this. Little bit of medicine; makes it all go away."

Suddenly the world was light again, clear and sharp and bright.

It's them or us.

Caede took a breath. *Now!* She whipped out her arm, snatching up the knife. In one fluid motion, she pulled it to her chest and heaved herself around to face stocky Mike. Her arm shot forward.

The knife sunk deep into the soft flesh of the man's throat. Caede wrenched her arm away and blood followed, cascading into the air like a fountain, dowsing the floor around her. Mike threw himself backwards, gargling, screaming, vainly clutching his punctured throat as the life gushed from his body. Lee and Sid recoiled, shouting and shielding their eyes from the spray. Seizing her chance, Caede ducked under a display table. She scurried to the next aisle, then stood, wiping the blood from her eyes to face the two remaining men.

The skinny one, Sid, skidded around the display tables, approaching from the right. Lee glared at her from the other side, bristling with fury. A low growl escaped his lips as their eyes met.

"Come on then," Caede mouthed, gripping the knife in her hands.

With a roar, Lee leapt at her. Caede took off towards Sid, screaming a vicious war cry of her own. Before he could react, they collided, and she stabbed low, once, twice, again and again until her arm was red and slick with blood. Sid wailed in agony and fell to the floor, clutching his stomach as thick, hot liquid oozed out of him. Leaping over him, she bolted towards the escalators. Something snagged her foot, and she slipped, landing heavily on the floor. Then Lee was on her. The pair wrestled, Caede kicking and scratching as viciously as a wild cat. But this time he was prepared, holding her down with his body weight. He clamped his hands around her neck and squeezed.

Red spots filled her vision. Gasping and kicking, she clawed at his arms and bucked with all her might. Her hands darted out, swiping the floor for anything to use against him. Lee growled, lifted her head and slammed it hard against the floor. The room spun and began to fade once more.

It's them or us!

Her hand met something sharp. With the last of her strength, she brought it up, smashing the bottle against Lee's face. He yelped and reeled backwards, releasing his grip. Caede gasped, coughing and spluttering, sucking in fresh air. Lee clawed at his face, cursing as blood and bits of broken glass ran down his hands.

Glancing to her right, she spotted some cooking pots on the floor. She seized one and hurled it at his head. The metal struck with a loud clang and he roared, leaping up. He seized her wrist and twisted. Caede yelped in pain, and in response brought her knee up, striking him hard in the groin. Doubling over, Lee dropped to the floor and curled into a ball, moaning. Caede scrambled up to run, but something caught her eye. A large cast-iron skillet on the display table sat next to her. *Do it.* Raising it in her arms like a baseball bat, she turned back to Lee.

With a whoosh of air and a sickening crunch, Lee's face collided with the skillet and exploded. He wailed, writhing, hands raised up as if in prayer. Caede answered with a roar, throwing the skillet down like a hammer, spraying the wall fixtures with blood and chunks of white. She did it again, and again, and again, until the skillet met only the floor, and the air was thick with a metallic haze.

Lee's body twitched for a moment, then fell still. Caede let the skillet slide from her hands and she slumped to the floor, shivering and exhausted.

She sat there in silence, listening to the ringing in her ears while her lungs strained against her ribcage, desperate for a full breath but unable to get it. Throat stinging and tender, blood dripping from her hands and face. And pain. Creeping across her waist from her right side, dragging at her ravaged nerves with every intake of breath. She glanced down to see an inch-wide shard of glass sticking out of her flesh. Teeth gritted, she took the glass in her fingers and pulled gently. The shard slid out unbroken, with a pop and a trickle of blood.

We need to go.

"I need to sort this out first," said Caede, forcing herself up into standing position. Hand clamped over her side, she headed for the tills to find a first aid kit.

It took a few shaky rounds of picking out the chunks of glass embedded in her hands, and the alcohol wipes burned, slowing her progress, but she was able to clean and dress her wounds. Not perfectly–Ravi would need to have a proper look at them later–but well enough. The other *her* was waiting patiently at the base of the metal steps. Together they limped up the escalator, leaving the bodies of the men behind them.

As she reached the first floor, a rush of cold air swept over her, sending shivers cascading down her spine and goosebumps shooting up her bare arms. A movement to her left caught her periphery, and she froze, snapping her head in its direction. A mirror on a nearby pillar reflected back an unfamiliar creature, something strange and frightening, covered in blood and bandages. Like a movie monster from the 1950s, but gorier. She walked over to the reflection, staring hard. Oily red streaks stained her hair and face. A chunk of white rested inside the dip of her collarbone. She fished it out and flicked it away, its rattle echoing as it bounced under a display table, alerting her to the silence. The ringing in her ears had finally stopped. The mask and goggles were long gone; fallen off in her earlier haste. Pointless to wear them now, anyway, not with Stocky Mike's blood smeared all over her. Soon she'd be one of those things, if she wasn't already. It was hard to tell.

T-shirts and knit sweaters decorated the nearby clothes rails. She snatched up one of each and pulled them over her. The cotton brushing against her skin brought with it warmth and comfort, and she hugged the fabric, taking it in.

We need to go; the shadow urged.

Caede blinked hard in response, and it fell silent.

Before leaving the department store, she picked up a scarf and wrapped it carefully around her neck and chin. Tender and bruised from the fight, her throat burned in the cold air. She considered looking for the blue jumper Jon had given her, but the shadow was right. She needed to go.

Outside, the bitter air nipped at her face. Grey clouds hung heavily overhead, threatening rain, so Caede took up a slow jog. If all had gone to plan, Ravi and Kai would wait at the station for her—

but for how much longer she didn't know. Ravi had promised to wait an hour, and she was sure that time had already long passed. Small puffs of steam billowed in front of her as she limped on, grateful for the new trainers. They were warmer and better-fitting than the old worn-out ones she'd been wearing before.

Somewhere in the distance, a roar split the air. Caede flinched and ducked down behind some wheelie bins. Hunched up and breath bated, she hid, straining her ears for any sound. After a few agonising seconds, she peeked out from behind the bins. Across the street, a small group of people emerged from a building. First, a man glancing around nervously before stepping out and gesturing for the others to follow. Still hidden, Caede watched as the group moved along the pavement, the man scouting ahead, checking the insides of cars and doorways. Another hung back, protecting the rear of the group, the shotgun in his arms cocked and ready to fire. Between them were two women, a much older man, and a young child. One woman carried a baby, wrapped in fabric and tied to her body.

The roar sounded again, closer than before, and the group stopped dead. The child clung to the leg of a woman and snivelled in fear. She stroked their hair and lifted them up, whispering something to them, words of comfort perhaps, and the child wrapped their limbs around her body, clutching her, taking in the comfort of their mother. The man at the front gestured, signalling, and the group disappeared into another building. From the direction they were heading, it was likely they had also thought to leave the city.

The creatures are getting closer; the shadow whispered. *We need to keep moving.*

"We should help those people," said Caede.

What can you do? You're half dead.

"Fine. Let's keep going."

She left the shelter of the bins and continued, eager to gain as much distance as possible from the roars. It reminded her of the woman, that poor woman, writhing on the floor, blood spraying while those monsters devoured her stolen limbs. Maybe that's what Lee and the other monsters were going to do to her. The thought brought a shudder and quickened her pace.

That momentum didn't last long. Black spots burned Caede's eyes as she dragged herself on, forcing one foot in front of the other, waves of pain washing over her with every step. With every inhale, her throat burned. The adrenaline had long abandoned her, so on willpower–and the words of an old professor rambling about endurance–she kept going. *Just get to the station.*

Finally, the building loomed into view, sitting on the corner of the road, like an island in a storming sea. Two figures were at the entrance, one standing, the other sat in a wheelchair. Ravi and Kai, still waiting for her, even though she'd been far longer than an hour. Upon seeing her, they waved in celebration.

"Caede!" Ravi was running towards her, calling, his smile fading as he got closer.

She reached out a hand to him.

"You waited," she said, voice cracking.

As she stepped forward, her legs buckled, and the ground rushed up to meet her. The world spun and blurred, fading to white.

212

21

Visiting Hours

Elizabeth Ng-Parker 05.08.2030

Elizabeth here. Today is August 5th and we're running some preliminary tests on Sigma Delta Tau strain 12. The other samples our team retrieved from the lab were dead, sadly. We have been able to extrapolate some data from them, which I feel is valuable, nonetheless.

According to Terry's notes, within the modified viruses are Xenobots–pre-programmable DNA transfer mechanisms–that's Sigma. Basically, using the cell's own defence against it. We've been doing that for some time now. It's just... This can make dramatic changes in fully grown adults, instead of just embryos, at a ridiculous speed. And it's completely customisable. It's like CRISPR on steroids. This could mean the complete eradication of deleterious genes in human beings. Ten years ago–a month ago–I would have said this wasn't possible, but here we are.

There's got to be a darker use for this. I suspect we'll discover that soon. From what I've heard, the Americans are becoming quite interested in purchasing Sigma for their own use, now that Russia has made its move. I dread to think of what they would do with this.

-

Jon studied the small aerosol bottle sceptically, turning it over in his hands as he tried to make sense of the jargon on the label. "Is this going to numb it enough?"

"No," replied Efi flatly, "but since neither of us are trained to administer anaesthetic, it'll have to do."

"Fair enough. I'm spraying now."

"Have you washed your hands?"

"No, Efi, I thought I'd make things more interesting by starting my own bacteria farm in your leg. Aye, I washed my hands. Also, I'm wearing gloves, woman! Want me to bleach my eyeballs while I'm at it?"

Efi snorted and laid her head back down onto the pillow of her hospital bed. "I think I need a stiff drink."

"Hey, could you grab my wallet?" said Jon, nodding to Luna, who was sitting by the window in the armchair. "Just in my back pocket."

He looked up at Efi as he sprayed. "It's not a drink, but you can bite down on it. Bite as hard as you want, there's no money in there."

Luna reluctantly tugged the leather wallet out of Jon's back pocket, dabbed it down with an antibacterial wipe, and handed it to Efi before returning to the armchair.

The room was practically a luxury hotel compared to the shared wards of the rest of the hospital; clean, with newer paint on the walls, a nice picture of a sunset in a frame, and some accompanying furniture for visitors. Jon sat on a stool bedside, with a medical needle and thread, ready to begin stitching up the wound on Efi's leg. Samson had been quiet since their arrival, preferring to scope the hallways in search of supplies. Jon was happy to let him go about as he pleased; it kept him out of the way.

"Okay, I've sprayed it," said Jon. "How long does it take to kick in?"

"Give it about thirty seconds," Efi replied, keeping her face pointed at the ceiling. "That should be long enough."

"I'll try and make this as quick as possible, okay?"

"It's fine. It's got to be done."

"Has it been thirty seconds yet?"

"I think so. Sod it, just do it. Got everything?"

Jon chuckled nervously. "Yeah, I think so."

"Okay. Just like how we practised. You want the skin, not the fat. Don't go past the fat."

"Why can't you do this again?"

"Because," said Efi bluntly, "I'll pass out."

"You're a nurse! You must have done this before!"

"On other people! It's not the same. Now hurry up!"

He nodded and began to suture, jaw set in concentration, hands shaking as he pushed the needle through the thick flesh of her leg and pulled through the thread. Efi flinched and sank her teeth into the wallet. To her credit, she kept her body still, her hands only moving to grip the sides of the bed. Jon continued to stitch without too much effort, only failing to knot the thread once or twice, which

215

he thought was quite good considering he'd only done this once before, as practice, half an hour prior, on an old banana. By the time he finished, the sky outside was beginning to lighten.

"Anyone want a coffee?" said Jon.

Efi groaned and pushed herself upright. "Please."

She inspected Jon's handiwork as he washed up, looking carefully at the stitches. "It's going to leave an ugly scar, but I think it will be fine. You did good, Jon."

"Happy to help," he replied. "Guess it doesn't hurt to learn a new skill. Sugar?"

"No thank you," said Efi. "I'm sweet enough."

Jon headed towards the vending machines, his thoughts returning to Caede and Kai. They had been in that room, he was sure of it. *Where did you go?* He pressed his fingers against his pocket as he walked, feeling the outline of the ring, partly to make sure it was still there, and partly as a comfort, as if it were a token of good luck. A small part of him indulged the idea that all the while he had it, they would still be alive. It was the same level of superstition that dictated not stepping on pavement cracks or incurring bad luck by breaking a mirror. Logically, he knew that the universe was chaos, and didn't care one bit if he was holding on to some woman's engagement ring. And yet...

Pale pink light filtered through the window, spilling across the hallway floor. Jon paused and took it in, his mind wandering to the view from the rooftop of his apartment complex. The scream that sent him tumbling back onto the roof instead of over its edge. His chest tightened and his stomach ached. Had it been her scream that had saved his life? Given him a second chance? As signs from the universe went, it was a pretty strong one.

"I don't know if you're real, up there," he said, looking at nothing in particular. "Course you're not. If you were, none of this would have happened. But if you are, keep them safe for us."

"You think there's anyone listening?" asked Samson, leaning casually against the hallway wall. He sidled over to Jon and gazed out of the window, a strange melancholy etched into his regal face.

"I'm not religious," said Jon. "Couldn't hurt to ask, though."

"Some say prayer is the last refuge of the damned," replied Samson. "I'd say it was pretty fitting right now." He fell quiet, then chuckled to himself. "But what the fuck do I know? So. You worried about your girlfriend, huh?"

"Not mine to be worried about," said Jon, pulling the ring out of his pocket. Samson looked at it and nodded. "Found this in my kitchen. I think it's hers. Truth be told, I only met her and her brother yester-"

He stopped. Was it yesterday? No. He'd been in the garage all Saturday night, and underground pretty much all of Sunday. He leaned against the window ledge and stared out.

"We got separated. Been trying to get back here in the hopes I'd see them again. Bit sad, really."

"Nah, it's not sad," said Samson. "You're only human.... She fit?"

"What?"

"Is she fit?"

"Yeah…. Wait, that's not important."

"Oh really? Why else would you wanna find her so bad? Give her back a ring? Fiancé's probably dead, you know that?"

"It's not like that."

"What's it like, then?"

Jon fell silent. Maybe it was like that, but he didn't want to admit it.

Samson laughed. "Like I said, mate. You're only human. Surrounded by monsters who wanna eat us, and we're just following our dicks."

Jon snorted. "Yeah, I guess so." He turned to Samson. "Speaking of which, what the hell are you, anyway? Seriously, this time."

Samson chuckled again. "Honestly? I don't know, mate."

"So you just woke up, hairy, giant, and otherwise perfectly normal?"

Samson laughed. "No, dickhead, 'course not. I spent days firing from both ends, just like everyone else, and passed out. Woke up covered in my own vomit, surrounded by bodies. The bodies of my colleagues…"

Samson paused and turned his face downwards. He stared blankly at the glass in the window. "I survived. They didn't. I remember waking up, looking down at myself and freaking out. I ran away, and I've been alone since, hiding and just trying to survive. Then you lot come along, still human, still alive. Meeting you lot changed some things for me, you know?"

Jon shifted his weight, returning his eyes to the window. All that death. It had seemed unreal, something one would only ever expect to see watching a horror movie in a cinema. And he'd been removed from it to an extent, hidden in his flat, drinking posh whiskey with no-one left to lose but the pizza delivery man. Samson probably had friends here, family, people to miss and mourn. Who did Jon have? An ex and an estranged brother who was God-knows where.

"Shit," he said. "Listen, I'm sorry."

"It's alright," Samson replied. "I'm strong now. Before, I was weak and skinny, a right nerd. Now look at me."

"Don't you miss being human?"

"You think I'm not?"

"You look like a fucking Thundercat to me."

Their laughter lit up the corridor and for a brief moment the world felt normal again.

Jon wiped a tear away from his eyes as the quiet returned. "Why did they leave?" he asked. The words fell out of his mouth unexpectedly.

Samson lowered his eyebrows, suddenly concerned. "That's a good question."

The two men returned to the ward to find the lights switched off, and Efi and Luna sitting in the dark, their eyes white and wide. Luna raised a finger to her lips, then pointed to the window. Jon stepped slowly to it, peeking over the windowsill. Dark clouds filled the sky, spilling silver raindrops that danced ripples across the pavement and staff car park. Just beyond, by the hospital main entrance, stood a group of people.

Jon squinted, cursing his unwillingness to visit an optician before the world ended. He waved Samson over.

"Can you see them?" he whispered, pointing at the group.

"Yeah, I see 'em."

"They human?"

"Nope."

Jon peered back over the ledge. The longer he stared, the more the humanity of the group dissipated, as if washed away by the rain, revealing the increasingly odd silhouettes of the individuals, all shapes and sizes too unnatural to be human. One huge and round, one small and slender. One too dark to see properly in the rain. All of them facing the entrance doors to the hospital.

One of the group broke away, gliding over the pavement in a zig-zag motion, its white skin gleaming in the streetlight. A sickening sensation rose in Jon's guts. It was the snake, he was sure of it. The same one that had taken Kai's arm. Had it escaped on its own and followed Kai's scent? Had it been rescued by the others and led them here? Either question implied something equally terrifying.

The snake stopped just short of the doors and turned to the rest of the group, as if to discuss what to do. One of the others rose up and separated off. Even in the darkness, Jon could make out the size difference between it and its companions as it towered over them. The thing was a behemoth. A bead of sweat made its way down

Jon's back, and the urge to throw up rose inside his throat. He glanced briefly at Samson. The man was large. Huge. This monster made him look ordinary.

Tearing himself away from the window, he whispered hoarsely, "we need to go."

"Don't need to tell me twice," said Samson, already stuffing medical supplies into his rucksack.

From below, the sound of exploding glass roared through the halls, sending a tremor through the building. Efi whipped the drip out of her arm with a grimace and hastily bandaged it.

"There's something I need to get before we go," she said.

"What?" hissed Jon. "No. We need to go. Now!"

"It's important! It's on the way and it won't take a second. Ravi and I had an agreement. If one of us left, we'd leave a note. If Ravi left here with your friend, he would have left something to tell me where he was going."

"Fine. Where?"

"Uh," Efi paused.

Jon raked at his hair. "Where, Efi?"

"The office!" she said. "Ravi's office."

"What if he hasn't left anything?" said Samson as he slung the rucksack onto his shoulders.

She shrugged, heading for the door. "Then we just go."

Keeping low, they crept out of the ward, nervously glancing around with every step and jumping at every shadow.

Jon's heart seemed determined to claw its way out of his throat. He gulped it back down and tried to focus on getting away from the place and catching up with Caede and Kai. If this doctor had left something for Efi to follow, be it an address or just instructions to one, it could lead him their way. Efi was right; it was worth the risk. A voice in the back of his mind mocked him. He'd known them for a couple of hours. What was he going to do if he caught up with them? Be welcomed with open arms? Get married, live happily ever after? As if she'd even consider him like that. A graphic designer in an apocalypse who didn't know his arse from his elbow, who couldn't step over a dead body without pissing himself? She'd think he was a loser. A creep. His face burned with shame, and he glared angrily at the corridor ahead of him. He reached for the ring and twirled it in his fingers. The metal band felt warm to the touch.

The voice was right; he hadn't known her that long. But it didn't matter. Right now, he'd consider Efi his best friend in the entire world, and he'd known her for a day. Time meant nothing anymore. And their meeting wasn't by chance. If Caede hadn't screamed, he would be just another body on the pavement. A literal cry for help had saved his life. He'd saved theirs. If there was a God, they had a sick sense of humour, letting him reach the edge like that, only to snatch him back at the last second. Maybe the loneliness had finally gotten to him. Maybe it was because she was the first woman since Tara to cross his path and smile. More likely, he was forcing a narrative, and he'd finally slipped over the edge into outright insanity. A heavy weight took shape and settled in his stomach.

The screech of twisting metal and crashing furniture rang through the hospital as the creatures tore through the wards above.

A thumping began in the back of his head. He gritted his teeth and tried to ignore it. Just up ahead, Efi had stopped at a door and was waving him over. He stepped inside and looked around the room. It was an office, decorated in a style reflective of National Health Service budget cuts and bureaucracy, with a large desk in the centre and tall shelves sagging under the weight of folders and dust. Hospital bedding had been piled underneath the desk as if it were a nest. Efi darted across the room and began rifling through the desk drawers, muttering to herself. With a victorious tut, she seized some pieces of paper and a map book, and gestured for the others to gather around her. The paper contained a single line:

Big house, gated, visible from the main road. Page sixty-seven, Square D, Eight.

Efi opened the map book and flicked through the pages.

"Can we look at this after we're done running for our lives?" said Jon.

"This won't take a second!"

Confirming the details, she gestured for Samson to turn around. He obliged, and she stuffed the map book into his rucksack.

"Put this in your pocket," she said, shoving the piece of paper into Jon's hands. "Let's go."

A whine filled the air, the scraping of metal against a hard surface. The group froze, all eyes fixed on the ceiling. The sound was all around them, and much too close. Jon swore under his breath. He headed to the door and peeked out. Seeing nothing, he turned back to the others.

"We should just run for it."

22

Escape to the country

Justine Pearson, entry 10.09.2030

There's been a commotion with the military boys in the lab this morning. One of them has a tail. A tail! How incredible. That's thirteen at work there.

Of course, the poor boy will probably want it removed, and when they do that, I'll be taking a few samples. We'll see if there are any other lovely surprises waiting for us in those cells.

-

Kai fumbled in the wheelchair, his hand tugging at the drip in his arm, his legs kicking wildly to free himself.

"Caedey!"

Ravi swore and sprinted towards Caede. The plan had been to wait for an hour and then run, whether she had arrived or not. Of course, they had waited. Kai would have forced Ravi to look for her if she hadn't returned. Worse, if Caede had been killed, they would be alone, just him and Kai. Leaving her behind simply wasn't an option. So, when she appeared around the corner, the relief had almost overwhelmed him. But as she drew closer, that relief turned to bile in his throat. The bruising, the blood, her hand clutching the side of her waist as she limped. Hollow, grey eyes stared at nothing in particular. Her other hand rose in a strained wave, and she mouthed something before dropping to the ground. And Ravi ran.

He reached her, inspecting her carefully as she lay still on the pavement, fingers pressing the flesh of her legs and arms, testing for breaks or muscle trauma before turning her over. At her waist was a deep-looking puncture wound, and he could see where blood had stained her jogging bottoms. Now it dripped onto the pavement. He didn't know how deep it was, but it would need stitches at the very least.

"Caede," he said, "can you hear me?"

She groaned and nodded in response. A good sign. Ravi dragged her up, lifting her arm over his shoulders. He dropped a little of her weight to test her strength, and she responded well, knees locking and feet squarely planted on the pavement. She tried to say something but couldn't and pointed to her throat. He lifted the scarf around her neck, revealing a thick layer of dried blood, and underneath that, heavy, purple bruises.

"I can't see the extent of the damage properly," he said. "I'll need to clean away the blood."

She nodded and together they headed back to Kai, who sat twitching impatiently in the station doorway, almost wrestling the chair in agitation. He calmed when they arrived, and the three headed further inside the station entrance, settling by the lifts. Ravi lay a towel on the floor and gestured for Caede to sit. She obliged, and he handed her a bottle of water. She took small, painful sips, grimacing every time she raised the bottle to her mouth. Ravi waited for her to finish, then handed her a pack of antibacterial wipes.

"Caedey," said Kai, "are you okay?" He reached his arm out to her. She hastily rubbed her hands with one of the wipes and took Kai's hand. He looked at her, his eyes big and full of worry. "What happened? Did they hurt you?"

Caede shook her head at that, and whispered, "dead."

Ravi squirmed a little as the words left her mouth, and her eyes flicked to his for just a moment, but he said nothing. *Dead.* She'd said it with such finality. And with all her injuries, he could believe it. As for how they were dead, he couldn't fathom. Caede was only one person, too frail to put up any sort of fight against those monsters. She looked at him again and mouthed, "them or me."

He nodded in grim acknowledgement. A mouse cornered by a cat will fight viciously for its life. Why would humans be any different? From the moment he and Efi had locked the hospital doors, he had kept most of the horror outside and out of view, his survival only requiring that he stay quiet, stay hidden. But now, he was a part of it, and would have to change if he was going to survive. And it seemed Caede had the right idea. At that moment, she was far more at home here, covered in blood, dirt, and sweat. Like a wild animal, fierce and unforgiving, savage and ruthless as nature intended, the pretence of civilisation stripped away.

"The puncture wound on your abdomen," he said. "How deep is it?"

She gestured with her fingers, pointing to the second joint closest to the knuckle. Almost two inches deep. That wasn't so bad; certainly could have been worse. Ravi took off his glasses and rubbed at his face.

"I've cleaned it," she said, her voice barely a wheeze.

"Okay. That's a good start."

Ravi took out some supplies.

"I'll re-dress the wound and make sure it's sealed until I can stitch it up properly. I daren't do that here. We'll have to wait until we get to my uncle's. Just hold up the shirt for now. I'll be as quick as I can."

He set to work. The wound looked clean, thank God, and seemed calm, not red and irritated. If she was careful, it wouldn't become infected. The cuts on her hands were almost worse; they were dirty and full of glass splinters, and her wrists were swollen and bruised. Caede grimaced as he cleaned and re-wrapped them. Despite the heavy bruising on her throat, her windpipe didn't seem to be crushed. Satisfied, he wiped his hands and returned the supplies to the bag.

A question flared up in his mind, one that, thankfully, he had only ever had to ask once. It came with weight. Certain Kai wouldn't hear them, he moved his face close to her ear and whispered, "I have emergency contraceptives if you need them."

After a pause, she slowly shook her head. "They didn't," she whispered. A tear burst its banks and trickled down her cheek, but she blinked it away.

"Okay," he said. "Let me know if you need to talk."

She nodded, and he didn't press further. He thought of his sister. A man had grabbed her on her way home from a party, and tried to drag her into a van. It had been happening more and more in the last few years, but he hadn't expected it to happen to his sister. She had escaped, but was so shaken by the incident that she couldn't face going to the police, insisting that she just wanted to forget it ever happened. After that, she stopped going to parties. At that moment, Ravi had felt angry and helpless. And he felt it again now, burning in the pit of his stomach.

They rested inside the station for a few minutes, allowing just enough time for Caede to choke down some painkillers before moving on.

"I suggest we find a car," said Ravi, looking out at the road. "It's clearer here, now we're out of the centre. We could drive the rest of the way."

Caede and Kai nodded, and they headed off, peeking into car windows, checking for keys. None of the three knew how to hot-wire a car, and even if they did, the modern ones used digital keys, making it impossible. Some had their keys, but no battery life. Most had neither. After some time walking along and searching, they found one, its keys still in the ignition. Ravi turned the key, half expecting the car to fail, but to his surprise it shivered and grumbled to life. The three piled inside. Kai lay across the back seats, closed his eyes, and immediately began to doze. Caede and Ravi sat in the front, nervously glancing out through the windows as they waited for an attack to come. But no attack came. The buildings remained as still and grey as ever, and there were no sounds beyond the hum of the car's engine.

"Okay," said Ravi. "Let's go."

He began edging the car forward, testing the brakes a little, then picking up speed, moving into second gear. Caede inspected the map, reading out instructions where her voice would allow, and pointing directions where it failed. The roads were signposted well enough to navigate without her input, so they continued mostly in silence, slowly weaving through the other cars. More than a few times, Ravi was forced to stop and push another car out of the way.

By the time they reached the edge of the city, the sun was already dipping into the horizon, its orange rays filtering through the tower blocks. Nothing else moved. The streets stood silent, with no signs of life anywhere. As they approached the border sign for Kent, they passed an abandoned army checkpoint. Ravi slowed the car and gazed at the wall of sandbags resting against an armoured vehicle, with a sign on its front reading:

Stop. Checkpoint.

"This must have been put up for the evacuation," said Ravi.

"Then where is everyone?" said Caede.

"God knows."

They kept driving.

Millions of people lived and worked in or around London. Even with the number of corpses lining the pavements, it didn't account for a fraction of its population. So where was everybody? Besides being evacuated, many survivors would have fled the city to safety. A flicker of hope rose in his chest at the thought.

"It's an easier drive now," said Caede, checking the map. "But, I'm not sure which is better, the main roads or country?"

"I don't know," replied Ravi. "The main roads are wider, but the country roads might be quieter; fewer cars, perhaps."

"Country roads it is, then."

Ravi turned off at the exit and headed east, slowing the car as he approached a small roundabout.

"I think I know where we are," he said. "I'm sure I've been this way before."

Caede glanced at the map. "It says here to take the second exit."

Ravi followed. After thirty minutes of driving alongside fields, they spotted a road with smaller, adjoining paths that looked like long driveways leading up to private estates.

Ravi leaned forward over the steering wheel. "I think we're here. The turnoff should be any second. Where is that damn driveway?"

"Wow," said Caede. "These houses are huge."

"Yes. My aunt and uncle are quite wealthy. My aunt was an actress when she met my uncle. She went on to become a director. She directed Hiraeth."

"Really? I loved that film."

"Yes. She's directed a few blockbusters. I couldn't tell you all of them, not off the top of my head, but between her and my uncle they have quite the impressive portfolio."

He turned the car onto a small, pebbled road that sloped gently upwards. Tall, trimmed hedges lined it, their shadows retreating from the headlights of the car as Ravi drove up. After a few seconds, the line of trees receded, revealing a large manor house and garden. A Jaguar sat in a large, open garage attached to the main building. There were no lights on anywhere.

"It doesn't look as though anyone's home," said Ravi.

"What about that car in the garage?"

"That's just my uncle's old Jag. It's a passion project. I don't think he's ever driven it anywhere. He just likes to tinker with it."

Ravi peered out of the front window for a long time, staring silently at the Jaguar. Finally, he turned off the engine.

"Well then, I suppose we're here."

Caede unclipped her seatbelt and turned to Kai, gently nudging him.

"Hey, we're here."

Kai groaned and stirred, arching his back and blinking away the residue of sleep.

"Hmm?"

"We're here, Kai. We made it."

"Really?" Kai leaned forward and stared out of the windscreen. "Is that it? Wow!"

Caede nodded. "Massive, ain't it."

23

Enter the Dragon

Terry Howard, entry 10.09.2030

I have always sought to help people. At first, I thought I would do that by becoming a general practitioner, but this life has taken me further than I ever dreamed. Sigma-13 is my greatest creation. I will be damned if I let it stay in the hands of warmongers and politicians.

-

"What?" said Efi. "Are you mad? What if it's a trap? We'd be running right into it!"

"Fine," Jon replied, jaw tight. "Let's just wait here then, cover ourselves in ketchup, and put out the fucking welcome mat!"

"Oh my God, shut up, both of you!" said Luna.

Jon made a motion to protest, but stopped. Efi was looking at him with narrowed eyes. If looks could kill, she would have reduced him to ashes in an instant.

"Okay, fine," he said. "What's the plan, then?"

Over their heads, the ceiling panels trembled and groaned. They could hear the crash and clatter of furniture being tossed around as the creatures barrelled through the wards above, so close that Jon could hear their hisses and growls, as if they were talking to each other in some unknown, terrifying language.

"If I didn't know better, I would say they know we're here," Samson muttered.

"Aye," said Jon. "God knows how, but they know. They're not like the ones in the tunnel, are they? These ones are organised."

"No shit," said Efi.

Luna stared up at the ceiling, eyes bulging. "Can we please just go?"

"Yeah," Jon replied. "We'll go slow, but if anything happens, we run for it. How's that sound?"

Everyone nodded in agreement.

"I'll go out last," said Samson, a grin spreading across his face. "If any of those things catch up, I'll make them regret it."

"Alright," said Jon. "Just don't expect me to rescue you."

He cracked open the door, just wide enough to scan the corridor before stepping out, gesturing for the others to follow. They crept over the threshold, one after the other, until they were all in the hallway. Efi led the way, with Luna close behind. Jon and Samson followed.

Shadows of the trees outside crept through the windows and across the floor of the corridor, groping at the group as they passed. The rest of the halls were dark, silent and foreboding, contrasting against the maddening noise behind them. Jon was about ready to break and make a mad dash for the nearest exit. He felt like a rabbit scurrying blindly through a tunnel, dogs above him digging into the ground, waiting for their chance to snatch him up. Tiny flecks of something–dirt carried in from outside or bits of glass, he wasn't sure what–crunched underfoot. There was no way the creatures could hear, not with the racket they were making above them, but he flinched anyway.

They carried on slowly in a line, Efi checking each corner and gesturing for them to move forward. It wasn't until the group reached the corridor with the stairwell that he almost crashed into the back of Luna and realised Efi had frozen. As he saw what she was looking at, he realised it wouldn't have mattered if they ran. In front of them, blocking the stairwell to the car park exit, stood the behemoth.

It appeared like a man in shape, but stooped over, too tall to stand comfortably in the corridor, its long arms almost brushing the floor, legs bent slightly as if preparing to pounce. Any once-human features were hidden behind a mask of grey scales, thick as armour, with a heavy, elongated jaw sat atop a thick neck and powerful shoulders. The same scales covered the rest of its body. If it had wings, it could be a living dragon. A dragon towering over him. Bigger than the snake man. Bigger than Samson.

Black eyes stared unblinking at them. It cocked its head inquisitively at the group, regarding each of them, until its gaze met Samson. Its lips peeled back into a grin, revealing jagged, uneven teeth that looked as if they'd been filed to sharpened points. From inside its mouth flicked a long, black tongue that forked like a snake's. It danced malevolently, as if delighting in the fear-thickened air, sampling the collective terror of each person.

Jon seized Luna's arm and yanked her behind him. Samson stepped forward and shrugged off the rucksack, tossing it to Jon. The dragon's grin widened, and it nodded at him.

"Okoye," it said. Its voice was a deep rasping, an avalanche hidden behind a Russian accent. "I've been looking for you."

"Kalinov?" said Samson. "What happened to you?"

"Improvements," said the dragon. "But what of you? What is this I'm seeing? Poor choice, I think. Your stink is unbearable. I could smell you a mile off."

"Didn't get a choice, mate."

"Ah, desperate times. Did you hear, friend, Terry is dead?"

"I did, yeah."

"I was told he put a gun to his mouth."

"He did."

"The man was a coward."

Jon watched, his mind filling with terror and amazement. It could talk. It had a name. Just like the others, this monster had been a man once, a human being. How could it be talking? Its mouth seemed too wide, its tongue too thin. And it was talking to Samson like it knew him.

"Samson, you…"

Samson glanced back at him. "Run," he whispered. "I'll catch you up."

"Okoye," said the dragon, ignoring the rest of the group. "Terry put a gun to his head, yes, but what of Justine?"

"Wouldn't tell you if I knew, mate."

"As I suspected. Pity, Okoye, I thought you would have jumped at the chance to take this next step with us."

"I'll be honest," said Samson. "I'd rather die."

"I can respect that. You'll die like a man, at least."

Samson turned again. "You lot run," he said. There was an urgency in his voice now.

"You can't fight that thing," said Jon. "Just run!"

"Go!"

"Samson, fucking run!"

But the big man just stood there, staring down the monster in front of him. Jon imagined the air in the corridor heating, thickening, as if a wave of electricity had passed between the pair.

Jon's feet began sliding backwards, but Luna was stuck behind him, frozen in fear. He glanced around. Where was Efi? Suddenly he realised she was stuck between the giants, her back pressed against the wall. The dragon turned its head towards her and flicked its tongue.

"Okoye. You know, once you are dead, I will take this specimen. Lev would love to work on her."

"Lev can go fuck himself."

"I don't think you would say that if you saw what he did with the others. He could help you, you know. Help your friends here."

"I already told you: nah."

"Pity. Daisy did not seem to mind."

With that, Samson bristled with fury, shaking himself like a wild animal preparing for a fight, his skin seeming to ripple in anticipation. A low, primal snarl escaped his lips. For the first time, Jon noticed the elongated canines and black gums lining Samson's mouth, and he shivered. In response, the dragon stomped its colossal feet, accepting the challenge. Samson raised his fists up and uttered a growl.

"Keep her name out of your fucking mouth."

Chunks of flooring flew into the air as the dragon lunged forward and the two juggernauts collided. They gripped each other, wrestling, arms locked together, grunting and snarling. Suddenly, the dragon jerked sideways, throwing Samson into the wall. He roared and dropped under the beast, using its momentum against it, and threw up his arm in a vicious punch to its gut. The dragon hissed in fury and reeled back, crashing into the opposite wall, knocking the plaster from it in chunks. It lunged again, barrelling into Samson, and the pair landed heavily on the floor.

Jon blinked as he tried to catch the flashes of movement between the two. Red splattered the wall. Dust, fur, and scales flew into the air. Clouds of hot breath rose above hisses and growls. Then he spotted Samson kicking hard, and the dragon flew back, shaking the building with the collision and sending cracks weaving up the wall. Lumps of plaster rained down, filling the air with thick dust. The dragon recovered and threw itself forward, slashing at Samson with heavy sweeps of its arms, its huge hands lined with thick, blackened claws. Samson dodged, ducking and weaving like a boxer, returning each swipe with a hammering blow of his own to the dragon's arms and face. After a second it swayed, punch-drunk, and stumbled. A grin flickered across Samson's face, and he readied himself to deliver the knockout punch.

The dragon hissed. Furious, it launched itself, ducking under Samson's fists, snapping at his torso with its jaws. Samson skidded and darted backwards. A scream filled the air. It was Efi still stuck against the wall, covered in plaster dust, her hands over her ears. Samson glanced up, distracted.

"Efi, run!"

The dragon stopped and grinned. Lowering its head, it dropped to all fours. With explosive speed, it dug its fists into the floor tiles and hurled itself forward like a slingshot, hitting Samson squarely in the chest. With a gasp, he fell to the floor. The dragon followed, landing on top of him. It opened its mouth wide and bit down, clamping its jaws deep into the flesh of Samson's shoulder. He roared in pain and kicked, once, twice, tearing the monster off him, then lay panting on the floor, hot blood pouring from the fresh wound.

The dragon rolled over, winded, and lay still.

"Samson, get up!" Jon screamed.

Luna darted forward, a long hunting knife in her hand. There was no time to wonder where she had got it. Jon seized her arms and pulled her back, holding her tight. She screamed and kicked in fury, writing to get free. But he held on. "There's nothing we can do!" he said. "Come on!"

Luna relaxed and dropped her feet on the floor. Jon let her go and the pair edged to the wall, shimmying past the two bodies towards Efi. Jon reached out to her, and she took his hand. They stepped slowly towards the stairwell and waited, silently urging Samson to get back up.

But the dragon recovered first. It rose and looked down at Samson, a cold smile lining its blood-soaked lips. Then it turned, raising its black, empty eyes to face Jon. He felt the blood rush in his ears and a sudden cold sweep over his skin. His mouth turned to chalk. He began nudging Luna behind him, urging her to run, but she stood her ground, staring at the creature with a mix of fear and fury, and Efi held his arm like a vice, frozen on the spot.

"Run," said Jon. "Go!"

Neither moved. They stared wide-eyed at the dragon. It was moving now, with purpose, towards him. He urged his feet to move, but they were stuck. His eyes darted around for something to use. There was nothing but chunks of plaster.

Then the dragon stopped. It glanced down, confused. Jon followed its gaze to see Samson's fists clamped around its ankles, his face set in determination. With a roar, he pulled, snatching the beast's legs from underneath it. Tiles and shrapnel scattered as the dragon hit the floor face down and Samson rolled onto it, smashing his elbow into its back. It gasped and coughed, choking on the rising dust, and Samson leapt onto it, raining heavy blows down against its thick hide. Blood frothed from the dragon's mouth as it squirmed, hissing and gagging. It fell still once again. Samson dragged himself up and ran towards the others. "Okay, let's go!"

They ran, feet pummelling the stairs as they headed towards the exit. Bursting through the door, they poured into the car park, heading straight down the slope towards the ground floor and street. Waiting for them at the bottom was another one of the creatures.

The thing was resting at the entrance of the car park, more tumour than human; a mass of grey flesh squatting on the pavement, unnaturally obese, wider than Jon was tall, and standing just as high. Its head, wide and flattened, sat sunken into the flesh of its shoulders, almost drowning in folds of damp, mottled skin. Underneath that was a torso, bloated and corpulent, teetering between two grey stumps. Jon quickly realised they were legs, folded and facing outward like a sumo wrestler preparing for battle.

Spotting the group, it leaned forward, placing its hands on the pavement. Beady eyes stared at them through the folds. A chortle, wet and gargled, escaped its wide, lipless mouth.

Jon heard gasps behind him.

"Ugh!" Luna grunted.

"What the hell is that thing?" said Efi.

He didn't have an answer. No words came, and the chalky taste returned. Samson growled. Jon turned his head to reply and paused. The man didn't look right. Beads of sweat had formed on his face, and he was panting in short, sharp gasps. He groaned and slumped, legs giving way. Jon leapt forward to catch him, knees buckling as the big man landed, but he managed to tug Samson up and drape his arm around his shoulder.

"What are we gonna do now, eh?" Jon said.

Samson mumbled something in response, but Jon couldn't make out the words. A ribbon of crimson left his open mouth and fell to the pavement with a splash.

"Shit," said Jon. "You alright, mate?"

"What's the matter?" It was Efi, there in Samson's face, lifting his head up to look into his eyes, checking his pulse, her fingers pressed up against the man's thick neck. She frowned.

"Luna," she said. "Come here, would you? Hold him up for me?"

Luna looped Samson's other arm over her shoulders, sagging under his weight.

"Keep an eye on that thing, okay?" said Efi.

Luna nodded, her eyes narrowed and fixed on the sickening creature. Jon stretched his neck around to get a better look at the wound. The skin around the bite mark bubbled and withered. Whatever was on the dragon's lips, or in its teeth, had seeped into Samson's flesh, and was rotting it from the inside. The bite reminded him of something he'd seen in a nature documentary; the words *Komodo dragon* flashed into his mind.

"We need to get out of here," he said.

Efi nodded. "What's the other one doing?"

Jon glanced over her shoulder. "It's just sitting there. I think it's watching us."

"It's making sure we don't leave," said Luna.

On the level above came the crash of the side door exploding open. The dragon was back on its feet, and heading towards them.

Samson coughed and raised his head. "Just leave me."

"Absolutely not," said Efi.

"Yeah," said Jon. "What she said."

The big man chuckled. "Thought you didn't like me."

"I don't like you."

Samson's laugh turned into a dry hacking noise, and fresh drops of blood fell to the ground.

"You alright?" said Jon.

"I don't know," said Samson. "Can't feel my feet."

"You'll be fine, alright? Just keep moving, come on."

He nudged Samson, urging him to move. Efi took his other shoulder, and the pair shuffled forward, dragging Samson between them. Luna walked ahead, eyeing the creature, knife raised in her hand.

"Jon," said Efi.

"I know," he said, snapping his head around. The dragon was at the top of the slope, watching them as if he were waiting for something.

"Fuck, fuck, fuck," Jon muttered to himself. How did it know about the side exit?

"We need to run," he said. "I don't think that one can chase us."

"Not gonna argue with that," said Efi.

They began a slow, laboured jog, flanking the squatting creature and heading around the entry barriers, as far away from it as possible. The creature watched as they passed, and began shifting its weight, following their direction. Jon stepped past the barrier.

The creature threw its mouth open, stretching it wider and wider, the top of its head seeming to separate completely from its body. Faster than Jon's eyes could follow, something long and gelatinous flew out, hitting Efi squarely in the chest, bowling the three of them over. The thing whipped her up into the air and spun like a thread, encasing her arms and legs, pressing them against her torso. Her maddened wail cut into the air as the wet, grey tongue of the creature cocooned her. With a chuckle, the creature rolled its tongue and sucked, slowly pulling Efi into its cavernous mouth. She flailed helplessly, her screams muffled and her eyes shining white in the darkness. The creature's face opened wider still, and it began to gulp.

"Efi!"

Jon dropped Samson and ran towards her. Luna darted ahead, smaller and quicker, weaving towards the creature in a zig-zag. She shrieked and leapt onto the beast, driving her knife into its slimy flesh, again and again in a violent frenzy, screaming in savage delight.

Thick, dark crimson sprayed into the air, covering her. The creature wheezed in agony and raised its useless arms up, trying to bat Luna off, but she dug the knife in deep and held on. Its body began to sag. With a pained gurgle, its mouth fell open. Jon tugged against the tongue, unravelling Efi.

"Come on, lass," said Jon.

She wriggled her arms free, and he took her hands, pulling as hard as he could until she slid out, coughing and gagging.

"I'm gonna be sick!" she said between heaves.

"Jon!" It was Luna, pointing behind him.

He spun around to see the dragon, closer now, heading towards Samson.

Jon let Efi go and ran towards him. "Samson! Move!"

The big man stirred and began pushing himself up. Jon wedged himself under Samson's arm and lifted. "Come on, man! You've got to get up!"

The dragon was closer now, only a few feet away. It leaned down into a squat position, hands resting on its knees, and their eyes met.

"How well do you know this man?" it asked.

"What?"

"How well do you know this man?"

"I don't."

The dragon shrugged. "Then you won't mind when he dies."

With that, the dragon stood and began walking back up the slope towards the hospital. Efi and Luna ran over. Efi took Samson's other arm.

"What just happened?"

"I don't know," said Jon. "Let's just go before that thing changes its mind!"

The pair dragged Samson up and left as quickly as they could.

24

Nobody's Home

Terry Howard, entry 18.09.2030

I was on the phone to Lauren yesterday and she said they have some promising stuff ready. Hopefully all the data I sent helped them with their tests. They've got a man, a Doctor Okoye, in the team. Apparently, he's big into the gene editing movement, fancies himself a 'biohacker', so he's very excited to see what Sigma can do. As long as he's professional about it I don't care.

-

Ravi shut off the engine, plunging the car into darkness, and the three sat inside, waiting, jaws clenched as they stared out of the windows. The sun had fully submerged itself into the horizon, leaving streaks of mauve and scarlet in its wake. Nothing stirred in the darkness but the trees, their black silhouettes swaying in the wind. Slivers of moonlight danced between their branches, illuminating the gravel path and front of the house.

Ravi's whisper broke the silence. "I think it's safe."

Caede nodded, and Ravi slowly opened the driver's side door, pressing his foot into the gravel. If anyone, or anything, had heard their approach, they hadn't reacted.

An icy gust nipped at Ravi's exposed face and hands, and he shivered as he waited for any signs of life beyond the swaying bushes. He stood for a moment longer before peering back into the car.

"There's nothing out here," he said.

Ravi walked around to the passenger rear side, opening the door for Kai, and extending his hand to him. "Can you stand?"

"I think so."

Kai was looking a little better after his nap, but in the darkness, it was hard to tell and neither he, Caede, nor Ravi had eaten in hours. If anyone needed food right now, it was the boy. The body couldn't fight off an infection on an empty stomach, and even with the care he had taken to heal Kai's arm, it would be a while before he was truly out of the woods. Ravi could feel the hunger tugging at his own belly. Now that he had noticed it, he could no longer ignore it.

"Shall we head in, then?" he said, rubbing his hands together eagerly. "Get some food that isn't from a vending machine?"

"Yeah," said Caede, gingerly climbing out of the car. "I'm starving."

Ravi smiled and let relief flood over him. The hospital had been safe–as safe as one can be in the situation, but it wasn't the same as being somewhere familiar, somewhere like home. And in the absence of his, this one would do. It was still family. A pang of nostalgia, then sadness, tapped at the back of his mind. He let them in, let them flow through his consciousness, then sent them away again before the tap became a hammering. It wasn't time to grieve just yet. There was work to do. He blinked away the tears and headed up the stairs to the dais and large wooden front doors.

The house had been built specially for his aunt and uncle after they had purchased a plot of land some twenty years ago, and though technically not a manor–since Ravi's uncle was not a lord–it had the size and land to qualify as one. The design had been pulled right out of a countryside magazine shoot, with a Georgian exterior, large, panelled windows, and branches of wisteria weaving across its front. In the spring and summer months, the wisteria would bloom, and the petals would rain down in a cascading dance of lilac hues, painting the driveway and fountain. Ravi's uncle liked to leave the petals there. Now, the branches were barren, the leaves brown and withering on the vines.

Ravi tried to remember how many bedrooms it had. Not that it mattered. There were enough to house Caede and Kai without inconveniencing anyone. When he'd last visited, the inside had been decorated with soft neutrals, rich yellows, and warm terracotta tones, with items and artworks of decor reminiscent of Northern India, his uncle's homeland. It was a mesh of modern, minimalist design and flashes of rich colour and familial history. It would have been nice to visit India as an adult, if only just once, but he'd never been able to find the time.

He pressed the button for the doorbell and waited a few seconds before trying it again. No answer. "I don't think anyone's home," he said, as if confirming out loud something he already knew. He tried the handle. Locked, of course. And his mother kept the spare keys on her, reasoning that he would only lose them. He headed back down the stairs and began walking along the side of the building, following a path of decorative low shrubs lining the windows.

"I take it the door's locked," said Caede, trotting up to him.

"We might have to find another way in," he replied. "There's a side gate and back door. Worst-case scenario would be that we might have to break a window. We will soon find out."

They returned to the car and lifted out the wheelchair.

Caede frowned. "I don't think it's going to go over the gravel," she said, letting out a sigh. "Kai, wait in the car while we look for a way in. And stay quiet, okay? We might need to get away quickly."

"I can walk," Kai replied. "Let me come with you?"

"Just do it, aright?"

Kai nodded, sulking as Caede closed the door. "We won't be long, I promise," she said.

They left the wheelchair in the boot and headed around to the side gate.

"Should I get out the torch?" said Caede.

"Not yet," said Ravi, voice low. "I don't want to draw any unwanted attention."

"The car would have done that," she replied flatly.

"True, but let's not tempt fate any further."

If Ravi's memory served, the gate would have a bolt at the top, but no padlock. He reached up and felt for the bolt, sliding it back, and the gate swung slowly open.

"I can't see a damned thing," he said.

"Just let me get the torch. There's obviously no one here."

"Okay, fine. Just keep the beam low."

Caede clicked the torch on, sending white light spilling across the pathway. They stepped lightly, ears straining for any sounds, glancing around for sudden movements. To their left, the path forked, winding through a large garden lined with tall shrubs and a gate beyond it. The path continued onwards to somewhere neither Ravi nor Caede could see, so they ignored it and pressed on.

A large conservatory came into view. Caede flashed the beam across the windows and the pair peered cautiously inside. The room was filled with orchids and miniature orange trees housed in ornate pots that rested on low tables. A set of wicker chairs and a coffee table sat in the centre. A tablet and empty cup sat on the table, but otherwise there were no signs of any recent activity. Seeing nothing amiss, Ravi tried the door handle. It opened with a satisfying click.

"For once, I'm thankful that my uncle doesn't take home security seriously."

A wave of warmth hit them as they entered the room.

"God, it's like an oven in here!" Caede gasped.

"The heating must still be working," said Ravi. "I won't complain. And if the inside doors are locked, we can break in without losing any warmth."

He walked across the conservatory towards a pair of sliding doors connecting the inner house. Pressing his face against the glass, he peered inwards. "Shine the torch in here, would you?"

Caede directed the beam into the room, holding it steady while Ravi stared through the window.

"Doesn't seem to be anything out of place," he muttered. "I'll try the door."

He turned the catch on the patio door upwards and tugged. The door slid heavily open. The smell of sandalwood and vanilla wafted out to greet him, filling his head with memories of childhood summers spent with his cousins, playing in the garden, sitting in the library with a blanket and a book, sleepovers where they'd all pile into one big bed and curl up together like kittens. His eyes began to water, and he blinked. He felt Caede's hand rest gently on his shoulder.

"Are you okay?" she whispered.

"I'll be alright," he replied. "My aunt and uncle are smart. And they aren't short of money. I'm sure they're somewhere safe."

"Okay. Well, I guess it's safe to bring Kai in now; we should go get him."

Ravi nodded as he turned back towards the garden. Suddenly, he caught a movement in the corner of his eye and he froze. From outside the conservatory, a small, white face stared, pressed up against the glass, looking directly at him.

"Bloody hell!" he yelled, jumping backwards into Caede, who yelped in response, dropping the torch. As it fell, the beam cast over the ghostly face and it recoiled.

"Argh!" it groaned. "Caedey! Are you trying to blind me?"

Caede quickly righted herself and spun around.

"Kai!" she said. "What did I tell you? I said wait in the car!"

Kai opened the conservatory door and crept inside, clutching the saline drip still attached to his arm. "Well, I didn't."

Caede sighed in exasperation, slumping into one of the wicker chairs. "You're recovering from surgery! What if something had happened to you?"

"It didn't. And what if something had happened to me while I was in the car?"

Ravi frowned and returned to the patio doors. "Well, Kai, since you're here now, we should head inside."

The three had entered a large lounging area with comfortable-looking chairs, bookshelves, and coffee tables. Ravi remembered the patio doors being open during the summer. He and his sister would run out into the garden to play in the swimming pool. The adults would sit inside and drink tea while he played, his mother on standby with a large towel for when they had enough. Someone would bring a huge plate of sandwiches and the children would sit in the sun and eat, all wrapped in their towels. Ravi basked in the nostalgia for a moment longer before moving on. "We'll check the house first and then have some dinner. How does that sound?"

Caede turned the torch back towards him. "Sounds good to me."

Together they tiptoed from room to room, casting the torchlight around to make sure each was empty before moving on to the next. The downstairs of the house featured what appeared to be a series of lounging areas, a home office, small library, games room with its own billiards table and built-in bar, dining room and large kitchen. Eventually, they made it to the front of the house.

"Do you think we could get some lights on?" Caede asked as they tiptoed into what seemed like a large hall.

"If they even worked, I'd advise against it for now," he replied, glancing around as he stepped into the room.

"Fine," she shrugged and continued onwards to a wide, regal-looking central staircase, Kai following close behind her. Moonlight trickled in through two large windows that stood aside a small entryway opposite the stairs. Their footsteps echoed through the empty hall as they ascended, their shadows stretching out in front of them as if eager to reach the top of the stairs first. When they reached the balcony, Caede shone the torch across, wiggling the light in front of each doorway to see if anything stirred within the rooms.

"We should check each room before anything else," she muttered, peering into the darkness.

"Shall we start from the left and go from there?" suggested Ravi.

Each of the eight bedrooms was immaculately decorated and kept guest-ready with clean linens, silk throws and fancy pillows adorning the dark wooden sleigh beds. The master bedroom, distinguished from the rest in both size and decadence, featured a huge four-poster bed with jacquard silk curtains draping down from the sides and a towering, intricately carved wardrobe. Fine art lined the walls; paintings and prints rich in colour featuring vibrant splashes of orange, red, purple, and gold.

Unlike the other rooms, this one had been used recently. The bed covers had been peeled back to air out and a small pile of clothing sat abandoned in an armchair beside it. How much time had passed between his relatives leaving the house and Ravi arriving, he couldn't guess, but the room still smelled of warm fabric and sleep. After checking inside the wardrobe and finding nothing, they continued onwards to the equally huge ensuite bathroom.

"Is that a jacuzzi bath?"

Ravi peered over the inside of the tub, marvelling. "Oh wow. I don't remember it being this lavish. My uncle always seemed more of the practical type."

"Maybe it's for hydrotherapy?"

"Perhaps…"

They left the master bedroom and padded over to the other side of the balcony, finding the main bathroom, home gym, a games room, and more guest bedrooms. Ravi's cousins no longer lived with their parents, having families of their own now, so there was no need for a nursery or personalised bedrooms anymore. They wrapped up their inspection, satisfied that nothing was out of the ordinary, and headed back down the grand staircase towards the kitchen.

"Hopefully, we'll be able to find something to eat," Ravi muttered as the group headed down the hallway. He glanced nervously at Kai. The boy's pale face was set, his jaw locked, determined to stay upright and not make a fuss. He needed to rest, and the pain relief must have been wearing off by now. Ravi had packed morphine and paracetamol, but during the journey out of London Kai had slept, so he hadn't taken anything for at least a few hours.

To Ravi's surprise, the fridge light flickered on as he opened the door. "I guess that answers our question about the electricity," he said as he inspected the contents. The vegetables were somewhat wilted, but they could be cooked without poisoning anyone. He bypassed the pack of chicken on the bottom shelf and reached for a large carton of eggs, still just within the use-by date on the label.

Caede trotted over to one of the ovens and began inspecting the dials. "Does that mean we can actually cook something?"

"Maybe. Are they gas or electric?"

"I think they're electric–flat hob and no spark button. Must be."

"Looks like the universe is our friend today. Does omelette sound good?"

25

Rest

The bed linens were cool to the touch against her fingers. And soft; softer than Caede had expected. Better than the bedding at the hospital–or a cold pavement. And, after rifling through a chest of drawers, she'd found some clean pyjamas. Her own dirty clothes she left on the floor by the bed. She could wash them later. Exhaustion crept over her as she lay down, and she yawned, closing her eyes. But something wasn't right. She sat up. Maybe it was the room? She closed her eyes again.

"Calm down, love…"

She jumped up with a yelp, sweat-drenched hair covering her eyes. She'd definitely heard it. Had they followed her? Where were they? *No,* she thought. *They're dead.* She tried lying back down but couldn't. Moonlight crept across the floor of the bedroom, bringing with it wolfish shadows and whispers of the day before.

Deciding a walk might help her settle, she padded out of the room, heading to Kai's. She peeked through the doorway to make sure he was asleep, not just to reassure herself that he was still there, still alive.

After an argument with Ravi about noise and light, she had convinced him to let them all shower and switch on some lamps. Kai had to sit in the bathtub of his ensuite with Caede and Ravi carefully washing him, reminding him that keeping himself clean would be the key to not getting an infection in his stump, and that he should appreciate the warm water while they still had it. Caede felt secretly certain that Kai would rather go through losing his arm again than sit in a bathtub being washed by his sister and some stranger, and honestly, she couldn't blame him.

Now he lay sleeping in his new bed. Ravi had set the room up as a makeshift infirmary, with the supplies taken from the hospital spread out on the vanity table by the window. Ravi had even attached a new drip to Kai's arm and sat with him, monitoring his condition for a while after he'd fallen asleep. The wheelchair sat next to the bed in case Kai needed it during the night. Caede tidied up his clothing, folded them and set them gently on a bedside table. As she watched his chest slowly rising and falling, she frowned. Kai didn't deserve this. Any of this. She choked down the guilt and quietly left.

She tiptoed back into the hallway and glanced across the balcony. Down the stairs, yellow light emanated from the open door of the library. A library! She couldn't believe the place had a library. Ravi had disappeared in there when she'd gone to bed. The books must have been a distraction. Maybe he just needed something to read to help him sleep. Maybe being proactive made him feel better. After contemplating the light for a while, she began to agonise over the possibility of its warmth and the company that shared it. Loneliness and fear tugged at her chest. Before she realised, she was walking towards the door.

She'd barely reached it when it opened suddenly, and Ravi was standing in front of her. Borrowed pyjamas hung from his slim frame. Suddenly, she felt foolish.

"Sorry, Ravi! Um…listen, this is going to sound really stupid…" She shifted her weight awkwardly.

"It's okay," he said softly. A sort of sad smile formed on his mouth. He adjusted his glasses and lowered his face to the floor. "It's odd being alone right now, isn't it? Bit embarrassing, really."

He stepped to one side, welcoming her into the room. "Have a seat."

The library was less of an actual library, and more of a large bedroom that had been filled to the brim with bookshelves, with a central window and comfy leather chairs. Ravi had a duvet covering one.

"Apologies if the light disturbed you," he said. "I've been doing some reading. I couldn't get to sleep."

Caede settled herself into the chair next to his. "No, it's fine. I just wanted…"

Ravi held a book in his hand, absentmindedly flipping the cover open and closed. He placed his hand on it and put it on a table next to the chair. "When this all kicked off, Efia, Holly and I slept on the floor of the office, even though there were beds in the wards. It was the only place we felt safe. I couldn't get to sleep up there. I thought a bit of reading would help."

He rubbed his temples and sighed. "Kai didn't have any trouble getting to sleep, did he? Thirty seconds and he was gone!"

The pair laughed.

"He's probably just exhausted," said Caede. "He's been through so much."

"It helps that I slipped him some morphine," said Ravi. "Just enough to help with the pain; he'll sleep better with it."

Caede nodded and sniffed. Her eyelids trembled. She leaned back against the chair. The siren-song of sleep called, drawing her deeper into its warmth.

"Are you okay, Caede?"

Caede yawned and forced her eyes open. "Not really, no, but I will be."

She saw Ravi hovering, unsure of what to do.

"I'm sorry, Ravi. I can go back to my room if you want."

"No, no, please stay. It's alright, honestly. I'm grateful for the company."

He placed his glasses delicately on a table that looked as if it was worth more than Caede's entire living room suite. "I was just trying to decide whether to go to sleep or keep reading. I thought that maybe I'd stay up for a little longer, but actually I'm quite tired."

For a moment they sat in silence, Caede staring awkwardly at the bookshelves, counting the seconds as they dragged by. Eventually, Ravi's hushed voice cut through the air. "I hope Efi and Holly are okay."

Caede turned to face him, thankful to dispel the oppressive quiet. "Do you think they'll be able to find us?"

Ravi kept his gaze on the ceiling. "I'm not sure, to be honest. Hopefully, they'll find the note, and if they want to, they can follow the map. They might not want to. I think I may have been more of a burden than a help, to be honest."

"Were you guys close before all of this?"

Ravi slowly shifted to face Caede; his eyes heavy with the same sadness he'd worn earlier. A couple of strands of black hair fell across his face, and he brushed them aside. He seemed tired. More than tired; somewhere between deep exhaustion and outright passing out. The weight of the last few days was etched into the corners of his eyes.

"We worked together, but I like to think we were also friends," he replied. "We'd go out for a drink every so often, you know, with other people from work, and we'd get the same tube train home."

He fell quiet. "Efi and Holly were the only ones willing to stay and help. I don't know if I would have survived otherwise."

"I know what you mean," Caede whispered. "Jon helped us get away from that monster. He saved Kai's life. He literally died trying to help us."

Fresh tears spilled over her eyelids and poured down her face. "We didn't even know him, and he died helping us."

Ravi leaned forward in his chair and took Caede's hand. "When I said family was the most important thing, I meant it. That man had probably lost everything. I'm certain he helped you knowing the risk. Don't let his sacrifice be in vain. You take good care of your brother, whatever happens. My fiancé, Farha.... She wanted to go to a wedding fair at the ExCel centre last weekend. I was stuck in A&E surrounded by what I thought were Ebola patients..."

He let go of her hand and leaned back in his seat. They stayed there quietly for a minute, each of them lost in their own thoughts before suddenly, flustered, Ravi stood. "I should really go to bed. It's been a long day."

"Yeah, you're right," she replied. "I never said thank you for helping us."

Ravi stood and gathered up the duvet. "No need," he replied. He walked slowly to the door and paused before leaving. "Good night, Caede. Try to get some rest."

26

Off to the shop

Justine Pearson, entry 01.10.2030

People will think we're evil. Maybe they're right, but we are trying to create something incredible here. No more disease, no more cancer, no more watching our loved ones dissolving into husks of their former selves.

Oh, Seb, my beautiful Seb... How could you leave me? How could you leave me alone in this world when we fought so hard? When I fought so hard to keep you in it... Couldn't you have waited just a little longer?

-

Jon and Efi dragged Samson's body onwards, their pace slowed to crawling by his deadened weight. Samson quietly groaned with each step; the only sign that he was still alive as they struggled onwards.

"The bleeding won't stop," said Efi. "We need to do something, or he's going to die."

"What do you suggest?" asked Jon with a grunt, as he shifted Samson's weight over his shoulder. Carrying him was becoming increasingly tiring, and the slick blood pouring from his shoulder made him more difficult to keep hold of. Jon didn't want to give up on him, but a thought plagued his mind: Samson might be dying and carrying him was a wasted effort if they wanted to get away from the immediate danger. The immediate danger, that, for whatever reason, wasn't chasing them down right now. The words *Komodo dragon* filled his thoughts once more. He tried to remember the documentary, but he'd only been paying half attention when he'd watched it. What was it the narrator had said?

"There's a pharmacy nearby," said Efi. "If it's not been looted, we can stop there."

"Alright."

They turned a corner into a smaller street, then took another onto a narrow road, barely wide enough to fit a car. If he hadn't known the street, he would have thought it an inconsequential alleyway, used to keep wheelie bins, but further down the sign of the pharmacy could be seen, and with renewed vigour the pair lumbered on towards it. Luna ran ahead and peeked into the windows. She looked back at Jon and waved before testing the door and disappearing inside. Jon quickened his pace, eager to get away from any more danger. As he approached the building, he was surprised to see the front windows still intact. The looting of the day's prior had left most shopfronts smashed in. This one must have been forgotten about.

Luna held the door open as he and Efi dragged Samson inside then ran ahead, moving aside the larger debris as they lugged him in. They spotted the service counter across the shop floor and hauled him behind it, laying him gently on the floor. Luna peered nervously over the desk, keeping watch while Jon and Efi sprang into action.

"How much blood has he lost?" asked Efi.

Jon looked nervously at the trail of blood on the floor, then back at Samson. "I don't know. A lot? Maybe too much."

"Shit," she hissed, disappearing into the storeroom behind the counter. After a few seconds of rummaging noises, she reappeared with a box full of first aid tools, bandages and antibacterial wipes. "Get him cleaned and wrapped up. I need to find something to stop the bleeding." She dumped the box next to Jon and dived back into the storeroom.

Luna hopped down from the counter and she and Jon quickly set to work. Using scissors, Jon cut away Samson's shirt, revealing his torso. Dark purple and blue welts covered his chest and abdomen. Fresh blood continued to drip from his nose and mouth. "Wipes aren't gonna help here," he whispered to himself.

"Huh?" piped up Luna.

"Nothing, don't worry."

"Is he dying?"

"I don't know."

Luna was around the counter now, leaning over Jon's shoulder. "Ew! He looks fucked!"

Jon ushered her away. "Don't look at that. Go sit over there or sumat. Tell you what, keep an eye out for us."

She ignored him and returned to the counter.

Efi reappeared with more boxes, muttering to herself as she examined what looked to be an instruction booklet, her eyes straining against the darkness.

"What's that?" asked Jon, glancing up as he bandaged Samson's shoulder.

"It's something to slow down the bleeding. Open his mouth, please."

Jon obliged and held Samson's mouth open as Efi snapped off the top of a small ampoule of liquid and tipped it in. "Massage his throat," she instructed. "Make sure he doesn't choke." Jon rubbed at Samson's throat until he coughed and gurgled the liquid down. He glanced up at Efi. "What was that?"

Efi opened another ampoule. "Coagulant, and not enough of it. The military developed this stuff a few years ago to stop soldiers bleeding to death. Obviously, it didn't work that well, so the NHS got the rest of the stock. It's like trying to plug the Titanic with a bottle cork. We'll just have to see if it helps slow things down."

Jon glanced back at Samson's ruined torso. "I'm not sure anything's gonna make a difference at this point." He shifted uncomfortably on the spot, lowering his voice. "Is he going to survive this?"

"He might if we can get the bleeding to stop."

"He's going to die," said Luna. "Look at him."

Efi emptied the second ampoule into Samson's mouth and massaged his throat. "Maybe you could try helping instead of making comments?"

Luna scowled in response. "You're wasting time when we could be escaping."

"Child, he saved your life!"

"I'm just saying, we don't know what kind of poison that is, and they could be coming after us any minute!"

Jon stood and put up his hands. "Woah, woah, woah. Come on, now. Luna, just stay over there for now, alright? Tell us if anything's coming."

Luna sauntered back around the counter to lean against the other side. Jon returned to the floor. "She's got a point, Eff. You just said it yourself. We could be trying to plug the Titanic here. I don't want to leave him behind, but…"

Efi slammed her hands on the floor, tears erupting from her eyes. "Just shut up and help me!" She looked at him and suddenly he felt like the smallest man in the world.

"We need to help everyone we can," she sobbed. "You think this isn't important? We could be all that's left. And he helped us. We look out for each other. The least I can do is try to help him."

Jon's thoughts turned to Caede and Kai. *Shit.*

"I know," said Jon. "I'm sorry."

"I'm a nurse, Jon. I'm supposed to be able to help people, and I feel so useless!"

Jon leaned forward, taking her shoulders in his hands. "You're not useless. I wouldn't be here without you."

"Stop being so loud," said Luna. "Someone's going to hear us."

She was right. The dragon and his crew of freaks could be the least of their worries for all they knew. What if there were others worse than them? He thought of the men who chased them into the underground, the spider, and the things in the tunnels. Were all the other survivors like them? If it was a virus, was their little group somehow immune? Thoughts buzzed and flitted through his mind.

"Why didn't they chase us?" Luna asked.

"Huh?"

Luna glanced down from the counter and repeated her question. "The monsters. Why didn't they chase us?"

"They didn't need to," replied Jon.

Luna cocked an eyebrow, turning briefly away from her post. "Why?"

"What do you mean?" said Efi.

"I think I know what creature it came from," said Jon, unwrapping some fresh bandage. "Now, hear me out, 'cause this is gonna sound a bit out there. I watched this nature documentary a while back, and these huge lizards were on it. Komodo dragons, the presenter said. In the documentary, they'd bite something and let it go. They've got venom, right? They bite their prey and just let it run off. They don't need to chase it, they can just follow the scent, take their time, wait for the prey to die. The fella back there reminded me of one. He bit Samson and just let him go. And the blokes in the tunnel–remember what they said? They were talking about a dragon."

Jon paused, contemplating.

"They're waiting," he said. "For Samson to kick it, then they can pick us off easy peasy. Samson's too much for them to fight alive."

"Go back to what you said about Komodo dragons," said Efi.

"What about them?"

"They're animals–real animals."

"Right," said Jon. "What are you saying?"

Efi collected herself and returned to Samson, checking the bruises on his body.

"I think the mutations come from animal DNA." she replied. "The mutations in the patients we saw were all animalistic in nature."

"Like spider girl."

"Yeah."

From the floor, Samson stirred. He coughed and groaned, trying to turn himself over.

"What's going on?"

The three whipped their heads around.

Efi let out a gasp. "Oh, thank God. We thought you were dead!"

Samson tried to turn himself over. "I feel like I've been hit by a bus."

"Do you remember what happened?" Efi asked, as she dropped to inspect his shoulder. Suddenly, she stopped. "Jon…look at this."

Jon shifted himself closer to Samson. Around the puncture sites, the blood was coagulating and hardening, forming scabs right in front of his eyes.

"What the fuck?"

Samson waved at the pair dismissively. "I'm fine, I'm fine. Don't worry about it."

Jon sat quietly in disbelief. "How?"

"Huh?"

"How are you fine? Mate, you've bled enough to fill a pool!"

Samson coughed again, spitting a glob of bloody phlegm onto the vinyl floor. "I think it's this thing. It does something to you."

Jon snorted. "Does what? Turn you into fucking Superman?"

Samson made a sound that could have been a chuckle if he hadn't also been coughing his lungs up. "Sort of."

"You know what? I believe you. The shit I've seen today, I'll believe anything." He stood up, dusted his legs with his hands, and stretched. "We should get going before your mate and his gang show up."

"Not just yet!" Efi's hand shot up in a gesture to stop Jon. She looked at Samson and pointed sternly. "You need to rest for a minute, because you say you're fine, but your body says otherwise."

Then she pointed at Jon. "He'll need sugar, salts, and hydration before we can move. Can I trust that to you?"

"I don't need it," Samson said, but Jon was already out the door.

Stepping out into the alleyway, he glanced left and right, checking the dead streets for any signs of movement. Satisfied, he headed towards a small supermarket across the road. The sky, empty of stars thanks to the wintry cloud cover and streetlamps, lay like a dark blanket over the stark black blocks of the buildings. Jon shivered and continued on.

The shards of what remained of the windows crunched under his feet as he hopped over the low window ledge of the supermarket. At first glance, most of the shelves stood bare. He grabbed a basket, walked over to one of the aisles and stopped, the smell of rotting fruit and vegetables filling his nose. Recoiling, he retreated and headed instead to the chilled goods areas.

Pacing the aisles, he checked for anything that might still be edible. The meat aisles were completely empty, except for some torn packaging and the small bones of what could have been chicken carcasses scattered across the floor. Jon kept moving.

He seized a couple of large bottles of water, then headed to the snack and confectionery aisles. Luckily, the shelves were still stocked enough for Jon to grab something to eat for everyone, including some chocolate for Efi. He had no idea if she even liked chocolate, but it might make an acceptable peace offering for his earlier transgression. *Can't go wrong with chocolate*, he thought. The alcohol aisles were empty, short of a lonely-looking bottle of supermarket brand red wine. He took it.

Once the basket was full, he headed back to the front of the store. A fleeting thrill of mischief rushed over him as he bypassed the tills without paying for his goods. Just as he neared the main entrance to the building, the jarring crunch of glass underfoot somewhere nearby cut through the air. Jon darted to the nearest till and ducked down, his breath caught in his throat.

"Hello?"

The voice sounded female and young, high-pitched and soft. He left the basket on the floor and cautiously looked around the side of the till to see a young woman with thick black hair and dark brown eyes standing at the entrance, a cricket bat in her hand with nails sticking out of it.

He waved awkwardly. "Uh, hi."

The woman slowly raised the bat in response.

"I won't hurt you," said Jon, arms raised in a gesture of peace as he stepped out from the till. "Look, I'm unarmed, love. Just another survivor."

"That's what the wolves said," she replied coldly, the cricket bat pointed at him. "Who are you?"

"Jon, just Jon. I'm human…. Did you say wolves?"

"Okay, Just Jon, I'm Nila. And yes, I said wolves. They look like men, but they act like wolves, preying on people like animals."

"Five of them, right? I know who you mean."

She nodded. "They said they just wanted to talk to me. Luckily, my dad's got a gun. They ran off pretty quick after he aimed it at them."

"Smart man. He still about?"

"Why do you want to know?"

Jon kept his hands up. "It's not good for a lass to be travelling alone right now, is all."

"Good thing I'm not alone then, isn't it?"

Jon heard a metallic click from somewhere behind him. Despite the frosty air, beads of sweat began forming on his forehead. He gulped.

"Look, uh, Nila, is it? I'm a little pressed for time, so why don't I just let you go on your way and I'll go on mine? How's that sound?"

The woman's face remained impassive as she lowered the bat. "Alright. I need to keep moving, anyway. Is there anything left to eat in here?"

"Just junk food; all the fresh stuff's gone off," said Jon. "But it'll do if you're hungry. I'm surprised the, uh, creatures haven't eaten it all."

"They won't eat that stuff," said Nila. "I saw a group of them trying some and they just spat it out. I don't think they can eat it."

"Sure it's not just personal preference?"

"No. I heard one of them say 'oh, I love popcorn' and then started heaving after they tried eating some."

"More for us then I guess," said Jon.

"Yeah. Well, it was nice meeting you, Just Jon," she replied. "No offence, but I'm going to watch you leave before I continue. You can take your basket; we won't rob you. We're not animals just yet."

Jon slowly picked up the basket and began walking towards Nila. As he passed her, he quietly asked, "those wolf men, d'you know which way they were heading?"

"The last time I saw them," Nila replied, "they were chasing some poor blonde girl into a shop in Lewisham. That was yesterday. I didn't wait around to find out what happened to her.

27

Confessions

Jon returned to the pharmacy and began handing out the food. Efi accepted Jon's peace offering of chocolate. The group sat in a small circle, accompanied by torchlight and the sounds of packets ruffling.

Jon quietly excused himself to the back to drink the wine, hands shaking as he opened the bottle. He expected the familiar warm haze to wash over him as he chugged, but it didn't come. Suddenly, his stomach lurched. Before he knew it, he was bent over, gagging and spitting wine over the floor.

"Jon?" It was Efi. She looked at him, then the half empty bottle still in his hand.

"Aye."

"Are you okay?"

He daren't look up. He just nodded and wiped his face with the back of his sleeve. "Jus' needed a drink is all."

"How often do you need a drink?"

"Not often. Promise. Look, Efi, I'll be fine."

"If you are alcohol dependent, you shouldn't go long periods without a drink. You could do more damage and–"

"Efi, love, I'm fine. Jus' leave us alone for a minute, alright?"

"Okay. But if you start getting bad, please just tell me. I'm a nurse. I can help."

He nodded silently, and satisfied with that response, Efi left. He stayed kneeling in his own bile for a minute before getting back up.

Returning to the others, he plucked up a cereal bar from the basket and chewed, eager to get the taste of cheap wine and vomit out of his mouth.

Samson was already sitting up–still looking peaky, but far more alive than he should have been. It reminded him of Kai. The injury was serious enough for an adult, let alone a child, but the kid was almost fine, as if he'd only lost a finger. Jon hadn't dared say that to Caede. Of course, she wasn't stupid. She must have been thinking the same thing.

And just like Kai, there was Samson, alive and well, following a mortal wound. Losing enough blood to fill a reservoir. The parallels were troubling.

"Ah, shit," said Samson, wiping his mouth. "I thought Sigma would stop this from happening."

"What?" said Efi.

"Huh?" replied Samson.

"What's Sigma?" said Efi.

Samson waved a hand weakly. "Ah, it's nothing. I'm just talking shit."

"What's Sigma, Samson?"

The irritation in Efi's voice rose as the question left her mouth.

Samson closed his eyes for a moment and rubbed his face. "I was wondering when the best time would be to tell you. Before I do, though, I need you to promise something."

Jon frowned. "Can't promise anything I haven't heard, mate."

Samson let out a sigh, then chuckled. "Don't give me that. Listen. Kalinov ain't gonna just let me go. You need to promise if anything happens to me, you'll get what's in my bag to the right person."

"Who's the right person?" said Efi.

"Justine Pearson," said Samson. "She's an old mate of mine—well, I say, mate. More of an acquaintance."

Samson nodded at his rucksack. Jon held it up, then slid it over to him. Samson took it and rifled through the main compartment, taking out some papers and a small metal lock box. He flicked through the papers, separated two sheets from the pile, and passed them to Efi.

"No offence to the rest of you," he said, "but she's the only one here who might understand."

Efi took the sheets and began reading, her brow low in concentration as she scanned through.

"What does this mean?" she finally asked.

"I found these in the lab I was working at before all this kicked off."

"You never said you worked in a lab," said Jon.

"You never asked."

"Oh no, don't give me that shit. You know way more than you're letting on here."

"Who is Terry?" Efi asked, eyes narrowed at Samson.

"Oh yeah," said Jon. "That dragon guy said Terry!"

Samson glanced away, avoiding her gaze as the words left his mouth. "He's the one responsible for all this."

Jon turned to Efi to see her standing up and shaking, the paper screwed up in her clenched fist, her expression a mixture of horror and rage.

"You knew?" she whispered through gritted teeth.

"Yeah."

"Did you help make this thing?"

"Nah. I only studied it. I observed it in a lab setting."

He looked up at Efi pleadingly. "I'll tell you everything I know, alright?"

"Why bother?" Efi snapped. "Look around you. The damage has been done!"

"No, no." Jon stood up and paced the floor behind the counter. "I think we need to know."

"Where d'ya want me to start?" asked Samson.

"I don't know," Jon seethed. "The fucking beginning would be nice. And you better make it quick, 'cause your mate's probably gonna come find us soon, and I don't wanna be sitting here, waiting for him with my thumb up my arse, ready to be lunch!"

"Alright. I'll give you the short version. Like I said, I worked in a lab. We were commissioned by one of these ethics' organisations,

SETA. They investigate reports of animal cruelty, unethical testing, GMOs–all that shit. We got a tip-off from this guy, Terry. He said his team was working on some new technology. Xeno-technology, called it Sigma Delta Tau. It's supposed to be a new form of gene therapy. You know, make people better, stronger. Fix eyesight, cure diabetes, regrow lost limbs, everything. A real panacea."

Samson paused and rolled his eyes.

"So, earlier this year, we found out that it's a military-funded project. Top secret. Not only that, they were testing this stuff on civilians without consent. Unwilling participants. Apparently, they tricked some poor souls into believing it could cure their cancer. To be fair, the finished product probably could–from what I saw."

"What happened?" asked Efi.

Samson rubbed his eyes, suddenly appearing exhausted. He kept his head aimed at the floor, his face hidden behind his hand.

"They died, and it was all covered up. Incomplete strain, you know? I guess Terry finally had enough, because he got in contact with the organisation. They've got some tactical division–or so they call it–and they broke into his lab, took some samples and sent them to us. That's where I come in. See, this thing, whatever it is, is at DNA level. They used lab made viruses as a delivery mechanism; some synthetic version of Ebola, I reckon..."

He stopped to take a breath. Jon found himself sitting on the floor next to Efi. Luna was cross-legged on the counter, watching Samson intently.

"Sigma Delta Tau, strain 13, does this," he said, gesturing at himself with a wave. "Makes you better than you were before. You can pick and choose the DNA, customise it, like CRISPR. But, unlike other gene therapies, this can't fix itself. It doesn't need multiple treatments. If I have kids, they'll have my new DNA. You get me? What got leaked," he gestured to the café and the air around him. "Was Sigma strain 12."

"What's CRISPR?" Said Luna.

"Ah, that's just a gene editor–it's like scissors for DNA," said Samson.

Jon felt his fist curl into a ball. His jaw had tightened without him realising, and his teeth ached. He caught a glimpse at Efi as she stared at Samson.

"Samson," she said. "How exactly did this 'Sigma 12' get out?"

"I don't know," said Samson.

"What do you mean, you don't know?"

"You need to understand," said Samson, holding his hands up. "I didn't know anything about this until I got the samples. And all I did was test them on some mice. Same thing that happened to everyone else, happened to me. 'Cept I managed to infect myself with thirteen before I passed out. I woke up surrounded by my dead colleagues… and made a run for it. Everything I know is in this bag and in that lock box. That organisation was investigating this for months. We only had it a few weeks. Our senior virologist couldn't even tell me exactly how this thing works. It's something we've never seen before. Completely new technology. Somehow it got out."

"You said it was a virus," said Jon.

"Nah, I said it uses viruses as a delivery mechanism. It piggybacks off synthetic viruses to spread more easily. The thing itself is like programmable DNA."

"And you injected yourself with it?!"

"Only as a last resort, mate. Thirteen stops you getting the other one."

"Have you got any more of it?" said Luna

Samson shook his head. "I did, but it's gone now."

"How the fuck did it get out, Samson?" said Efi.

"I told you, I don't know! Maybe someone didn't clean up the lab properly. Maybe Terry did it himself. But I can't ask him, 'cause he's dead."

Efi bristled with rage. "Everyone's dead, you fucking idiot!"

Samson sat quietly, too tired to react. "I'm sorry," he whispered.

"Yeah, well," said Efi. "It's done now."

"I think it's better like this," said Luna from the counter.

"What?"

Luna turned her face to the window. "People are evil. They just hurt each other, anyway. And the planet. At least now it'll get a chance to heal itself."

"You don't know what you're saying," said Efi.

Luna shrugged and continued looking out.

"There's more," said Samson.

"What?" said Jon.

Samson tilted his head towards Efi. "Your leg still hurting?"

Efi looked confused for a moment, then looked down. "No," she said, "it's not. It feels fine."

Samson smiled. "I gave you something to stop it."

Efi unwrapped the bandage around her leg. Jon shuffled over to her to see. The stitches were still in place, but the flesh had completely re-sealed itself, healing so rapidly that all that remained of the wound was a faint, red line. Jon stared, open-mouthed at it.

Efi glared at Samson. "What did you do to me?"

Samson shifted his weight and met Efi's eye this time. "Sigma-13. It's more aggressive than twelve. More predictable. Safer. You were gonna change. I saved your life."

Efi said nothing. She just stared at her leg.

After eating and waiting for Samson to be able to stand without swaying, the group set off. Jon was eager to be moving again. What Nila had said back at the supermarket troubled him, and he felt a renewed urgency to catch up with Caede and the boy. He checked his pocket for the ring, rubbing his thumb over its edge.

The group scurried along the main road, sticking to the edges of the buildings and avoiding the streetlights as much as possible. Samson limped, supported by Efi, as they pressed onwards. Luna and Jon scouted ahead, each holding a torch, checking the shops and cafés for signs of life, or anything that could make the journey easier. Sweat dripped into Jon's eyes, and his shoulders ached under the weight of the already full rucksack. But he was willing to put up with it if it meant finding something useful. A decent compass, for one. And where was his knife? Had he dropped it? Or was it in the bag he'd left with Caede? He'd have to pick up a new one from somewhere.

The road widened and split into two as they left the suburbs and reached Lewisham high street. There was much of the same here as the other shopping areas they'd passed through. London, he thought, seemed to be made up of small towns and villages, all pushed into a circle, and each of them had their own version of a 'high street'. Lewisham had an ancient church sitting right next to a Taco Bell. Jon wondered how long Taco Bell had been selling in the UK. Wasn't that an American restaurant?

He was wondering if there was anything worth eating inside, when a streak of bright red on the pavement caught his eye.

"That's fresh," he said. It surprised him that he'd said it out loud.

Luna was on the other side of the street, inspecting the contents of an abandoned handbag. "What?" she called.

"There's blood over here," he said.

There was a streak, or rather, a smear–smear was the best word for it, because it looked as if some poor sod had dragged themselves along for a while. Jon looked around, but couldn't see a body that he could confidently say it belonged to. It was coming from inside a large department store further up the road. A weight settled in Jon's stomach. *Some poor blonde girl.*

"Shit."

He followed the smear until he reached the store entrance. It was a shop in Lewisham. The weight grew, settling itself further into his guts. He stepped over the threshold of the shattered front doors and looked around. The shop floor opened out into sections: men's clothing and footwear, gifts, tech, a sign for the café…. The blood was thicker here, and in drips, little ruby droplets forming patterns on the floor, weaving between the clothes lines.

"Jon?" It was Luna, stepping into the store.

"There's more here," he called. "Look!"

"It's just blood," said Luna. "There's blood everywhere."

"This is fresh," said Jon. "Look at it!"

An urgency tapped at the back of his head.

"Jon?" Efi now, with Samson in tow. "Are you okay? What's going on?"

He didn't reply. The blood led a path towards a set of escalators in the centre of the shop floor. Jon followed it and glanced around, his eye catching a pile of crumpled fabric on the floor. It was a denim jacket. He knelt down to inspect it. The jacket was worn, old, and dirty. It looked just like Tara's old jacket; the same one he'd given to Caede. *Poor blonde girl.* The words echoed again, and his chest tightened. He brought it up to his nose and sniffed. The familiar scent of his own laundry detergent, stale sweat, and dust hit his nose. Tara's old jacket.

"Jon?" called Efi again.

"Over here," he replied, voice cracking.

He turned the jacket over. It was Tara's jacket, alright, but Caede had been wearing it. Maybe she'd found something warmer?

"Hey." It was Luna, standing just behind him, head cocked curiously at the jacket.

"What's that?" she asked.

"My ex-girlfriend's…" he said.

"There's some jeans up there," she said.

"What?"

Jon stood and looked up. Luna extended her arm towards the escalator, pointing at another pile of fabric halfway between them and the second floor. "Just there," she said.

He followed the steps up, ascending the escalator until he was eye level with the pile. She was right, it was a pair of jeans, ripped at the knees, with a small, white paint stain on the left leg. Tara had been painting the hallway that time and accidentally splashed some on herself. The same jeans Caede had been wearing. He picked those up, too, hands shaking.

"Stay there," he said to Luna. "I'm gonna look up here for a sec."

"Okay."

The first floor, women's wear, opened out into clothing sections, formal wear, sports, casual, accessories and footwear all neatly in their own spaces, signs hanging above them.

Jon reached the shop floor, taking a few steps before almost slipping on something soft underfoot. He tilted his head down to see a single pair of women's underwear laying discarded on the floor. He moved his foot aside and stood, staring at them for a moment, before crouching to inspect them further. The underwear was old, faded from white to off-grey, with the lace beginning to unravel on the leg holes. They had recently been worn.

A high-pitched ringing filled his head as he stared. A foul taste hit the back of his throat, and his vision blurred. He turned immediately and retreated down the steps. Luna, Efi and Samson were waiting for him at the bottom of the escalator. Efi stood, looking up at him with concern. Luna and Samson were sitting on the floor, leaning against the escalator wall.

"What is it?" asked Luna.

"Jon?" said Efi. "Are you feeling alright?"

"Caede was here," he said. His voice sounded distant, quiet, like he was floating away from his own body. Nausea followed, dragging him back down.

"Your girlfriend?" Efi gently took the clothing from him. "You sure?"

Jon felt his teeth press together. "Yes, I'm sure. I gave her that jacket. She was wearing those jeans when we got separated."

"You don't know that for sure," said Efi.

Jon's face flushed with heat. "She was here! She was right here, in the clothes I gave her! Those bastards chased her in here and..." he couldn't finish the sentence. His skull throbbed. He pressed his fingers into his temples, massaging it away.

"There's no blood on these," she said, turning the jeans over in her hands. "Maybe she stopped to change clothes?"

"But why?" said Jon. "The clothes she had on were perfectly fine. Why would she stop just to change? She was with her brother, and your doctor mate–why didn't they change? Where's their clothes…. And wouldn't they be in a pile all together?"

"Jon," said Efi. "Calm down, okay? Let's have a look around. We can figure it out. I'm sure she's fine."

"While you guys look," said Luna. "I'm going to get some new stuff."

"Get us a hoodie, would ya?" said Samson.

Jon and Efi headed to the first floor. She inspected the underwear, her expression contemplative.

"These are old," was all she said.

Quietly, his face close to Efi, Jon said, "When I went to get food earlier, there was a girl in the supermarket."

"Another survivor?"

"Aye, had her family with her. Said her name was Nila. Anyway, she said she saw a group of men chasing a lass into a shop just like this one. She said the men were like wolves."

Efi nodded solemnly. "You're sure it was this shop?"

"Know of any other department stores 'round here?"

"No idea. It's where posh people shop."

"What if she was talking about Caede?"

"Pretty big coincidence, if she was. What are the odds of this random girl seeing her?"

"And what if it's not, eh?"

They continued up to the second and third floors, each time finding nothing, so they made their way back to the ground level. Samson had managed to pull himself up, and he leaned against the wall as he removed a large hoodie from its hanger, chuckling to himself.

"Might as well get some fresh drip while we're here!"

"Oh my God, you're old," said Luna. "No one says drip anymore."

Using the wall as balance, she tugged on a pair of expensive-looking men's jeans. A designer T-shirt and hoodie lay on the floor next to her.

"There's women's clothing upstairs if you want to change," suggested Efi.

"These have bigger pockets."

Jon ignored the others and continued around the floor until he reached the escalator that led to the basement floor: Home appliances, kitchenware. A bloody trail, and the tang of iron, marked the descent. Swallowing the knot in his throat, he followed.

It was a massacre. Red was everywhere, covering the display tables, chunks of pink and white viscera splattered on the floor between them. Two bodies lay stinking in their own pools of congealing blood. Jon doubled over, heaving. He spat bile at the floor before recovering and psyching himself up to have a proper look.

One had half his head caved in. A heavy-looking skillet rested next to the body. Judging by the blood and bits covering it, that must have been the murder weapon. The other was lying face down by a display table covered in broken bottles and storage jars. But there was no Caede, and no sign of the other men in the pack.

He started searching, sweeping through the shop floor, finding no sign of her body. There were only drops of blood, each following the other in a jagged line between the displays. There was a bloody handprint. Some red smears. He kneeled down and looked under the tables and shelves. All he could see were patterns of disturbed dust. Caede had been here, he was sure of it. Something terrible had happened to her here. He pictured her being dragged away by the pack as they laughed. In desperation, he threw a table aside and inspected the floor underneath. More blood splatter, but no sign of Caede.

"Where the fuck is she?" he shouted at nothing.

No answer came. The bodies of the men, were they the same men who tried to take Efi? Their bodies were right there. All... How many were there? Five? One had been caught in the tunnels, he was sure of it. Did that leave four or three? He couldn't remember. And where was the boy? And Efi's doctor friend? *Think. Think!*

"Jon?" It was Efi, standing by the escalator, her eyes on the bodies.

"Down here."

"Shit," said Efi. "What on earth happened here?"

"God knows."

"Are you alright?"

"Do I look alright?" said Jon, gesturing at the bodies. "No, I'm not fucking alright!"

She fell quiet, and he stood up, annoyed. Suddenly she seemed small and timid, something he'd never seen before. So far, he'd only seen Efi, the straight-talking, no bullshit survivor. This person wasn't her, just another stranger looking at him with pity and fear. He didn't have time for this. He needed to find Caede.

"Jon?"

"What?"

Efi paused, then said gently, "I don't think she's here."

Her hands were raised and outstretched towards him as she edged closer, all tentative, as if he was some kind of lunatic. Like she was afraid, or saw him as a child in the midst of a meltdown. In an instant the anger dissipated, and a weight settled in his chest, pulling him to the floor. Efi must have run over to him, because she was in front of him now, hands on his face, her eyes big and dewy. The tears came in heaves and lurches. He couldn't stop them. All he could do was sink further into the floor until his head met Efi's knees. She let him rest there, stroking his hair and cooing softly at him like a baby. He cried, then screamed all his pain and anger into her lap, until his lungs burned and his head pounded. It wasn't just over Caede. He barely knew the girl. It was everything. It was Tara leaving. It was his dad dying. It was not knowing if his brother, or his friends, were alive. It was being so fucking useless that he couldn't even kill himself properly.

Finally, throat hoarse and eyes raw, he sat up.

"I'm so sorry, Jon," said Efi.

He kept his head down, focusing on breathing. "It's okay," he said, finally. "I didn't really know her that well. I just…. It doesn't matter. Jus' would have been nice if they'd made it."

"Oh, yeah. Her brother. I remember you saying."

"Yeah. A wee little lad, looked like he'd keel over in a breeze."

"Maybe they're not here because they escaped? You never know. If she was with Ravi and Holly, well…"

Jon looked back over at the bodies. "What was it that those blokes said to us before they chased us into the underground?"

Efi grimaced. "They wanted who they thought was your woman."

"Yeah. If there's no sign of Kai and your doctor friend, then…"

"Then they must have separated them somehow."

"Or they've been taken, too."

Jon stood up and walked over to the bodies. He'd not seen any of them for long enough to recognise them individually, but their shapes were familiar. The one with his face missing was tall and broad-shouldered. The one on the floor was shorter, stocky too, and starting to bloat. He kicked that one hard, and it felt like kicking lead. It felt good. He kicked again, just because he could, and something fell off the corpse. Jon knelt to look at it and saw that it was a Swiss Army knife. He picked it up and turned it over in his hands, eyes widening.

"Shit," he said. "No way."

"What is it?" asked Efi.

"It's my knife. Caede had it in the rucksack I gave her. She must have used it…. Do you think Ravi could have helped her? Fought these guys off?"

Efi shook her head. "He's too soft for that."

Jon nodded, slipping the knife into his pocket.

"There's no way Caede did this by herself," he said.

"Looks like she put up a hell of a fight, though." Efi looked around at the men. "She wasn't turned, was she?"

"They were both still human when I met them."

"The people I saw turned gradually."

"She's not one of them, Efi."

He must have sounded angry again, because she fell quiet once more. He wondered why he was getting so many chances. Tara would have screamed at him by now, slapped him, made him wish he'd never been born. It was refreshing to be feeling something again, to get angry, to care. Maybe Efi knew that.

Crying's not going to fix anything, lad. His father's voice this time.

Fuck off.

That felt good. The anger had felt good, too. But it left so quickly, and swept through him like a hurricane, leaving him exhausted and ashamed in its wake.

The pair continued searching for any evidence that Caede had left alive, finding nothing. If she had died in there, her body would still be there, surely, but it wasn't. Either way, nothing good could have happened. Jon was relying on his memory of the men, and how many there should have been. There were only two bodies, and there had been a whole gang chasing them into the underground. Did the creatures only get the one guy in the underground, or both? There was no way that girl could fight off a gang of those monsters, not alone. She had to be dead, or worse. He didn't want to think about it anymore.

"I give up."

He stood and started walking towards the escalator. Efi followed, trotted behind him.

"Jon?" she said. "What are you doing?"

"I'm done," he said without looking back. "I only wanted to give the girl back her ring and I can't even do that. So I'm done. I'm out."

"What are you talking about?"

He stopped and turned to Efi. "I'm going home."

"What?" she said, pulling a face. "I don't know if you've noticed, but there's not really a home to go back to. We need to keep going and catch up with Ravi and Holly."

"No, you need to catch up with Ravi."

"For God's sake, Jon, stop being a child! We need you with us. We need to stick together. And you said so yourself, you don't really know this girl. You've known me longer than her. We've already survived so much together. And what about Luna, and Samson? Doesn't that mean something?"

"Look. I don't care. I just want to go home now."

"What have you got there, eh? Stuff? You're going to risk your life just to sit at home by yourself with some stuff?"

"No."

Jon turned and kept walking. Efi ran in front and stopped him, her hands resting flat on his shoulders.

"You think you're the only one who's lost everything, Jon? What about Holly? What if she was with her? You think I'd give up if there was a chance to save her?"

"Your girlfriend's dead, Efi."

Efi's face fell. "What?"

Jon let out a sigh. "I saw another woman in the garage when we woke up, but she was already dead. Red hair, blue eyes, right?"

Efi's eyes widened, filling with tears. She brought her hand to her mouth and looked up at him with an expression worse than anger or accusation.

"I'm sorry," he said. "I didn't know it was her, and at the time—"

"It's okay," she whispered, her face aimed at the floor. "I understand. I think…I already knew..."

"I have to go."

"Jon, please. Stay with us. Come on, we need you."

"No, you don't," he said, his voice quiet.

"You're not leaving," she replied. "I won't let you."

He gently pushed her aside and headed up the escalator, passing Samson and Luna on the ground floor without a word.

"Jon?" Luna's voice.

"Yo, Johnny?" called Samson. "Where're you going, bro?"

Jon ignored them and kept walking. He was going to keep walking until he got home, keep walking until he reached the roof, then he was going to walk right off the edge, like he should have done Saturday. All this effort, all this trying…. It was just a delay. A distraction from the inevitable.

28

The Chase

The others didn't follow. *Good,* he thought. He left the store in a daze, and walked slowly, weaving around the cars and bodies, heading back towards the city centre with little regard for hiding or being quiet. About ten minutes in, a thirst struck him—the familiar kind, and he considered breaking into an off licence before deciding against it. It wouldn't make a difference anyway, not now. He kept moving.

An hour passed before he heard the voices.

A male voice rose, pleading. "You need to believe me! We really did. We had her!".

A female voice shot back, accusing and furious, intensified by a thick Eastern European accent. "You're going to stand there and lie to us? To him?"

"I'm not lying! Swear down! Look at me! Look what she did to me…."

Jon darted behind some parked cars. He lay flat against the pavement and watched from under the cars as some figures came into view. Immediately, he recognised the dragon, his colossal frame towering above the rest of the group. They were confronting a man, small and skinny, with brown hair covering his body, his nose an elongated snout like a dog's. Jon recognised him as one of the men who had chased him and Efi into the underground.

He was clutching his stomach and stood hunched over, panting with effort. Blood dripped from a wound somewhere under his arm and ran down his legs. The man held up one hand in surrender and kneeled in the group's presence, seemingly in equal measures repentance and exhaustion.

Jon counted them. The woman was small, lean and slick, her face short and wide, with large eyes reminiscent of a gecko. She had a short blonde bob, cut sharp and slicked back behind her ears. Then there was another, a male, stout and covered in spiny scales. There were three more behind those two. One was the snake man. Six of them in total. Jon tried to remember how many of them had been at the hospital.

The woman who had spoken before stepped forward again, words heavy as she spat them at the man.

"Are you telling me you idiots couldn't even catch one single woman?"

"She must have been turned already," replied the man. "She was too fast for us..."

"So, what you're saying to me is that you're fucking useless. Because that is what I'm hearing. We saved your miserable lives, and this is how you thank us?"

The dragon stepped forward and spoke, his voice a deep, low rumble, somehow barely audible, yet it carried across the street as clear as a roar.

"That will do, Alina."

The woman fell silent, lowering her head in reverence, retreating behind him.

"She killed Lee?" he asked the smaller man.

"Yeah! She beat his fucking skull in! I couldn't stop her! She stabbed me! Look..."

Jon listened to the exchange, staring open-mouthed in wonder. There was no way Caede could have done that to grown men. It was her against three. Three of those monsters. He thought of the bodies. Lee, was that the taller one? He was the one outside the tube station with the shit-eating grin on his face. Jon smiled at the thought. The arsehole had it coming, certainly.

"Where is she now?" asked the dragon.

"I don't know...she left. Got up and walked off, talking to herself about a station."

"He must mean Blackheath Station, or Lewisham," said Alina.

The dragon nodded, hand resting on his chin. "Kelsey," he said.

One of the others, a tall woman with long, black hair and pale, almost white skin, raised her head and stepped forward. "Yes?"

"Run ahead, get her scent and see what you can find. Seems we're about to get a new addition to the ranks."

The group smiled at each other. One hopped a little, clapping their hands together like an excited teenager. Kelsey grinned and took off, running so fast that in an instant she had disappeared from Jon's line of sight. The dragon returned his gaze to the man at his feet. "What about the other group?"

"We lost them in the underground," he replied, stammering. "The hive got 'em."

"Pity."

Jon lay in a daze. Caede was alive and heading out of London. She must have been following Kai and Ravi if she hadn't already caught up with them. His mind raced. Of course, she'd survived. How could he be so stupid? He pressed his fingers against the outline of the ring still in his pocket. Could he catch up with Efi and the others now?

A yelp and a crunch hit the air. Jon snapped out of his trance and turned back to the group. The small man lay in a heap on the road. The dragon stood over his body, dusting off his hands.

"Alina," he ordered, and she obeyed, stepping beside him. "Report back to Lev. I have the scent of the traitor and his pack. We will follow them and bring back the females. I will take care of the traitor personally."

"Of course. Be careful, my love," said Alina.

"I will."

The pair shared a kiss, and Alina left the group, running swiftly in the opposite direction. The dragon shook himself, raised his head to the air, and breathed in deeply. He lowered his head and exhaled, flicking out his tongue. It danced in the air before returning to his mouth, and he closed his eyes as if to register the new information. For an agonising second, he turned his head in the direction of the car. Jon froze and clamped his eyes shut. Finally, he heard the man's voice.

"Let's go."

Jon waited, breath held, until the group disappeared from view. Then, confident they were out of earshot, he scrambled to his feet. His head pounded as he tried to process what he'd just heard. The traitor? Did he mean Samson? And Caede was alive! Maybe not for much longer if he didn't do something.

He'd have to catch up with the others. Warn them. But Efi had the map, and he didn't know the area well enough to guess. London, sure, but where they were headed was outside. Kent, was it? Jon glanced around and noticed a Waterstones further along the road. He sprinted over to it and wrenched open the door, running around like a lunatic until he found the section for travel and map books. He grabbed one and rifled through it, swearing quietly at himself. He remembered the paper in his front pocket with the instructions from Ravi. He unfolded it, and finding the right page, ran a finger over the route. *Okay,* he thought, *this is a start.*

He left the store and started walking. He walked for an hour before stopping. His legs burned and his stomach ached with hunger. If he was going to catch up with the others, he needed to find a better way.

He frantically began looking into each of the car windows. *All the cars abandoned and not one of them has any keys? Come on!* He was about to give up when he glimpsed an old Mitsubishi Lancer parked neatly in a space next to the curb. He walked over and glanced inside. A bloated body lay curled up in the backseat, a set of keys and a large knife encased in their hands. The car itself must have been well loved, because it was in immaculate condition, its cherry red paint polished and gleaming. He'd always wanted to own one, but with his paltry graphic designer salary and the lack of parking on the road where he lived, he could never justify the cost. The closest thing he'd ever had to a powerful car was his father's thirty-year-old Subaru Impreza that didn't like being in second gear and always tugged slightly to the left, no matter how many garages he'd taken it to.

Jon opened the rear passenger door and fell backwards, heaving as the smell of concentrated death poured out into the air. For a split second, he thought about looking somewhere else. He turfed out the corpse, wrenching the keys from its fingers, and waited for the car to air out before jumping into the driver's seat. He glanced at the gear lever. It had been a while since he'd driven a manual, but, just like riding a bike, the muscle memory would kick in and he'd soon remember it again.

"Please let it have fuel," he whispered, turning the key in the ignition.

The car rumbled, sputtered, then roared into life, shaking itself off, as if it had been sitting there, bored out of its mind. The sound made him jump at first, and he wondered if the lizards would hear it and double back. *No point waiting*, he thought. An unexpected smile crept across his face as he checked the fuel gauge. Half a tank. Enough to get out of the city. Tentatively, he put the car into first gear and pressed his foot to the accelerator. The Lancer responded with a growl and a shudder from inside the bonnet, and it began to ease forward.

He tapped his pocket, checking for the outline of the ring. It was still there.

"Alright," he said. "Let's see those bastards catch this."

29

The Doorbell

Terry Howard, entry 29.10.2030

We're the rabbits now.

Blind, bleeding, suffering...mad. We finally became the victims of our own folly. We tried to play God, but therein lies the problem.

There isn't one.

It's all gone wrong. Oh God, it's all gone wrong... Lord knows how but they've unleashed it. It's all my fault. It's all my fault...

By the time you hear this... if anyone survives long enough to hear this, I will be... gone. I'll be gone. Samson, if you're watching this, if you access my daily logs—you know where to look—you'll find everything you need. I'm sure you'll have questions, but you won't get any more answers from me, I'm afraid.

I want everyone to know that what I did, I did to protect the people I care about. I did it to save people. I never meant for this to happen. I'm so, so sorry.

Forgive me.

Caede's eyes opened to a sliver of daylight resting across her face. She blinked, groaning, and turned away from it to see Kai standing in the doorway with a mix of confusion and disgust on his face. He wrinkled his nose.

"It's gone nine," he said. "Look. It's light outside!"

"Oh," said Caede, annoyed. "I didn't realise you had such important plans for today, your majesty!"

"God, you're so grumpy. You're like an old person!"

Ravi appeared behind him in the doorway. "Everything alright?"

"I'm fine," said Caede.

"Oh, good," said Ravi. He turned to Kai, still in the doorway. "I need to check your arm, Kai, and we need to take proper inventory of the food and supplies. If we're going to be staying here for a while, we need to make sure there's going to be enough for us to live on."

"Fine," said Caede, "but can I get dressed first?"

After the three had dressed and eaten, they headed outside to the gardens. They'd each borrowed a pair of wellington boots from the mudroom. It was less of a room, and more a large cupboard, for keeping the things you didn't want to bring into the main house, but couldn't stay outside. Back in London, Caede would have had to just put out some newspaper by the front door and hope that Kai remembered to take his shoes off before running straight up to his bedroom. A mudroom would have saved them from many arguments. But that was why the rich were so much happier, wasn't it? They had a room for their dirt. The less fortunate had to scrub it from the carpet.

She stepped out onto the patio to join Kai and Ravi, watching her breath dissipate into the chilled morning air. The sun brought with it a whisper of warmth, and she closed her eyes, taking it in and wishing she had a cigarette. A cigarette, her dressing gown and slippers, and a rusty old garden chair to sit on while she listened to the birds chirping out their morning hymns. But here, there was only silence. And no cigarette or rusty chair, just endless fields. Was this home now? In a week, or maybe even a month, would she be thinking fondly of a tiny patio for a garden, or the sounds of the morning traffic, or the constant reminders of her mother's absence in family photos, framed and lined along the walls at eye level? The tears should have come, but they didn't.

The first of the gardens was large and open plan, a family area dedicated to summer barbecues and children's play. The second, guarded by a gate and tall shrubs, was laid out like an allotment, with neat rows of plants hidden under a protective cover, two great water butts, and a greenhouse in the corner.

"This looks promising," said Ravi.

They moved through the allotment to the third garden and found another gate. This gate was padlocked, the key still jammed inside it. Security, clearly, was less of an issue in the countryside. Ravi unlocked the gate and they found themselves in a small field surrounded by low shrubs and a fence, with rows upon rows of solar panels on metal mounts standing in the centre.

"I didn't know this was here," said Ravi. "It explains a few things."

"Like what?" asked Caede.

"These panels probably generate electricity for the house. We have them at the hospital, though to be honest I never thought to ask how they worked, or even how much energy they produce."

Not knowing what to do with the solar panels, they left the field, locking the gate behind them, returning to explore the allotment. Caede inspected the shrubs that lined the land, finding a fence hidden behind the branches. That was good. It would keep out more than just a few nosy neighbours or unwanted pests. Not that she could see traces of either. There was only farmland on the other side.

She turned to find Ravi's head under the protective covering, inspecting the crops. Kai stood next to him, vacant and looking off into the distance. Despite the treatment and the blood transfusion, he still looked grey. Thinner than she remembered, sharper too, as if the events of the last few days had stripped him of the last of his puppy fat, and he'd been left with the sinewy form of a fledgling adult. Like his body was finally catching up with his mind. Kai had always been wiser than his years. Too often he was the mature one, and it left her frustrated and furious with herself.

"You okay?" she asked.

"I'm fine," he replied. "Just thought I heard something."

"I can't hear anything," she said. But she hadn't been listening for anything, so why would she?

"Yeah," he said. "It's probably nothing."

Ravi poked his head out from under the cover.

"I found a marrow, and some pumpkins," he said. "There's enough still here to see us through the next week. I'll see if I can roast this, or we could make a curry? There's rice in the pantry, and I'm certain I saw some recipe books in the kitchen. It shouldn't be too difficult to whip something up."

"Just one of the things we'll have to learn if we're going to survive here, I guess," said Caede.

"My thinking exactly," Ravi replied. "I don't think life will ever be the same, moving forward."

"Yeah," she said, her mind half elsewhere.

Kai and Ravi had headed to the library and the pair sat, taking up one of the olive-green leather armchairs each, their faces planted firmly in a book. Leaving them to it, Caede headed to the foyer, continuing up the central staircase to the second floor. For the first time in years, she had nothing to do, and no idea what to do. There was no routine here yet. She could join Ravi and Kai in the library, but she wasn't in the mood to read. All the evenings she'd spent studying had ruined the hobby for her, anyway.

She decided to check the bedrooms. In Kai's new room, she found his old bandages discarded in a pile by the bed. They would need to be boiled if he was to use them again, so she put them aside, making a mental note to heat some water. She gathered up the dirty clothes and headed to her room, then Ravi's, where she did the same. Laundry. A menial task, but necessary, and it might help clear her thoughts. She agonised over whether to just use the washing machine while they still had electricity, before deciding against it. It seemed wasteful and unnecessary. Armed with a pair of Marigolds and detergent, she stuffed the clothing into a basket that she found in the laundry room–the place had a laundry room too– and returned upstairs to the main bathroom.

The wound in her side burned with every step, and tugged too, as if it was about to split open again. Ravi had applied butterfly stitches to keep it closed. She wondered if it needed something stronger.

She dumped the clothing and a generous dose of the detergent into the bathtub and filled it with cold water. As she scrubbed, she wondered how long they would even have tap water, heating, or anything besides basic shelter. Well, this was a little more than basic shelter, but it wouldn't mean much without food and water. There were other bathrooms in the house. They could fill the bathtubs with water, keep a stock of it?

A sudden knock made her jump, and she turned to see Ravi idling in the doorway.

"I wondered where you'd gotten to," he said, smiling, glasses twirling in his hands. "Tea? I've put the kettle on."

She pulled off the gloves and set them on the edge of the tub. "Yeah, please. I'd love one."

"You shouldn't be doing that," said Ravi, pointing his glasses at the clothes. "You're still injured. You won't heal properly."

"Oh, I'm fine," she said, doing her best to sound chipper.

"Did you sleep okay?"

"Yeah, I did, thanks."

Ravi shifted his weight in the doorway. "I wanted to thank you for your company last night. I've always had trouble falling asleep, so I thought some light reading would help. Farha's another story. Her head hits the pillow, and she's out like a light…"

He laughed softly, then fell quiet.

"I know what you mean," Caede replied. "It's hard to fall asleep with everything that's happened."

Ravi nodded in response but said nothing.

The pair hovered, stuck in a conversational stalemate. Caede never knew what to say in situations like this. Too often she'd been accused of being cold or awkward. Truth be told, she was used to being alone. Small talk made her uncomfortable. She'd rehearsed enough of it to survive her shifts at the pub, but at home there was only Kai, and he was nearly always in his room.

"I haven't had free time in ages," she said, finally. "And look at me. I'm doing laundry."

Ravi chuckled. "I understand. Usually I'm up to my arms in patients. By the time I've gone home, helped with dinner, helped my sisters–they always want me to help with homework or recitals. Nila drives me mad; she makes me practise lines with her for hours…" He turned his face to the floor and put a hand over his eyes.

"You said they weren't at home, right?"

Ravi nodded.

"I'm sure they're fine."

She tried her best to sound genuine, but the words felt empty, a weak attempt to comfort him.

"I'll get on with that tea, shall I?" he said.

Before Caede could reply, a rumble filled the air.

"What the hell?"

"Is that a car?" said Ravi.

Caede scrambled up from the floor. The rumbling stopped just outside the house. A few seconds later, a knock echoed through the hall and across the balcony, causing them both to jump.

Caede glanced at Ravi. "Is that the front door?"

The knock repeated, clear and loud. Suddenly she realised Kai was alone.

"Kai's downstairs!"

"Okay," said Ravi, taking her hand. "Let's go."

Before they could get to the staircase, Kai's excited yells rose from the foyer below.

"Caedey! Ravi!" he shouted. "Get down here!"

The pair ran to the stairs in time to see him opening the front doors. A tall woman stepped into the foyer, thanked Kai, and looked up, pausing to stare in awe at the size of the room. She was followed by an even taller, broader man, and a shorter girl with faded dyed blue hair. They stood in the entranceway, their heads turning this way and that, looking around in wonder.

Kai waved at someone beyond the door, and a man with scruffy brown hair stepped over the threshold. They exchanged a look, then embraced, happy to see each other. Kai hopped up and down and pointed up at the stairs. Caede stood at the top, looking down at the visitors, mouth agape.

Smiling awkwardly up at her was Jon.

30

The Reunion

A knot formed in Jon's throat as they pulled up to the house.

He'd found Efi, Samson, and Luna on the motorway at the edge of the city, inspecting an empty car. They'd watched as he approached but jumped when he'd sounded the horn. After a punch on the arm from Samson, a nod from Luna, a big hug from Efi, and some swearing, the four were driving fast, Jon at the wheel and Efi navigating. He'd lowered the window to let the air whip at his face, enjoying the speed, elated to be back in the countryside. The sweeping hills, the lush green woodland, the vast fields stretching endlessly out alongside the road; it reminded him of Yorkshire. Luna and Samson sat in the back, laughing and playing 'I spy'. The drive had taken a little over an hour, and they'd seen no signs of the creatures. Jon had started to wonder if they would bother tracking them this far out. The nagging sensation in his gut said otherwise. There were no other survivors either. The roads were clear, too. Any cars they did pass were either parked up on the hard shoulder, or pressed alongside trees and bushes, as if they had been left there on purpose. The drive had been easy, all the way up to the house.

Jon gulped down the knot, letting it settle amongst the butterflies in his stomach. An attractive roadster sat in a tall, wooden carport next to the house. He pulled up next to it and shut off the engine.

Was this the right place? He agonised over the question, hands gripping the steering wheel. Efi had seemed to think so. It was the only place around and the address matched the one left by her friend the doctor, so it must be right.

Efi called to him. She was already out of the car, Samson and Luna too, the three of them walking towards the main doors of the property.

"Jon?" she said. "You coming?"

"Just give me a sec, would you?"

"Okay."

Why was he nervous? Maybe Samson was right, and he was just thinking with his dick, after all. The girl was engaged, and there was literally, absolutely no sign of her having any sort of attraction to him. Did calling him an idiot count? No. Expectations. That was it. He just needed to drop any expectations, leave those in the car. He didn't want to be like that, like some desperate starving dog following home a stranger, because they were the first person to throw him some crumbs.

He got out of the car and headed towards the others. The front of the house was a soft grey, Georgian in design, but more modern, as if it had been built in the last twenty years, and sickeningly large, draped in twisting wisteria vines that had long since flowered, with only the reddening leaves intact. Something out of an estate agent magazine, if such a thing still existed. It looked less like a house and more like a wedding venue. Did people really live in these things?

The dark wood doors were detailed with delicate carved floral patterns, sat atop a dais flanked by two huge white columns. The doors were already open, and Efi and the others were stepping inside, greeting someone just out of view. As Jon approached the front steps, he realised it was Kai.

"Oh my God!"

"Ay up, lad," said Jon, stepping over the threshold to embrace him. "Nice to see you again. How's the arm?"

"It's fine," Kai replied. "It doesn't even hurt anymore. Ravi fixed it for me." He paused, a grin forming on his face. "Caedey is not gonna believe this."

"Kai?" said a voice.

And there she was. Jon looked up to see a grand staircase splitting off to two balconies, the steps and banisters matching the dark, rich wood of the front doors. At the top stood Caede. He stared up at her, taking in every detail in case she was little more than a mirage. Jogging bottoms, blue sweatshirt—not the one he'd given her. This one was darker and baggier. Her hair was tied back into a ponytail, some strands falling across her face. Eyes grey as a winter sea, one bloodshot and half closed, the skin around it marred with purple and yellow bruises. More bruising around her throat. His chest tightened at the sight of her injuries, Nila's words echoing in the forefront of his mind. Still, she was alive. Injured, but alive, and looking right at him with a strange expression. Suddenly, he was very aware that he'd been staring for far longer than was polite, and his hand found the back of his neck.

Efi shot him a look and he caught it.

A man was standing next to Caede, holding her hand, someone he'd never seen before. The man looked down at Jon inquisitively. Jon pressed his hand against his pocket, feeling the outline of the ring. It jabbed him in the leg.

Then the man's eyes settled on Efi, who had stepped forward from the entrance way. "Ravi?" she said.

"Efi?"

The man's face lit up, and he broke into a trot, bouncing down the stairs with the same energy as a Labrador, almost knocking her over as they collided into an embrace, laughing and smiling. She pulled away and looked him over, brushing him down and fussing over him like a mother.

"How the hell did you get here?" she said. "I thought you'd never leave that bloody desk!"

"I'll have you know," he replied in a faux protest, "I'm quite the survivor, actually."

Jon turned his attention back to Caede, who was still standing at the top of the stairs.

"Uh…you alright?" he said, smiling awkwardly.

She moved, pummelling down the stairs towards him, stopping just short of arm's reach.

"Holy shit," she said. "I thought you were dead."

He wanted to reach out and embrace her as fiercely as Efi and the doctor, but he couldn't bring himself to move. *What are you so afraid of?*

Sweat settled at the base of his spine. He became acutely aware of the last time he had showered or brushed his teeth. Why hadn't he changed his clothing at the department store? Stolen some cologne? He could have showered at the hospital, washed his arse at the very least...

"I…"

"But that thing snatched you! We–I thought she'd killed you. How did you get away?"

"Did you kill it?" asked Kai, now at his side, looking up at him with big eyes.

"What happened to you?" asked Caede.

Jon wondered if he imagined a tremble in her question. Had she been worrying about him? A strong urge to run and find a bathroom surged through him. Instead, he laughed, high and nervous.

"Listen," he said. "I was trying to find you two. Spider girl kinda put a spanner in the works, then some pricks chased us into the underground.... You look hurt."

"I'm fine," said Caede.

"Did you kill it?" Kai repeated.

Jon laughed. "Yeah, I did."

"We killed it," Efi corrected, pointing a finger at him.

"Fuck off," said Jon. "I fought the bloody thing while you were busy crying over a little cut on your leg."

Efi laughed and tutted. "I distinctly remember stabbing it in the head while you were falling over some boxes."

"After I did all the work!"

Efi waved her hand dismissively. "Whatever. We're here now."

Samson bounded over from the front door with a broad grin across his face, Luna shuffling apprehensively behind him. He nudged Jon playfully with his fist and nodded at Caede. He winked and smiled at her.

"You gonna introduce us then, Jon?"

"Uh…"

Efi spoke, taking the reins with a hand placed softly on Jon's shoulder. "Sorry, Rav," she said, "we brought a couple of extras with us, I hope that's okay? This is Samson, and that's Luna."

"Of course," said Ravi, eyeing Samson, one eyebrow cocked as if he was unsure of the man. "The more the merrier…. Where's Holly?"

Efi said nothing, but turned her face to the floor, and an uneasy silence fell over the group.

"I see," said Ravi. "I'm so sorry."

"It's okay. Well, it's not. It is what it is."

She exhaled, blowing away the sadness. At least, that's what it looked like. Jon wondered if, in a way, Efi was similar to Caede, a stoic.

"Rav," said Efi. "Look. We need to tell you something. We're not safe here. Jon, tell them." She nudged him with her elbow.

"Right, right. A group of those things are after us. I don't know how long they're gonna be, either. I overheard a bunch of 'em talking. They're after Samson, and they're after the girls."

Caede's eyes widened. "What?"

"Why?" asked Ravi.

"I don't know," said Jon. "He said something about recruits."

A ripple of fear spread through the group.

"I'd better get the kettle on," said Ravi.

They gathered in the dining room, around a large oval table of dark wood, polished to the nth degree by somebody who was no doubt fastidious and dedicated to its care, suggesting the extent of its expense to whomever cared to notice. The chairs, just as luxurious as the table, featured burgundy velvet, giving the impression of soft comfort, but the chairs were stiff against his aching back, not soft like his old armchair. The whole place was like it: decadent, over-designed, stuffy, the kind of house you'd expect someone with too much money to live in. The contrast seemed especially stark with the group sitting around the table, their clothing torn, caked in dust, sweat, and blood. It was almost comedic.

He sat in silence. A weariness had taken over, and he found himself weighed down in that mahogany and velvet chair, desperately trying to keep his eyes open.

"Why are we just sitting here?" said Luna. "Shouldn't we be doing something?"

"Relax, kid," Samson replied. "Resting is doing something."

"But we could be getting weapons, boarding up the windows. We should–"

"Luna," said Efi, voice calm. "We can't do anything without a plan first. We're going to have a nice cup of tea, get our strength back, and then we'll decide what to do, okay?"

Luna kissed her teeth in response and crossed her arms, sinking back into the chair.

Jon was only half paying attention to the conversation, his mind drifting. He was here now. Out of London, still alive, and miles away from that rooftop. Caede and Kai were okay, despite all odds. He let his mind continue to wander before noticing a mug hovering in front of him. A plate of biscuits had appeared in the centre of the table. Caede placed the mug down on a coaster, taking a seat next to him.

"Oh! Uh, thanks."

He leaned across the table and snatched up a couple of digestive biscuits, dunking them in the tea before chomping them down. It was the first proper cup of tea he'd had in almost a week. He nursed the mug, savouring the warmth.

Ravi passed out cups to the rest of the guests–guests being the only term that seemed to fit in Jon's mind and took a seat opposite Caede. They shared a glance. He raised his eyebrows and lowered his chin. Jon's eyes flickered to Caede in time to catch a faint nod. Suddenly, he felt foolish. Caede and this guy had been holding hands at the top of the stairs. Had the doctor been her fiancé this whole time? A picture of them formed in his mind, the pair laughing, sharing a moment together. It made his stomach churn. He choked it down with the rest of the biscuit.

"So it's decided," said Ravi.

"It's the only way we're gonna keep the kids safe," Efi replied. "And they can escape if anything happens."

"I'm not a kid," said Luna.

"I doubt they'll find us," said Samson, ignoring Luna's protests. "It's one thing to have our scent in London, but we're miles away— we travelled by car. They were on foot, right, Johnny?"

Had he missed something? He must have zoned out. The others were looking at him, waiting for him to say something. It was just like one of those team meetings where your mind had wandered off, and suddenly the boss was asking you what you thought of this or that, and you had to blag it and hope for the best.

"Uh, right," he said. "They're fast, but they're on foot. They didn't check any of the cars when I saw them."

"How many were there?" asked Ravi.

"Must have been five, maybe six of 'em."

"I guess all we can do is keep a lookout, then," said Ravi. "We'll need to decide who's first and take shifts. My uncle has a pair of binoculars in the library; we can use those to watch the roads."

"I reckon," said Samson, "if they're following us, and they're on foot, they'll be here by around three or four. Might be timing it to arrive when it's getting dark."

"How do you know?" asked Efi.

"Walking distance," said Caede. "It takes roughly ten hours to walk from London to Kent. Less time if they run."

"That's right," replied Samson. "And if they're on foot, they'll be quieter. You probably heard us coming for miles in that beast."

"I did," said Kai. "I knew I heard something! Didn't I say I heard something?"

"Yes," said Caede thoughtfully. "You did."

"So, then," said Ravi, matter-of-factly. "We have five adults and two teenagers. None of us are trained in any sort of combat. We don't have weapons. Where does that put us?"

"We have a defensive position," replied Efi. "We might not even have to fight them directly if we can hold them off. Does your uncle have any guns?"

"I don't imagine so. My aunt and uncle are both vegetarians. He doesn't hunt, and he's never mentioned anything about clay pigeon shooting. I could be wrong. It's certainly worth looking for one."

Ravi stood and began pacing slowly beside the table, as if deep in thought.

"Samson," he finally said. "I'm going to need your help if we are to survive this possible encounter."

"What do you need to know, mate?" he replied, turning on his chair to face him.

"Well, you're clearly living with the effects of this, and your additional experience could give us some much-needed insight. You are also the first chimaera I've come across who isn't aggressive to humans."

"It's 'cause I'm still human, bro. Tell you what, I'll tell you what I told these guys and give you the full rundown, everything, but I need a shower or somethin' first, 'cause I stink."

"Agreed," said Efi. "We're all tired and filthy."

"Of course," Ravi replied. "There are several bedrooms upstairs, each with an ensuite, if I remember correctly. Make yourselves at home. We'll reconvene in an hour and begin preparations. Lunch will be roasted squash with rice."

"Why is everyone so calm?" Luna stood with her hands pressed against the tabletop. "Those things are coming for us. Why are we talking about lunch?"

"Luna," said Efi, more sternly.

"We should be fighting them! We've already killed one, and it wasn't even that hard!"

"Chill out, lil sister," said Samson. "Nothing we can do about it if they're coming. Keep calm and carry on, n' all that."

"We'll be ready," said Efi. "We're not going to let anything happen to you."

31

The calm

Jon scrubbed himself down with the towel and flopped onto the bed. The fresh bedding was soft against his skin, somehow cool and warm at the same time. To be clean–to lie on a bed in this five-star hotel of a house–felt like a marvel. The shower was lukewarm, but preferable to being covered in sweat, and far better than the icy spray of his own shower at the flat. It felt good to watch the blood and dirt spiral into the plug hole, to wash away the stress and fear. And, his rib wasn't broken, likely just bruised, according to the doctor–who wasn't Caede's fiancé, it turned out. He'd just have to take it easy for a while and it would be fine.

After some slightly guilty rifling through the wardrobe and finding nothing to wear, he let himself be naked, relishing the air on his skin for a while longer before he'd have to put his old T-shirt and jeans back on. The ring was still in his pocket. He'd kept it there to not lose it, but soon he would have to reunite it with Caede.

He should have been more concerned. The things, chimaera, whatever they were, were coming. If Samson was right, they'd reach the house before nightfall. Or they'd time it to arrive as nightfall came. He wondered how his little group would be able to fight off those monsters. That one female had moved faster than he'd ever seen. Could they all move like that? And the dragon. They'd need a tank to bring that bastard down. They had Samson, and he'd almost fully recovered from their previous fight, but could the dragon heal like that, too? There were so many questions, and not a single answer his mind could offer would satisfy. He closed his eyes.

A knock at the door jolted him awake. He swore and sat up, wondering how long he'd been asleep. Without thinking, he said, "yeah?"

The door opened, and Caede's face appeared. Her eyebrows raised, then she quickly glanced away.

"Should I come back later?" she asked.

The realisation sank in. Jon threw himself across the bed to seize his clothing, silently praying that she'd seen nothing condemning.

"No, no…I'm decent!" Jon scrambled into his jeans and shirt, making his way across the room rather indignantly. "Jus' caught me off guard."

Regaining some of his composure, he opened the door.

"So, uh, what brings you to my neck of the woods?"

Her face remained passive, all but for one eyebrow, still slightly raised. It was hard to tell if she was annoyed, amused, or intrigued.

"Lunch is ready," she said.

"Great," said Jon. "I'm starving."

Caede shifted her weight in the doorway, her fingers picking at one of the nails on her left hand, wearing a new expression, another in the list of her expressions he couldn't place. Hunger gave way to nausea, and he swallowed, hoping to keep whatever might be rising in his stomach down.

"Can we talk for a second? Just really quickly, please?" she said.

"Course. What's up?"

"Can I come in?"

"Shit… yeah, sorry. Course."

He gestured into the room, quickly heading over to the bed to reset the duvet and pillows, making space for her to sit. "Here."

She took a place on the edge of the bed, next to him, and said nothing, her face pointed down, as if to study the intricate patterns of the Persian rug or the knots in the hardwood flooring. Finally, she looked up, her face a mixture of anger and sadness, or grief. He thought he saw a flash of colour in those grey eyes.

"I… I'm so sorry, Jon," she said.

"What?"

Why was she apologising?

"You saved my brother's life, and when that monster attacked us, I just left you for dead. I should have helped, but I just ran. I didn't think. I just ran and left you, after you helped us… Christ… It's all I seem to be fucking good at!"

"Hey, hey," said Jon. He shifted his weight closer and put an arm around her shoulder. "What are you saying sorry for? It's okay. You had to help your brother. And I'm fine, see? I'm tough. Takes more than a big spider to kill me. Not like you southerners, eh?"

Caede sniffed and let out a small laugh, rubbing her face with the back of her hand. She snapped her head up.

"Hold on," she said. "Did you just call me weak?"

For a second he thought he'd fucked up, but then he saw that she was smiling. *Thank God.*

"Oh no, none of that," he said. "We both know us northerners are sturdier than you lot. Bit of snow and you all lose your bloody minds."

Caede snorted and gently shoved him. "Idiot."

"Made you laugh, though."

"Shut up," she replied. She flicked the hair out of her eyes and looked at him in a way that made his face hot and his stomach churn, and he glanced away.

"Well," she said. "It's a good thing you're alive. We'll need a sturdy northerner when those things get here."

With that, she rose and padded over to the door, pausing at the threshold to turn back and throw him a glance. The light from the window skimmed her face, and she smiled, but it was offset by the bruising around her eye and throat. Nila's words echoed once more, followed by his own. *Don't ask.*

"Are you coming?" she said.

"Yeah, just gimme a sec."

She left, striding down the hallway towards the balcony, calling behind her, "food's getting cold!"

He sat for a second longer, wondering what the hell had just happened, before jumping up to follow her downstairs. He sprinted down the hallway, almost skidding over the edge of the balcony thanks to his socks sliding on the polished floor and hoped that she hadn't seen. Caede was halfway down the stairs already. She stopped and turned to let him catch up. If she had seen his less than graceful approach, she didn't say anything. Maybe it was his imagination, but the air felt thicker for some reason, hotter, and hazy, as if he'd had one too many to drink. Had the heating come on? He glanced at Caede.

"I need to ask you something," he said.

"What?"

"Listen," he started. "You don't have to answer, but, uh…I met this lass on the way here and she said she saw a woman fitting your description running from a group of blokes. Same ones who chased us into the underground. She said they'd followed the girl into a shop in Lewisham, not far from the station. That was you, wasn't it?"

"Yeah," she said bitterly. "I didn't know anyone else was around. Nice of her to help."

"I'm sorry," Jon replied. "Look, you don't have to say anything, but we found the shop. We found the bodies. What happened? Did they hurt you?"

"I'm fine," she replied.

"Were you alone?"

"Yes."

"Where was that Ravi bloke? The doctor? Where was he?"

"He was with Kai."

"So he wasn't there to help you?"

"I said I'm fine, Jon."

She stared at him now, jaw clenched, eyes furious and pleading.

"I'm sorry," he said.

"It's fine."

"It's not fine," he said. "I said I'd help you. If I'd been there, I could have."

"Actually, you did help me. You left a knife in your rucksack. Made it easier for me."

"But I should have been there. I promised–"

"And I told you before, don't promise me things."

She looked away. They stood next to each other, but facing opposing directions, as if miles apart, Caede staring at the wall and Jon the ceiling. From inside the dining room, he could hear the others chatting to each other, the screech of the chairs sliding against the hardwood floor as they gathered around the table.

"They were hunting us," said Caede finally, her voice low. "There was a group of them, like a pack of dogs. It was my idea. I told Ravi to take Kai and hide. I tried to distract them. It worked, I guess. One of them wanted to..." she trailed off. When her voice returned, it was a whisper. "I killed him first."

"Good."

He hadn't expected to say that. He hadn't expected to say anything, but the word left his mouth before he could do anything else.

"They deserved it," he confirmed.

"Did they? One of them was just a kid–a boy! He couldn't have been much older than Kai! And they didn't even have a choice, Jon.

The tall one, Lee—he said it wasn't personal, that if it wasn't me, it would have been them."

"Didn't have a choice?" Jon replied. He almost spat the words out in disbelief. He took a step down, lowering his face to meet hers. "From where I was, when they were chasing us into the underground, they seemed pretty happy. Don't believe any of that bullshit. Them or you.... They deserved what they got."

"What if someone finds out? What if things go back to normal and people find out? I'm a murderer." The words tumbled out, and she wrung her hands in agitation. "They'll take Kai away. They'll put me in prison…"

"Hey, hey," said Jon. "Breathe, alright? Just breathe. You were defending yourself. No one's gonna convict you of 'out. Who else knows?"

"Just Kai and Ravi."

"You've got nothing to worry about, then. And even so, you're not a murderer, Caede; you're a survivor."

Caede said nothing, but shrugged and sniffed, and they were silent again. Jon fidgeted. His hand found the back of his neck. Finally, he said, "are you alright?"

"No," she replied. "But I will be."

Jon offered his hand, and she took it, stepping into him, her forehead pressing against the top of his chest. He wrapped his arms around her and closed his eyes.

"There was a moment," she said quietly, "when Lee was going to let me go. I could have just left, but I didn't. That sounds terrible, doesn't it?"

"I'm not the best person to ask," he replied. "I'm just sorry I wasn't there to help–not that you needed it, eh?"

Caede's eyes flickered upwards, meeting his, then settled somewhere just below, between his mouth and his chest, and suddenly he was acutely aware that they were still standing close enough together that she could probably feel his heart as it hammered against the wall of his ribcage. He stifled a gulp.

"Remind me never to piss you off, by the way."

Caede laughed at that, a real laugh, warm and inviting. He stepped back to give her space, but also to take some for himself. This was something–definitely something akin to attraction, friction even. It was both thrilling and terrifying. After months of feeling nothing, it seemed almost alien. He wondered if he'd been less afraid in the tunnels of the underground than here, standing in front of this woman.

Caede tilted her face up. "We should join the others."

Lunch lasted all of a few precious seconds, the group too hungry to talk, and grateful for a warm meal. The only sounds made were the scrapes of cutlery against ceramic.

If Ravi was as good a doctor as he was a cook, Jon reckoned they'd be alright. For nothing but squash, rice and a few spices, it tasted pretty damned good, and he gulped it down, pleased to have a full stomach.

Dessert consisted of more biscuits and a round of tea. After that, the group sat and chatted, comparing stories of their journeys out of the city. Samson was standing, gesturing wildly and, Jon thought, exaggerating the details a bit, as he told the others about their escape from the underground and hospital. Jon's eyes wandered to Caede's face. She glanced back and his eyes shot down. She waited for Samson to finish, then gave her recollection of the events on the rooftop, speaking in hushed tones as she described what she'd seen. When she'd finished, the group sat in silence, enraptured and horrified.

"Shit," said Efi.

"That's what they're going to do to us, isn't it?" said Kai.

"No," said Caede. "We won't let them."

"We've already killed some of them," said Luna. "I killed one. That big gross frog thing."

"How did you do it?" asked Kai, leaning forward in his seat.

"I just stabbed it," said Luna. "Again and again. Just don't think about it, and it's easy."

"You won't need to do anything like that," said Efi quickly. She shot Luna a stern look, but the girl didn't seem bothered.

"They probably won't make it out of London," said Samson, leaning back in his chair. "We're miles out of the way here. A lot of effort to go through just for some prey, you know?"

"It's interesting that you call us prey," said Caede.

"It's how you gotta think," said Samson. "Cause that's how they see you."

"I already know that's how they see us," said Caede, pointing to her face and throat. "How is it that you don't?"

"How is everything?" interrupted Ravi, hovering about the table with a teapot in his hands. It was reminiscent of how Jon's mother dealt with arguments, particularly when it came to him and his father.

"Tea top up?"

"Rav, relax, babe," Efi cooed, patting the seat next to her. "Come, sit. We need to get this sorted out."

Ravi obliged and settled into the seat, pouring himself a cup of tea.

"Listen," said Efi. "Sam's not one of those things. He's different."

"How so?" said Caede.

"Different strain for a start," said Samson, sitting down. His demeanour had changed, more serious than before. "I'll explain properly, I promise you love, but right now we need to decide what we're gonna do if they follow us."

With that, he shrugged away Caede's accusation. "Me, Efi and Ravi have been talking, and I think we've got a plan. It'll mean everyone's got a job to do though—even you, little man."

He nodded at Kai, who turned bright red in response.

"I reckon you're up to the task, am I right?" Samson continued.

Kai nodded, suddenly too shy or embarrassed to answer.

"Awesome," Samson continued. "Right then, I need you and Luna to find anything that looks like a safe or gun cabinet. It's a big metal box that'll be fixed to the wall–probably hidden in a wardrobe or something. Can you do that?"

Kai nodded and jumped up from the table. Luna rolled her eyes and stood, sidling out of the room behind him.

"Right. That's the kids out the way," said Samson. "The rest of us need to make sure the downstairs windows are boarded up. Front doors, back doors, side gate, any entrance to the house on the ground floor–it all needs to be locked and blocked."

"We'll also need weapons if they can't find anything," said Efi. "Samson and I will see to that."

"I'll get on with boarding up the front windows," said Jon. "Is there a ladder anywhere? Tool kit?"

"I'm not sure," said Ravi. "There must be one in the shed or garage."

"Alright, I'll have a look."

"What do you need me to do?" asked Caede.

"Think you could give Jon a hand?" said Efi.

"Sure."

"Uh, who's left?" said Samson. "Ah. Ravi, my man! Mate, you've already done enough, but we need to take inventory of everything we've got. Food, water, anything we'll need to survive, attack or not. And a plan of the building if you got one."

"Of course," Ravi replied.

"We've got heating and hot water, right?" said Samson. "Does this place have its own generator or something? Like an independent boiler or what?"

"There's a solar panel farm in the land just beyond the back garden," said Ravi, "and a biomass boiler system. It seems my uncle was a bit of an eco-enthusiast. Luckily for us, the panels are generating quite a lot of the electricity we've been using since we've been here."

Samson stroked his chin. "They'd still be connected to the grid, right? What is it, a battery storage system?"

"I'm not sure, to be honest. They look similar to the ones we had at the hospital, though. It sounds like you know a little about them, Samson?"

"Call me Sam if you want, bro, but yeah, it's something that interests me; a hobby, if you will. I can help with the panel stuff, no problem."

"Okay, that's great. Thank you."

"Chimaeras first," reminded Efi. "Power is going to be pointless if we're all dead."

The five adults fell silent.

"You know, there's still time to leave, if you want," said Ravi. "We could always come back once the danger has passed?"

"No," said Caede. "If they're following our scent, and they're this determined, they'll just keep following us wherever we go... I'm sorry, this is my fault. I told us to leave the city. I killed three of them. If we'd stayed at the hospital, we could have all left together, and this wouldn't have happened."

"Babe, listen," said Efi. "You haven't put anyone in danger. We were already there. All we can do now is prepare and hope they don't come."

"Very well put," said Ravi. "With that in mind, we should make a start. I need to run some check-ups on Kai, and then I'll be in the library for the remainder of the afternoon."

"I'd like to see the boy's arm as well," said Efi. "Just quickly, and I need you to have a look at my leg. I think the infection has passed, but I'd like a second opinion."

"Of course."

They all helped gather up the cutlery and mugs, stacking them on the draining board in the kitchen to be washed later, and then went to work.

32

Nightmare

Staring out of the window seemed like the thing to do. Night was falling quickly, giving way to a crisp, clear sky sparkling with stars, the distant fields bathed in blue moonlight. The window, low with a wide ledge, the kind designed for sitting and enjoying views, or reading books, had quickly become her favourite place in the house. From her vantage point, she could see the countryside and roads for miles. Wrapped in the duvet, Caede sat, taking in the view. Despite the circumstance, it really was peaceful, far more so than London. The silence out here away from the city didn't seem out of the ordinary, as if it was how things should be. Should always be. No cars, no shouting, no sirens, just the gentle breeze brushing through the trees and her thoughts floating along uninterrupted. It was easy to forget her little garden and rusted chair with such peace. All she needed now was a cigarette and it would be perfect.

She picked a splinter out of her finger and flicked it away. The cuts from the glass were still swollen and angry, and despite wearing bandages while they were boarding up the windows, underneath her hands were raw and cracked from the effort.

In the garage they'd found a ladder and a pile of spare floorboards, enough to cover a few of the windows. For the rest, they had to take apart some of the furniture. Ravi gave them permission, certain that his aunt and uncle would rather he and his friends were safe than preserve a few tables. The front of the house had ten windows. Too many to board up, but at least the ones at ground level were done. It was enough, hopefully, to put off a small group of potential attackers. Better than nothing, anyway.

Jon turned out to be pretty handy with a hacksaw, and the pair worked quickly together, Jon cutting the wood to size, Caede with the drill. They'd kept chatter to a minimum—not that there was the energy for banter between sawing and drilling. Jon had an estranged brother, Mark, two years younger, who had moved to New Zealand and cut contact with the family shortly after the United Kingdom left the European Union. He had voted remain, and it had become a point of contention between him and their father, the proud Yorkshireman and 'leave' supporter. Not that they needed any additional fuel to the fire. Jon's father had spent most of their lives convinced that he could toughen his boys up with hard labour, and the belt, if Jon or Mark even dared to shoot him a defiant eye. His mother was soft-spoken, gentle, almost coddling, abstained from voting in any form of election, and refused to get either of her sons vaccinated. She insisted that viruses were invented in Chinese laboratories, and vaccinations were a means of government control. How the family had functioned at all was a wonder.

"Wow," Caede had said. "Family dinners must be something to behold at your house."

"One of the reasons I moved to London," said Jon. "Had to get away from it all. What about you?"

"Not much to tell."

"Oh no, don't give me that," said Jon. "I shared mine, s'only fair."

"You already know most of it. We lived in Wales as kids and moved to London after the country declared independence. Then mum died, and my grandparents took custody of me and Kai until I was old enough to become his legal guardian. Since we'd inherited the house, we moved back to London, and I worked on my master's degree. Then this all happened."

"What were they like?"

"Who, my parents?"

"Yeah. You said they were divorced, right?"

"Yeah. They were fine, I guess. Dad was a lecturer in Architectural Design at Cardiff Metropolitan. Mum taught primary school kids. They worked a lot... Then we found out about the cancer and the affair. He divorced mum to start his new family and left us to suffer. I caught them at it, you know, while my mum was at a hospital appointment. In our home, in my mum's bed. I hated him for that. I never said anything. I left and stayed at my aunts for a while, but mum was getting worse, and Kai was still little, so I had to go back. I couldn't leave him. I thought about running away a lot, but Kai always kept me back."

With that, the conversation stalled, and the pair resumed drilling and sawing. Kai and Luna had found a gun cabinet, much to Ravi's surprise, with a well-maintained double-barrel shotgun and a small stock of shells that they assumed fitted it. Being the only one to have fired a shotgun before, Jon was handed the weapon and instructed to keep it in his room. Combined with the boarded windows, Caede wondered if they could get away with just shooting the creatures from afar. If they shot the big one, the rest might just leave. And if they fell as easily as the wolf men from the department store, it wouldn't be too difficult to pick them off either, one by one.

The group discussed options. If the gun failed, they'd need something else to defend themselves with. There were numerous decorative swords hanging on the walls of the library, so those were gathered and handed to each of the adults. There were cricket bats in the shed, and some brooms in the mudroom, so Efi got to work weaponizing them. She duct-taped kitchen knives to two of the brooms and sharpened the ends of the other three.

Ravi had also activated the intruder alarm and security light, muttering disapprovingly that his uncle was too negligent when it came to personal security. If the chimaeras came during the night, the group would have fair warning. All in all, the odds were pretty good.

Finally, with no sign of their impending arrival and the preparations complete–as complete as they could be with limited time and resources–the adults assigned a look-out rotation and went to bed.

Caede had spent her time wandering the halls, listening for any sounds, and found nothing out of the ordinary. She'd checked in on Kai, fast asleep and tucked up in his duvet. One of those *things* had taken his arm. It was all they would be taking if they did come. She silently swore it. She continued on, passing Jon's room, pausing briefly to listen at the door for any sign that he was still awake. His earlier words had resonated. And there was something there, too. Some kind of kinship, or mutual understanding. Caede wondered if he felt the same way. He seemed as though he knew something of loneliness, something she could relate to. An ache formed in the pit of her stomach, a fluttering she wasn't expecting. What was it, though? Guilt, perhaps, for leaving him behind after he'd helped her? Relief to find him still alive? Good old-fashioned lust, the brain mistaking adrenaline for desire, in the face of surviving the unthinkable? It was hard to place. She returned to her room, continuing her watch from the window.

As she gazed out, she expected fear, anticipation, dread, something, but there was nothing. Only the ache, and a sense of calm. Pale flecks of moonlight filtered between clouds as they drifted lazily over the hills and woodlands. A fox scampered across the grounds and paused, glancing around, before darting into the trees. A short series of knocks on the door let her know that her shift was over. She walked over to the door and knocked back before returning to the window ledge. She let herself sink into the pile of pillows she'd wedged against the wall and closed her eyes.

The department store appeared hazy, distant, and out of focus. She was running, but as if through syrup, her movements slow and strained, limbs impossibly heavy. The main doors were just there, ahead of her, then suddenly they were far away, miles away. The floor shifted and stretched, and the air filled with the laughter of the wolf pack as they closed in around her. She tried to scream, again and again, but nothing came out. Her mouth was empty, and the world was empty. Suddenly she was dead and rotting, back amongst the pile of bodies in the road.

"Caede?"

Someone's voice was calling from far away.

"Caede, wake up."

She bolted upright, sweating and shaking, heart beating against her chest like a jackhammer. Someone was holding her arm. She screamed and kicked out her leg. The figure let go, cursing as they tumbled backwards.

"Hey, hey!"

It was Jon, sitting on the floor in a T-shirt and pyjama bottoms. "Calm down, it's okay. It's just me."

"Jon?"

"My fault. Shouldn't have grabbed you."

A beam of yellow light fell across the room. At its source were Ravi and Efi, both looking groggy and dishevelled. Ravi's too-big pyjamas were half falling off him, his glasses hanging askew. Efi fared no better, her tightly curled hair flattened on one side of her head, and dark circles sitting heavily under her eyes. In her raised hands was a cricket bat.

"What's going on?" she demanded.

"Woah, woah, woah, it's not what it looks like!" replied Jon, hands in the air.

"It's okay," said Caede. "It was just a nightmare. I'm fine."

Efi lowered the bat. "You're sure?"

"I'm sure," said Caede. "False alarm."

"Thank God," Efi replied. With a yawn, she took the still dazed Ravi by the arm and left the room.

"Sure you're alright now?" said Jon. "What happened?"

"Yeah, I'm fine. You know those dreams where you're trying to run, but you're not going anywhere, and it's like you're wading through treacle? It was like that. I couldn't get away. It was horrible."

Jon reached out, offering a hand, and she took it.

"I know what you mean. I've had dreams where I'm having a fight with someone, and I'm hitting and hitting them, but nothing's happening. They're just standing there, looking at me like I'm an idiot."

"Funny," she said, "mine are always me trying to run from something."

Jon helped her up. "Come on, let's get you to bed. What are you doing, sleeping on a window ledge for, anyway?"

"What are you, my dad?"

"God, I hope not," he muttered.

"How old are you?" said Caede.

"Thirty-five, you?"

"Twenty-four."

"That makes me eleven years older than you. I'm not even sure it's possible to be a dad at eleven. Can you imagine? That'd be messed up."

Caede laughed. "You're right."

She replaced the pillows and hopped onto the bed, pulling the duvet up to her chin.

"Hey," she said. "Don't leave?"

"Want me to read you a bedtime story now?"

Caede snorted. "Fuck off! Just stay with me for a minute, okay? I don't want to be alone right now."

"Are you sure you want me here? I can get the doctor, or Efi, if you prefer female company?"

"I don't know Efi," said Caede.

"You don't know me, either," said Jon. "You said so yourself."

"I just trust you, okay?"

"Alright," he said. "I'll stay."

She patted the other side of the bed, gesturing to him to climb aboard.

"Come, sit."

He did, settling himself against a propped-up pillow, arms crossed. Caede could feel her eyes getting heavier, so she let them close.

"Glad you're still alive," she said.

Jon said nothing, waiting until Caede's breathing had slowed and settled into a steady rhythm. He leaned his head back and closed his eyes.

"Me too."

The sound of rain woke him. A beam of light shone through a gap in the curtains, resting on his face. During the night, he must have fallen asleep and slipped down, as he was no longer sitting against the pillows. He was lying under the duvet, and there was an arm resting on his abdomen. For a split second he wondered what the hell had happened, almost choking when he turned his head and saw Caede still asleep next to him. He considered sneaking out. There was no way she'd want to wake up and see him there. He said he'd stay so she could fall asleep, not get into bed with her. Worse, her arm was pressing on his bladder. As carefully as possible, he slid from the bed and made his escape to the ensuite.

Caede stirred and raised her head, casting her eyes across the room to the window. Through the gap in the curtain, she could see the grey sky and the rain she'd been expecting, finally. The typical British autumn. And no chimaeras. They hadn't come, after all.

There was a flushing sound from inside the ensuite. So Jon had stayed, then. Caede sank back into the duvet. A strange sensation crept over her, and the ache returned. What was it, exactly? It had been so long that, if it was attraction, she wouldn't know what to do with it. The ensuite door clicked open and Jon stepped out, drying his hands. He caught her eye and froze.

"Hey."

"Hey."

He relaxed a little, shifting his weight awkwardly in the doorway, raising an arm to the back of his neck. "Sorry. Must have fallen asleep."

"Don't be," she said. "It's fine. Come."

He walked over to the bed, the beam of light falling across his face as he passed through, and the ache worsened. His hair was all messed up from sleep. Thick hair, the colour of chestnuts, falling over hazel-coloured eyes. Week-old stubble had formed along his jawline and chin. His face carried the friendly, earthy character of someone kind and funny. Maybe she was just projecting a tick list of desirable traits onto the man and assumed kind and funny were included in the package. No. He was funny. He caught her eye and smiled–not a big, wide smile, but small and slightly lopsided, as if he was unsure how she would react to his presence. When he reached the bed, he sat on the edge, one foot anchored to the floor. His shoulders pivoted to face her, as if he was afraid of being too close.

"Did you sleep alright?" she said.

"Too well. It's light outside," he replied. "Shame about the weather, eh?"

"Isn't that what people talk about when they can't think of anything to say?"

She wondered why she'd said that. What could he possibly reply to something like that?

He shrugged and chuckled. "Just wait till I've had a coffee. Then you'll want me to shut up."

"I hate small talk."

Why did she say that?

"Well," he said. "If you want big talk, you'll have to take me to dinner first."

Caede laughed and turned her gaze to the window. "The things haven't come."

"Aye," he said. "I hate to say Samson's right about anything, but he might be on the money. They'd be here by now if they were following us."

"I don't trust him."

"Samson? Nah. He's a prick, but he saved us, and didn't just fuck off when shit hit the fan. And I'm sure it was him those lizard freaks called the traitor. I don't think he wanted this anymore than we do."

"I guess we'll find out soon enough."

Jon watched her, trying to make heads or tails of her expression, but her face remained mysterious, as if her mind was elsewhere, as if it were drifting out to sea.

"You alright?" he finally asked.

"My stomach hurts a little," she replied.

"Hang on. I'll get you some water."

Before Caede could reply, Jon had hopped off the bed and disappeared into the ensuite again. After some splashing noises, he returned with a tumbler of water. She took a sip. The liquid was soothing against her bruised throat. She tipped it back, drank the rest, and handed him the glass.

"Thank you."

Jon put it on the bedside table and turned to face her.

"I could get the doc to have a look at you."

Caede wasn't listening. Her stomach was churning, and her face burned. The man was close enough to simply pull towards her. But that was just the loneliness talking. Selfish impulse, nothing more. It was almost childish, some pubescent, hormone-driven high that she'd been swept up in. Or maybe he just made her feel safe, and she didn't want him to leave. The ache peaked, giving way to an unbearable fluttering in the pit of her stomach. She was caught up in a moment, that was all. This wasn't new. One-night stands, guilty flings–short-lived, drunken affairs that had failed to become anything more. They never lasted. Nobody wants to carry someone else's baggage.

And it wasn't Kai's fault, not really; it was just the situation. Kai was still a child, and he had to come first. She couldn't ask someone to just take on a child, and she couldn't commit to anyone knowing that it would fail the second they asked her to prioritise them instead. This turn of events was no exception. Yes, he was a fine man. Yes, he'd saved her life, and her brother's, more than once. Yes, there was something there, she was sure of it. And the monsters had stayed in London. They were safe. They were free. But this was no different from before. She still had to think about Kai. And Jon would be living with them in this house. What if she ruined whatever *this* was? There would be no avoiding the fallout, no escape from another fuck-up in a lifetime of fuckups.

Jon had almost sprinted to the bathroom for that water. He turned on the tap and splashed his face, reminding himself that this was not, absolutely not, the time. He'd strengthened his resolve. But as he'd handed her the glass, and she drank, throat rising and falling, cheeks flushed, something had stretched that resolve to breaking point. And those grey eyes. What was she thinking? He'd give anything to know what she was thinking. Then he could act on something, follow her lead, and he wouldn't have to face the crushing rejection that came with putting yourself out there. He chastised himself for being both a horny lech and a complete coward.

Before he could do anything, he felt a hand press against his waist. A lump formed at the back of his mouth. He gulped. Where was the glass now? It was on the side table. How had it gotten there? Was he sweating? His eyes flickered over to the bedroom door. It was closed. Why did it have to be closed? He chewed the inside of his cheek, agonising over what to do, but his brain seemed to be slower than his body, because he was already moving towards her, and she was clinging to his T-shirt, her nails digging into the fabric, rubbing against his flesh in a way that seemed to electrify his every nerve. *Fuck.* This was too soon. But God, he wanted this. All those times Tara had rejected him, pushed him away, made him sleep on the sofa… Caede's leg brushed his, and he felt the warmth of her skin against his own. That warmth was maddening. It was as if he had been reduced to something less evolved, something prehistoric, existing only for instinct. Eat and fuck. He wanted to devour her. Maybe she wanted to devour him, too. A quiet, desperate groan escaped him as her face drew closer.

Stop.

Why? What are you so afraid of?

Stop. It's not right.

He pulled away, taking her hand from his waist.

"What's wrong?" she said.

Nothing. Everything. If he stayed there another minute, he wouldn't be able to stop himself. If he had to smell her sweat, inhale the dizzying pheromones radiating from her flesh for a second longer, he wouldn't be able to stop himself. It would ruin any chance of a friendship. Or worse. The nausea returned.

"We should, uh, get up," he replied, flustered. "They're probably all wondering where we are."

He looked at her, studying her face. Was she disappointed? Angry? Her bottom lip disappeared behind her teeth, and her eyes met his, then turned down.

"Yeah," she said quietly. She shivered as if to rid herself of the malaise and looked up. "Alright. Just let me brush my hair first."

33

Cat DNA

They headed into the dining room to find the rest of the group sitting around the table. On a serving plate at the centre of it was a small pile of toast and next to that, some boiled eggs in a basket, one for each of them.

"Afternoon," Efi called, smirking from the inside of a teacup, an eyebrow raised. "Nice of you to join us."

Jon shot her a look, and she glanced away coyly, stifling a snigger before flickering her eyes back at him as if they were kids in a playground and she was mocking him for having a crush on the cool girl.

Ravi sat next to her; an eyebrow raised as he fiddled with his glasses. "I trust nothing untoward happened when we left you last night?" he said without looking up.

"I don't know what you're suggesting, pal," Jon replied, "but I look after my mates, so no. Nothing untoward happened. We're not savages just yet."

"Jon sat with me while I got back to sleep," said Caede, taking a seat at the table. "We must have overslept, sorry."

She patted the seat next to her, gesturing for Jon to sit down. Without thinking, he did, and caught a glimpse from Efi. It read, *what did you really get up to last night?* He looked away, face burning.

"No need to apologise, Caede," Ravi sniffed. "Please, help yourself to some breakfast."

"Caedey!" Kai yelled from the other side of the table, jumping up excitedly. "You need to hear this!"

"Need to hear what?"

Kai waved a hand at Samson. "Tell them!"

"Alright, little man, calm down," Samson said with a laugh. He took a swig from his mug, then helped himself to a slice of toast. "Okay, where was I?"

"Kai's arm," said Efi.

"Oh yeah. So, I was just telling everybody about my, er, minor part to play in all this.... Long story short, Kai's arm might grow back."

Caede glanced at Jon. He raised his eyebrows and shrugged. She looked back at Samson. "What?"

"His arm," Samson replied, "might grow back."

"I knew it," Jon whispered, not quietly enough, as Caede turned to him.

"Knew what?"

Jon shifted in his seat. "I think Kai's got whatever this thing is."

Caede slowly turned towards her brother, her lips moving as if to speak, but nothing came out. She pushed her chair away from the table as she stood.

"Now, Caede, please try not to get upset," Ravi urged, his own chair squeaking against the polished floor as he began moving towards her.

"I've been like this for ages," said Kai. "I'm fine. Look at me. How have you not noticed? I'm literally grey! I look just like our cat."

"How?" Caede breathed. Suddenly, her legs buckled, and she slumped. Jon shot out an arm to catch her and lowered her back into the chair.

"We don't know," Ravi replied, "it's impossible to tell how he contracted it, but luckily he's healthy, and his arm is healing well–remarkably so, in fact."

"How didn't I notice before?" said Caede to no one in particular.

"It must have been the shock of everything happening," said Ravi. "And the transfusion must have delayed the effects of the infection."

"The kid's gonna be just fine," Samson interjected. "The strain that got out, it's an unfinished version of what it's supposed to be, so it could have been a lot worse. You're lucky you've got a cat."

"What?" said Caede.

"Right. So, as I was explaining to these guys, this thing, it's like an accelerated gene-engineering device. I don't know exactly what it is, but when we were investigating it–me and my team, that is–we noticed that it aggressively interacts with DNA. It's like a sped-up diagnostic tool. It finds problems, seeks out the faulty wiring and cleans it up, fixes it, fills it in with something new, something usable. When I was still in the lab, before all this went down, we were testing it with mice. Gave them all kinds of ailments to test on, you know? One had cancer, one elderly, one haemophiliac–you know, all that shit. This thing cured them. All of them. Only problem, the DNA it uses to fill in the gaps–it's gotta come from somewhere. The strain that got out, it's not the finished product. It's missing stuff. It's unpredictable, it-"

"What do you mean, unpredictable?" said Caede.

"It's not consistent. Most of the people who got it, they just…well, you've seen it. Multiple organ failure. Probably why you thought it was Ebola, Rav."

Ravi nodded.

Samson turned to Caede. "Kai said you've got a cat, right?"

"Yeah…"

"So it would have taken a profile from your cat, anything it thinks would be useful, and transferred it to Kai. Having access to that DNA, it had transferable data to use."

Caede stared at Samson with a mixture of confusion and fear. She looked at her brother, then turned back to Samson. "I don't understand."

"S'alright," Samson replied. "I was gonna sit everyone down later and go through it all. I know it sounds like some crazy voodoo shit, but I'll clear it all up. I got slides' n' everything."

Caede nodded slowly, eyes on the surface of the table now, glassy and vacant. Jon took her hand tentatively. "Remember when you two got to my flat?"

"What's that got to do with this?"

"Kai had lost so much blood. That should have been the end of him."

She turned to face him with eyes burning so hot he had to glance away.

"Well, uh, I saw something similar happen to Samson after we were attacked. I think this thing saved Kai's life."

"And how the fuck does cat DNA save my brother from bleeding to death?"

"You're gonna freak out when you see the tail," said Kai. He erupted into laughter. Luna smirked in her seat next to him, and Samson grinned, clearly pleased with himself, but said nothing. Efi raised her eyes to the ceiling and Ravi shook his head in disapproval.

"Kai! This isn't the time to be joking around," said Caede.

"Ah, come on," said Samson. "Let the kid have a laugh. He needs it."

"We all need it," said Efi.

With that, the group fell silent.

"Look, Caede, right?" said Samson. "Like I said. I'll explain it all–swear down on my life, my honour as a man."

"I think," said Ravi, hands pressed flat on the table. "We should address the matter at hand."

Met with only silence and slight nods, he continued. "Efi and I have drafted up a rota of sorts to help things run smoothly while we're here. I think everyone can agree with what we've written so far, but if you think we've missed anything, just say and we can make amendments. I don't want anyone to feel as though they've drawn the short straw."

He held up a small whiteboard displaying the days of the week and a table of chores, each square filled in with a name. "Efi and I left Kai and Luna out of supply runs because of their age. So we'll need two volunteers to fill in for them."

Caede's hand shot up. "I'll do it."

Before Ravi could say anything, Jon followed suit. "Me too."

"Okay. That was easy," said Ravi, filling in the blank boxes. "Anyone who goes out for supply missions will be in teams; I don't like the thought of anyone going out by themselves. There's a few villages not far from here that we can do regular runs to. There might even be other survivors there."

"I was thinking," Efi chimed in, "that we go out twice a week for supplies, me and Samson one day, and Jon and Caede the other. How's that sound?"

"That's an excellent idea," said Ravi.

34

The Crash

Getting the group to agree on everything took an hour. Luna and Kai were on clean-up duty, so they took the empty plates into the kitchen and began washing up. The adults gathered in the garden and got to work.

The rain from the morning had cleared, leaving a patchwork of white and blue clouds drifting lazily across the sky. Efi and Caede picked all the vegetables from the allotment, gathering them into a basket to put them into storage. The winter frost was yet to set in but leaving them outside wasn't worth the risk of losing the entire crop if it arrived early.

Samson, Jon and Ravi had gone to inspect the solar farm at the end of the gardens. Ravi intended for them to start up the home generator and get the panels disconnected from the grid. He'd mentioned something about a renewable energy boiler for the house as well. Heating through the winter seemed more of a possibility, and, Caede reckoned, crucial for their survival. They could last a long time with little food if they were warm and had access to water.

Efi hacked at the branch of a large pumpkin. "If Sam and Ravi can get those panels generating independently from the grid, we'll be able to cook all these up and keep them frozen for a while. We'll have a decent supply through winter."

"Yeah," Caede replied absentmindedly as she clipped at a courgette stem. Jon stood further down the garden, holding a large sack of wood pellets over his shoulder. His hoodie sat tied around his waist as he spoke to Ravi and Samson. He caught her eye and smiled. She glanced down, returning to the vegetables.

"I wanted to look at the panels," said Efi. "It's typical: get the women to pick vegetables while the men do the fun stuff. Holly would know what she was doing with this. She loved gardening."

"Who's Holly?" said Caede. "Ravi mentioned her, but I never had the chance to ask. Everything's been kind of a blur at the moment."

Efi snipped a swede from its stem. "My girlfriend. I was going to ask her to marry me. I was thinking and thinking about it. I never said anything to her... Kai's your little brother, have I got that right?"

"Yeah."

"He's precious, you know? So well behaved. My brother was a nightmare at that age. He had so much energy; you couldn't get him to sit still if you paid him."

"Where is he now? Was he evacuated?"

A sad smile formed, then faded on Efi's face as she spoke. "He died three years ago."

Caede felt a pang in her chest. "What happened?"

"He met this kid. Me and mum didn't like him, but Mo said he was alright. Something always bothered me about that kid. Dead behind the eyes, you know? He was a bit older than Mo, too, and I wondered, why can't that kid find someone his own age to hang out with? He was a bad influence. I've seen it with so many kids where we used to live, before we moved to the UK. All they know is violence. Mo got into an argument with him. One day, the kid accused him of owing him some money. Well, Mo's not like that. We had plenty of money. He wouldn't have needed to borrow anything from anyone. We later found out the kid had joined a gang, and it was all part of this initiation ritual to start a fight with someone and stab them."

Efi paused and gazed distantly at the ground. "He killed my little brother over a ten-pound note. Mo would have survived if those little shits had called an ambulance, but they left him. Just left him there on the ground in an alleyway. He managed to drag himself far enough to knock on someone's door and they got help, but it was too late. By the time the paramedics arrived, he'd lost too much blood. My poor mum. She gave up everything she had to get us here, and after that, she sort of died, as well. Like the light had gone from inside her. My mum was educated. Intelligent. We could have gone anywhere. She chose England because it was supposed to be safe. We didn't know that they'd stuff us into a shitty council estate full of monsters like that kid. She didn't know..."

Efi put her tools on the ground and rested her face in her arms, shuddering with shallow gasps as agony took her over. "My brother was precious too," she sobbed. "I've lost everything. My poor mum, Holly, Mo. And now I'm sitting here, gardening when I'm not even a fucking gardener!"

Caede put an arm around Efi's shoulder, hugging her tightly. "Oh, Efi. I'm so sorry."

As Efi cried, Caede caught a glimpse of movement to her left. The men had noticed and were heading over, their faces confused and concerned. She gestured quickly, waving them away. Their reactions would only make it worse. Sometimes you just needed to cry, get it all out, then it passes. It always did.

"Holly should be here doing this with us," said Efi. "She was the most beautiful person, you know? It's like she just lifted me up every time we were together. After Mo, every day was a struggle… until I met Holly. And mum loved her. She'd say 'oh yes, Efia, this is much better than a man! You can keep this one!'"

Efi laughed sadly and shook herself off, busying herself in the vegetables once more.

"I'm sorry," she sniffed. "Seeing Kai just brings back the memories."

"Don't be," said Caede. "You've been through a lot. We all have. My mum died of cancer when we were kids. My dad abandoned her. Turns out he'd been having an affair for years. He left to play happy families with his coworker while my mum withered away. I haven't spoken to him since. He didn't even come to the funeral, the coward."

"Jesus Christ," said Efi.

"It is what it is," said Caede, wiping her face with the back of her arm.

"It is what it is," Efi repeated quietly. "Is that how we deal with it? The grief?"

"I guess so. I tried counselling for a while but stopped. I didn't want to talk about it, and they don't give a shit, anyway. Tried drinking it away too. I took up running, fencing, gymnastics... They helped a bit. After a while, I just became numb. I've tried talking to Kai about it, but he was so young when it happened. I don't think he remembers."

"That's probably for the best," said Efi. "Better for him to not remember that pain."

"Yeah."

They lugged the vegetables back inside the house to find Kai and Luna in the kitchen, whispering in agitation to each other.

"Alright, what are you up to?" said Caede.

"Nothing."

The pair looked guilty as hell, but Caede didn't push the matter. Kai would tell her later if it was that important.

"Well, since you both clearly have nothing to do," said Efi, "we've got a job for you, haven't we, Caede?"

"Can you give these a wash, please?" Caede gestured to the basket of veg.

The teens glanced at each other briefly.

"Really?" said Luna, her voice a drawn-out whine.

Caede's eyes flickered to Efi. Her face remained passive but for the smallest twitch of an eyebrow.

"If you want to eat," Efi replied sternly, "then yes, really. You're still a child the last time I checked, and I won't have you sitting around idling now we're here."

Luna groaned. Caede shot a look at Kai and he conceded, nodding in acknowledgement. Caede suspected Luna might be used to disobedience, but Caede's mother never let things slide, and neither did Efi, it seemed, so neither would she. For the most part, Kai was a good kid, but she couldn't afford to be soft on him in front of a peer. If she started treating him differently now, he'd accuse her of pitying him, and he hated that.

"Fine," said Luna. "But after this can we relax?"

"After this, you can do whatever you want," said Efi. "Just stay out of trouble."

With that, Efi left the kitchen to join the others at the solar farm, jogging steadily up the garden. Caede went to follow and paused. She was sure Efi's leg had been wounded. How was she jogging now? A whisper came from inside the kitchen, distracting her, and Caede paused, ear bent in its direction.

"Ugh, Efi's being such a bitch," said Luna.

Kai laughed. "Why?"

"You heard her, acting like she's my mum or something… Yeah, well. If she's not careful, she'll end up just like her."

Kai laughed again. "Whatever."

Making a mental note to talk to Kai later about what that exchange meant, Caede returned to her laundry mission from the day before. Now that everyone else was here, there would be more of it, so she decided to go ahead and use the washing machine. The grid hadn't given up yet, so this once would be fine. She gathered up anything sitting around unworn, including the still damp clothing from the day before, and dragged it to the laundry room. While the machine ran, she wandered the house at leisure, allowing autopilot to take the wheel.

The billiards room seemed nice, with its regal, leather armchairs and tall, deep shelves filled with board games and puzzle books. It was surprising that Kai and Luna hadn't already abandoned their vegetable washing duties for this room. But then, Kai would stay to finish the task, one arm or not, the little jobsworth. She didn't mean that. But he was her opposite, in so many ways. Would things have been different if he had been the eldest? Would things have been better?

She ran her hand along the edge of the pool table, absentmindedly knocking a couple of the balls into the pockets. Life without endless study, without work, without grades and cocktail-making courses and scrolling through Tinder profiles.... Somehow it felt both relieving and empty. Like old habits that needed to be dropped. Once again, she didn't know what to do with herself. Usually, there was always something to do.

Kai's face appeared in the doorway.

"Hi."

"Hey," she replied. "You okay? I feel like we haven't spoken in a while."

"Yeah. I'm fine. It's raining again, by the way. Everyone's come in. Luna said she wanted to go to her room so, me and Ravi are gonna go to the library. He wanted to read about the panels and stuff."

"That sounds like a good idea. How's your arm?"

"Ravi checked it this morning and said it looks good, so I guess it's fine."

"Do you remember what happened yet?"

Kai shrugged. "Not really, it just happened really fast.... I'm gonna go join Ravi if that's okay?"

"Sure," Caede sighed. "Go for it."

He disappeared fast enough to leave a cartoon dust cloud in his place. He really was a good kid, taking it all in his stride, so she couldn't fault him now. In many ways, he handled things better than her, but she reasoned it was because he was more accustomed to chaos. She was already a teenager at the time of her mother's death. Kai was too young to understand what had happened, and what it meant for them. He'd grown up with uncertainty. He was better equipped to deal with this situation. Caede left the billiards room and headed upstairs. Her hands ached, and her head throbbed with a steady, intolerable drumbeat. The laundry could wait.

Jon, Samson and Efi sat on the floor, dabbing themselves with towels. Samson had taken off his jacket and shirt, and Jon could see the golden sheen of short fur overlaying his black skin. Jon wondered if it was a side effect of the–what did Samson call it? The strain? Samson had said he would go through it all with them after lunch; he could wait an hour for answers.

"Typical British weather," said Samson. "One-minute, glorious sunshine, next it's pissing it down."

"What were you expecting?" said Efi. "A heatwave? It's November. In Britain. Course it's going to rain."

"True, true."

Jon rested the towel over his shoulders and stood to leave.

"Yo, Johnny," said Samson.

"Yeah?"

"You off to see your girl now, yeah?"

"What?"

Samson chuckled and nodded at Jon. "I got some condoms in my bag."

Efi spat out a laugh, shoved Samson, and looked up at Jon with a wink. "Go get her, tiger."

"What are you talkin' about?" said Jon.

"Oh, come on, Jon, it's obvious," she said. "What really happened this morning?"

"Nothing. Nosy parkers, the pair of you."

Efi laughed. "You dragged us halfway through London to give that girl back a ring, and you're telling us there's nothing going on? Do I look like a fool to you?"

Jon's face burned. "You're daft, woman."

"Mate," said Samson. "I'm just saying. I got 'em if you need 'em."

"Have a laugh," said Jon. "We're just friends."

"I think she could use some company," said Efi. "I saw her, sneaking glimpses of you in the garden. She likes you."

"Oi," said Samson. "You said she was a ten. She's a seven at best. She's got no arse for one."

Efi shoved him again. "Don't be a pig!"

Samson laughed, feigning contrition. "I mean, she's a seven… compared to you."

Efi rolled her eyes in response. "So romantic."

"Are you two done?" said Jon. "Cause I'm gonna go get changed and erase this conversation from my memory."

"See you later, stud," said Efi, grinning.

He threw her the bird and with a grin of his own, left. Reaching the top of the grand staircase, he paused. If he continued up the right-hand staircase, he'd be heading towards his new bedroom. Left was Caede's room. He still hadn't returned her ring. A very childish part of him didn't want to. He turned it over in his pocket, agonising over what would happen if he gave it back to her.

What are you so afraid of?

He headed up the stairs.

Caede couldn't sleep, so she had settled for just lying still on the bed with a damp flannel on her forehead and her eyes closed, letting her mind rest. After a couple of paracetamol capsules and some water, the throbbing in her head had calmed enough for her to be still and enjoy the silence. After a while, a knock came.

"Come in," she said.

The door clicked open.

"Hey," said Jon's voice. "You alright?"

"I'm fine; I just had to lie down for a bit."

"I can go if you want."

Caede gestured, tapping a space on the bed next to her. "Come, sit."

He did. "I meant to do this sooner," he said. "I think this is yours."

Caede sat up and saw Jon taking something from his pocket and dusting it off. For a moment, she was confused. Then her face lit up as she recognised the sapphire and the smaller, surrounding white stones. Jon settled himself onto the edge of the bed and pressed the ring into her hand.

"Oh my God," she said.

"I found it in my flat as we were leaving," said Jon. "Funny story. I thought it was the one I'd bought for Tara at first. Sorry–I meant to give it back to you as soon as we got here, but with everything going on, I forgot."

Caede turned the ring over in her hands, marvelling at it, then slipped it onto her middle-left finger. "You've had it in your pocket this whole time?"

"Yeah, sorry–didn't mean to."

"No, I mean, you followed us all this way to give this back to me?"

"Nah–not just that. I also need to bill you and your brother for the damages to my flat. You have any idea how much it's gonna cost a cleaner to get rid of all that blood?"

The pair broke into laughter. It passed quickly, and a heavy silence fell over them.

Jon cast his eyes to the floor. "Ah, well. What's there to go home to, anyway? Everything I have is here, now."

"What did you say?"

"Nothin'."

"Liar."

Jon shifted his weight and looked up. "Alright, alright. I said, everything I have is here now."

"I understand," said Caede. There was a soft melancholy in her answer that she hadn't expected. These people were now the closest things to friends and family, failing Kai. Everyone else was gone, evacuated from the city and somewhere far away… or perished. She hoped for the former, even if, for her, it was only an aunty in Wales, and her grandparents.

"It's funny," she said. "I've known you, what, a day? And I feel like…" she paused and fell quiet. "No. Ignore me, it's stupid."

"Oh no," said Jon. "You can't do that. Just start something and leave me hanging. What were you gonna say?"

"Promise you won't laugh, then."

"Oh, so now I'm allowed to make promises, am I?" Jon grinned, feigning annoyance.

"Just promise, idiot."

"What if you say something stupid?"

Caede shoved him playfully. "You know what? I'm not saying it now."

Jon laughed and feigned falling, hands up in surrender. "Aw, don't be like that. Come on."

"Nope," she said. "Moment's passed."

Jon sighed and settled himself, leaning back on his elbows against the duvet.

"So," he said. "Who's the lucky fella, then?"

"What?"

He nodded at the ring. "Your fiancé?"

"Oh!" said Caede. "I'm not engaged. God, no. This was my mum's ring."

She turned the ring around on her finger, eyes trembling as she brushed her finger over the stones.

"This is all I have left of her now."

A tear ran down her cheek. She sniffed and wiped it away with the back of her hand. The ache in her chest returned. She pushed down the urge with a deep breath and hoped he hadn't noticed.

"Thank you. I don't know how I can ever repay you–again."

"Don't worry about it," he said, shrugging.

She turned to face him. He sat and met her eyes with a smile. He looked natural, relaxed, inviting.

"What do you mean, don't worry about it? I literally owe you my life–my brother's life. And now this!"

That seemed to agitate him. His expression shifted from jovial to serious, and he sat up. "None of that now—you don't owe me a thing. Got it?" He paused. "If anything, I owe you."

"How's that?"

"One day, I'll tell you… maybe."

"Oh, come on, that's not fair."

He laughed. "Hang on. You wouldn't tell me what you were gonna say. Don't tell me what's fair and what's not, bloody hypocrite!"

"Ugh, fine."

Jon nudged her with his shoulder. "You're giving up that easily?"

Caede looked at him and rolled her eyes, nudging him back.

"Look, I'll tell you," he said. "Just now's probably not the best time."

She cocked her eyebrow. "Why's that then?"

Suddenly, they were both tip-toeing a line of mutual understanding. They were facing each other, close enough that she could feel the heat of his skin and the smell of his sweat. In her free hand, she gripped the bed sheet, twisting the fabric around in her fingers. His eyes flickered from hers to her mouth and rested there.

She could make the move, take the risk. The others were all busy. She imagined Efi and Samson playing a game of pool in the games room, Kai sitting with Ravi in the library, books piled around the pair as they studied. Luna, languishing in her bedroom at the other end of the hallway, earbuds plugged firmly in her ears. It was just Jon here, in this room, with her. She rested with bated breath, silently urging him to move closer.

"Promise you'll tell me, then."

A grin spread across his face and faded. "What if I don't want to?"

"Promise me," she demanded.

His eyes flickered from hers to her mouth, and he smiled again, moving closer. His fingertips brushed hers. The grin returned.

"Make me."

Checkmate. Caede took his shirt in her hand and tugged, connecting her lips to his. For an agonising moment, he retreated, as if in disbelief. Then he returned, pressing his lips against hers with such force that it almost hurt. She pulled harder on his shirt, retaliating, biting his lower lip, and he groaned, shuddering, surrendering. He fell onto her, his hands on her face, in her hair, stealing desperate gasps between kisses. She pushed back with all her might, twisting her fingers into his hair, gripping the back of his head, holding him tight.

Then his arms were around her, underneath her shirt, running up her back, over her breasts. A sound escaped her that she didn't recognise, a moan, a gasp, a shiver of ecstasy. The shirt disappeared over the edge of the bed. His own followed. She let herself fall back onto the mattress, inviting him to follow with a soft tug on his arm. He lay over her for a second, resting on hands and knees, dazed and misty-eyed as he took her in. Finally, he lowered his body, and she raised up her legs, wrapping them around his hips, pulling him closer until she could feel him grind against her.

"Ah, fuck," he gasped.

She let go, and he shifted his body, kissing her breasts and waist, working his way down to her navel. He paused at the puncture wound on the side of her abdomen, and the butterfly stitches holding it together.

"Does it hurt?" he asked.

"No," she said. "Not anymore."

He kept looking at it. Then he looked up at her face with a pained expression. "We should stop," he said.

"Really, it's fine."

"It's not fine, Caede," said Jon. "This ain't right."

He sat back, distancing himself from her, face lowered as if in disgust.

"What are you talking about?" said Caede.

"I'm sorry... I shouldn't be doing this to you."

The air sharpened around her, pricking at her skin, and she pulled the duvet up to cover herself. A weight settled itself in her stomach and her eyes burned. She wanted to pull the duvet tighter around her and disappear inside it. She wanted to ask him why, why lead me to this point? Did you see something that put you off? The only thing she could do was choke out the words, "it's fine."

"Caede," said Jon, apologetic, almost begging. "I'm sorry. I just don't wanna take advantage. You're injured, you've been through a lot…. And, uh, look, to be honest I'm going through some stuff right now myself, and…"

The prickling felt like knives now, jabbing at her flesh. Jon scrambled off the bed and scooped up his shirt, holding it bundled in his arms as he stepped backwards towards the door.

"Honestly, it's fine," she muttered. If he stayed a second longer, the tears would come, and she wouldn't be able to stop them this time. If he didn't want her, he could have just said. She wouldn't have been that upset, really. She could have accepted it, and it would have been fine. *Just fine.*

"Are you alright?" Jon asked.

"I'll be fine."

"You sure?"

"Can you just go, please?"

"Okay."

He turned around and left, closing the door softly behind him. Caede pulled the duvet around her, tight as she could, and the tears came. She shook, sobbing quietly, letting the bitter wave consume her. She was alone, always. Why would anything be different now?

She almost didn't hear the crash from down the hall. It took a few seconds for her to recollect herself, and her thoughts turned to Kai. She swore and leapt off the bed, tugging her clothes back on as she ran out of the room.

35

Before the Storm

The books were everywhere, lining each shelf across the entire room, short of the far wall, which held the window. Kai and Ravi sat, each in their own leather armchair, face deep in a book as the rain hammered outside. Kai shifted his weight and fumbled with the pages. It was tricky to hold the book and turn the page at the same time with just one hand. For a moment he wanted to cry, to throw the book across the room, but what was the point? It wouldn't solve anything. It wouldn't bring his arm back. Ravi glanced over and raised his eyebrows.

"Are you alright?"

"I'm fine."

"Don't worry, Kai," said Ravi. "Things might be a little difficult right now, but you'll get there. You're already ahead of any other patient I've seen in your condition. Try to take it easy, okay?"

"Okay."

Ravi nodded and returned to his book: a manual for solar panel maintenance. He'd been keen to learn more about the ones in the garden. He said they could keep the electricity and the boiler running so they wouldn't be cold through winter. It wasn't something Kai had ever worried about before. He'd once thought

Caede had been stingy with the thermostat, but actually, they had never been really cold. Something he'd taken for granted, maybe.

Ravi would need help with both things, he decided, so he would learn about them too. He didn't mind helping, or chores for that matter. Unlike Luna…. She had been in a foul mood since they were asked to wash the vegetables and had gone straight to her room afterwards. Cleaning wasn't fun, but he didn't get why she was so angry about it. And what was that joke about killing her parents for? It seemed insensitive, given that he'd told her about his own mum. She'd still joked about it, even suggesting that she'd do the same to Efi. The more he thought about it, the more she sounded like a liar. He didn't know how to feel about her. She was cool and funny—and older. His friends would have been dead jealous to know he was now living with an older girl. They talked about girls as if they were some kind of mythical beings, elusive and impossible to understand. If living with his sister had taught him anything, it was that girls were just like boys, and did all the same things boys did—even the gross stuff. The difference was that girls seemed to understand boys far better. Kai really didn't think anything of girls. He supposed it was a puberty thing, but he also wondered a few times if he was gay, or if he just wasn't interested in any of that stuff. He liked Ravi a lot, but he couldn't figure out what way he liked him. A mentor? An older brother, perhaps? Maybe because Ravi was kind and patient, nothing like his loser dad. Or was there more to it than that? He didn't really want to think about it.

The sky had gotten darker as the morning progressed, with black, swollen clouds bruising the horizon, and Kai found himself having to squint to see the words on the page. It made his head hurt, so he left Ravi to his studies and headed upstairs. Ravi had stressed to him that getting plenty of rest was critical to his recovery, and Caede would only worry if he didn't. Afterwards, they could have lunch and spend the rest of the afternoon playing board games. Ravi's uncle had plenty to choose from.

The stairs were a struggle. Logically, he knew it was on that side he'd lost the arm, but he kept forgetting. He'd started up the stairs on the wrong side. He kept reaching for the banister, and almost toppling down sideways when there was nothing to grip it. He screwed up his face and told himself to keep going. If someone had offered to help, he would have declined. He needed to do this by himself, and it was only really the stairs now, and the books.

He had to pass Caede's room to get to his, and paused at her door, deciding whether or not to see if she wanted to hang out. Then he heard a noise. He thought he heard Jon in there. Kai pressed his ear to the door and listened for a second before recoiling. Humour and disgust fought for dominance in his gut, and he stifled a laugh as he continued to his room. He couldn't be sure, but it sounded like they were doing things. Adult things. *Gross*, he thought.

Once in his room, he wobbled over to the bed and lay down, pulling the duvet up around him. He wondered if his friends were somewhere safe, if their parents had taken them away from the city in time. So many times, they were his comfort, his reminder that monsters weren't real, that he wasn't alone in the world. Now, there were only the adults, and a girl who seemed like she'd sooner stab him than anything else. The humour turned to sadness, and he cried quietly under the duvet until the exhaustion took over, and he fell asleep.

The sound of glass shattering woke him–not like someone dropping a drink on the floor shatter, but the shatter of a window, loud and mixed with the screeching of its frame, as if a brick, or something larger, had burst through it. Hurried, anxious voices carried through the hallway, then the door knocked and opened. It was Caede and Jon. They were sweaty and breathless, as if they'd been running.

"Kai?" Caede called.

Kai scrambled from the bed to his sister, hugging her tightly. "You heard it too?"

"Yeah," she whispered. "Are you okay?"

"Uh, huh. What is it?"

"Get dressed into something warm. Now. If we have to leave, I don't want you freezing."

"What about the others?"

"No questions," she said. "Just make sure you're warm. Boots on when we get downstairs."

The three left Kai's room to find Samson, Efi, and Ravi at the top of the stairway.

"Heard it too, huh?" said Samson, brow low. His mouth was twisted into a concerned grimace. Efi clutched a cricket bat in her hands, eyes wide, and Ravi stood with his arms crossed, still holding the book about solar panels.

"Any idea where it came from?" said Jon.

Samson shook his head slowly, and the group stood in the dark, listening intently, waiting for anything that differed from the steady hiss of the rain outside.

"Where's Luna?" said Efi.

"She went to her room," replied Kai. "I'll go get her."

"Not alone you won't," said Caede.

"It's alright," said Ravi. "I'll go with him; we can check together."

Kai looked at his sister, and she nodded reluctantly.

"Be careful," she said. "If anything doesn't look right, come back immediately. Do you understand?"

With a nod, Kai and Ravi headed down the hallway towards Luna's bedroom. The rest of the group continued to listen.

"I can't hear anything," said Jon.

"It was a window smashing, right?" said Efi.

"Yeah," said Samson. "You boarded up the ground floor, Johnny?"

"Aye," said Jon. "All 'cept the conservatory."

"So that leaves upstairs. This place got a loft?"

The others shrugged or shook their heads.

"No idea," said Jon.

Before anyone could reply, through the rain rose a roar, so loud and close that the group jerked and ducked as if it had been a grenade landing at their feet.

"What the fuck was that?" Efi hissed.

Samson turned his head to the front doors. "Sounds like I owe you lot a drink," he said.

Another roar tore through the air. From down the hallway came a scream.

Caede took off towards it. "Kai!"

"Caede!"

Jon rose to follow. A hand seized his wrist. It was Efi's. "Get the gun," she said.

36

Ophidiophobia

Kai and Ravi crept along the darkening hallway, feet padding lightly and ears straining. They'd checked Luna's room and found nothing. Kai wondered if she'd run away, or if she was hiding somewhere, but that didn't seem like her. Then, he'd seen the flicker of movement in a doorway up ahead, in the far bedroom. Something disappearing into the darkness beyond the door.

"Luna?" he called.

No answer.

"We need to be careful," said Ravi. He pushed his glasses nervously up his nose as he stared at the doorway. Kai nodded, and they continued towards it, slowly pushing it open. Light from the hallway spilled into the room, past his and Ravi's silhouettes, casting shadows this way and that as it bounced off the dark wood furniture. The pair gazed in, eyes searching for any signs of life.

"I can't see anything," said Kai, glancing up.

Ravi shrugged and stepped back towards the hallway. Just as Kai began to follow, he heard a noise. The sound was coming from the ensuite bathroom. A wet, gagging sound.

"Luna?" he said.

"What is it?" said Ravi.

"I don't know."

The pair crept through the room, towards the ensuite. Reaching the doorway, Kai looked into the bathroom and froze. He recognised the figure standing in front of him, with its white, nightmarish face, and long, fishlike body, now covered in gashes and bruises from what Kai could only guess was the result of being trapped in that lift shaft. The lift shaft it definitely couldn't have escaped, not without help. Sweat formed and dripped down his spine.

The snake was looking away from him, standing in the middle of the ensuite, jaws unhinged and open wide, head rising and falling in a juddery motion, like a gannet. A pair of feet poked out of its mouth. Resolve abandoned him, and Kai screamed, tumbling backwards. Arms caught him and yanked him away from the monster, and he ran out of the ensuite, socks slipping across the polished floor of the bedroom, Ravi in tow. From inside the ensuite, the snake groaned and staggered after them, but couldn't move. The pair froze, caught in fear as they watched it shudder, then fall on its front. It began to heave, the muscles in its neck flexing and undulating as Luna's body reappeared. With a final lurch, it spat her out, and she landed heavily on the floor.

"Oh my God," Ravi gasped.

The creature looked up and flicked its long, black tongue at them. It reared up, abandoning Luna, and hissed angrily at the pair.

"Run!" Kai screamed, seizing Ravi's arm.

They bolted out of the room, almost colliding with Caede. At first she looked confused, then her eyes raised, and her face twisted in horror. She spun on the spot and all three ran. From behind him,

Kai heard a sharp intake, and suddenly Ravi was on the floor, black liquid covering his back, sizzling away the fabric of his cardigan and shirt. As the venom reached his skin, Ravi screamed.

"Get it off!" Kai yelled.

Ravi tore off his cardigan and shirt, hurling them over the banister. Kai could see Samson and Efi running towards them, yelling something he couldn't make out. Maybe they were just screaming. He had to warn them about the venom.

"Don't let it spray you!" he cried as they drew near.

A second jet of black tar flew, hitting the wall to his left. Samson and Efi skidded to a halt and stumbled back, watching in horror as the yellow wallpaper bubbled and warped away.

"Shit!" said Samson.

Efi grabbed his arm and turned back. "Run!"

Something tickled the back of Kai's ear. Like a gust of wind, or a breath, something inside him screamed at him to duck. He yanked Ravi's arm and threw himself into an open doorway just in time to avoid the creature as it cannon-balled past. He knew what it would mean if those teeth collided with him again, and hoped Efi and Samson could dodge it. Gripping Ravi's arm, the pair crawled through the bedroom, ducking under a bed.

"Ravi," Kai whispered between strained breaths. "What do we do?"

"I don't know," said Ravi shakily. He went to push his glasses back up his nose and his fingers met air. "Oh God, my glasses..."

"Where are they?"

Ravi let out a frustrated sigh. "Probably at the bottom of the stairs with my cardigan."

"If you can't see, then… I'll fight it," said Kai.

"Absolutely not. Your sister entrusted me with your safety. We're not going anywhere near that thing."

"Caedey!" said Kai. "Where's Caedey?"

"I don't know. She's probably dealing with it. Let's just wait here and…"

Kai was already shimmying out from under the bed. From a gap between the ajar door and its frame flickered a black, forked tongue. Then the door opened. The snake glided into the room and rested its eyes on him. Kai froze and stared up at the creature. It had found him. And it was going to take his other arm now. And his legs, and his body. Why was no one stopping it? Where was Caedey? Why wasn't she here? But she was never *here*, was she? He was going to die alone. And he was always alone, wasn't he? She was always busy. Busy with work, busy with studies. His eyes filled with tears, blurring the outline of the monster, and the doorway, and the rest of the room. He didn't want to die. Ravi was tugging at his ankle, trying to pull him back under the bed, but it was too late. The creature was close now, so close he could feel the heat of its breath on his face, and this time it would swallow him up, just like it did Luna.

At least I'll see Mum again.

Something struck it from behind. It screamed and reared its head back, and Kai looked up to see Caede, gripping its neck in an armlock, her teeth clenched together with effort as she squeezed.

"Stay the fuck away from him!" she roared.

The snake bucked and threw itself back, hitting the wall. With a grunt, Caede let go, and she fell, but her arm caught something. The ornate brass handle of a sword was sticking out of the beast's back. With a savage cry, she wrenched it down, and the monster screamed again. She ducked and shouted something towards the hallway.

Samson's voice rose in response. "Head shot it!"

There was a bang, so loud it made Kai's ears ring, and a red mist filled the air where the monster's head was supposed to be. Two empty shotgun shells bounced on the hallway floor, and the snake slumped forward into its own pooling blood without a sound. Jon held the gun up from the other side of the doorway, arms shaking. He lowered it, rubbing his shoulder with his free hand as he stepped into the room.

"Fuck, that hurts!"

"Kick-back," said Samson. "Gotta be careful with it."

"Next time you shoot it, then!"

"You two!" barked Efi. She walked over to Ravi and helped him onto his feet, throwing a look at Jon and Samson.

"Stop bickering. Jon, cover the windows. We need to know how many of those things there are."

Jon obeyed, springing to action. He settled himself on a window ledge and began hastily reloading the shotgun. Caede tugged the sword from the monster's back and tucked it into its sheath, tied at her waist with a belt. She ran to Kai, wrapping him up in her arms, and held him tight. He hugged back and buried his face in her shoulder.

"Are you okay?" she said.

He mumbled something back and sniffed. Caede said nothing and stroked his hair. He pulled away after a moment, nodding reassuringly at his sister. He wanted to tell her he was alright now, to thank her, but the adrenaline was wearing off. Suddenly, he felt like a stone, like he needed to sink into something soft and stay there for a while.

"Come on," said Caede, leading him to the bed. "Sit here for a second, okay?"

With Efi and Caede's help, Ravi lowered himself into the bathtub of the ensuite, and Efi took the showerhead and began hosing him down with cold water. He grimaced as it hit his back, making pained noises through gritted teeth.

"Jesus! It's like a burn," said Efi.

"It feels like it," said Ravi. "There are sterile dressings in Kai's bedroom. Antiseptic cream as well. Blue rucksack by the bed."

"I'll get it," said Kai from the doorway of the ensuite.

"I told you to sit down," said Caede.

"Let him get it," said Efi. "He's a strong one, isn't he?"

"Yes," said Caede. "Sometimes I wonder who looks after who."

Jon shouted something from the window.

"What?" called Efi.

"I said, I can't see anything," said Jon from inside the bedroom, voice carrying over the sound of the shower. "Where's Luna?"

"What?" said Efi.

"I said, where's Luna?"

Samson walked into the room with Luna's body in his arms. "She's here."

He took Luna over to the bed and set her down. She sat hugging her knees, shivering and wheezing, not saying a word. Caede ran over with a towel and washcloth for the girl's face.

"It's okay now," she said gently, draping the towel around Luna's shoulders. She dabbed Luna's face with the cloth. The girl recoiled and shot her a look.

"I'll keep an eye on her," said Samson.

Caede handed him the cloth with a nod. "Thank you."

"Guys!" called Jon from his spot by the window. His face was drained of colour, and beads of sweat lined his forehead. "We've got visitors."

37

Thunder

Shit. There was a group of them, ten, maybe twelve figures at a glance, all standing gathered next to the fountains in the front garden of the manor. There were meant to be six. He had been sure it was only six. Through the curtain of rain, one stood out, its silhouette a dark and menacing obelisk, haloed by the water ricocheting off its body. The Komodo dragon, Kalinov.

"Fuck!" Jon spat. He punched the floor in frustration and turned away from the window, eyes closed as he leaned against the wall and rubbed his knuckles.

"What is it?" asked Efi. She crawled towards him and peeked over the window ledge. "Oh my God."

"Aye. Samson owes me a pint."

Samson approached the window. "Shit, how many's that?"

"Ten, I think," said Efi. "It's difficult to see."

"How're you feeling now?" Jon asked Samson. "Think you got another round in you?"

"Bit stiff, yeah, but I reckon I could take the big guy. Might need a bit of help, though."

Caede was at the window now, eyes wide as she gazed out at the monsters beneath them.

"They knew," she said.

"Knew what?" said Jon.

"They knew the weather was going to be bad today."

"It's November," said Efi. "It's bad every day."

"But it was clear yesterday. They could have attacked while it was clear, or during the night. They waited for this."

"Why?" said Efi. "Why would they wait? It would have been better to attack at night?"

"Welp," said Samson. "Don't matter now, does it? They're here."

"Aye," said Jon. "And it's gonna be a bugger to aim."

"That's why," said Caede. "Even at night you could aim, if you had a torch. And, if we didn't have a gun, we'd have to go out there in the rain. We'd be at a huge disadvantage."

"We're already at a huge disadvantage," Jon muttered.

Kai walked into the room, rucksack in hand. He trotted over to the window and peeked out. "What's going on?"

"Get back from there!" Caede hissed, pulling him away by his sleeve. "Come on. I told you to sit down. Go sit with Luna."

"But I can help!" Kai protested, pulling back at her.

"Listen to me," said Caede. "This isn't a game, okay?"

"You think I don't know that?"

"Just sit on the bed and wait there. Right now. No arguments."

"Better listen to her, bud," said Jon from his spot by the window.

Kai's shoulders sagged, and he obeyed, slumping onto the bed next to Luna. Caede took a spot next to Jon.

"You alright?" he said without looking up.

"I'm fine."

"You're not," said Jon.

"We can talk about this later."

"Might not happen, love."

She opened her mouth to protest, then closed it.

"Listen," said Jon. "If we survive this, I won't chicken out again. I promise."

"Better survive then," Caede whispered.

Jon glanced at her and smiled grimly. He felt fingers tangle with his and curled his hand around them.

Efi sat Ravi down on the bed and began applying one of the creams from the rucksack. He cringed as the cream touched his skin and shifted his weight uncomfortably.

"I think I'll stay with the children. Luna needs urgent care, and I'm in no position to fight any more monsters."

"Are you sure?" said Efi.

"You'll need me here if you get injured," Ravi replied. He went to take off his glasses, to rub them against his shirt, but neither was there, and he lowered his hands and sighed.

"I'll get you a towel," said Efi.

Ravi grabbed her arm. "Efi," he said, voice quiet. "We both know I'm not a fighter, and I can't see a bloody thing without my glasses. I'm much better with the aftermath."

"I know," said Efi gently. "It's okay. Stay with the children, make sure they don't get hurt."

He nodded obediently. Efi bandaged him up before heading to the window, settling next to Jon.

"What's the plan?" he asked.

"We use the advantage we have," said Efi. "We're shielded here. They're not. How many rounds have we got?"

"It's twenty per box," said Jon. "And we have a couple of boxes, so we've got enough to pick off a few of 'em, even with my aim."

"Do you know what you're doing?" asked Caede.

"Took care of snake man, didn't I?"

"What are they doing down there?"

Jon squinted as he tried to make out the group. They hadn't moved any closer to the house, but now they were huddled in a circle as if they were talking to each other, assessing, trying to decide which part of the house to attack first, maybe.

"I don't know. Wish they'd all just fuck off and leave us alone."

"Shoot them," said Caede. Her eyes met his. "Do it before they attack."

"Alright. Open the window."

But Caede just stood there, staring out at the rain.

"Caede?"

"Where have they gone?" she said.

Jon snapped his head towards the window. The space where the group had been was now empty. His guts tightened.

"Shit."

Efi stood and headed to the other window. Samson was already there, looking out.

“I can’t see them,” he said.

“How good is your eyesight?”

“Better than it used to be.”

Efi stared hard through the glass, unblinking, then with a sudden inhale, she leapt back.

“Left! Luna’s room!”

“Shit!” said Jon. He leapt up and ran towards the sound. Caede darted ahead of him in a fluid motion, sweeping past him as if he were wearing lead boots, and he almost tripped over himself. By the time he was at the door, it was already open, and Caede was halfway down the hall with one of the swords in her hands, Efi close behind her. He heard a scuffle, a sharp gasp, a thud, a grunt, and the two women staggered out of Luna’s room covered in red.

“One down,” Efi croaked.

“How many left?”

Efi shook her head. “God knows.”

“I’ll man that window,” said Jon, heading back into the bedroom. He settled on the window ledge, gun ready.

Samson appeared at his right. “Kalinov’s still down there, then.”

“Oh yeah, your scientist mate.”

“You wanna make a bet?”

“Yeah, go on then.”

“How many punches do you reckon it would take for that fucker to tell me where Daisy is?”

“Who’s Daisy?”

Before Samson could answer, a crash came from down the hallway.

"Fuck!" said Jon, pushing himself up.

The pair ran back out. There were three of the creatures, one with a sword stuck through its chest, hobbling across the landing. It swayed, crashing into the banister, and fell to the floor below with a crunch. The other two were entangled with Efi and Caede, all of them wrestling and striking at each other with pain-fuelled grunts. Samson leapt forward, seizing one of the figures, freeing Efi. Jon recognised her as the sprinter with dark hair. Samson roared, throwing her down over his raised knee, and with a crack she arched, gasped, and fell to the floor, unmoving. Caede was still wrestling with the third, punching and clawing at it like a wild cat. Jon raised the gun, but couldn't get a clear shot.

"Samson!" he yelled, and the big man seized the creature–a male, skinny and grey as a corpse, with hardened spines speckled along his arms and back. Samson lifted him by the throat and hurled him towards Jon. Jon fired, and the thing's head exploded into a red mist.

A scream rose from the bedroom.

"The kids!" yelled Efi.

The four darted into the bedroom. Luna and Kai were on the bed, screaming and yelling, "kill it! Kill it!"

Ravi was on the floor, desperately trying to fight off one of the creatures. Jon couldn't even get a look at it before Samson barrelled it over, knocking it out of the window. With a shriek, it fell, dashing its head on the ground below. A bellow rose in response, and the group froze.

"Okoye!"

Jon skidded over to the window and looked out. It was Kalinov. The rest of the chimaeras stood with him, the group smaller now, but it didn't feel like a comfort.

"Okoye!" Kalinov repeated, his chainsaw voice rising over the hiss of the rain. "Come out of there. Fight like a man, and I will let your friends go!"

"Ah, shit," said Samson. "He's got me there."

A small voice rose from the bed. It was Luna, propped up against the pillows, staring at Samson. "You should go."

Efi shot her a look. "Be quiet," she said.

"But I'm right!" Luna shot back. "He should go. They only want him!"

"Listen to me, child," said Efi, pointing a finger. "We don't sell out our own. You do not say that again. Do you understand me?"

"It's okay, Eff," said Samson calmly. "She's right."

"You're not thinking of going out there, are you?" Efi snapped. "Are you crazy?"

"Nah," said Samson. "They won't stop until I square up."

"Sam," said Efi. "If you're going out there, I'm coming with you. I will not let you fight that thing by yourself."

"Same," said Caede. "They're going to kill us, anyway. Or worse."

"Might as well make it a pain in the arse for them," said Jon.

Efi and Caede nodded.

"Nah, guys," said Samson. "I can't ask you to do that."

"Chale," said Efi. "You helped us. Now, we will help you. We're all we have left."

"Depressing, ain't it," said Jon.

Samson laughed, then rubbed his face with his hands.

"Alright," he said, finally. "Let's do this."

"Not to doubt you or anything," said Jon, "but soon as we get out there I'm shooting the fucker."

38

Rain

Jon rested his hand on the front door handle. "You sure you wanna do this?" he asked.

Samson looked at him, brow low. "Don't think we have a choice, Johnny."

"Weapons ready?"

"If you can call a broom with a knife taped to it a weapon," said Efi, "then yes, the weapons are ready."

Jon nodded grimly and pushed his hand against the door. Just as it was about to open, Samson stopped him.

"Wait a sec."

"What?"

"Listen," said Samson, addressing the group. "Far as I know, there's only two people in this whole world infected with Sigma 13. Me and Efi. I reckon Kalinov's given these guys 12 and they think they're stronger than they are. Still, be careful. Shoot 'em in the head. Scramble their brains–they'll die. Same if their heart's damaged beyond repair. A body's a body. Damage it enough and it's down. You get me?"

Jon nodded. "Headshot it is, then."

The chimaeras were waiting for them on the lawn, just beyond the gravel driveway and fountain. Jon shivered inside his overcoat as the icy rain pummelled his face and neck. He'd borrowed that and a pair of wellies from the mudroom. The boots were too small and tight around his feet, but better than his old trainers in the current circumstance. He gripped the gun tightly to his chest for reassurance. Next to him were Efi and Caede, each of them holding a makeshift spear, swords tucked into their belts.

Samson walked a little ahead, stopping at the edge of the lawn to cock his head towards the group. "Alright!" he shouted. "How are we doing this?"

Kalinov the dragon stepped forward and grinned, baring his sharpened teeth. He gave a slow, wide sweep of his arm. "Here is fine. Unless you prefer inside."

"I don't like this," muttered Efi.

Jon said nothing. He just nodded and tried to focus on not falling over and shooting himself. The heavy rain had softened the lawn, leaving it slick and boggy, making every step forward an effort. If he was about to die in a fight with a bunch of lizard people, he was going to go with whatever dignity he could. *Here lies Jonathan Taylor; graphic designer, alcoholic. Died slipping on his arse in some mud.*

The chimaeras hissed and growled as the group approached, shifting excitedly on the spot.

"Thought I'd never see you again, Kalinov," said Samson.

The dragon said nothing. Instead, he raised a hand high as if to salute, and dropped it. Two of the chimaeras stepped forward from the rest of the group; a skinny female with a wide jaw and huge hands, and a stocky, muscular-looking male. Kalinov let out a hiss, and the pair attacked.

Quicker than Jon's eyes could follow, the female was right there in front of him, knocking the wind out of his lungs as her feet landed squarely on his chest. He flew backwards into the mud, coughing and gasping. The gun disappeared out of sight, lost in the rain. To his right he heard a scream.

"Jon!"

One of the broom handles landed next to him and he grabbed it. He caught a movement to his left and instinctively rolled. A foot landed heavily in the empty space. He shot his arm out, seizing the chimaera's ankle, and yanked hard, dragging her down. She was quick, but she wasn't strong, and she crumpled under the force of the pull. He rolled again, pulling her leg under the broom, and pressed down with all his weight. With a loud pop, her shin snapped. The chimaera screamed, letting go of Jon, and she writhed on the ground, clutching her broken leg. Wasting no time, Jon forced himself up and ran to the spot he thought the gun had landed, but he couldn't see anything, only mud and grass. He glanced around to see Caede and Efi, fighting the stocky male, Caede gripping her sword.

His punishment for not paying attention came in the form of a vicious bite to his lower leg. The chimaera's teeth sliced through the thick rubber of the boot, puncturing his calf. He cried out and jabbed down with the spear, catching her in the shoulder. Thick crimson spurted out, spilling over the ground, and the lizard recoiled. Seizing his chance, he stabbed again, hitting her in the chest, and the knife's blade stuck fast, wedging itself into the centre of her ribcage. She flailed around, screaming and trying to free herself. Jon gripped the spear and prayed the duct tape holding the knife to the broom would hold. He pushed again, forcing the blade in further, until suddenly she stopped moving and slumped to the ground.

No time to relax, lad. Jon yanked the makeshift spear free and turned to see Efi and Caede finishing off the other one. Caede ducked, then launched herself forward, raising the sword up under the chimaera's chin. With a scream, she drove it home, and the chimaera dropped in a heap on the ground.

How many is that now? he thought. Behind him came a roar, and he snapped his head round. Samson was striding through the mud, his path set towards Kalinov.

"Samson!" he shouted, but the big man couldn't hear him.

Pleased by the challenge, the dragon shifted his shoulders and puffed out his chest, laughing murderously. The two juggernauts began circling, staring each other down once again. Before Jon could take a step towards them, the next fighter stepped forward, issuing his own challenge. This one was thicker set, his arms sinewy and muscular. He approached Jon slowly, cautiously, a hunting knife in his hand. Jon shook off the pain in his leg and raised the spear up close to his chest. A high-pitched whine began filling his ears.

S'alright, son; all you need to do is not get stabbed. Easy peasy.

The lizard leapt forward, whipping its arm out like a slingshot. Jon threw himself backwards, barely avoiding the slash of the blade. He swore and jutted the spear forward, jabbing at the chimaera, forcing him backwards. They circled again before the chimaera threw his arm forward, striking fast. Jon jumped back again. As his foot hit the ground, a sharp pain shot up his leg and he slipped, landing on his back in the wet grass. With a hiss, the chimaera leapt down, knife pointed at his face, ready to strike. Without thinking, Jon threw his arm forwards. In an instant, the lizard stopped moving. It was impaled on the spear, blood pouring down the shaft. Jon let the spear go, letting it fall to the side with its victim, and he lay still, lungs and ribs burning, to catch his breath.

A scream cut through the air. It was Efi, shouting something at him. He jumped up. Samson and Kalinov were standing, arms locked together in a stalemate. Dark red blurred with rain on Samson's hoodie. Half a broom handle stuck out of Kalinov's thigh. The pair panted with strain.

Efi shouted again. "Help Samson!" A chimaera appeared behind her, knocking her over. Caede leapt at it, sword in hand. "Go!"

Suddenly, Kalinov's head collided with Samson's face. He let out a yell and leapt back, spitting blood at the ground before steadying himself and raising his fists.

Samson punched. The dragon feinted, left, right, retreating steadily backwards, just as it had at the hospital. Jon tried to call out, but the two giants couldn't hear him. Samson threw a left hook, catching the dragon's jaw, knocking its head sideways. Kalinov shook it off and seized Samson's arm. He punched with the other, then suddenly his arm fell limp.

Swaying on his feet, Samson tried again. He hadn't fully recovered from the fight at the hospital, from the venom, and he was tired. Jon's eyes flicked downward to his spear. If he could get to Samson quick enough… but the mud was thick, and Kalinov was laughing now, loud, and he'd pulled Samson close to his face.

Jon started wading towards the pair. "Samson!"

He looked up again to see Samson's arm hanging limply at his side, his other arm gripping the dragon's throat in desperation.

"Samson!" Jon bellowed, running faster. "I'm coming!"

Kalinov batted Samson's arm away effortlessly and laughed. Jon's muscles screamed as he urged his legs to move faster. Not fast enough. Kalinov was already gripping Samson's hair, wrenching his head back.

"Samson!"

The dragon roared and threw its head down, clamping its mouth over Samson's exposed throat. Samson screamed as the dragon's neck swelled and contracted. Thick, black liquid poured out from between the gaps in its teeth and ran down Samson's throat and shoulders. Blood erupted from Samson's eyes, nose, and ears. He twitched and gagged sickeningly as the dragon pumped the venom into him. Then it ripped its head away, taking Samson's throat with it, his blood spraying into the air. It let go and Samson slumped to the floor, no fight left. He stayed on the ground, lying still as the rain washed his blood into the earth.

The dragon looked over at Jon and smiled, its crimsoned teeth bared.

39

Lightning Strike

The sky darkened, and the rain pounded harder into the ground, transforming the already soaking manor gardens into a freezing quagmire. Jon struggled to keep his balance, and the rain cascaded over his face, dripping wet hair into his eyes. Through the blur, the dragon approached. It towered over him, grinning in triumph.

Jon stepped carefully sideways; his eyes locked with it. He wasn't a fighter. He'd been in fights, sure, but those were childish skirmishes in school, or a scuffle outside a pub over a rugby match. None were fights for his life, not until the last few days, anyway, and none against a foe so monstrous, and so utterly terrifying. And he had a broomstick to defend himself with. He gripped the makeshift spear a little tighter, and tried his best not to piss himself, or fall over, as he trembled under the monster's shadow.

The dragon gave Jon a nod. "You are braver than most!"

"Fuck off!" shouted Jon. "Samson's dead, right? The traitor? That's what you called him. You got him. So why don't you just piss off and leave us alone?"

The dragon chuckled. "The traitor is dead, yes, but that is not only why we are here. You have something we need. I am here to collect it."

"Eh? What are you on about?"

They watched each other, the dragon slowly circling him, its feet leaving a trail through the crushed grass and mud. From somewhere behind him, Jon could hear the yells of his companions, ordinary people fighting heavyweight champions. And he'd dropped the frigging gun, hadn't he? The only weapon that stood a chance against this bastard. And he'd lost it.

Useless.

Before he could even blink, the dragon shot forward. Jon's feet found themselves above him, right in the air. It was so fast he was surprised he still had his boots on. He heard the slap of the mud, and a ringing noise filling his ears as he landed. The spear was gone, landing in the grass, just out of reach. Jon lay on the ground, dazed and groaning, sucking in shallow breaths. This was it. He was dead. He must be, because nothing else was happening. Everything sounded far away, dulled by the ringing and the sound of his own heartbeat.

A scream cut through the haze.

"Shit…"

He wrenched himself onto all fours and tried looking around. White-hot pain seared through his right eye. He tried to open it, but couldn't. Something warm oozed from his forehead and down his face. He felt a hard lump floating around in his mouth and spat it out. Wiping his face with his sleeve, he forced himself to stand. The dragon was waiting, either to mock him, or it was following some unknown code of honour–don't murder the shit out of a man while he's down. Jon cursed. There was a flash of envy for Saturday Jon, the Jon on his way to the rooftop before all this kicked off. The dragon loomed over him, wearing the same grin from before, long, black tongue flickering lazily in and out of its mouth, lingering, as if to savour his suffering.

And what could he do about it? Sod all is what. He'd at least die on his feet, like a man... fighting a literal dragon. He imagined his father nodding in approval.

The dragon reached down, seizing him by the throat with one colossal hand, and lifted him into the air. He gasped and kicked, flailing uselessly as an infant against the monster's arm, and it laughed that avalanche laugh, pulling him close to its face. Jon closed his eyes and let his arms fall limp.

This is it, lad.

Death didn't come. Something was distracting it. Caede and Efi, darting around the beast like wasps, spear and sword in hand, ducking low, stabbing, viciously stinging its legs and torso before leaping backwards.

The dragon roared in fury as it swatted at the women with its free arm. But they were smaller, faster, dodging every swipe. Jon lifted his arm and his hand brushed something in his pocket. The Swiss Army knife. He grabbed it, flicking the blade up, and sank it deep into the dragon's arm. He twisted the blade and yanked down. The monster roared again and let go, and he fell to the ground with a thud.

Throat burning, Jon coaxed himself back onto his feet, shaking off the throbbing in his head and chest. He spotted the broom handle sticking up out of a patch of grass and scrambled towards it. He had to help the girls. They were quick, but–he heard a short, sharp scream and a loud thump.

Jon whipped his head around to see Caede lying face down in the mud.

"Caede?"

She didn't respond.

"Caede?!"

The rain bounced off her body as she lay motionless in the grass. A weight formed in his gut and settled there. He moved. The mud sucked at his boots, pulling at his feet as he dragged himself towards her, as if it knew, and was warning him not to approach. The ringing sound returned, louder than ever, pulsing in his ears, filling his brain with static. The sounds of the fighting and the rain faded into the background.

"Caede? Caede! Talk to me!"

He was close enough to touch her now, and reached out, nudging her arm gently. She didn't respond. He yanked her up into his arms, vision blurring. *You promised her.*

From somewhere far away, Efi's scream echoed.

You promised.

"Jon!"

More shouts, closer now.

Useless.

"Jon!"

Pathetic.

"Jon! Help me!"

A wave of ice-cold fury swept over him. The burning in his chest and eye faded. Jaw clenched, he laid Caede down, picked up the spear and dragged himself back towards the battle. As he approached, he could see Ravi and Kai had joined in now, stabbing at the beast with sharpened broomsticks of their own. Ravi had his glasses back on, one of the lenses cracked. Efi increased her efforts, jabbing at the dragon, the broom handle black and slick with its blood. She caught Jon's eye and darted left, turning the dragon's attention towards her. Blinded by rage, it followed, swiping madly at her, then at Kai and Ravi. Kai leapt back quicker than Jon could see and ducked close to the ground. Efi filled the space he left and struck, jabbing it savagely in the gut.

With every step, the freezing rain lashed mercilessly against Jon's face, his feet throbbed, and his bones ached. He drudged onwards, jaw set and teeth gritted. Finally, he reached the dragon.

Some advice he'd been given years ago–maybe by his dad, maybe rugby, he wasn't sure–materialised in his mind. *One foot back, lad. Ground yourself. Steady your shoulders.* Gripping the spear in his hands, he gulped down the ball of fear sitting in his throat, gathered his strength, and bellowed.

"Oiii!"

Everything stopped. The world around him fell silent. Even the rain battering the grounds seemed to cease above him, its veil circling him and the dragon alone, isolating the pair from the rest of the universe, as if some divine being wanted to witness the moment of his certain death. The dragon paused and turned in slow motion, flexing its broad shoulders; a Goliath towering over the frail, utterly ordinary human frame that quivered beneath it. Acid burned in the back of his throat. Jon set one foot back to ground himself.

Efi appeared beside him. For a split second, the dragon twitched its head towards her. Seizing his chance, Jon hurled the spear up with all his might. With a deafening crack, it pierced the dragon's throat and burst through the back of its skull, spraying thick crimson into the air. For a moment, it looked confused, then its black eyes rolled back, and its face twisted into a scream. It lurched sideways, hissing and thrashing, throwing itself around as the life sprayed out of its body. Jon let go of the spear just in time to avoid being dragged under it, and he stood panting, hands on his knees, as he watched the monster writhe and shriek. Finally, it fell, slumping lifelessly to the ground.

"We did it," he gasped. "We fucking did it."

Efi approached the body, weapon in hand. "Is it dead?"

"I bloody hope so," said Ravi. He leaned against his own makeshift spear, wheezing. Efi raised hers into the air and threw it down, thrusting it deep into the dragon's flesh. The beast didn't move.

"Yup," she replied. "Definitely dead."

Kai walked up to the body and looked down, eyes bulging at the sight. Then he looked up and around, suddenly panicked. "Where's Caede?"

Jon opened his mouth to answer, but the world around him had turned sideways, and the ground rose up to meet him as he passed out.

40

Aftermath

Blurred shapes floated around his periphery, and muffled sounds echoed as he returned to consciousness. He tried opening his eyes, but only one responded. He was met with a beam of amber light stretched across a white ceiling. The familiar faces of Ravi and Efi stared down at him behind goggles and surgical masks. They said something, but he couldn't hear what. A dull ache consumed him, and a ringing sound filled his ears. His eye began to burn, so he closed it again. Jon moved his lips to speak, but nothing came out. He groaned and tried to sit up, only to fall back again.

"Don't sit up," said Ravi. "You've been unconscious for a while, and you're on a lot of medication."

"We had to strap you down," said Efi.

Jon opened his left eye again.

"Don't look at me like that," said Efi. "We had to make sure. And you wouldn't let us..." she trailed off and glanced at Ravi.

"I'll start with the bad news," said Ravi.

He spoke calmly, with the practised formality of a doctor accustomed to delivering unwelcome news. Jon tried to nod. Whatever the news was, he wouldn't be able to escape it, so he might as well just lie there and listen.

"There's no easy way to tell you this, Jon, but during the fight, your right eye was severely damaged. We tried to save it, but we were unsuccessful."

"I'm so sorry," said Efi.

Jon lay still, as images of the attack flashed through his mind, and he remembered being struck by the dragon. Thinking about the strength behind the monster's fists, things could have been a lot worse. He could live with one eye, he supposed. People did it all the time.

Then it hit him. *Caede.* He remembered her lying there on the ground, mud on her face, her eyes closed. What did they do with her body?

"Cae…" he croaked, pulling against the makeshift restraints as he tried to sit up. Coughing, he lay back. Tears burned the corners of his eyes and rolled down his face.

Efi reached over and stroked his hair. "Shhh, it's okay, babe. It's going to be okay."

"Caede," Jon tried to whisper, reaching his hand to Efi. She took it and held it as she looked at Ravi, her face hard to read behind the mask. Her eyes seemed different behind the goggles. They'd been dark brown before, almost black. Now they were a golden yellow, and her pupils were an odd shape. Jon wondered if he was hallucinating because of the meds, or maybe it was just trauma. Efi turned back to Ravi, and Jon assumed she hadn't heard him.

"Samson, as you probably already know," Ravi continued, "did not survive the encounter."

Efi closed her eyes and grimaced, tears freely pouring, forming wet patches on the mask as she gripped Jon's hand. Ravi leaned on the edge of the bed and pulled the mask down to sit under his chin, fingers massaging his nose.

"Luna is alive but has sustained a number of significant injuries. She will be bedridden for the foreseeable future."

Jon screwed up his face and focused on making a sound beyond just croaking. "Caede?" he said.

Finally hearing him, Ravi nodded. "Caede is alive."

The words reverberated around the room as Jon took them in. Relief and elation knocked him back against the pillows, flooding over him, washing away the fear and grief, and suddenly he felt much lighter. The ringing noise fell quiet.

"Caede suffered a heavy blow to the head during the fight," Ravi continued. "I can't say with certainty that she will make a full recovery, but she is resting in the other room with Kai. The next few days will be crucial."

Jon said nothing. He just lay on the bed with his eyes closed.

41

The Change

Justine Pearson, entry 01.11.2030

If anyone is listening to this, my name is Justine Pearson. I'm the lead scientist for the Sigma Delta Tau project. My team and I created Sigma-13 as part of a military-funded genetic engineering operation. Out of my team, I am the only human survivor. I'm alive, I'm safe, and I'm going to continue my work, in hiding, until I can find a way to fix this mess.

I will make this better, somehow.

-

The days following the funeral passed slowly, with the weight of the attack hanging over the survivors. Samson's grave–more a shallow flower bed, dug in the far corner of the garden by Ravi and Efi–was marked by a small, handmade wooden cross with his name written on it in marker pen. It was one of several, each of them labelled with the names of lost loved ones.

Jon, Caede, and Luna were all too injured to attend, so after burying his body, Kai, Efi and Ravi stood together in quiet reverence. Samson's belongings, a rucksack filled with printouts, notebooks, and USB sticks, were now in Efi's care. For the chimaeras, Ravi took tissue and blood samples from each. Then he and Efi dug a pit in the next field over, as far away from the house as possible. For a while, they considered burning the bodies before deciding against it. Too much fuel to waste, too much noise and light. The last thing they needed was to shine a beacon out to any remaining chimaera–or humans, for that matter–who might intend them harm.

Kai, desperate to be useful, spent his time assisting Ravi and Efi with the others' care–despite their insistence that he didn't have to–or curled up in the library with a fourth edition copy of The SAS Survival Handbook.

A successful scouting mission by Efi sourced the group enough medicines and tools to convert two of the spare bedrooms into temporary infirmaries, with Caede and Luna in one room, and Jon in the other. She and Ravi had even scavenged a suitable prosthetic to replace Kai's arm. Once charged, and with a bit of tinkering, Ravi was able to fit it to the boy.

"Good thing the hospital had its own 3D printer. I was a little concerned that they wouldn't have anything on site. It's hard to know how up to date these rural hospitals are. We actually found a few prosthetics. More than we could carry. These newer models have built in wi-Fi and fitness trackers–not that either would be useful at this moment in time, but you never know. And this one will help with the phantom limb syndrome. It will actively manage your pain. How does it feel?"

"It's a bit heavy," said Kai.

"That's normal. It will get easier the more you wear it. Try flexing your fingers."

Kai obliged; face set in concentration as he stared at the hand. After a few seconds, one of the fingers twitched.

"I can't do it," he said with a huff.

"Don't worry," said Ravi. "It's only your first try. Soon enough, you'll be able to move it just like a real arm."

***

Jon rested mostly, at first only leaving his bed to use the bathroom or take short walks around the manor. He'd found himself surprised that the water was still running, that the toilets still flushed, and he wondered when it would stop. He made a mental note to ask what the long-term plan would be for water. Were there any rivers nearby? Could they collect rainwater and use that? Would they need to filter it? There was so much to consider, so much he had taken for granted. You turned a tap and water came out. He'd never really thought about it beyond that.

Also surprising were the sudden and intense migraines. One minute he was fine, the next, he was on the floor, curled up in a foetal position, clutching his skull in agony. Ravi had warned him not to exert himself, but even with as much bed rest as he could tolerate, they would come, the pain all-consuming.

He resented staying in bed day in, day out, and wondered how he'd been able to do it back at the flat. Once upon a time he'd happily spent days at a time indoors, in his pyjamas doing bugger all, but suddenly he couldn't stand it. Efi would check in, only to find him doing pull-ups on the ensuite door frame, and she'd yell at him to get back in bed. He didn't dare argue. Through everything, she'd been there, working tirelessly, taking care of everyone–her and Ravi. The pair had been miracle workers.

Then there was the change. It had swept through Efi like a storm. Ravi hadn't told him until he'd recovered more, but just after the attack, she had fallen ill with a high fever, bedridden for at least a day, puking her guts up. Then, she was fine again–better than fine. *Changed.* Her face shone with gold, as if blessed by some ancient Grecian Goddess. Patterns ran down her skin, mottled dots and semi-circle lines akin to that of a jaguar or leopard. And the change had given her strength–strength beyond that of any human. Speed too. He wondered if she could have matched Samson in a fight.

No one could figure out where the DNA had come from, either– not until Efi had rifled through the contents of Samson's bag and discovered the other syringes, each labelled with a different animal type. They concluded that, due to the markings on her skin, it had to be a big cat of some kind.

Kai had visited too, every day, to show off his new arm. The kid delighted in picking things up with it, then dropping them. They'd tried a handshake at one point but had to be separated by Ravi after the arm had nearly crushed Jon's hand.

A week passed by with no change to Caede's condition. Another passed before she could return to her own bedroom. Multiple times Jon had approached her room, only to falter at the door handle and walk away.

"Give it time," Efi had said. "She needs rest. She's lucky to be alive."

Truth be told, Jon didn't want her to see him. Every time he left that door, he'd return to his room, head for the ensuite and just stare at himself in the mirror, taking in all the bruises, the bandages, the medical eye patch covering the hole where his eye had been. He wasn't vain, and he'd never been particularly insecure about his face before–you didn't play rugby and care about how pretty you were–but this was different. He'd lost his eye. What would she think? Would she still want to see him? And after he'd left her hanging, too. The first lass in years to show him an ounce of attraction, to be happy to see him, to kiss him, to actually want him… and he'd bottled it.

Another week passed, and the power from the grid finally failed. The group had anticipated the loss, and in a continuation of their miracle streak, Efi and Ravi had managed to revive the back-up generator. They'd even figured out the solar panel battery system and the biomass boiler, ensuring some light and warmth for the house. Most of the electricity was saved for food preservation and medical apparatus. Efi, ever sensible, had taken steps to prevent water loss by filling the unused bathtubs from the taps. She had also positioned the large water butts in the vegetable garden to catch as much rain as possible. Ravi had curried and frozen all the vegetables from the garden and taken stock of the pantry. Between that, the bags of rice, and the canned food, Jon reckoned they were in a pretty good position to get through winter. There were worse things to survive on than tinned food and vegetable curry.

Finally well enough, Jon made attempts to help out where possible. With Efi and Ravi busy taking care of Caede and Luna, Kai had been left to pick up the domestic chores and was grateful for Jon's help.

Jon had been wringing out some jumpers in the tub of the master bathroom, letting his mind wander, when he found himself standing in front of the mirror once again, inspecting his eye. Ravi had changed the bandages earlier that morning and mentioned something about a suitable false eye. Jon wasn't sure how he felt about it. He opened his mouth and checked his teeth. The dragon had knocked out two of them in the attack, leaving an unsightly gap in the right side of his gum line. It could have been worse. He was starting to look like his old self again. He'd even convinced Efi to give him a haircut and help him shave, and she'd done a good job, too, even if she was a bit trigger-happy with the clippers. And–he looked down to confirm–he'd lost weight. The mirror was his friend today. Maybe it was time.

He leaned on the sink and stared at the plughole. Would it be awkward? Would she be put off? Upset? He imagined her recoiling at his eye and began pacing around the room.

"She asks about you," said Kai.

Jon jumped and spun around. *Shit.* He'd forgotten the boy was there.

"Huh?"

"She asks about you," Kai repeated.

"What?"

Kai dunked a pile of clothes into the tub. "Yeah. She thinks you ghosted her."

"Not gonna lie, bud. It's weird to hear you say 'ghosted'."

"I'm not a little kid; I know what it means. Did you really?"

"No!" said Jon. "I mean…I didn't mean to…. Look at me. Would you want to see this after going through all that?"

Kai looked back at him with a blank expression.

Jon sighed. "I should just go, shouldn't I?"

Kai nodded and returned to the laundry. It was decided then. He left the bathroom and strode over to Caede's room. He stood at the door, hand hovering, suspended in front of him. Finally, he willed it to make contact with the wood, and tapped. He waited.

This is a bad idea.

Why? What are you so afraid of?

He pivoted on the spot a couple of times, hopped up and down, and puffed air out of his cheeks. Just as he decided to leave, he heard a familiar voice.

"Come in."

Fighting every urge to flee, he turned the door handle and stepped over the threshold. The room was dark, save for a sliver of daylight from between the curtains eking across the room, just enough to see the shapes of the furniture and the dust particles floating languidly in the air. There was a familiar smell here too, hiding underneath the cleaning chemicals, the scent of well-worn bed linens and sleep, reminiscent of weekend lie-ins and lazy Sundays. Caede was sitting in the middle of a large four-poster bed with a small tray across her legs, on it a deck of cards set up for a round of Solitaire. A pile of books sat next to her. One of them he recognised. A science fiction classic about space travel and sand. He'd read it a hundred times as a teenager. Seeing it next to her made his stomach ache.

"Bit dark in here for reading, ain't it?"

Caede glanced up. A card slipped from her hand and fluttered onto the others, disrupting the careful set-up.

"I haven't started them yet," she said. "I tried reading one, but it hurt too much. I'm still getting headaches on and off. The cards are a bit easier."

"Do you want some painkillers? I can get some. It won't take a sec."

"I'm fine. Where have you been?"

Compared to the ringing sound filling his ears, her voice was barely audible. For a second, he thought he was about to get another migraine.

"I...uh, well...I did come see you a couple of times, but you were asleep. I didn't want to disturb you."

"I haven't been asleep for three weeks," said Caede.

Jon swallowed hard. "I know. I'm sorry."

He stepped into the light and gestured to the medical patch covering his eye. His hand found the back of his neck as he watched Caede's reach her mouth.

"What happened?"

He said nothing. Somehow saying it out loud would confirm the fact, even though he'd been living without the eye for weeks already.

"Had a bit of a scrap with some lizard prick," he said. "Told me he broke a pool table, so I had to sort him out."

Caede grinned, stifling a laugh. "Did you kill it?"

He felt himself smiling. "Aye."

"Good."

He shifted awkwardly on the spot. The room was suddenly equal parts unbearably hot and freezing, and a line of sweat was forming in the centre of his back.

"Are you okay?" asked Caede.

He chuckled again and rocked on his feet. "Ah, don't you worry about me. I'm tough, remember? I'm just glad you're doing alright." He could feel himself stepping backwards, retreating to the door. "I'd better get you them painkillers, eh?"

"Why did you leave?" she asked.

Jon paused and glanced back. Caede had set the tray aside and was slipping from the bed. She had on the same baggy jumper and jogging bottoms she'd been wearing when he had first arrived at the house. She walked over to him, stopping just short of arm's reach. His stomach churned.

"Please," said Caede. "Can you just tell me? I don't mind. I just wanted to know why."

"I, uh, should let you get some rest."

"Oh, come on, Jon. I've been resting for nearly a sodding month! I've barely seen anyone…"

She folded her arms. "Look, whatever it is, I'm a big girl. I can take it."

He stood halfway in, halfway out of the doorway, knowing that if he turned around and met her eyes, he wouldn't be able to leave. He would be drawn into their depths, only to sink and drown. If he was being completely honest with himself, it was too late. It had happened the moment she had looked up at him in Mrs Brown's kitchen. He could have returned to his lonely flat and drunk himself to oblivion. He could have taken that trip to the roof again. *But no, you had to follow her.* And now, something was different. He wanted nothing more than to walk over to the bed, continue where they left off.

"Caede…" he said, almost pleading, before trailing off. He felt a hand rest on the small of his back, and another around his waist. He took it in his and went to pull her away, but then he remembered the warmth of her body under his, the smell of her sweat, the softness of her hair. And those eyes.

Why are you resisting? he thought. *Why the fuck are you resisting, you daft prick?* He gritted his teeth.

What are you so afraid of?

"Caede, I…"

He turned to face her.

What are you so afraid of?

"Jon, look," she said. "I'm sorry. I just thought…"

He met her eyes and took a deep breath. Before he knew it, the door had closed, and he was kissing her, lifting her up, and she was wrapping her legs around his waist, gripping him so tightly it made his ribs ache and his head swim. He gasped, and she relaxed, pulling back, her eyes full of sudden concern.

"Are you okay?"

"Yeah."

A smile flickered across her face. "Promise you won't leave this time?"

Epilogue

"It's recording? Oh, okay. Cool, cool. We can edit this bit out, yeah? I mean, it's not live, is it? Alright, cheers, mate. Starting now…"

"Hi everyone. As you know from my previous videos, my name is Samson Okoye, and today I am here with my colleague, Doctor Elizabeth Ng-Parker. Now, listen up. Today's video, it's gonna be a bit different from our usual routine. If you're new to the channel, normally we like to have a bit of banter, speculate on the genetic makeup of horror movie monsters, game monsters, all that. Today we're gonna discuss some real work, and the tone is gonna be a little more serious. As usual, I've put links in the video description, and if you have any questions, leave them in the comments and I'll get back to you… uh, probably from my soon to be prison cell. We're pretty sure the feds are gonna be here soon to shut us down, so I don't have long.

I want to go through some stuff today that I think is going to affect all of us very soon. I know it sounds conspiratorial, but I promise you, you'll want to see this. The feds don't want this getting out.

A while back, the ethics organisation SETA hired us to perform some tests on what they are calling a government sanctioned biological weapon. They got this weapon from our contact; someone I will not name because I'm not a nark.

I'm gonna explain in easily understood terms so you guys get what we're dealing with here. What we actually have is something like gene therapy on steroids. In this vial is something called Sigma Delta Tau–I'll be calling it Sigma for short. If you've watched my previous videos, we've covered gene therapy discoveries such as CRISPR, so you'll know already that we can use the cells' own mechanisms to snip and alter DNA. The problem with current gene editing technology is that, through natural selection, treated cells are rewriting themselves and returning to their pre-edit states. This is a spanner in the works, and I don't know about you man, but if I get sick, if I get cancer, I can't afford multiple treatments, even with insurance.

Sigma changes everything. This is a mechanism that not only cuts DNA, it replaces it in record time, with permanent results. I'm talking about dramatic cell change and replication. DNA, completely rewritten. The end of genetic disease in our lifetime. Better yet, you can customise the DNA you receive, or you can pre-program it to look for problems and actively fix them at the cell level. And, unlike current gene therapies, the benefits will be passed down to the next generation. Say you got Spina Bifida. Consider it fixed, fam–your future youths too. It's like AI for your DNA.

I know what you're thinking. It's a pretty bold claim, right? That's what I thought when our contact brought these strains to my lab. I'm not gonna lie to you. We mostly do private jobs for zoos and the like, taking blood samples and testing for disease. Above board stuff that usually doesn't affect people. So, when we are brought something like this, we have to be extra careful, hence why we've got on all this PPE.

So, back to Sigma. Sigma uses artificial viruses as a delivery mechanism. It's like programmable proteins that go into your cells and look for problems, weaknesses, all that. Today I'm gonna show you what I mean.

So, we have here some strains of Sigma, and we're gonna take a look at some of their effects. I'll start with Sigma-9. This is a defective strain and won't be in production, according to our contact. All existing strains of nine are on ice. Needless to say, it's not gonna be on pharmacy shelves any time soon. Same for strains 10 and 11. Apparently these were too unpredictable.

The live samples I do have, 12 and 13, will be demonstrated today. Strain 12 is an unfinished product, prone to erratic mutation due to the type of viral delivery mechanism used to administer it, so it won't be developed further.

Apologies in advance to any animal lovers out there–you might want to stop the video here or look away. In these cages I've got some lab mice. I'll refer to them as subjects one, two, three, four and five.

Subject one was injected with Sigma-12 approximately twenty-four hours ago. As you can see, she doesn't seem to be showing any symptoms. Subject two has not been injected but has been housed with subject one during this period. She also seems fine.

Subject three has also been injected with 12 approximately twenty-four hours ago, and I am measuring his progress. As you can see here, he appears to be experiencing the effects of extreme dehydration, with similar symptoms to that of haemorrhagic fever—like Ebola, to you and me. Without proper treatment, our patient here will soon be deceased. I need to add a disclaimer here–this will affect mice quicker than humans. Their bodies are much smaller than ours, with much higher metabolisms, so keep that in mind while you're watching.

Subject four has also been injected with Sigma-12. Of all the subjects we've studied so far, this is the only one that has been affected in this way. It's like nothing I've ever seen before. Twenty-four hours ago, this was a mouse. Now it's…shit, I don't even know. Just look at it. Is it a mouse? Is it a lizard? Can it survive outside of lab conditions? Can it breed? Who knows? I've got a lot of questions, and not one of them I want an answer for.

The last sample we have here is Sigma-13. Now this one is our golden goose. This is the one they are preparing for human trials following approval. Approval by whom, we are yet to find out.

Subject five, at first glance, seems like a pretty ordinary lab mouse. She's perfectly healthy. If I pick her up and show you here, she's fine, alert, aware, looking good, right? Now, watch this clip of her a week ago. See how she's moving there? She's elderly, on her last legs. I administered Sigma-13 a day ago. She's not only revived, she's passing all the tests we would expect her much younger peers to complete and more. She's increased in size too. She's faster, stronger, more vibrant. It's incredible. I don't know about you, but I certainly wouldn't mind getting hold of some of this one.

Okay, so, you remember our poor little Sigma-12 patient here? Well, watch this. I'm administering a large dose of Sigma-13 to his spinal cord. In an hour, he'll be fit as a fiddle.

This all sounds great, right? So, my question is this: why is the military funding the development of revolutionary gene-editing technology? SETA thought it was a weapon, but I can't see how unless they're trying to make super soldiers. I wouldn't put it past them.

And on that note, I've gotta clean up the lab and get going. Goodnight, folks. See you on the other side."

END.

PREY

Sneak peek of Book 2: Delta

Caede bolted, running for the front doors of the pub, leaving the pandemonium behind her. Damn the cold. It wasn't far from her home, anyway. She'd hidden for long enough and couldn't just sit there, shivering in the dark anymore. She tore out into the street, unsure if the thing had followed. It was asleep after having its fill of the patrons, after splattering their blood across the bar, so she'd seized her chance.

The creature had crashed through the window, flailing about in what she could only imagine as feral, animalistic panic, destroying half the furniture, sending chairs and tables flying. Then it turned on the regulars, tearing at their arms and legs, biting and clawing at them like a maddened beast. Caede and Danny had fled to the kitchen and hidden there, hoping that it hadn't noticed them. She'd looked at Danny. His face seemed unfamiliar and distant as she tried to remember him. She remembered his screams as she fled.

"Caedey?" Jon's concerned tone summoned her back to the present. The cold air struck, biting into her already chapped lips. Reluctantly, she breathed it in and let it fill her lungs before allowing it to escape, taking with it more of her body heat. She shivered and watched the puffs of steam dissipate into nothingness.

As if the weather wasn't bad enough, it had to snow. Awful stuff. Cold, wet and usually followed by ice, which was even worse.

She cocked her head towards him. "Hmm?"

"You okay?"

"Just thinking about food," she said. A half-hearted reply. But she didn't want to worry him. She was hungry. That was true. Starving, even. The sensation of it was both maddening and exhausting at the same time; the cold only exasperated it. But the memories of the event–as they'd agreed to call it–were returning little by little. She couldn't remember exactly how long she'd stayed hiding in the pub before finally running and ending up on the pavement, but it didn't really matter now, anyway. The memories didn't change the outcome, nor could they help in their current situation. They were still starving, still cold, and it was still snowing.

The village was a few fields over from Ravi's aunt's house. It came into view as they crested a hill, quaint and picturesque as a scene on a Christmas card, with its thatched snow topped roofs and kitsch shopfronts. Nothing much had changed since their last visit, save for a few footprints. Other survivors most likely, though that raised some concerns. They could be a blessing, or a curse, depending on how friendly they were. Caede thought no more about it for now.

Jon checked the prints over, confirming them as boot prints. "Human," he said. "Must be one of the locals."

"That's a relief."

Jon noted the direction of the prints and together they headed towards the shops in the little high street. The general store, and the many pubs, had been helpful in providing enough snack food to stave off the maddening hunger. But if she had to eat another bag of Scampi fries, Caede was going to scream. Most of the pubs and shops were empty now, anyway.

"Where do you want to start?" Caede asked.

She turned to face Jon and saw him pointing over to the post office on the other side of the street.

"Check it out," he said. "Was that open before?"

Caede studied it for a moment. The front door was ajar, and the snow at its base had been recently disturbed.

"I don't think so," she replied. "Look at the snow."

Jon hummed in agreement. "Alright. Better investigate."

The pair moved cautiously towards the door, doing their best to step lightly, despite the loud clumping of the snow under their feet. Another reason to hate the stuff. As they approached, a whisper could be heard from within the shop, and the pair froze. Raising a gloved hand, she gestured to Jon to the door. He readied himself next to it, placing his hand against the wood as he prepared to push it open. Caede gripped the spear—a wooden broom handle they'd sharpened to a point—in her hands and waited as Jon counted silently from three to one. He pushed the door open and Caede leapt in, spear pointed ahead.

About the author

Jesse Brown is a millennial with an anxiety disorder and too many cats. Growing up in a council estate, Jesse often disappeared into books, video games, and horror movies as an escape. At college, Jesse studied Art, English Language & Literature, Philosophy and Psychology. After obtaining their degree, Jesse worked as a Graphic designer, marketer and writer for a number of small businesses across Kent before moving to Berkshire in 2017. When they're not writing, they're on the treadmill, training for the zombie apocalypse, or playing Legend of Zelda.

Author's note: Thanks so much for taking the time to read EAT! If you have a few minutes to spare, it would mean the world to me if you could leave a review. Reviews really help indie authors like me reach a wider audience, and help other readers find new titles, so whatever you thought of the book, say so! I won't be offended, I promise. Thanks again!